Dear Reader,

Look what the stork brought!

This month Silhouette Books delivers a heartwarming collection of love stories celebrating motherhood by three award-winning authors. In *Birds, Bees and Babies*, Jennifer Greene, Karen Keast and Emilie Richards examine the many facets of love, romance and family in three powerful, poignant and touching tales.

For the three heroines in this book, all roads lead to the one-horse town of Junction, Missouri. The squat, red-brick building of Junction General Hospital isn't very prepossessing. And Room 232—complete with hospital-green walls and wheezing radiators—is hardly a glamorous place to be. But it's the place where magic happens, where three new lives are brought into the world by capable, competent Nurse Mary Condrey. Whether the mother in question is first time, fourth time or adoptive, lives are changed, secrets are shared . . . and love blossoms.

This book is a celebration of family—of the bonds formed and strengthened by shared experiences. Come share them with us!

All the best,

Isabel Swift
Editorial Manager
Silhouette Books

Birds, Bees and Babies

JENNIFER GREENE
KAREN KEAST
EMILIE RICHARDS

Silhouette Books®

Published by Silhouette Books New York

America's Publisher of Contemporary Romance

SILHOUETTE BOOKS
300 E. 42nd St., New York, N.Y. 10017

Contents

Riley's Baby

JENNIFER GREENE

A Note from Jennifer Greene

I love babies. If there are forty adults and a baby in the room, I inevitably gravitate toward the baby.

My love of babies is in no way a measure of my ability to raise them. My husband and I have two children. Ryan was a brilliant and precocious baby. He decided, coming out of the womb, that there were strategic times to cry—like whenever I needed to eat or sleep. I can remember adjusting our dinner hours anywhere from three minutes past lunch to 10:00 p.m. It didn't matter; that first wail would kick in as soon as I picked up my fork. I can also remember, many nights, vacuuming my living room carpet at three in the morning with Ryan in my arms. (He slept wonderfully until I turned the vacuum off.)

When Jennifer was born, I was older, tougher, wiser. I threw out the seventeen childcare books I'd read for Ryan and started right in the hospital with lies and bribery. "If you don't cry for the next fifteen minutes, I'll hold you for the next forty-eight hours straight," I'd promise her. It didn't do any good. She had me figured out before we left the delivery room.

It's a miracle that my children survived their babyhood. Both kids knew I couldn't stand to hear them cry. Both, accurately, played me for a sucker early on.

I'm just as much a sucker for a love story and always have been. Love stories involving motherhood, though, reach me like no others.

Motherhood is mystical, special, timeless, wonderful. It also takes you out of yourself. Selfishness doesn't survive a baby. If a relationship has holes, they get bigger with the advent of diapers. Babies have a way of putting a major dent in candlelit dinners, champagne and spontaneous lovemaking.

From where I'm sitting, though, motherhood can be the starting point for the greatest romance a woman can have.

When you have a child, you put a different value on love. When you have a child, you test everything you've ever believed about love...because you have to. You have to fight for the time to be together; you have to find something to give when you're as limp as a dishrag; you have to be understanding when your sole goal in life is burying your head under a pillow for eight hours of uninterrupted sleep.

That kind of love takes work—lots more work than a candlelit dinner—but in the process you build something as strong as cement. Real love, tough love, the kind that hurts, the kind that matters, the kind that lasts—this is magic of the most powerful kind.

My story is not about a married couple, but a single one. They *have* love...but not a love that's been tested yet. There's no cement. Their whole concept of romance is the magic created when the two of them are alone together. They think that's all there is. They don't know how big, how strong, how powerful the scope of love can really be. They're just starting their real romance, but they'll have to discover that for themselves.

Jennifer Greene

Prologue

Mary smoothed, folded and tucked with an efficiency the army would have admired. Technically it was the nurses aide's job to make the bed, not hers. Just as technically, of course, it was a doctor's job to deliver babies, but Mary had delivered her share for more than twenty years. Hospital administrators liked to make rules and regulations and policies. She'd been a nurse too long to pay much attention.

She finished with the bed and straightened, her eyes narrowing on the rest of the room. It didn't look like much—just a bed, monitor, table/tray and a worn out Naugahyde chair squeezed into the corner. The clanking radiator didn't add much to the decor; neither did the faded green paint on the walls. Most would say the room looked barren and sterile, emotionless.

They'd be dead wrong.

Junction General Hospital was too small to have a formal labor room. Room 232, at the end of the hall, was reserved for expectant mothers. Mary personally made the bed in the room. She also personally ensured that no dust touched the windowsill, no water spots marred the sink in the bathroom, no crease disturbed the smooth white cotton blanket.

Bringing life into this world was a hard and intimately personal business. Mary knew—she'd done it five times herself—and over the years she'd watched times change.

Twenty years ago a mother was sedated almost upon arrival. Now a woman in labor rarely received any drug unless it was absolutely necessary.

Twenty years ago, almost every mother was married—and nearly every father was shooed to the waiting room. Now, mothers delivering for the first time were just as likely to be fourteen as forty. No one asked if they were married, and fathers—wed or not—were often enough part of the birth.

Twenty years ago, the women wore the earrings. Now, heaven knew, the fathers occasionally did. At least in one ear.

Mary fiddled with the backs of her own earrings—red garnet studs inherited from her great-grandmother, and her only vanity. She heard herself being paged, strode for the door and hesitated. She gave the room one last glance to make sure it was right—not right and prepared by anyone else's standards, but by her own. It could be days before a young woman was admitted to this room. It could be minutes.

Maybe the details of life had changed over the years, but some things never did. Babies were always going to arrive in their own good time, and never conveniently. Expectant fathers were always going to be more difficult to deal with than the mothers, and it took pain to deliver a baby. No philosophy or pain killer or Lamaze classes were ever going to change that.

Mary heard her name paged again, yet she still didn't move. She'd seen more than twenty years of babies born in this room. Twenty years of life—and love—and stories she'd never told and never would tell.

Those stories had given her a different perspective than most. If anyone asked Mary—and no one ever had—the cycle of romance didn't start with Adam and Eve and an apple, but nine months later. Stories of birth were stories of searing privacy, unforgettable pain, joy, anticipation, fear that tore at a soul . . . and the renewal of birth that mended it.

Room 232 wasn't just a place. It was a moment in time, in which two people had the chance to experience the ultimate romance of love and life. A moment in time when a man and a woman could make or break each other. Mary had seen it go both ways.

Certainly babies were a jolt of reality, between diapers and night feedings and burpings and colic. Giving birth, though, was the single greatest jolt of reality there was. This was it. Everything that mattered. And either the right kind of love went into the making of a baby, or it didn't.

The prices were all paid here. In room 232.

Chapter One

You're pregnant."

"I can't be." Adrienne Bennett's voice was quite firm.

The doctor stepped away and plucked at her vinyl glove. "About eight weeks along."

"I *can't* be."

"My guess is early December—"

"My guess is that you have the wrong rabbit, because mine couldn't have died." Adrienne lifted her feet from the blasted stirrups. The paper blanket tried to flutter to the floor. Agitated, she grabbed it. "Come on, Liz. I'm thirty-three years old, which you know as well as you know me. I've never believed in luck, never played Russian roulette, and I sure as heck have never been careless about birth control. *Never.*"

Dr. Liz Conklin reached for a pen and the prescription pad, but her gaze focused on her old friend. She wasn't fooled by Adrienne's exasperated attempt at humor. "Take it easy," she advised. "These things happen no matter how careful a woman is. Give yourself a chance to get used to the idea before you panic."

Panic wasn't even a word in Adrienne's vocabulary. Or it didn't used to be. "Two thousand years of medical science. They cured polio. They can give you a new heart. So how is it that we're about to reach the twenty-first century without a foolproof method to guard against pregnancy? It's unbelievable!''

"Riley won't be half as upset as you are," Liz said calmly.

"Riley will divorce me," Adrienne immediately contradicted her.

"He can't divorce you. You aren't married."

"Which is far worse. If you're married and surprised by a pregnancy, that's one thing. If you're just living together, that's another. Riley didn't sign on for this kind of complication."

"Neither did you, but this kind of 'complication' takes two. I'm almost sure that our mutually favorite industrial relations attorney has a good idea how babies are made. He also happens to worship the ground you walk on. You don't suppose there's a chance—a slim, remote chance—that Riley won't be half as upset as you are?"

Because Liz was trying to be soothing, Adrienne wanted to make a light comeback, but couldn't. Her whole body was cold—chill cold, fear cold. Her heart felt as heavy as lead. She was famous for her sense of humor, but couldn't dredge up an ounce of it now. Babies were a subject she had always taken very, very seriously, which was the precise reason she had been so careful to never become pregnant.

All Adrienne had to do was close her eyes to conjure up a mental picture of Riley. The cliché about tall, dark and handsome had probably started with him. So did the one about electric blue eyes. But his lethally sexy looks had never captured her attention. She couldn't care less what a man looked like as long as he was compassionate and intelligent and had a long dollop of integrity.

Riley had a long dollop of the devil. Other men had been scared off by her cool reserve. Riley had been amused by it. Most men were predictably threatened by a strong, successful woman. Riley had made Adrienne laugh at herself. *No* man had any difficulty understanding her when she said no and meant it. Riley had taken her no's all the way to bed with them, and then had the unprincipled gall to make the experience so devastating, so delicious, so terrifyingly special that she couldn't think straight.

She'd known from the beginning that he was a flirt with a rogue's reputation. Throw a party, and women tripped over themselves to get to Riley's side. He loved that. The problem with Riley was that he was one of those rare men who honestly liked women. He also knew them. Too well—so well that she'd had a heck of a time covering up her symptoms until she had the chance to make this doctor's appointment. "Look, Liz, there has to be a chance you're wrong. I only missed one period. That happened before, and the only thing wrong was an innocuous little fibroid cyst."

"There's a definite difference between a cyst and a normal, healthy uterus eight weeks into pregnancy." Liz said firmly, "Knowing you, you guessed you were pregnant before you walked in, so let's get serious here. I want to do some blood work and get you on some vitamins, and you're built on the small side, kiddo, meaning that your pelvis isn't equipped to take a watermelon. With very careful control of the baby's weight, you shouldn't have any major problems.''

"Believe me, I have a *major* problem."

"Talk to Riley."

"I—"

"Adrienne, go home and talk with Riley!''

At five minutes to twelve Adrienne, dressed in a red blouse and businesslike white suit, was standing at a pharmacist's window with a handful of prescriptions. Somewhere behind the counter, there was an open bottle of alcohol. The odor made her stomach roll. *Talk to Riley?*

Once her prescriptions for vitamins were filled, she walked into an adjoining deli to grab a quick sandwich. The tantalizing aroma of corn beef made her mouth water, but the same smell made her stomach pitch acid. She quickly walked out again. The first day of April was balmy and redolent with the scents of spring. She didn't notice. *How could she possibly talk to Riley?*

It was only a short fifteen-minute drive through midtown Indianapolis to the law offices of Reeder, Small and Burkholtz. It wasn't fair. The moment she stepped in the door, she was starving to death. The coffee room only yielded a box of stale crackers, which she munched frantically before her first afternoon client.

The firm's specialty was divorce, and if Adrienne continued her success rate with clients, Reeder, Small and Burkholtz were going to be stuck adding ''Bennett'' to the partnership. The boys may have hired her with all the right mumbo jumbo slogans about equality, but Adrienne knew the score. They never really thought she'd cut it. Women attorneys didn't abound in divorce. The field was too ugly and too tough.

At one o'clock, she heard out the ravings of an embittered wife who'd stayed in an abusive relationship too long. Her second client of the afternoon was a man, who was determined to take his unfaithful wife for everything she had right down to her false eyelashes.

Both cases were ugly; both were tough. Adrienne's colleagues claimed that no divorce attorney sustained any ideals or romantic illusions for long. Luckily she'd never started with any romantic illusions, but ideals were another story. She had specifically chosen divorce as her legal specialty because of an ideal: to help people get divorced as painlessly as possible.

Her parents were one of those unfortunate couples who never had the good sense to get a divorce. As in most marriages, it took two to tango. Her father was certainly guilty of numerous infidelities...but her mother had incomparable skill at saying just the right thing at just the right time to wound and emasculate. As far as Adrienne could tell, the two had spent thirty-five years living to hurt each other.

At five o'clock, she left a desk full of work and took her queasy stomach home. Her work as a divorce attorney only reaffirmed values she'd learned as a child. Love was a powerful and positive force. Marriage, regrettably, had nothing to do with love. Enter possessiveness and ties and forced responsibilities, and the relationship went *"pffft."* Every time.

The exhaust fumes on the expressway nearly took her stomach out for good. Riley knew exactly how she felt about marriage. Everyone argued in a relationship—an occasional spat was the spice of life—but the only times they'd ended up shouting at each other was about marriage. Riley had finally, permanently, dropped the subject.

Adrienne was terrified it would come up again when he discovered she was pregnant.

Either that, or he'd walk out on her.

In her head, she knew Riley wasn't the kind of man to walk out on any woman in trouble. But in her heart, Adrienne had been waiting for Riley to walk out from the day she'd met him. Men liked soft women. She wasn't soft. She was terribly hard and terribly cynical and cold—good grief, at five years old she'd had to learn to be cold!—but Riley just didn't seem to see her that way.

Riley might be the best thing that had ever happened to her, but a pregnancy changed everything. Their whole relationship was based on mutual needs and matched respect and sharing—not dependence. Never dependence. Adrienne knew precisely what happened to a relationship when either partner was cornered into forced feelings of responsibility. The result was shambles.

Talk to Riley, Liz had advised. Well, she would. She'd talk tough, blunt, practical, hardheaded common sense; she'd make absolutely positive he was off the hook. Blunt, tough realism came naturally to her. The talk wouldn't be any problem at all.

A horn blared from the merging lane of the freeway. She hadn't seen the aging Chevy. Her eyes had been too filled with tears.

Swinging a briefcase full of labor contracts, Riley ignored the elevator and took the stairs two at a time. He'd missed his morning jog as well as his usual half hour on the handball court at lunch. The only muscles he'd used all day had been in his rear end. Every nerve was singing with pent-up physical energy.

Halfway down the hall, he dug into his pants pocket for the apartment key. He was whistling when Mrs. McFadden stepped outside her door for the evening paper, dressed in a housecoat that barely camouflaged her Buddha-like rolls. He winked a hello at her, and she blushed to the roots of her newly tinted pink hair.

You still got it, Riley. At least with the geriatric set. He was laughing at himself when he turned the key, then mentally swore when he discovered he'd locked the door, not unlocked it. Adrienne regularly promised to lock herself in when she arrived home first. She never remembered. She also never remembered to fill her car with gas, that food was required sustenance for all human beings, and that he really did hate perfumed soap.

None of those monumental faults had ever affected his feelings for her. Dropping his briefcase, he pushed off his shoes and shrugged out of his suit coat. Adrienne had decorated the place, which was why there was a brass rack and table waiting for the debris he inevitably stashed at the door.

"Adrienne?" Ambling through the hallway, he peered into the kitchen—a study in oak, stained glass, and leftover-breakfast coffee cups.

She wasn't there, nor was she in the second bedroom they'd turned into a study. The matching desks were empty, the bookshelves untouched. He'd argued with her about using "midnight blue" paint because the room was already dark, but as usual, Adrienne was right. Coupled with soft light, her "blues" made for a restful, serene work area for both of them in an evening.

The hall took a turn and twist before reaching the living room. Unlike the dark blue study, she'd made their living area all light and color.

The overstuffed couch and chairs were man-size, in deference to his six-two frame, but the splashes of feminine color were uniquely Adrienne. No question she liked spice, and the contemporary oil over the white marble fireplace picked up her favorite paprika, cinnamon and vanilla. The tables were brass and glass, relieved from a cold contemporary look by textures. The coffee table sat on a thick white fur rug. She'd hung South American *molas* on the far wall. Adrienne was a big believer in pillows—huge, fat ones, the kind a man could sink his head in after a long, hard day.

Every time he walked in, he remembered how much he'd hated the singles scene and coming home to a bleak, cold apartment alone. Adrienne had done more than change the colors; she had ruthlessly altered the place until a man found comfort in every niche and corner. She was a hopeless nurturer—a label Riley knew she would promptly and pithily deny.

He spotted her from the doorway. She obviously hadn't heard him come in because she was slouched on the couch with her back to him. All he could see was the crown of her head. For a moment he paused, wondering—not for the first time—why he'd had to fall for such a complex and troublesome woman.

Adrienne didn't look like trouble, and he happened to know her body intimately well. She was built lithe and long, with legs that didn't end and hips so small they were swallowed in jeans. She had no vanity. Her breasts came right out of a man's fantasy. They weren't big. Just firm, white and responsive, with nipples no bigger than buttons. If you tried to compliment her she'd laughingly exhibit her feet, which she thought were huge. She was wrong.

She'd kissed a dog when she was three, who'd taken a chunk out of her fanny in response. She still had the embarrassing scar. He'd spent a lot of time worrying how many other men had seen that scar, also how many other dogs she'd kissed in the figurative sense. There couldn't have been many because Adrienne was no fool, but something or someone had given her a defensive edge that she never quite lost, a fiercely guarded independence that she never quite forgot.

She cultivated a professional image. Her hairstyle was short and sassy, just a thick swirl of chestnut with a sweep of bangs on one side. She inevitably chose clothes that tooted the same picture—bright, quick, practical and capable. Her self-image, although inarguably accurate to a point, was not at all how Riley saw her.

More than once, he'd mused that he'd like to get her in front of a mirror and show her the Adrienne that he knew. Drowning soft brown eyes. Fragile, translucent skin. Small lips that could readily be coaxed to laughter and an irreverently tipped nose. She walked with an exuberance, just a bit of a feminine swish that advertised confidence in her own sexuality. Riley loved that feminine swish, even recognizing it for the storefront it was.

No human being on this earth could be more easily hurt than Adrienne.

Riley soundlessly walked up behind her and leaned over. He barely caught the startled flash of surprise in her eyes before sealing his mouth over hers. Beyond a first taste of something unexpectedly cold and candylike on her lips, reality disappeared for several moments after that. It always did when he kissed Adrienne.

Her scent had seduced him first. She liked perfumes that drove a man crazy, a hint of soft dare, a hint of something elusive and teasing. It was the first thing he'd noticed about her, the first thing that made him decide she was bad news and better avoided. The second thing he'd noticed was how she kissed. Adrienne melted in layers, first an extraordinary shyness, then warmth, then a layer of yielding and yearning passion that went straight to a man's head.

After their first kiss, he'd cut her from the pack of men who used to surround her as relentlessly as a stag isolated his chosen doe in the fall.

Adrienne hadn't been easy to corner. She was even tougher to protect, partly because she considered herself one tough self-reliant cookie. And partly because Adrienne, from the first, had turned his world upside down. Riley wasn't a stranger to a love affair, and most women found him laid back, accepting, easy to be with. Not violently protective. Not caveman-possessive. Never aggravated. Never stressed to the absolute limit of his patience, which used to be considerable. And never turned on to the point of madness by the simplest kisses. Except with Adrienne.

After a year and a half he should have been used to her ability to surprise him, but tonight was different yet again. When he'd leaned over her, all he'd intended was a peck, a simple "hi, love" smooch.

It started that way. But *she* was the one who twisted around so her arms could sweep around his neck. Her head tilted to encourage the crush of his mouth. He crushed, obliging her. Desire sliced through him, fueled by her warmth and willingness. Adrienne could take when coaxed. She rarely demanded, yet her fingers speared through his hair, anchoring him still, ensuring his closeness.

Her skin smelled like the lilac soap he hated on him, and adored on her. So soft. He found her tongue. Her response was wild, deliciously desperate, a murmur lost between them and treasured more than she knew, but his thumb abruptly discovered that the pulse in her throat was trembling.

It took him another minute to realize that she was trembling all over.

Startled, he pulled back—not urgently and not far. With his palm still cupped in her hair, he murmured teasingly, "Hey, that was quite a homecoming welcome."

No one could jump out of emotional waters faster than Adrienne. "I don't suppose you'd believe that I thought you were the mailman?"

"No."

"Ah, well. I suppose it must have been you I was glad to see."

"Rough day?"

"Long and traumatic," she admitted blithely.

He could see that—now. In fact, on a mental level the red phone just rang in his personal White House. There were no tears in her eyes, but her lashes were damp. He'd never seen Adrienne cry, and the lamplight was too dim to guarantee he wasn't misreading the faintest redness in her eyes. Confusing him further was the package on her lap. Unless he was having hallucinations, she was holding a spoon and a pint of fast-melting butter brickle ice cream.

"Since when..." he began.

"Oh, quit grinning at me, Riley. I saw it was on sale at the convenience store at the corner and wandered in. I haven't had butter brickle since I was a kid. It's unbelievably good," she said feelingly, and as lithe as a cat—as if nothing was wrong—swung off the couch.

"You actually polished off an entire pint?"

"It's not like junk food. Ice cream is absolutely loaded with nutritional things. Like calcium—"

"And butter brickle." When he swung an arm around her to steer her toward the kitchen, he knew for sure she'd cried. He also knew he wasn't going to get anything out of her until she was good and ready. Adrienne could be pushed—about as easily as a mountain. "I don't suppose you're in the least hungry for some real dinner after your...um... appetizer?"

"Are you kidding? I could eat half a whale."

Again he paused. For the past two weeks, Adrienne's appetite had rivaled that of a hummingbird's. Further, she never went on an eating binge without reason. He considered whether Burkholtz had put the move on her, whether one of the custody issues she handled involved an abused child, or whether her mother had called. "Anything interesting happen today?" he asked casually.

"First thing this morning I had the meeting with the Laughlins. Property settlement, I told you? They argued over every spoon and ashtray."

"Stressful?"

"Not really. More humorous, particularly when they got to the ashtrays." She looked up with a dry grin. "Neither of them even smoke."

"Burkholtz hit you with the review schedule?" He knew the issue of her potential partnership would come up with the spring review.

"No time, never even saw him today. How about you? How'd the meeting go with the union lawyer from U.B.R.?"

He followed up with chitchat, keeping a careful eye on her at the same time. Letting Adrienne loose in a kitchen had similar repercussions to giving an untrained puppy the run of the house. Riley had learned a long time ago to give her some innocuously harmless task—like tossing salad.

In principle, it wasn't fair to give her anything to do. They split the chores. He did the cooking and the laundry. She did the shopping, cleaning and taxes. He had no problem with the fair division of labor; it was Adrienne who got the feminine guilts when he worked in the kitchen.

As he sautéed the chicken breasts, he only hoped her problem *was* the feminine guilts. She was shredding lettuce into bits too microscopic to see. "Your mother call you?" he asked lightly.

"No. Why should she—Riley, don't."

"Don't what?" His white shirt cuffed to the elbows, he was cleaning the season's first asparagus under the open faucet.

"Not asparagus. Not tonight."

He raised a brow. "You love asparagus. It's your favorite—"

"*Please*. Not asparagus."

Adrienne didn't have a fussy bone in her body, but hey, everyone had an occasional whim. By the time he'd rearranged the menu to cater to her appetite, though, dinner had deteriorated into bland chicken, dull peas and plain old potatoes. She managed the peas, pushed the rest around her plate, and finished off with a slice of unbuttered bread. The half a glass of wine he poured her remained untouched. She wanted milk. They'd lived together for a year and a half. She'd never wanted milk.

It was easiest to clean up when there were no leftovers. Heaven knew, he didn't want to save anything from the dinner. He carried and scraped; she rinsed and fed the dishes to the dishwasher, talking shop at the same time. "So Wednesday, I'm probably going to be stuck in court all day. The custody hearing's going to take all of the afternoon. I've been looking forward to coming up against Dailey for a long time. If he thinks he's going to win one off his reputation this time, he's living in a dream world. How do you feel about abortion, Riley?"

"Pardon?" Last he knew, she was discussing hanging a fellow attorney out to dry.

"Abortion. I'm just curious how you feel about it. I never happened to ask you." Her back was to him. She'd taken a glass out of the cupboard and was holding it to the light. Adrienne hated water spots. "Are you for it or against it?"

"Well . . ." He swiped at the table, his eyes on her back. "Overall, I'm against abortion ever having been made into a legal issue. I think it's a mistake to pretend we can legislate morals and ethics, nor does the legal system have any business intruding on people's individual personal and religious beliefs—"

"Stash it, Riley. I wasn't asking for a courtroom speech. I was just curious how you felt on the subject."

She was still holding up that glass. At least, until he came up behind her and stole it from her hand. He couldn't identify the emotion rolling in his stomach, but he had the abrupt sensation of falling in quicksand—as if the rest of his life could be affected by the next few seconds and he didn't know any of the parameters, the edges, the rules.

That feeling intensified when he turned Adrienne around by applying gentle pressure to her shoulders. He only caught the briefest glimpse of her eyes—she lowered them too quickly—but there was time enough. His so "tough," so sassy, so fiercely controlled Adrienne was scared. The look in her eyes was as haunted and desperate as a cornered doe's.

"So..." he said softly. "We're pregnant, are we?"

Chapter Two

Riley's voice was tender, but Adrienne saw what mattered. His whole body had locked still and his eyes were a blank, stunned blue.

She had never expected him to react with a delirious whoop of joy—good grief, neither of them wanted a pregnancy—yet her heartbeat suddenly dragged and she was curiously tempted to cry. Silly weakness. When his hands tightened on her shoulders, she firmly ducked from the contact and averted her eyes. "*We* are not pregnant, Riley. That's a medical and metaphysical impossibility. I'm the only one pregnant. This is my problem, not yours."

"I believe it takes two."

She was ready for that. "And that would have stuck you in the hot seat of responsibility if we lived in the eighteenth century. Luckily we live in the twentieth." All Ms. Efficiency, she hung up the dish towel and punched the button to start the dishwasher. "It doesn't take two people to handle the problem these days. I know you don't want a baby—"

"Actually, I don't believe we've ever discussed it," Riley said quietly. "Come here, honey."

She didn't want to "come here." If she came anywhere near him, she was positive she would do something stupid, like drape herself all over him, or worse, cry. Besides, the kitchen was clean. She shut off the lights and strolled to their bedroom as if it were any other night. After dinner, she always fed the fish.

The aquariums took up one whole wall in their seablue bedroom, and she didn't need to turn on the overhead because the tanks were illuminated. Silver dollars swam over iridescent stones in one tank; angel fish danced near the bubbler in another; and the last held a school of darting, bright neons. Riley had bought the first pair of fish, but Adrienne was the one who'd expanded their shared hobby—not because she was so crazy about fish, but for a far more private reason. Romance. He would surely laugh at her if he knew—the whole world knew she didn't have a romantic bone in her body!—but she had a hundred memories of Riley, naked, his skin catching the light and shadow of shimmering reflections, his whispers backdropped by the muted sound of bubbling water, his eyes and hands...

She stiffened when she realized he'd followed her to the doorway. Damn pregnancy hormones. They had her feeling all shaky and vulnerable when she wanted most to be strong—for his sake much more than her own. She fumbled with the cap to the fish food. "The thing is to stay calm, Riley. At least try to relax! The only way to discuss the problem is logically and rationally, and getting upset doesn't solve anything at all—"

"Honey, I am calm."

"So am I. Completely." Except that she abruptly spilled a tablespoon's worth of fish food in the tank. They were only supposed to be fed a pinch. Frantically she reached for the green scooper. "I've *never* been more calm."

Riley swiped a hand over his face. "Could we backtrack before we have any further discussion on who's calm and who's not? You've been to a doctor. Probably Liz?"

"Yes."

"You're okay? Totally okay, completely healthy?"

"Yes."

"And there's no question—"

"None." She saved the neons and moved on to sprinkle food into the angel fish tank. "Look, I know you can't be happy about this. Neither am I. You signed on for living together, not for this kind of problem—"

"I passed puberty a few years ago. Way back when I was aware that when a man and woman make love— particularly as often as we do—a baby is always a potential repercussion. And that we might have to deal with that, love."

Riley, at his most dangerous, used a certain tone of voice. Adrienne thought of it as his naughty tone, because that same male husky timbre had persuaded her into bed, teased her into trying lobster, and coaxed her into believing that living together was a practical, logical, sensible option. He could magnetize a stone with that voice, and worse than that, he was confusing her. When you drop a bomb like an unexpected pregnancy on a man, surely he should react a little more volatilely than to stand in a doorway and pop a butterscotch?

Unless Riley'd already assumed how they would handle the problem. Her throat went suddenly dry. "I asked you in the kitchen how you felt about abortion. But I didn't tell you how I feel."

"That wouldn't take a mind reader," he murmured. "You may have never handled an abortion case, but you've taken on more than a few clients involving women's rights, love."

"Yes," she agreed. She was so busy feeding the fish that she couldn't spare a moment to look at him. "The constitutional interpretation of equality affecting women—"

"Is a fine theoretical subject for another night. Tonight we're talking about you. You're sneaking around the fence, Adrienne. It isn't like you. Are you trying to tell me you want an abortion?"

She couldn't answer without facing him. Riley was one of those men who rarely stood still—he was too physical, too full of energy—yet he hadn't budged an inch from the doorway. The aquarium lights made his white shirt look iridescent and harshened his strong-boned face. By contrast, his eyes rested with infinite gentleness on her face, waiting... for an answer she couldn't give him.

She spoke as carefully as if she were tiptoeing through a mine field. "What I'm trying to tell you is that I can't involve you in this choice, Riley. I know that's not fair and I know you don't want a baby and I do care what you feel... but I'm asking you to understand. An abortion is not a choice I can live with, not like this, not for me. I'm sorry."

She had no idea Riley was holding his breath until he closed his eyes and let out a gust of a sigh. With disorienting speed, he crossed the room and grabbed on to her. Tightly. So tightly that her cheek felt the numb of his collar button, and her eyes were on a level with the pulse beating hard in his throat. Then her eyes started stinging and her vision blurred into rainbows. "I thought you'd be angry," she whispered.

"That's pretty obvious."

"I was positive you would want me to have an abortion—"

"That's pretty obvious, too, my darling doofus."

She knew he wanted her to smile. No matter how serious the subject was, a light touch helped keep things in perspective—she'd taught him that—but she couldn't have smiled at the moment if her life depended on it. "You can't want a baby. You have to resent the idea."

"I hadn't planned on one, no. And if you don't mind, I'd like a little more than ten minutes to get used to the idea before I comment on babies."

"You don't have to do that. I've already thought it out. There's obviously only one answer here, and that's for me to move out."

Riley's hands stopped making slow soothing circles down her spine.

She forged on stubbornly, her cheek still matted against his shirtfront. "You talked me into living together, and you did it with logic, Riley. If I remember right, there came a point where neither of us knew where our toothbrushes were, where your shirts were hanging in my closet and my shoes had accumulated in yours. We couldn't even cook dinner because the vegetables were all in my fridge and the meat was all in yours—you said it was foolish, and you were right. You said that just because people didn't want to be married shouldn't mean they had to spend a lifetime alone. You said that if our circumstances changed, either of us had the freedom to walk out at any time—"

Riley brushed his lips against her hair. "Maybe I once said too many things."

"We made a relationship that freed us both—not tied us down. As far as I know, neither of us have hurt each other, and we've both always been honest." She closed her eyes. "And I'd like to be honest now. You know what I was most afraid of, telling you about the pregnancy?"

"What?"

"That you'd jump in blind with some silly idea about us getting married."

His hands suddenly clenched a little too roughly on her shoulders. "That would have been...silly, wouldn't it?"

"You know it would be."

"I know exactly how you feel about marriage, yes."

He was holding her far too tightly, but she didn't care. Maybe he'd never hold her this tightly again. No woman held a man by cornering him, and she wouldn't—*couldn't*—do that to Riley. His breath smelled like butterscotch, though, his skin like soap. Both scents were familiar, as familiar as the emotions invoked by his arms around her. He had a gift for making a woman feel protected, cherished, almost— sometimes—safe. All day long she'd felt so shaky. "If there's no abortion and we're not getting married, that only leaves so many choices, and if I'm going to do the right thing, I have to say that my keeping the baby isn't one of them." She had to gulp to get that land-mind truth out, then rushed on. "The best solution would seem to be adoption."

"Honey—"

"But adoption is not the issue right now—the pregnancy is. Everything's changed now. You know it has. You work for a conservative company—you can't just live with a woman whose stomach is about to swell up like a balloon. It isn't right, and those complications will only get worse, not easier. The obvious answer is for me to move out."

"You're not moving out."

"I really think—"

"Adrienne, would you do me an enormous favor and *quit* thinking? You mind is galloping a hundred miles an hour faster than mine. You may have had a chance to think about this, but I haven't. How about if we leave just a few of these decisions until tomorrow?"

She lifted her head and met his eyes. "Waiting won't change anything. I'm not going to live here and have you grow to resent me. That's what would happen."

"You sound very sure that's what would happen."

"I *am* very sure that's what would happen."

Riley felt as if he'd recently been run over by a semi... and that the offending semi kept backing up for a return hit. He hadn't come in the door expecting to be assaulted with the subjects of pregnancy, babies, abortion and adoption. Even if he had, he'd never found a way to anticipate Adrienne's complex and distinctly feminine mind. For a woman so quick she could probably outthink—and certainly outtalk—Einstein, he was regularly amazed at the insane ideas she could produce from thin air.

For example, that he would ever come to resent her.

She didn't respond to his first kiss. Her head was obviously on babies, not desire. Maybe his head should have been on babies, too, but he'd had his fill of hit-and-run semis for the evening. Babies were an obligingly long nine-month process. Adrienne was upset now. Her eyes were haunted with strain, her face white with tension, and as far as this business of his ever resenting her... she started to say something.

He kissed her again, deeply, thoroughly. His hands slipped behind her to nudge open her skirt button, then handle the zipper at the back. The skirt obligingly whooshed to the floor. Adrienne tried to say something else.

She fired for the feel of his palms cupping her bottom, always had. She liked the earthy rub of his arousal pressed against her, always had. She liked a petal-soft tongue at the base of her throat; she loved her eyes kissed closed; and textures turned her on—his palm skimming her nylon stocking, his hands gliding her silk slip against her skin. It went against everything his feminist and independent lady believed in, but the truth was Adrienne loved being swept away. What she craved even more was being loved.

A fish splashed. Bubbling waters muted the cry of yearning he coaxed from her. By the time she was beneath him on the comforter, she was bare. The aquarium lights pearlized her skin. Her brown eyes were lost, pleading, promising, but it was the hint of despair in those soft eyes that drove him beyond the limits of reason.

A man, at times, simply had to be ruthless about tenderness.

When it was over, she lay shuddering and limp beneath him. "Riley—"

"Sssh." He heard both the bewilderment and confusion in her voice. Neither of them ever got used to it, the explosion of flint and flame whenever they came together, but tonight had even been more. Maybe he should have realized before why her breasts had become so tender, so sensitive. Maybe there was even a medical reason for her heightened desire, her ardent sensuality and uncontrolled responsiveness—namely a pregnancy. He didn't care what the reasons were. She'd come to him like wildfire.

"I don't know what happened. I never expected—"

"Neither did I." His lips found her forehead. "You're beautiful, love. Inside, outside, everywhere."

"I—"

"Sssh." He held her long after she fell asleep. With her eyes closed and her body limp and curled around him, she looked precisely what she was. His lover. His lovely, lonely frightened mate who had spent a childhood and a career surrounded by hurtful relationships.

She had never told him she loved him. For a long time, though, he believed she did, and for just as long he'd known she didn't trust him. For a year and a half, she'd been waiting for his interest to wane, waiting for the explosive passion between them to fizzle, and—most of all—waiting for him to leave her.

No, she didn't tell him any of those things. But a man couldn't live with a woman—not a woman he cared about, not a woman he loved—without gaining some knowledge of how her mind worked. The slightest reference to marriage was enough to raise Adrienne's blood pressure thirty degrees. She would never admit to needing anyone, because that onus would put an invisible rope on the other person's neck. Needing was a capital crime to Adrienne. It was okay for her to take care of him, but she fiercely shielded him from any hint that she might need taking care of, too.

The lady was thirty-three years old. Damn young to be so bullheaded. And damn old to have never had her first experience with trust.

Riley's eyes squeezed tightly in the darkness. He'd always figured he could teach her trust in time. Her pregnancy, though, changed things. He no longer had the luxury of time.

And unless he was extraordinarily careful, he knew darn well he could lose her.

Even before she heard the buzz of the alarm clock, Adrienne knew something was terribly wrong. Her eyes still closed, she rolled over to wrap around Riley for a last-minute snuggle…and discovered him gone, the sheets next to her empty.

Either there had been a tornado, or Indianapolis had had its first earthquake. Riley never woke up before the buzzer. Not that she didn't love him but she knew him. Riley had all the liveliness of a sludge before 9:00 a.m. Worried, Adrienne jerked out of bed, and abruptly felt an attack of dizziness like a bullet of reality. *Yes, you're still pregnant, Miss Bennett.*

She collected a black skirt and white blouse with black piping from the closet, and took her rolling stomach to the bathroom. Even after a fast shower, her reflection in the vanity mirror appalled her. Her cheeks had a glow, her eyes held a sleepy satisfaction, her mouth was a sting of red.

She looked like a woman who had been made love to thoroughly and well—but making love with Riley had not been on the agenda last night. Babies had been. The baby she was not prepared for, the one she was sure he didn't want, the one that explained once and for all why unmarried couples shouldn't live together—and how she'd ended up making love with Riley was beyond Adrienne.

Beyond the closed bathroom door, she heard him moving around. It wasn't hard to hear him. Riley get-

ting ready for work was no noisier than a herd of elephants. Trying to hurry, mentally chanting prayers
that her stomach would stop pitching acid, she
climbed into her clothes and then reached for the tubes
of war paint in the medicine cabinet.

She had one eye subtly brushed with a layer of
mascara when the chants stopped working. The un-
controllable wave of nausea hit her as fast as a summer storm. She barely had time to lean over the sink—
and at the same time, she could hear Riley whistling in
the hall.

Riley didn't whistle in the morning; he snapped and
growled. Furthermore, their mutual world was falling
apart and he was walking around out there as blithe as
a bumblebee. Could he have forgotten she was pregnant? Blocked the trauma from his mind? Had he totally flipped out? And she'd woken up dominantly
aware that he had not mentioned marriage the night
before. She'd have argued with him if he had. She'd
have fought him if he had. But still, Riley had some
hopelessly archaic ideas about honor and women, and
she'd been so sure . . .

At the moment, she felt sure of nothing. She managed to run the water taps on full to cover the sound
of her being sick, then groped for the cleanser to cover
her tracks. After that all she could do was lean against
the porcelain, weak and shivering. Unfortunately the
pitiful whistling rendition of "Rag Town" ceased just
outside the door. He rapped once.

"You okay in there, brown eyes?"

"Just fine," she sang out.

"You're not sick or anything, are you?"

"Heavens, no! I'm just fin—" Too late she saw the knob turning.

Riley peered in, took one look at her and shook his head. "So...we're not feeling so chipper this morning?"

She felt like last year's leftovers. "Riley, please go away."

"Okay," he said cheerfully, but he didn't. In one fell swoop, he had her sitting on the toilet seat and was running warm water on a washcloth to wash her face. She didn't want her face washed. She wanted to curl up somewhere in the fetal position with a blanket over her head. "This is why you've been spending so much time in the bathroom these past mornings, isn't it?"

"No," she denied.

"Yes, it is." Riley mopped her face, then ran cold water and squeezed a layer of toothpaste on her brush as if he thought she'd totally lost the capacity to do it herself. "Naturally you're staying home today."

"I'm not staying home, there's no reason to. The whole thing goes away as fast as it comes."

"Does it?" he asked interestedly.

She simply couldn't sit there and discuss morning sickness with Riley. Looking at him was tough enough. He must have showered before she did because his hair was still damp at the edges, coal dust with a sheen. His gray suit always made his shoulders look like a linebacker's. His face had clean, strong, angular lines, not a boy's features but a man's, and there wasn't a woman this side of the Atlantic who wouldn't look at Riley twice. He was good-looking. He was sexy. He had eyes that could strip a woman in three seconds flat and a natural virility that made a woman's nerves tingle.

She had to look like she felt. A woman who had just thrown up. The way Riley's eyes rested on her, you would think she was the last brownie in the pan, and his inexplicable cheerfulness seemed additional proof that he had a seriously unhinged mind this morning. In fact, she was concerned enough about his behavior to test it. "Did you remember that we have a dinner with your boss Thursday night?"

"Hmmm?"

"You have to go."

"So we'll go. That's Thursday and this is now. You put your face on and I'll fix breakfast, some nice bacon and eggs—" he glanced at her face "—some nice soda crackers and tea."

Adrienne stared after him. He'd been grousing about the dinner with his boss for weeks. Riley usually rated business dinners lower than snake bites, but now he was whistling again.

Ten minutes later, Adrienne appeared at the breakfast table. He'd put out a fork and knife to go with a small plate of soda crackers. She had the brief inclination to hold her head in her hands. "Riley?"

"Hmmm?"

One of them had to behave rationally. It was obvious to Adrienne that she was the only volunteer. "I'm not keeping the baby," she said quietly.

"No?"

"No." She finished the four crackers he'd arranged on the plate and stood to reach into the cupboard for the package. The whole package. Riley's sudden smile was unnerving when she sat down—he just didn't seem to realize how terribly serious a subject this was. "You know my mother and grandmother—nurturing women don't exactly run in my family, and I haven't one reason to think I'd be any different. I faced a long time ago that I wasn't maternal material."

Riley, noting her polishing off the crackers, slid half of his scrambled eggs on her plate.

"Are you listening to me?" she asked fiercely.

"To every word," he assured her.

"Maybe I never planned a pregnancy but that doesn't mean I don't care. If I'm stuck having this baby, I'm sure as brass going to make sure it ends up with a mother who knows what she's doing and would do everything right. A child belongs around a mother who—" she hesitated "—can make chocolate-chip cookies." Her eyes searched his. "We both know I can't boil water."

"You're exaggerating. You do a beautiful job of boiling water. It's just when you try to do something tricky like opening a soup can that you—"

"Riley, this is not time to tease." She dived into the scrambled eggs. "The only diaper I've ever seen was in an ad on TV. I've already had two horrible nightmares about diaper pins—dammit, don't smile. I'm telling you they were *nightmares*."

He wiped the smile off his face and said soberly, "You should have woken me up if you were having bad dreams."

She waved the sidetrack comment aside. "There's nothing wrong with working moms, but if I had my choice, I'd want the child around a mother who'd be there when he got home from school. Who was good at patching skinned knees, who always had time to read, and listen, and be there. A good mother creates a whole nurturing atmosphere." She lifted a hand in a helpless gesture. "I spend all day, every day, surrounded by people who are doing their best to tear their lives apart—that's the kind of atmosphere that I know. You think I'd risk bringing that home to a child?"

Riley's first impulse was to tease her silly for worry about such crazy, irrelevant nonsense. Parents learned to diaper babies; a child's whole future was hardly dependent on homemade chocolate-chip cookies; and she had as much in common with her mother as 14-carat gold did with the rings that came out of a Cracker Jacks box.

His impulse to tease her died a quick death when he realized she was serious. His intelligent Adrienne was actually afraid of a diaper. His perceptive courtroom counselor had no concept of her own giving and loving instincts, and his strong, self-reliant lover was worried sick about things he'd never conceived she'd be worried about.

Since she'd finished the crackers and most of his eggs, he forked two slices of bacon onto her plate. He didn't know what else to do.

"So having the baby adopted is the best possible answer," she finished finally.

"If that's what you want."

Adrienne saw him glance abruptly at his watch and frown. Lurching to his feet, he carted plates to the sink. He always had to leave ten minutes before she did. She trailed him as far as the hall. "You understand? Why adoption is the best option for the baby?"

"I understand why you feel it is." He buttoned his suit jacket and reached for his briefcase.

She automatically straightened his tie. "So if we agree on adoption, the rest of the solutions fall into place. I move out. A little more than seven months from now, I have the baby. In the interim, I have fifty states to find the absolutely perfect couple to adopt the child. In that way, the baby can have the best possible home and—"

"Adrienne."

Most mornings, Riley was pliable. Most mornings he was awake enough to respond to an air raid. When he nudged up her chin with his thumb, Adrienne was again aware that he just wasn't himself. His hand gently cupped her cheek, but his eyes were intensely blue, bold and battle bright.

"You were so sure I was going to argue with you last night," he murmured, "and I think you woke up even more sure I was going to argue with you this morning. Only that's not going to happen, love. We're going to deal with this your way—totally and completely—with only one teensy exception. You are not moving out."

"Riley—"

"You try it and I'll find you. You try moving into a cave and I'll find that cave. You are not going to be alone and pregnant, so wipe that thought permanently out of your mind." His tone was rock hard one instant, soothing and easy the next. "And now we have that clear, give us a kiss, because I'm sure as hell not going to be able to make it through the day without one."

She didn't give him a kiss. He took one. Just one, in which her sanity hovered somewhere between the crush of his mouth and the overwhelming warmth of his body. He tasted like coffee and peppermint toothpaste. He smelled like clean soap and lime. And he felt like the man she had hopelessly, desperately fallen in love with.

When he closed the door, though, she felt despair. Maybe she'd been crazy to think Riley would walk out on her, but staying together was equally impossible. He didn't understand. Everything had changed.

A treasured, well-savored memory popped into her mind that underlined her low mood. When was it, weeks back? She'd been soaking in a hot tub after a perfectly rotten day. Riley had shown up naked in the doorway, shut off all the lights, brought in a candle and two glasses of champagne and slid into the tub with her.

What happened after that was typical of her impulsive, wildly romantic Riley... but what would happen if he tried that now was the point. For openers, she'd have to turn down the alcohol because of the doctor's orders. Even assuming she ignored the doctor's orders, the first sip of champagne would undoubtedly make her throw up. And weeks down the pike, even a dark candlelit room wouldn't conceal a most unromantic, burgeoning tummy.

She wasn't going to stick around and see it happen—patience instead of passion in his eyes. Riley's natural impulsiveness squelched under forced responsibilities he'd never asked for. He was the only man with whom she'd ever come close to feeling secure, not just in bed but in living and caring and sharing every day with him. That security, though, came from knowing their relationship was based on an equal exchange of needs.

Nothing was equal now. What they had was unforgettably special, but Adrienne had always known that the best of relationships deteriorated when either partner was tied down or cornered.

She'd a thousand times rather call it off now than let that happen, and as far as this baby... unconsciously Adrienne's palm slipped down to her abdomen. Except for the smallest protrusion, there was nothing there, nothing she could feel to explain this terrible anxiety and panic.

It's obvious why you feel it—you don't want the baby in any way, she told herself fiercely, frowned, and abruptly raced for the kitchen.

The morning had been so traumatic that she'd nearly forgotten to take the baby's vitamin that Liz had prescribed.

Chapter Three

Riley canceled a lunch meeting and picked up some fast food en route to the bookstore. Inside, the clerk frowned at the sight of his paper-wrapped hamburger. He shot her a wink and a smile, and the next thing he knew he had more help than he could handle.

The teenage clerk was very sweet, very young and very crush-prone. It took all his tact to convince her that he didn't need any help, which as it happened, was a lie. Another woman wandered into his aisle and plucked a book off the shelf faster than the snap of a finger. How the hell did she find it so easy?

There seemed to be more than a hundred books to choose from, starting with Spock and ending with space-age concepts of parenting. There was a *Mother's Almanac*, a *Father's Almanac*, books on pregnancy, books on child raising, books on how to increase the intelligence of a fetus in the womb, books on discipline, books on childbirth underwater, books on...

In the end, he scooped up everything he could carry. The clerk's eyes widened at the size of the stack on the counter. "I take it you're gonna be a father?"

"Yes." The moment she started punching buttons, he knew he wasn't carrying enough cash.

"First-time dad?"

"Yes." He flipped through his wallet for a gold card.

"Do you care whether it's a boy or a girl?"

"No." Actually he cared about Adrienne, which was why he was buying the books. She was so shook. So shook, so worried, so scared, and so sure the whole world had turned upside down—and maybe it had. All Riley knew was that for the past twenty-four hours he felt as if he'd fallen into a bowl with a food mixer on high speed. Adrienne's mind was on babies; his was on her. Maybe the books held no answers, but they were a start to understanding what she was feeling.

With his gold card retrieved, he reached for the book sack—which seemed to weigh between a ton and a ton and a half—and used his shoulder to open the store door. An April breeze whipped through his hair, the wind crackling through the new spring leaves like rustling taffeta. Halfway to his car, it hit him with all the surprise of the first bomb of Pearl Harbor.

He was going to be a father. Him. Riley Stuart. A father.

He had been whistling that morning for just that reason, of course, but then the connection had only been a vague emotion. A family and children had always been an equally vague plan in his mind—sometime, after he finished law school. Sometime, after he got himself established. Sometime, after he had a job that required no traveling.

Sometime had just arrived, and with it a slow thrumming beat in the middle of his chest. He wanted it. He wanted the child, suddenly and fiercely and totally. Adrienne's daughter, with her pride and sassiness and soft vulnerable eyes. Or a son, with her smarts and his shoulders—he'd die if a daughter got his shoulders. If it were a daughter, she'd have to go in a convent before she was ten if she looked like Adrienne. But his son . . . his son could go to Dartmouth.

An old man bumped into him, glared and mumbled past with some comment about people blocking sidewalks.

Riley's step picked up, but his focus was blind. Always, there had been a woman in those "sometime" fantasies. Not just *a* woman. *The* woman: lover, mate, wife, friend. From the day he met her, Adrienne fit all the niches but one.

Numbers were particularly relevant because a family started at three. Something was wrong in the scenario of just father and son, or just father and daughter. The snapshot without Adrienne didn't work. Life without Adrienne didn't work. Convincing her of that was obviously going to be tricky, particularly since he didn't dare mention marriage.

And he had no idea where he was going to hide all the books.

For the first time in weeks Adrienne felt like herself. She'd won her case in court, nausea hadn't plagued her all day and she had energy and good humor to burn. Humming something catchy, she pulled the emerald-green dress over her head and reached back for the zipper. Nothing ever went wrong when she wore the green dress. Maybe it wasn't new, but it had always been as lucky as a rabbit's foot for her.

She zipped it past her hips, then frowned. The zipper didn't want to squeeze any farther. Her tummy seemed to have popped out three inches in the past twenty-four hours. She hesitated, then took it off and reached for the jeweled print chemise in the closet. All right, so she couldn't wear her favorite. Who needed a rabbit's foot, anyway? Absolutely nothing was going to spoil her mood tonight.

"I hate going to these things."

Adrienne stepped out of the closet, and noted with amusement that Riley's scowl was as dark as a thundercloud. "I know you do," she said soothingly.

"There's no reason to go. I'll just call Brown and tell him we both caught the bubonic plague."

Smothering a chuckle, she watched him jerk a tie around his neck as though he intended to strangle himself. Riley in a temper had a lot in common with a baby in his "Terrible Twos." Serene and calm, she walked over to button his shirt cuffs. "You make this huge fuss every time, and all for nothing. You always end up having a great time and even if you didn't, it's only for a few short hours—"

"*Wasted* hours. Listening to Brown rant on about his right-wing policies. And his wife's as charming as a barracuda. She'll probably feed us raw fish. She did last time."

"Riley, this is your boss's way of telling you you're doing a great job."

"Yeah? He wants to do that, he can give me a raise."

"He gave you a raise. In fact, he gave you two this past year." Adrienne patiently removed the gold-and-green tie and replaced it with a blue-and-gold one. He was wearing a blue suit—her choice. If she'd left it to Riley, he'd be wearing a hair shirt and sackcloth. "He's vetting you for the head of the industrial relations department. You know that."

"He's not *vetting* me. He's pushing me toward it."

"He knows you're considering hanging out your own shingle. You can't crucify Brown for offering you every possible nugget to make you stay—it's your own fault he thinks you're irreplaceable—and tonight is hardly as complicated as all that. I don't know why you let yourself get so worked up over one dinner, one evening." She finished tying his tie and patted it down. Mad or not, he looked wonderful. Virile and vital and blue-eyed—but regretfully, stubborn.

"We're not going," he said flatly.

"Okay," she agreed, all soothing smiles, and then did what any other red-blooded woman would do— dragged him to the car.

An hour later, they drove past the wrought-iron gates into Andrew Brown's estate. The three-story sprawling mansion was built of white stone, its elegance suiting the life-style of a man who owned an international manufacturing company with subsidiaries all over the world. Brown had a full staff of attorneys whose specialties ranged from corporate law to industrial relations. Riley was the lawyer Brown called in the middle of the night to settle a labor problem in Germany. Or in Japan. Or in Topeka, Kansas.

Riley might have dreams of starting his own practice, but as Adrienne knew well, the corporate life hadn't hurt him. Riley adored those labor disputes; the tougher the better. As she also knew, once she got him inside he would not only behave nicely but shine in the crowd. He always did. The only trick was getting him inside.

"We could still back out," Riley muttered as he escorted Adrienne to the door. "Brown would never know we were here. I didn't see anything wrong with the bubonic plague excuse."

If he were a two-year-old, she would have stood him in a corner. Since he was a grown man, she swung her arms around his neck and kissed his mouth. There was lovemaking and then there was sex. There were occasions when nothing worked as well as plain old sex on Riley. His prickly mood dissolved the minute he felt the snuggle of her body, the deliberate rub of her lips. They both knew she was manipulating him. They both liked it. "You're not only going in there. You're going to have a good time," she informed him.

He considered that while he took another kiss. "I'd rather go parking." He wanted more than another kiss. When he nuzzled her throat, he discovered she'd chosen a wicked scent tonight. Deliberately. "When's the last time you were made love to in the back seat of a car?"

"Never."

"Never?" He lifted his head and most leisurely surveyed her mouth, her throat, her eyes. He looked until a streak of coral climbed her cheeks, delighting him. "We're going to have an awfully good time, taking care of that serious lack in your education—"

"Riley!" She rang the bell, her nerves tingling. He did it to her all the time. Made her feel desired and special. Made her feel like no one mattered but the two of them, that they could conquer anything as long as they were together. That's always how it had been with them, at least until she discovered the pregnancy... but quickly, quickly she banished the pregnancy from her mind. Not tonight. She was in such a radiant mood that nothing could disturb it.

Her mood dipped just a hair when their hostess answered the door. If Maud fit the stereotype of her name, she'd be staid and proper. Instead Brown's second wife had a long white throat uniquely suited to the wearing of diamonds, a smooth coil of Egyptian-dark hair, and a shrewd eye for an up-and-coming man— particularly if he was a looker. She smiled a lambent welcome at Adrienne, but made a point of bussing Riley before ushering them both through the marble foyer.

"What's new in divorce settlements, Adrienne?" Maud asked, although her attention still focused on Riley as she led them toward the intimate—a mere twenty—dinner party. "You and I never seem to have the chance to just sit down and talk."

"Maybe tonight," Adrienne murmured, annoyed that she felt unsettled instead of amused. Maud's antics had always been a source of humor, not stress. If Maud hadn't made a token play for Riley, Adrienne would have had the kindness to immediately call the paramedics, knowing the older woman was ill. Maud was just . . . Maud.

Typically, when Riley freed his arm, Maud made certain her breast brushed his wrist. Just as typically, Riley shot Adrienne a comical look. Any other night she would have chuckled with him, but somehow her mood had shifted another tiny hair. Riley could handle himself around far more skilled barracudas than his boss's wife. It was just . . .

Just nothing, you goose. Within minutes of entering the living room, she automatically deserted Riley and did what she did best: worked the room. Riley wouldn't care if she curled on a couch with her shoes off, but Adrienne did—he hadn't quit Brown's yet, and until he was certain of that decision, she had a job to do. She listened to Andrew Brown's political monologue, circulated around the corporate heads and made careful small talk with the wives.

It wasn't Adrienne's favorite kind of evening, but she'd walked in confidently prepared to enjoy it. There was just no reason for the inexplicable sensation of isolation that kept creeping up on her. The Browns always invited a similar group. Ambition dominated the ambience, and an itty bit of back stabbing and in jokes dominated the conversations, but those dynamics came with the corporate world. Adrienne knew the game and was more than willing to play it for Riley. He was hardheaded about honesty; it didn't hurt to be nice. Most of the men in the room had wives to play diplomat, but Riley...

Didn't have a wife.

She shook off the word "wife" and plastered a radiant smile back on her face. Maud found her just before dinner. "For a change I put you on the other side of the table from Riley, darling. Dinner conversation's so boring when we stick couples together, don't you think?"

Adrienne mentally released a humorous sigh. Maud tried her best to stir things up at a party, so it was no surprise to see that her hostess had settled Riley between two women—the only other two women at the party who were single.

As she eyed his companions across the table, she thought wickedly that the two ladies were in for a treat. The tall, quiet blonde had looked desperately nervous when she first walked in; the younger brunette had painfully shy dark eyes. Neither, clearly, had expected to walk into the fiercely competitive atmosphere of Maud's "little" dinner. Riley, of course, would have them at ease before either knew what hit them.

Adrienne had known from the day she met him that Riley attracted women and also that he loved to flirt. She'd never called him on it, because there was no point. He hadn't gone blind the day he met her. He liked women, always had and always would—and what was the harm? You can't hold a man with jealousy or by misunderstanding every casual conversation he had with another woman. If a woman was going to hold a man, it had to be with what they had together.

The dining room was a massive business in mahogany and gold. Candles winked from sterling holders and silverware clinked for the opening course of vichyssoise. Adrienne took one look at the potato soup, felt her stomach warningly pucker and glanced again across the table.

The gentle-eyed brunette was smiling now. Adrienne hadn't noticed before that she had on a form-fitting white knit dress . . . and a stomach as flat as a pancake. So did the tall, quiet blonde, who suddenly wasn't so quiet. Riley had said something to make her laugh. Nervousness forgotten, the blonde's face took on animation and life—she was really very attractive, with intelligent, bright eyes and a natural warmth in her laughter. Adrienne was sure she would like her. Riley had never gone for airheads. He did like a lithe, long figure, a woman in control of her life, a woman . . . who wasn't pregnant.

Someone passed a plate of asparagus in front of her. Riley caught her eye over the table and winked. It was a sexy wink, an intimate wink, a private message passed just between the two of them. *We'll be out of here soon,* his blue eyes promised her.

Not soon enough. To Adrienne's utter horror, a lump filled her throat too thick to swallow and a wave of unmanageable emotion started to engulf her.

"Would you excuse me a moment?" she murmured to the man next to her and slipped away from the table. Although it couldn't be ten feet to the doorway, the distance seemed like ten miles, and once out in the hall, she had no memory of where the powder room was.

By the time she found the almond-and-gold powder room, she had a direct problem with a flood—pouring uncontrollably out of her eyes. *Good grief, what is the matter with you?* Too shivery to stand, she dropped to the edge of the almond tub. The whole thing was crazy. Huge, crazy hiccuping sobs kept emerging from her lungs and wouldn't stop. Tears streamed from her eyes like an unplugged dike. She mentally called herself a hundred names, but it didn't help.

Someone knocked on the door. Mortified, she gulped back a new flush of tears and called out, "Be out in a minute!"

"Adrienne, open the door."

As fast as she recognized Riley's voice, she reached for one of her hostess's impeccable guest towels and doused it with cold water.

"My boss is going to be irritated with me if I break down his door, love. It would be a lot easier if you'd just unlock it."

"Can't." She was positive her voice sounded normal, yet his response was immediate.

"I really will break it down, honey."

He wouldn't, she promised herself, but there was a brief second when she wasn't absolutely sure. Plastering the towel over her eyes, she jerked the lock and the door. "I just got a little something in my eye," she said blithely. "It's all taken care of. For heaven's sake, go back to the dinner party!"

Riley closed and latched the door behind him. The spacious powder room abruptly became crowded, particularly when he loomed close enough to peek around the corner of the towel. He didn't need more than one quick look at her eyes. "All taken care of, hmm?"

If he'd just sounded appalled or impatient, she could have pulled herself together. Instead he sounded so damned *dear*. Her lungs heaved out a horrible sound and the tears started pouring again. "I'm sorry. I don't know what's wrong with me. This is so stupid!"

"It's okay."

"It's not okay. It's disgusting. Nobody killed my dog. Nobody started a world war. Nobody hurt me. I was just sitting there and everything was fine—"

"Adrienne, it's okay. It's perfectly normal. There's a whole section on blues starting on page 78 of the pregnancy manual." He plunked down onto the toilet seat and pulled her on his lap, jamming her cheek to his shirt and wrapping his arms around her.

"What blues? What pregnancy manual?"

"Shh." He rocked her. She was shaking so hard, crying so hard, that for a while he couldn't do anything else. He heard something about a green dress that didn't fit, some woman's flat, flat stomach, and that he had every right and freedom to talk to a beautiful blonde.

She lifted her head to repeat fiercely, "Every right, Riley." He jammed her cheek back to his chest. In good time the tears finally slowed, even hurricanes had to quit sometime. He patted his pocket for a handkerchief before he remembered that he had never in his life carried a handkerchief. The Browns had several thousand dollars' worth of brass fixtures, recessed lighting, marble and fancy towels, but no tissues. He unraveled some toilet paper and made her blow her nose.

"I just can't believe I'm doing this. It's so stupid!"

"It's not stupid."

"It is, too! I've never been moody or overemotional in my entire life!"

"You were never pregnant before in your entire life." He smoothed back her hair. She really was a mess. He couldn't recall ever seeing Adrienne such a total disaster before. Her nose was red, so were her eyes; her cheeks were blotchy and her hair, well, he'd messed up her hair. Dammit, he loved her!

"You have to go back to the party."

He expressed his feelings about the party in a simple four-letter word.

"Riley! This business dinner is part of your work. There's no way I'm going to let me—or this pregnancy—interfere with your job. That's the exact reason I told you that we'd both be better off if I looked for another place and moved out."

"Then you could have the blues all by yourself?"

"What is this 'blues' business? I don't have any blues; I just went temporarily bananas. And you don't have to be nice when someone behaves like a total fruitcake.''

"The blonde is a no one, honey. Just someone sitting next to me. I was just talking to her."

"You're welcome to talk to her."

"I can see that."

"She was beautiful—"

"Heavy mascara. Bad teeth. Hips like an army tank," he improvised rapidly.

"She looked so smart."

"She had the IQ of a frog."

"She did not. She looked smart. And not only smart, she looked nice."

Three of the pregnancy manuals had sections on blues. None of them exactly equipped Riley to handle this. Adrienne was the most sensible, practical woman he knew. Until now. And until now, she'd never had a jealous bone in her body. "Okay, she was nice. But she wasn't you, love."

"Me? You *have* to get it through your head, Riley. You like svelte and slim. I'm going to look like an elephant in another few months."

"I like elephants."

"Not ugly out-of-control elephants." From the deep blue—from absolutely nowhere—she suddenly whispered, "I'm so scared."

So he kissed her. And when her arms went up around her neck, he kissed her again.

By the time he kissed her a third time, the blood was humming through his veins and his heart was full. Her responsiveness had nothing to do with passion and—

whether or not she knew it—everything to do with trust. For those few brief moments he had a taste of it all. The compelling power of loving her. The devastating weakness of knowing she loved him just as much, if she'd just give that trust a chance.

In due time, of course, it occurred to both of them that there was something less than romantic about necking on a toilet seat in his boss's house. Adrienne was the first one to start chuckling—an honest chuckle. She was back to herself again.

Riley left her to seek out Maud. When his boss's wife forgot to play vamp, she had a decent head on her shoulders. At the same time Maud made their excuse of sudden illness to the dinner party, Riley was sneaking Adrienne out the back door into a star-speckled April night.

The sneaking wasn't strictly necessary, but it was fun. Racing to the car made them feel like kids playing hooky, and Adrienne was breathless with laughter when she climbed in the passenger seat. If Riley had anything to say about it, it wasn't the last time she was going to laugh that evening. He wanted her to forget that upsetting bout of blues.

Even more than that, he wanted her to know that he'd be there for her—not just for the laughter, but the tough times as well.

April finished off cool, but the whole month of June had been hot and sweltering. As she walked into the apartment, Adrienne welcomed the flush of air conditioning with a heartfelt sigh. Pushing off her

shoes and laying down her briefcase, she made a bee-
line for the kitchen.

Riley had a late-afternoon meeting, which meant
dinner would be late, which in any moral framework
on earth justified an immediate snack. She bypassed
the butter brickle ice cream, the Muenster cheese and
the caramel corn, all of which appealed to her last
week. This week it was spinach. Freshly washed and
raw.

Until this pregnancy, there wasn't a soul in her life
who could have accused Adrienne of greed. If Riley
had been there, she'd have delicately plucked a leaf or
two. Since he wasn't, she pulled the whole bag from
the lower shelf of the refrigerator. Munching ravenously, she sorted through the mail, and when her snack
was finished headed for the bedroom to change
clothes.

She peeled off her work clothes and pulled on a pair
of cotton pants, discovered they wouldn't zip—much
less button—cast them off and tried another pair. Five
minutes later, her entire summer wardrobe of slacks
had been rejected—none of them fit—and she was
fingering through Riley's closet, muttering about the
weight-gaining potential of spinach.

She was tugging on one of his oldest, softest blue
oxford shirts—Riley hadn't commented on her
usurping his shirt wardrobe any more than he'd mentioned her recent love of spinach—when she noticed
the stuffed animal.

It wasn't your usual small, cuddly teddy bear. It was
a unicorn, white, soft-furred, and half as tall as she

was. Although Riley had tucked it in the far corner beyond the aquariums, it wasn't the kind of thing one could miss for long.

Although she continued buttoning his shirt, she couldn't take her eyes off the toy. She had deliberately "missed" a great deal over the past few weeks. She hadn't noticed the *Father's Almanac* buried under Riley's *Wall Street Journal*, for example. She had also paid no attention to the pregnancy manual under the bathroom sink, with its earmarked pages and highlighted paragraphs.

Twenty-five pounds of white unicorn was tougher to ignore. The look of the toy made her feel as though a rug had been swept out from under her.

For the past two months, Adrienne had done the best she knew how to pretend the pregnancy didn't exist. Since the dinner party, she had temporarily, warily, dropped the idea of moving out. Riley simply became totally irrational on the subject. But she had only agreed to stay until the baby was born. And only, she promised herself, if she could make their relationship work as it always had.

For his sake, she hadn't mentioned babies. He'd caught on to her cravings, but she'd carefully hidden her queasy stomach and bouts of blues from him. A dozen times, she'd tactfully told him that he had the same freedom to leave he'd always had. If his life was negatively affected in any way by this pregnancy, she was prepared to pack her bags.

She'd worked hard to make sure nothing was changed for Riley. She was changed, though, and there was no fighting it. No matter how often she told herself she didn't want the baby, sometimes this elation would sweep through her...sometimes an extraordinary sensation of softness...and sometimes her crazy hormones had an embarrassing erotic and exotic effect when the lights went out. She couldn't seem to keep her hands off him, which thoroughly delighted Riley, the rogue.

The passion was real, the pretending becoming increasingly hard. She *was* pregnant. Their lives *had* changed. Decisions *had* to be made about the baby. Soon, those things had to be faced and dealt with. She'd already dealt with the reason he hadn't brought up marriage. *He never wanted a permanent relationship with you, Adrienne. You understood that from the very beginning.*

She couldn't understand his buying the unicorn at all.

The apartment door slammed. She was still sitting on the bed when Riley strode in. He was always a dynamo of energy after a desk-bound day. By the time he found her, he'd already peeled off his suit jacket and was tearing at his tie.

He took one look at her dressed in his shirt and pounced. You'd think he hadn't seen her in a week the way he kissed her. You'd think the man was magic the way she responded...and she did respond, eyes closed and blindly reaching for him. It was a foolish illusion in her head, she knew, yet Riley had the dreadful gift of making her feel cherished, wanted, needed.

He also wasn't happy until she was good and unraveled. Straightening with a merciless grin—a promise for later—he strode toward his closet. "You have to wait until after dinner."

"Do I smell the reek of egotism in this room?" she wondered aloud.

"You want me. Go ahead, admit it. I won't tell."

"You? Of the hairy chest and the bony knees?"

"You love my knees."

She did, it was true, but that was only because she was insane about the man, in bed and much more disastrously, out of it. Her mood dropped like a plummeting boulder, though, when her gaze darted back to the unicorn. "What are you doing, Riley?" she asked quietly.

"At this precise instant, stripping." He exhibited one hairy leg around the closet door as proof, then momentarily reemerged in cotton jeans. "It's one hot night out there."

"That's not what I meant. Who is that stuffed animal supposed to be for?"

He saw where she was focused. "The baby?" He tugged a T-shirt over his head. "I suppose you think it's a little big for a newborn."

"I think it would be a big toy for a baby cow," she said wryly. "Only we're not having a cow. We're having a baby that both of us have agreed would be best off given up for adoption."

"I was fairly sure you hadn't changed your mind about that."

"You know I haven't."

He nodded. "I also know that your standards are pretty tough—some might say impossibly tough, since you've totally rejected every adoption agency you've talked to. So I've been doing a little research, and came up with someone to adopt the baby for you. Someone you know. Someone where you'd be able to keep track of what happened to the child, and someone where you can be positive the baby will be raised with values you value."

For a moment air seemed locked in her lungs. None of the adoption agencies she'd talked to had offered those things. They'd told her she was making "impossible demands." One caseworker in Chicago had had the nerve to suggest that Adrienne did not sound emotionally sure she could give up the baby, which was totally untrue. She was relieved and reassured that Riley had found someone. It was just, momentarily, difficult to breathe.

"Who is this 'someone'?" she asked hollowly.

He shot her a fast grin. "Me."

"You?" But as fast as she lurched off the bed, Riley had ducked through the doorway and left the room.

Chapter Four

Adrienne bolted after him, and found him calmly reaching for a spoon in the kitchen drawer. "You can't possibly adopt the baby!"

"No? Why not?" He lifted the lid on the earthenware pot that had been simmering all day. Immediately the scents of orange peel and garlic and red wine spiced the air. His French *Boeuf en Daube*, an old favorite of Adrienne's, was done.

"For all the hundred obvious reasons starting with the most important one." Adrienne sank onto the kitchen chair as if it was the last seat on the bus. "You don't want the baby. If you'd wanted it, you'd have told me a long time before this."

He gently contradicted her. "Actually I always wanted a child or two, but the idea always went on the back burner—after law school, after establishing myself in a career, after I had a house." He carefully didn't mention marriage as part of those plans. He knew her reaction to the word too well. "I guess I always thought there's be an obvious 'ideal time' to be a father, but I'm thirty-five now. I don't want to be so gray haired and arthritic that I can't swing a bat in the yard with my kid."

"You never said any of that before," she said in a small voice.

Carrying the salad bowl to the sink, he fluffed her bangs. Poor baby, she looked so shell-shocked. She was also past four months pregnant, and time was running out. For the past few weeks Adrienne had taken up the nasty habit of catering to his every whim, laughing at his worst jokes, shielding him from every little stress. Little stresses like a pregnancy, for instance. She seemed determined to pretend the baby didn't exist. He'd tried it her way, but the days kept passing like a time bomb. He had to do something to get through that sweet thick head of hers that her lover was not deserting ship.

"I didn't talk about it before for a lot of reasons." He handed her the silverware to set the table. "I think both of us wanted some private time and space to adjust to the idea. And besides that, you've hardly invited any discussions about the baby."

"Because I didn't want you to feel obligated. I had no reason to think you wanted the child." Her voice caught on a reedy breath. "Riley, if I've been blind or insensitive about your feelings—"

He nipped that one fast. "Honey, you're sensitive to other people's feelings to a fault." Except her own, he thought fleetingly. "I never mentioned adopting the child, because when you first told me you were pregnant, I could see all the obvious obstacles. Sure, I can picture my carrying an urchin on my shoulders, but what do I know about chicken pox and colic? Then there's my job—working for Brown, I'm on the road too much. And I don't like the idea of raising a kid in an apartment. Then there's the whole thing of 'single dads.' There are lots of single moms out there, not half as many single dads, possibly because we're not half as good at the job.''

He watched her carefully set two knives around his plate, two forks around her own. Then she started folding napkins. Enough for a week.

"Anyway, as far as colic and chicken pox, I figure I could learn. And as far as being a good father, I figure I could work at it. Hard. The job—hell. It'd be a tough financial go for a while, but in the long run I always wanted to hang out my own shingle. And the apartment isn't any problem at all. You like it, sweet, and you also keep telling me that one of us has to move the minute the baby is born.''

Her head shot up. "Babies don't belong with living-together couples, Riley. It's just not right.''

"I totally agree. So you keep the place, and in the meantime I'll look for a house. Something small, with a little lawn and trees. You wouldn't object if I were the one to adopt the baby, would you?''

"I . . . no, of course not.'' She pleated another napkin. A cinema of snapshots flooded through her mind—Riley rocking a baby, carrying a little one on his shoulders to the zoo, playing Santa Claus. In every mental photo, the child looked deliriously happy, and why not? No one had more patience than Riley; he was affectionate and warm, perceptive and accepting—an absolute natural as a father. "I think it's a fine idea,'' she said brightly. "I just . . .''

"You just what, love?''

She just felt like someone had smashed her in the teeth. He wanted the baby, but not her. If he'd wanted her, he would have brought up marriage. Okay, okay, possibly she'd reacted like a cat on a hot spit any time he'd even mentioned wedding rings in the past, but bigger truths dominated her mind now—the same bigger truths and insecurities that had haunted her since the start of this pregnancy.

From the very beginning, she had never expected the relationship to last; she had always expected him to leave her. The power of being in love had a lot in common with a newly opened champagne bottle. Nothing beat the fizz and the sparkle, but the bottle left open over time lost both. She'd seen it with her parents and she saw it every day in divorce court, but she'd always hoped—fiercely hoped—that it might take Riley just a little more time to realize he wasn't in love with her.

"What's wrong, honey?"

"Nothing," she said. He whisked the pile of napkins out of her hands, leaving her nothing to do. "I just don't know how a father goes about adopting his own baby."

"Neither do I. Pretty humorous, isn't it? Two attorneys in the same house and neither of us knows the laws affecting adoptions. Still, it'll be easy enough to find out...as long as you're sure you don't mind."

"Why on earth would I mind? It's your child."

"Yours, too," he reminded her casually. "So maybe you'd better be very sure of that, too, love."

"Sure of what?"

His gaze was as blue and intense as a hot summer sky. "That you don't want the child."

She suddenly blinked hard. Sometimes when she thought of the baby, this huge, wallowing sweet emotion engulfed her—she'd even dreamed of the three of them together, her holding the baby so tightly, Riley smiling, so happy, so proud. Maybe it was that picture of pride that made her wake up in the night, shivering all over, confused and upset and afraid.

It was so easy to hurt a child. She knew. There was no point in denying it; she came from a line of cold women. Her grandmother was as loving as a porcupine; her mother had been distant and insensitive. "A woman has to be tough to survive in this life," her mother always told her, but Adrienne hadn't been tough as a child. She'd been hurt, too easily and too often. Not anymore. As a grown woman, "You're just like me, darling" was her mother's favorite phrase.

Just like her. Adrienne couldn't seem to shake the phrase from her mind; it followed her as mercilessly as a shadow.

"Honey?"

She touched two fingers to her temples. "We've already discussed this. I want nothing to do with this baby. Nothing, Riley."

She knew she sounded coldhearted and insensitive. Hard. Like her mother. Which made it particularly difficult to understand why Riley brushed a soft, silent kiss on her brow as he set dinner in front of her.

He dropped the discussion, and she tried to put it out of her mind. It was one of those nights when Riley had work after dinner and she didn't, so when he holed up in the study, she fed the fish and did the dishes, then sneaked a wash load of his shirts downstairs to the laundry. Riley's job was the wash, but she knew he liked his shirts with a little starch and he never took the time.

She checked on him later. From the spread of papers, she could see that he was three-quarters done, so she brought him a weak whiskey—his way of winding down—and turned on an extra light. Riley would read in the dark if she let him. And outside, the night had turned cool. She switched off the air conditioning and threw open the windows, especially in the bedroom. He didn't sleep well if it was stuffy, and there was nothing stuffier than air conditioning.

"Adrienne!"

She pelted back to the study.

Black-rimmed glasses perched on his nose, he motioned to the place next to him on the couch. "Sit. Before you wear yourself out."

"I wasn't worn out."

"Sit!"

"Wow," she murmured. "I'm real impressed. That sounded like a dictatorial, chauvinistic order, and here I thought you were such a cupcake."

Unfortunately he was within reaching distance of her wrist, and Riley did like to wrestle. By the time he'd tired of his acrobatics, she was lying on the couch with her head in his lap, she was well kissed, and his glasses were back on his nose.

Legal pad pages shifted past her. "Riley?"

"Hmm?"

"Your choosing to adopt the baby shouldn't have anything to do with our living together. They're two separate things. Nothing's changed. It's still not necessary to stay together because I'm pregnant. You have the same rights in the relationship you always had. If at any time the situation becomes awkward or you don't want to be here—"

"I know. I'm free to leave, which you tell me so often that my ego's beginning to feel like a chipped tooth," he said dryly. He closed the last law book and stacked it with the others. "Could you not try to kick me out of the house tonight? I'm too beat to pack."

She missed his small joke because she was so busy inhaling a lungful of air. "When we were talking before dinner...I know I must have sounded selfish and hard. Riley, I can't help it if I'm not maternal or nurturing."

"You just don't have a single caretaking instinct," he murmured helpfully.

"You know I don't." She tried to move, but his arm sliced off her attempt with a gentle stranglehold across her neck.

Riley would have loved to do more than strangle her. Earlier in the kitchen, he'd done what he set out to do—made sure she knew he wanted their child, and forced her to picture him in the role of father. When she hadn't rejected either idea, hope had sprung eternal. Maybe over time, if he were tiptoe careful, he just might be able to sneakily bring up rings without her bolting for the door.

Eternal hope hadn't lasted long. It was going to be damn tough to mention marriage when the pregnant lady in question said flat-out she didn't want the baby. *His* baby. He had wanted to hang up on that bruising hurt, and he probably would have—if Adrienne hadn't been the one with the bruised, panicked eyes and skin as pale as parchment.

And she was still jumpy. Still pale.

"Is there some reason," Adrienne asked delicately, "that you have your arm locked around my neck so I can't move?"

"Yeah." He dropped the legal pad and pencil on the lamp table. "You were about to jump up and pour me another whiskey. I don't need one—nor did I ever want or expect you to wait on me."

"I was never waiting on you!"

"I know," he said mildly. "You have no nurturing instincts whatsoever. Lightning would probably strike if you got the insane idea that you take care of everyone around you."

She knew he was teasing her, but she couldn't smile because of the huge lump in her throat. It wasn't easy to say what she wanted to say. "I just don't want you to hate me because I don't want the baby."

"Sweetheart, there isn't a chance in this life I could hate you. And whether or not you want the baby has nothing to do with that."

"I don't want it, Riley."

"It's okay."

"At all."

"It's okay."

She woke in the middle of the night with the strangest sensation in her abdomen. Lying on her side, Riley was curled against her spine. They always slept that way, her back spooned to his chest, the front of his thigh nuzzled against the back of hers. Nothing was wrong this night, nothing different...except for that tiny, vague feeling.

Blinking in the dark, she waited, disoriented and sleepy. It happened again. Not pain. Just the brush of a velvet flutter from deep inside her.

"Riley!"

She turned over and grabbed him. He didn't move. A siren next to his ear wasn't likely to arouse Riley from a sound sleep. She had to shake his shoulders hard, and even then he didn't open his eyes. "If there's a burglar, you handle it," he mumbled groggily.

"Dammit, would you wake up? This is serious."

She grabbed his hand and locked it over her abdomen in the darkness. Nothing happened. Seconds ticked past, then minutes. Still, the flutter movement didn't repeat itself.

"This has a lot in common with someone waiting for tax reform." Riley yawned. "If you're sick, love, tell me. If you're in trouble, tell me. If not, I'm going back to sleep."

"Please, Riley!"

It happened again. Nothing monumental, nothing huge. It simply felt the wings of a butterfly stirring inside her. "Did you feel it?" she yelped.

"No."

"It's real."

"What's real?"

"The baby!"

Although the aquarium lights were turned off, a full moon shimmered silvery light from the window. She saw him when he lifted up on one elbow and slowly skimmed his palm from her abdomen to her hip. "Not that you care about the baby," he said gravely.

She backpedaled like no one's business. "I never said I cared about the baby. It was just...you obviously do. Since you want to adopt it. So I thought you should know."

"Ah."

There was a definite smile on his face. A smug smile. An all-knowing male smile. Maybe that was why she kissed him—to wipe it off. Maybe she kissed him to divert him from traumatic deep-water subjects—like babies. Maybe she kissed him because she was sick of his being patient and accepting and kind when she knew darn well she'd been a pill to live with for weeks.

He didn't kiss back like he was all that annoyed either by babies or her.

For Adrienne, the future still loomed like an abyss. To bog Riley down because of her problems, though, was never what she'd wanted. The future was just going to have to wait.

Ruthlessly she pulled the pillow from behind his head and let it drop on the floor. With the chilling determination of a hunter, she cornered her prey by climbing on top of him and anchoring his head still between her palms. She nipped his shoulder hard, to show him who was boss, and she kissed his lips very softly, to show him how much trouble he was in.

Riley would undoubtedly look more threatened if he weren't chuckling so hard.

"All right for you. Put your hands above your head," she ordered mercilessly.

"Oh, God. Is this going to be one of those impossible choices about my virtue or my life?"

"This is one of those times when you have to take your medicine like a man. Try and be brave. Fight me and I warn you, I won't be responsible."

He didn't try to fight her, but it was tough to pull off the role of aggressive seductress when your lover was choking back laughter. A tickle put him in his place, but unfortunately Riley wasn't a gentleman. He retaliated.

Later, she remembered a splash of covers and a tangle of limbs, giggling and being out of breath and Riley leaning over her with laughter in his eyes. That laughter softened, muted, darkened. And then his lips found hers.

His skin was stroking warm and his taste alluring. She knew what he wanted and she knew what he loved. The night blurred into sensations—hunger and softness, quicksilver kisses and Riley's eyes, so full of need, so full of want.

There was the briefest moment when she felt his lips on her abdomen, a reminder of the baby that should have broken her mood, yet it didn't. The wonder of life inside her had started with Riley, and this night was about that kind of love. Wonder, precious and fragile, seeped into her senses, instilled her hands with feminine magic, filled her heart.

She pulled him down and took him in, a hundred times more wild than she knew herself to be, yet not so much with passion as tenderness. He was everything. She wanted him to know that, and in the darkness she gave him everything she was. With Riley, she had never had any other choice. With Riley, she had never wanted one.

Seven o'clock in the morning was no time to match socks. Riley scooped up the whole drawerful and tossed them in the open suitcase on his bed, his mood as pleasant as an irritated rattlesnake's.

He reached in the closet for a couple of white shirts and jammed them in on top of the socks. Adrienne was up and due out of the shower any minute. Like him, she'd been wakened by the telephone at six o'clock in the morning. It was his boss. There was union trouble in the West German plant. Riley's flight left in three hours. He had to hit the office first, and how was he supposed to remember where his passport was this early in the morning?

More relevant, he didn't want to leave. A year ago, he'd have jumped for the challenge of a European labor problem—dammit, they were fun—but a year ago Adrienne hadn't been pregnant.

The last place he wanted to be was five thousand miles away from her, and especially now. He knew she felt conflicting emotions about the baby, but last night she'd shown him what mattered. She wanted it. Desperately. He'd never seen her so hushed, so excited, so beautiful . . . or so suddenly scared as when she'd felt the baby's first movement.

He's guessed for a long time that her feelings about both the baby and marriage were mixed with fear. He understood her fear of marriage, but not her fear of the child. Adrienne could cope with corporate politics, a burned fuse, or survival in a blizzard, so nothing explained her irrational confusion over the baby except fear. Only one emotion excised common sense, overruled the brain, snaked up on you and locked its fangs where you were most vulnerable. Maybe Riley didn't understand why, but he sure as hell knew Adrienne was scared.

She hadn't been scared last night, and the memory still had him feeling dipped in honey. Hot? Her mouth alone could have caused a conflagration. Sensual? She had a tongue that ought to be licensed. And as far as love, Adrienne had redefined the word for him last night. She'd come to him with honesty and vulnerability, naked like he'd never seen her naked, and open from the soul.

He was going to marry that damn woman, and while one night didn't change the world, last night had surely made a difference. She trusted him. How could she have made love with him like that if she didn't? He'd be infinitely careful with her this morning, infinitely patient. She would undoubtedly be feeling sensitive this morning.

"Riley, I swear I could smack you. Get away from there!"

His head jerked up from the suitcase. "What's the matter?"

"You're going to get there with your shirts looking like accordions, and what are all these socks?" Adrienne bent over the case and dumped everything he'd packed. "Men! And you're not taking the gray suit. It has a spot. You're taking the blue one."

"Yes, ma'am."

"Don't touch those shirts!"

"Yes, ma'am." For that second "Yes, ma'am," she delivered the smack she'd been swearing about. Being Adrienne, the smack wasn't a hit but a kiss—and not at all the kind of kiss he'd counted on this morning. "Did you get your passport out of the top right-hand drawer of the desk in the den?"

"I was just going to do that," he said virtuously.

"I'll do it. I wouldn't trust you to find your own feet this early in the morning. You—" her finger wagged at him like a teacher's ruler "—get yourself a cup of coffee and stay out of my way."

Riley obediently poured himself a cup of coffee, brought it back to the bedroom, and stayed out of her way. For the next ten minutes he couldn't keep the grin off his face. There was no point in telling her he was a grown man, fully capable of packing his own suitcase. Adrienne took care of her clients like a lioness with threatened cubs; nothing was going to stop her from taking care of her mother; and there was no way he could entirely escape her protective instincts. She flew between closet, dresser and suitcase faster than a cyclone.

It took him a full ten minutes to realize she was flying a bit too fast, teasing a little too hard. He knew she was feeling well—the color in her cheeks was a giveaway—but she was working as hard as a banshee to avoid directly meeting his eyes. "Okay," he said gently. "What's wrong?"

"Wrong? Nothing's wrong, except that I can't find your red-and-blue tie."

"Forget the tie. What's bothering you?"

"Nothing!" She snapped the suitcase closed. Eyes still averted from him, she grumbled, "If you're going to comment, though, I'd appreciate it if you'd just get it over with."

A grown man developed instincts about when he'd failed to notice something. Riley sensed all the feminine radar, but he'd be darned if he could make a connection. Like a lost soul searching a map, he checked her head to toe. She was wearing sort of a classic-styled loose cream dress, low cream heels, gold buttons in her ears and what appeared to be an African scarf at her throat. "Ah, new earrings," he said heartily.

"Cut it out, Riley."

"The scarf—"

"You gave me the scarf."

"And it looks great with the—" he thought fast "—new dress."

The newness of the dress wasn't the problem. He knew from her too-bright laugh that it wasn't the problem, and Riley felt a slice of panic. None of the

pregnancy manuals had this particular test, and it was
obviously a critical one.

"Pretty funny looking, hmm? You would have
really laughed if you'd seen me shopping. All the other
maternity dresses had little sashes in back or bibs in
front—you'd think all pregnant women wanted to re-
gress to looking like Little Orphan Annie. I'm afraid
I'm into elastic waists for the count, Riley. No more
slim, no more svelte. I thought I could postpone it a
little longer, but there's just nothing in the closet that
fits anymore."

For a moment he was tempted to wave a hand in
front of her eyes, just to make sure someone was
home. Adrienne, vain? The same lady who blithely
vacuumed in his oldest T-shirt?

But when he touched her soft cheek, he saw the
fragility in her expression. This wasn't about her
looks. It was about his reaction to her looks. "You
thought I'd care, did you? No more slim, no more
svelte? You thought I'd care?"

"Maybe not consciously."

"I have to be the one to tell you this, love," he said
slowly, "But you have become more beautiful, not
less, in the past few months. That goes for the skin,
the eyes, the smile, and most definitely the little
growing package in front. How could you doubt it?"

The tension faded from her expression, yet still she
said, "My mother said I looked like a toothpick carrying a watermelon."

Riley's eyes narrowed. "How did your mother get
into this?"

"She went with me when I went shopping last Saturday."

"You didn't mention that." He wished she had. Every time Janet Bennett wanted anything, Adrienne leaped to help. Riley understood loyalty, but every time Adrienne did anything with her mother, she came back feeling cut down and like a failure as a daughter. Riley liked Janet Bennett just fine. He'd like her even better if she lived on the West Coast, preferably in the earthquake zone. "Forget what your mother said. Take it from me, you look absolutely terrific."

Aware of the time, both automatically moved toward the door, Adrienne snatching her purse and briefcase and Riley toting his luggage. She didn't have to be at work this early, but she could steal a few more minutes with him if she left when he did. "Come on, Riley, you don't have to go overboard. I haven't suddenly become so shallow that I care about looking 'terrific,' but I have to look professional. Burkholtz may have given me a raise, but he hasn't once mentioned the partnership since I told him I was pregnant."

"And one of us in this twosome happens to know labor laws inside out." He locked the door and escorted her down the hall toward the elevator. "If that turkey does anything to imply your pregnancy is an issue affecting your employment—or the partnership—I'll personally take the buzzard to court and hang him out to dry."

"Calm down," she soothed.

"I know what your work means to you."

"Well, I know how you drive when you're revved up in the morning. Forget Burkholtz and all this other nonsense—it's the last thing you need on your mind." Outside, the summer morning sun was blinding. Once Riley had stashed his suitcase, she reached for him, squinting as she retied his tie. "You're going to have a wonderful time."

"I don't want to go." It was the first chance he'd had to tell her.

"Of course you do." She patted the tie down with a thump but her hands lingered, softly, possessively, on his chest. "You thrive on these things, Riley, and no one's better at them than you are. I'm delighted you have this chance."

"It could still fall through. I'll make calls at the office before I actually take the flight. It's possible they've already settled things."

"And horses can fly. Brown never calls you at six o'clock in the morning unless he has a really good mess for you to wade into," she said humorously. "Heavens, you're not hesitating because of me, are you? I'm thrilled you have this chance to go. How many times do I have to tell you that you can leave me anytime you want to?"

She sounded so thrilled at the thought of him being five thousand miles away that Riley felt kicked, hard. Maybe he hadn't won last night's war but he'd counting on having won the battle. They'd been as close as a man and woman could be. He couldn't believe she was back to chasing him out of her life again.

He wanted to wrap his arms around her, fold her up, and kiss her so thoroughly that she couldn't see straight. That was what he wanted to do—and what he would have done, if she didn't steal his initiative.

She went up on tiptoe and kissed him, hard. So hard that her tummy rubbed against his belt, he could smell the hint of lavender on her skin, and desire pulled at him. Her lips hovered, then offered a second kiss, this one a tease, a blur of softness and promise.

When she finally pulled back, he felt all the masculine reassurance of having been kissed well and intimately, by a woman who very clearly loved him. That reassurance died when her eyes met his—briefly, fiercely, poignantly. "I want you to take care of yourself, and I want you to have a good time." She barely hesitated. "And if you find someone else, Riley, you're free. You always have been, you always will be. You don't owe me anything and never did."

Hours later, Riley stared blindly out the 747's window. He saw nothing below but a gray, endless Atlantic. Most of the other passengers were napping. He couldn't sleep nor could he concentrate on the contracts on his lap.

Damnation, she *still* thought he was going to stray. Hell, the woman had the same as invited him to find someone else. Maybe he'd been wrong about everything. Maybe she didn't love him, maybe she really didn't want his baby, and maybe it was crazy for him to believe he could sneak a ring on her finger given enough time, patience, love, and yes, dammit, trust.

Maybe he *was* wrong about everything, but every time he closed his eyes, he saw her reaching for him in the night, all passion, all fire. He saw her bearding Brown at the dinner party, listening to his boss's stories so he didn't have to. He saw her ravenously devouring a spinach leaf. He saw her sneaking a peek at the books he'd hidden away. He saw the way she'd looked, hiding in the Browns' bathroom, so upset with herself, so determined he wouldn't know. He saw her soundlessly place a short whiskey on his worktable at the exact instant he was ready to wind down. He saw her—the most beautiful woman alive—the moment she'd felt their baby move.

The pictures hardly added up to a woman in a hurry to end a love affair. He *knew* she loved him. That she wanted both him and the baby. And that if she'd ever needed anyone, she needed him now.

Oh, yeah, Stuart? So why is she halfway to labor and still trying to kick you out the door?

He swiped a hand over his face, feeling exasperated and confused. He had no answers except for the one obvious one. She was frightened. He wasn't giving her up, and Riley reminded himself that he still had months before the baby was born, months to convince her that there was no reason to be scared of him or anything they had together.

That didn't sound so hard. He'd be there when she needed him. He'd be more patient, more loving, more understanding. He'd be so damned trustworthy that she'd think he was a Boy Scout. He'd woo her until he dropped. And if that didn't work, he could always drag her to the altar, blindfolded and handcuffed. Maybe if the minister did the service in Arabic, she wouldn't realize what it was.

The image momentarily made him smile, but not for long. Adrienne, much as he loved her, could be as stubborn as a mule. And months had a way of flying past faster than the speed of sound.

Chapter Five

I can't believe how fast the time's gone! Just one more month, Adrienne," Liz said cheerfully. "So, how are we feeling?"

Adrienne mentally rolled her eyes. Liz asked the same question every time, then immediately bent over with a stethoscope hooked in her ears so she couldn't hear a thing. "Just fine," Adrienne murmured in her blithest monotone. "Nothing new. My ankles are swollen. I'm getting varicose veins in my legs. My belly button popped out. Say boo and I cry. I feel ugly, undesirable and klutzy. Two sips of water and I need a bathroom. I could sleep twenty-four hours a day—except at four in the morning, when the baby either gets hiccups or starts kicking—and I only get sick to my stomach three or four times a week now."

Liz lifted her head, pulled the stethoscope out of her ears and smiled. "The baby's doing fine and so are you from the look of you. At the start, I admit I was worried that you wouldn't take care of yourself, but obviously I was wrong. How's Lamaze going?"

"Riley's the ace of the class. He can breathe and pant like nobody's business." Adrienne glanced down at her abdomen, which more and more resembled a small beached whale. She pulled down her blouse and began the long process of shifting from a reclining to a sitting position. A crane would have helped. "He wants to be present at the birth. I don't. I don't suppose we could convince nature to switch things around in our case?"

Liz chuckled.

"How do you feel about drugs?"

"The same way I felt the last time you asked me," the doctor said mildly.

"Well, I still don't see anything wrong with sleeping through the whole process. Whole generations of women had drugs during childbirth—your mom probably did, and I *know* my mother did. Heck, we've overpopulated an entire planet with babies in spite of those drugs." Adrienne finally made it to a sitting position and wagged a finger at her friend. "Do not tell me the pain is an issue of mind over matter or all in the head. I saw the Lamaze movie on childbirth. The pain was not in her head."

"It's over faster than you know. And if it comes to the point where you can't handle it, we'll come through with something to make you more comfortable." Liz shook her head wryly. "I had this same discussion with Riley last week."

Adrienne's head shot up. "What do you mean?"

"Riley's called me once a week from the beginning. Didn't he tell you?"

"No!"

"You mean he didn't talk to you after the last time we did blood work?"

Adrienne's heart stopped with a squeeze. "Was there something wrong with my blood? Something wrong with the baby you didn't tell me?"

"No, no. That's not why we discussed blood work. I thought you knew—never mind. Riley will tell you. More relevant..." Liz's gaze focused seriously, a doctor suddenly more than a friend. "Are you still working?"

"My leave of absence starts Friday."

Liz looked relieved. "I was afraid you'd taken that partnership, and it's just not the best of times for you to have extra stress."

Riley had said the same thing, but Adrienne was the one who had surprised herself when Burkholtz had finally offered the partnership. She'd not only turned it down but requested a leave. Her work had once meant everything to her. She wasn't sure why, now, she couldn't dredge up an ounce of dedication. "You're sure the baby's all right?"

"The little devil's putting on more weight than you are. My guess is a boy." Liz hesitated. "We're talking a nice big healthy baby, Adrienne, but as we've already discussed, there is a slight chance we may end up doing a cesarean."

"And as we already discussed, that's fine by me. I could just wake up when it's over." Adrienne climbed off the examining table and frowned. "Except that I'd want to know exactly what kind of drugs you use for a cesarean, because if it's anything that could possibly affect the baby—"

"Hey. A moment ago I could have sworn you were bargaining for morphine."

"Oh, shut up, Liz."

Liz chuckled. "Do I need this grief? I've got a whole waiting room of patients who actually thrive on my advice, and here I'm taking my time up with you. Go on, get out of here, but take good care of him, kiddo."

"I thought I was. You said the baby was in great shape."

"The baby is. I was talking about your taking care of Riley." Liz winked.

Adrienne chuckled, but once Liz was gone, her smile folded like a bad poker hand. A small mirror hung over the sink in the examination room. The big-tummied, clumsy, soft-eyed woman in its reflection bore little resemblance to the Adrienne she knew. The Adrienne she knew would never have willingly hurt someone she loved.

She *hadn't* taken care of Riley.

She'd once sworn she'd never tie him down, never corner him with forced responsibilities, yet in the past few months Riley had unquestionably been the one to take care of her.

She'd let that happen—not because she'd suddenly turned into a heartlessly selfish woman, but because this last stretch of pregnancy had been debilitating. Not physically—emotionally. Nature didn't give an owl's hoot about principles. Especially in these past weeks, nature had made very sure that the life growing inside her had dominated everything she did, everything she thought, everything she felt. The overwhelming instinct was to protect the baby from every physical and emotional stress.

Riley hadn't complained. He treated her like coddled treasure, a fragile rose. Riley wasn't a man who ran away from responsibility, but that was just it. She had become a responsibility.

The thought turned her stomach, but the idea that she had been insensitive to Riley's needs made her heart ache. It was about time she faced up to decisions she'd made. It was past time, like Liz said, that she took care of Riley.

"You're sure you're up to this?"

"Positive," Adrienne said gaily.

"It's not like we couldn't have gone tomorrow. With this weather—"

"Now, Riley, it's just a little snow." Actually the November evening was as black as pitch and bleakcold. The car wipers were going like mad to accommodate the battering spatter of sleet. Riley had only taken her out when she'd insisted...and she'd insisted because she knew he'd wanted this for weeks.

"You're sure you're warm enough?"

"No problem."

"Uncomfortable?"

"Just fine," she fibbed blithely, although the question almost made her laugh. Comfort and a pregnant woman in her eighth month was a contradiction in terms. Her coat no longer buttoned around the middle. Walking was an exercise in waddling. Climbing into the car had a lot in common with stuffing a goose, and Riley had to truss her into the seat belt. She could no longer manage it, particularly after he'd consulted

Liz and modified the design to make the seat belt safe for her hippo-sized abdomen.

"Do you have to go to the bathroom?" Riley shot her a grin. "I already know the answer to that one, but we'll be there in another ten minutes."

"I can wait," Adrienne said serenely, but when she glanced at him, she felt guilty for waiting so long. Riley's shoulders were encased in an ancient suede jacket and his dark hair glistened, damp with melting snow. He looked incurably handsome, but even the shadowed car couldn't hide the circles beneath his eyes, his newly honed cheekbones. He'd lost weight in the past months, and his dollop-of-the-devil grins were becoming rare to come by. Her fault.

Well, he was happy tonight—so full of energy he couldn't sit still—and she intended to keep him that way.

Months ago, when Riley had returned from Europe, he'd set the wheels in motion to sever his employment with Brown, hang out his own shingle and go house hunting. Adrienne had supported his break with Brown, knowing how long Riley had wanted to make that move. She'd also enthusiastically gone office shopping with him, and once he found prime rental space, helped him move in and organize.

The house, though, was something else. She knew Riley's plate was too full, yet she'd avoided anything to do with the home he'd finally chosen—a choice that now struck her as selfish and, yes, cowardly. It wasn't supposed to hurt that he was going to live in the house with the baby and not her. Why should it? Both agreed that babies didn't belong with couples who weren't married. Both were too adult to fall into the pit of a shotgun marriage, nor was there a need for it. Riley wanted the baby; she was going to take the apartment and everything was hunky-dory.

To avoid seeing the house was the same as pretending she was unsure or unhappy or maybe even feeling devastated about those choices. That wasn't true, which she intended to prove to him tonight.

Riley turned the corner on a country lane. "You prepared for a surprise?"

"You bet." What she was really prepared for was helping him, which she should have done a long time ago. Riley may not have noticed, but she was dressed to work. There had to be things she could do. Wash cupboards? Line shelves?

But her mind blanked when he braked at the end of a long driveway. The sleety night blurred her vision, but not so much she couldn't see the sprawling ranch house, the giant fenced yard, the chestnut trees in the front. All of it should have been unfamiliar. It wasn't. About a hundred years before they'd taken a country drive on a lazy Sunday afternoon. "What a great house for a family," she said then. At the time, it had been just idle conversation.

Now Adrienne turned stricken eyes to Riley. "Yeah, I thought you might remember it," he murmured. "Come on, let's get you out of the weather. I'll put on a pot of coffee while you explore the layout. Only don't expect too much. There's barely a stick of furniture, and I've only had time to have the place repainted and carpeted." He led her up the snowy driveway, and switched on the lights just inside the house. "You're still feeling okay, aren't you?"

"Good enough to climb mountains," she assured him, which wasn't precisely true. He skinned off her coat, put water on the stove and left her to explore. She wished he hadn't. The house was laid out in an L, with the kitchen and living areas in one section, the bedroom wing in another. Maybe the house had no furniture yet, but there were other details to catch her eye.

She'd once said she loved skylights. There were skylights in the kitchen and master bedroom. She'd once said she loved fireplaces. There was a massive fieldstone hearth in the living room and a second smaller fireplace in the master bedroom. The living room was painted cream, the kitchen toast and the carpet Riley had chosen was a thick, plush paprika. Cream, toast and paprika were her favorite colors.

Riley, on stocking feet, stole up behind her with mugs of hot spiced tea. "Like it so far?"

"Very much." That was an understatement. She liked it to the point of pain and despair, but thankfully he didn't seem to realize that. His eyes rested on her face with the gentleness of calm, blue waters, and then he grinned.

"You haven't seen the baby's room yet?"

"No." She didn't want to. She took a bracing sip of the hot mulled tea and discovered she still didn't want to.

"I'm not sure you should," he admitted ruefully. "It's the worst mess in the whole place."

"It can't be that bad."

"It is."

"Riley…" He wasn't really pushing her toward the door closest to the bathroom, but his knuckle was pressed at the small of her back and he was definitely nudging. He flicked on the overhead switch and there it was.

The baby's room. And damn him, she knew she'd told him she favored yellow for a baby's color, and the room was distinctly painted a soft sunrise yellow. Her throat formed a lump so big she couldn't possibly swallow, not just in reaction to the baby's room but the whole house. She abruptly forced that lump back down.

She'd come to help him, and this was unquestionably the place where he needed it. As he'd said, the room was a total disaster. Every available space was filled with boxes. He'd purchased a crib, playpen, high chair, car seat, stroller and changing table. He just hadn't put any of them together. The job would take a skilled mechanic an entire day.

"I just signed the closing on the house three weeks ago," he defended the debris. "After that…well. You know how busy I've been, and I didn't figure I had to hurry in here with the baby not due for another three or four weeks—"

"Yes." Adrienne gulped another sip of tea. She had so carefully not involved herself in preparations for the baby, which had seemed a matter of principle. It was

Riley's baby, not hers. Not yours, not yours, not yours…the mental echo wailed in her heart like a lost wind, but she banished it as stubbornly as she forced down more tea. It was time to rally, not wallow—and to think of Riley, not herself.

Men invested an enormous amount of masculine ego in being "handy." Riley was a trace touchy on the subject. He should be. The last time he'd picked up a hammer, he'd made a hole in the apartment wall so huge she had to cover it with a picture.

"You know," she said slowly, "I think you and I have really done something special that'll go down in history."

"Pardon?"

"We've managed it. An honest role reversal, à la 1990. You know what I mean. If I'd gotten pregnant fifty years ago, I'd have been 'ruined' if you didn't marry me. Even if I'd become pregnant twenty years ago, I'd have been stuck with the entire responsibility, whether that was right for the baby or not." She'd been wanting to sneak in this little speech for weeks, so she had to talk fast. "Times have changed, for the man as well as the woman, thank heavens. I'm having the child, but you're keeping it, and we were both able to make that decision based on what was right for the child, didn't we? And both of us feel good about it." She smiled at him. "I'm so proud of you—but could you come just a little farther?"

"Beg you pardon?"

"Get me a screwdriver, love."

"What?"

"A screwdriver. Preferably several. A couple of regular and one Phillips head. And throw in an Allen wrench and a hammer?"

"Adrienne..." Whatever he started to say, he seemed to think better of it. He clawed a hand through his hair and sighed. Loudly. "You want to put together the baby's furniture? Now?"

No. If truth were on the line, she wanted nothing to do with the baby's furniture. Rather than touch one oak spindle on the Jenny Lind crib, she'd rather be outside in the sleet, as naked as a jaybird, cavorting around barefoot with her fifty-inch girth and freezing to death.

Dramatically freezing to death, however, would not help Riley. She could handle this. Every instruction she read, every screw she picked up, every fresh mug of tea Riley handed her—she promised herself that she could handle this.

Dammit, she had to.

They finished the crib. One side listed like a drunken sailor. "Only thirteen screws and this strange looking metal thing left over," Riley mentioned dryly.

For the first few minutes he hadn't gotten into it. She'd had to coax and tease—methods that were now, obviously, working too well. "The problem is that I read the directions. Everyone knows they never make any sense. Just hand me that metal part again."

He handed her the metal part. They rebuilt the crib. She started on the stroller; he started on the high chair. They switched projects midway, both seeking the promised greener grass on the other side of the fence.

It wasn't any greener. "There's nothing sacred about finishing all this stuff tonight," Riley kept insisting.

"Now, Riley. You just don't realize how much fun we're having." He rolled his eyes, and she had to laugh.

The stroller functioned if you didn't try to lock it. But as far as the playpen... "For heaven's sake, don't throw away that Easy To Assemble sign on the front of the box," Adrienne ordered. "On that sign alone, we should be able to put the manufacturer behind bars for a good hundred years. Talk about a shut-away case for fraudulent advertising."

"Adrienne, I know you think you're talented mechanically." At that precise moment, they were both sprawled on the floor, back-to-back, their fannies and spines bracing each other. The back of his head leaned against the back of hers, and both of them had their eyes closed. It took too much courage to open them. The whole room was a land mine of cardboard, spare parts, Styrofoam packing material and tools. "You are good with a screwdriver, I'm not denying it. I just think you take these projects too personally."

"Of course I do. This is a war. Both of us graduated from law school with honors, for heaven's sake. This is absolutely nothing by comparison." Adrienne surged to her feet, no small feat with her bulk, and pushed up the sleeves of her maternity sweater. "I could handle a hinge cover and drop-rail lock in my sleep."

"Which is the point. It's eleven o'clock, love."

"A terrific time to handle—" she grabbed for an instruction sheet "—the swivel wheel holder."

She wasn't really so stubborn. The point was his laughter. Riley hadn't laughed with her—not like this—in ages. Maybe it was late and maybe her back ached. She didn't care. Riley had been increasingly tense for weeks. Tonight the drawn look had disappeared from his eyes and he was relaxed and unquestionably sassy humored.

So was she, until the projects were suddenly done. For a few minutes they busied themselves stuffing Styrofoam and plastic leftovers back into the empty boxes, but then that was done, too.

Silence settled on the softly lit baby's room. A helpless silence. A too-precious-to-breathe silence. Without meaning to, her gaze wandered from the oak crib and high chair to the gay yellow print of the playpen pad. She touched the stroller handle, the shade of the little bedside lamp—it looked like balloons, yellow, red, blue.

"Did we do good or did we do good?" Riley demanded.

"We did good," she whispered, but her voice had an odd watery quality.

"Adrienne?" He crossed the room in three fast strides, and chucked up her chin too quickly for her to blink back the moisture in her eyes. He sucked in his breath and stood there.

"Everything's fine. I just—"

He didn't give her a chance to finish. "We're leaving. Now."

The snap in his tone startled her. They turned off lights and collected their coats, but it didn't occur to her until they were out in the winter-frosted night that he was bafflingly angry. Riley had never been angry, not at her. It didn't make any sense, but the signs were unmistakable.

Outside, the sleet had stopped. The night was as clear as black ice. He protectively grabbed her arm en route to the car, but once she was installed inside he didn't slam the door. He closed it with a shotgun-sharp little click. And when he turned the key, he glanced at her. He looked as if he wanted to get his hands around her throat. For eight months he'd been treating her like fragile china.

"You're going to have to tell me what's wrong, because I don't have any idea," she said quietly.

"Nothing's wrong. You warm enough?"

It was a relative question. The heater was going full blast, but the emotional temperature in the car threatened frost. "Something upset you," she persisted.

"Forget it."

She wanted to. She was cold and uncomfortable and tired. The closer she came to the end of this pregnancy, the more she felt fragile and scared and wary of walking into anything she couldn't handle. Riley looked as manageable as a two-hundred-pound stick of just-lit dynamite, and the alluring temptation was to ignore the problem until he'd calmed down. *Like you've ignored everything else, Adrienne?* "I want to know what upset you," she insisted.

"No, you don't."

"Come on, Riley. I'm not a cupcake. I don't crumble. If I said something to upset you, I want to know it!"

"You said—and did—things that upset me, all right." On the freeway, Riley changed lanes with caution and care, but on the inside, he was losing it. "All that business about role reversals à la 1990. About how values have finally, really changed for both men and women. About our having the freedom to make the *right* decisions about the baby's future. Maybe you could sell that con to a used-car salesman, Adrienne, but you're through selling it to me."

"What?"

"I bought the house for you, because you loved it on sight. You may not have seen the inside until tonight, but you loved it on sight, too. And no, don't start talking yet. Just answer me. Did you or did you not like the house?"

There was only one answer she could give him. "I loved it," she admitted softly.

"Yeah. Only I thought when you were willing to see it that you were finally..." He shifted gears. "Dammit, I've always understood that you had real, honest reasons to be wary of marriage. Watching your parents' relationship had to be a little bit of hell when you were growing up, and everything in your job has to underline the same messages. You see people hurting each other, relationships not making it, commitments abandoned faster than the change of seasons."

She could feel her face blanching of color. "Riley—"

His eyes leveled on her for bare seconds, as blue as ice. "I'm not responsible for all those other people, brown eyes. Just for me, and I know damn well how I feel—about us, about you, about commitment. I *love you*, and I'm tired as hell of your thinking I'm going to cut out on you at the first sign of rough waters."

She couldn't think when he was shouting. "Riley, you're not being fair. I never thought..." She hesitated. "Maybe when I first met you, I did. Believe you'd leave me at the first slam of a door. But believe me, that hasn't been true for a long time."

"No?" he demanded.

"No."

"You've actually come to trust me?"

Trust? There was a time the five-letter word hadn't been in her vocabulary, but that was before this pregnancy. For the past eight months Riley had been there for her—even when she was chasing him away, even when she'd been such a pill she'd have walked out on herself.

"Adrienne?"

She closed her eyes. "I wasn't hesitating for lack of an answer. I was just trying to find some way to answer you that didn't sound hopelessly corny. I don't want to embarrass you, counselor, but I'd trust you with my life."

She'd hoped her answer meant something to him, but Riley clammed up with a frown. Within minutes, they were parked outside the apartment. It was so cold that the windows started fogging up the moment he shut off the engine, isolating the two of them in the dark car. When she reached for the door handle, though, his hand clamped on her wrist.

"You trust me, Adrienne. And I think you love me. So I'll be damned if I can understand why we're not married."

She felt cornered, not so much by his hand on her wrist as his gaze. Everywhere she looked Riley's eyes were waiting for her, determined and harsh and demanding. "You haven't asked me to marry you," she said unsteadily, "at least from the start of this pregnancy."

Riley saw the prick of emotional tears in her eyes. Still he pressed. "Because you'd have bitten my head off. But you knew it was what I wanted." When she tried to avert her head, he cupped her chin in his gloved hand. She knew. "Maybe you'll never stop being wary of the institution, but you stopped being wary of me and what we have together a long time ago. I think you want a marriage as much as I do."

"No. You know how I feel about marriage."

"I know what you *say*. Just like I know what you *say* about the baby. You still think you plan to take a fast boat to China the minute the baby's born, and I think it's time we cleared up that horse manure. You should have seen your face when you touched that crib tonight. You want this baby so badly it's eating you up inside—it's on your mind day and night."

"No!"

"Yes." His hands closed on her shoulders. His face was gaunt, and the hollows beneath his eyes dark. "All this time I thought it was me you were afraid of, but it's the baby, isn't it? You're so scared of this baby that you can't think straight, and I have no possible way to understand that unless you talk to me. Why, Adrienne? It's a baby we both want and both love, so why is it tearing you apart?"

"Riley, leave it be!" He grabbed her arm again, but she managed to wrench open the door and stumble out. She had never so desperately needed to be alone, just for a minute, just long enough to escape the smothering small car and Riley's relentless questions.

Cold air slammed into her lungs and froze the tears on her cheeks, and she suddenly hurt everywhere; inside, outside, all over.

He didn't come after her. It was an hour later—she was curled up in bed with her eyes wide open on the ceiling—before she heard his key in the lock. Another hour passed and he still hadn't come near her.

Confused and lost, she stared in the darkness until she was positive he was asleep in the other room. Still, it took her a long time to find the strength to do what she had to do. She felt sure of nothing...except that she'd hurt Riley enough.

Chapter Six

She wasn't running away. Maybe she'd taken off at three in the morning without a stitch of luggage, but that hardly meant she was running away. She'd left Riley a note so he wouldn't worry; it was hardly criminal to need some time to herself, and it wasn't as though she didn't know where she was going.

At least, she decided where she was going as soon as she stopped at a gas station, which happened quickly. Predictably her fuel tank was on Empty. The station obligingly provided machines where she could pick up a cardboard container of milk, and more relevant, maps.

There were other choices, but it was the map of the Ozarks that captured her attention. She had a sudden memory of the greens and quiet and peaceful dark woods from a childhood vacation in the mountains. It seemed an ideal place to calm down and think through her decisions in the weeks before the baby was born.

No matter which route she took, it was an enormously long drive. She told herself it didn't matter. The farther the better. She could always stop at a motel when she tired, and maybe she wasn't loaded with cash, but her wallet had half a dozen credit cards and a padded checkbook.

The dark night spit snow as she crossed the Indiana border into Illinois, and the blacktop loomed ahead of her, endless and bleak. Her abdomen rested against the steering wheel and the weight ached, but it troubled her that the baby didn't kick tonight. Because mature, grown women didn't run away?

So we're dealing with your basic immature coward, little one. Just goes to show I was never the mother for you.

She nearly missed the turnoff for Route 72 because her vision was blurred by tears. Riley didn't understand. He thought she loved him. He thought she wanted to marry him. He thought she wanted the baby.

Dammit, he was right about all of that, but he didn't *understand*. She had no business having a baby; she never had. If Riley loved her, he had fallen in love with the Adrienne he thought she was: a career woman, competent and independent, self-reliant and sure of herself. Before the pregnancy Adrienne had been just that, but she'd had eight-plus months to remember that she was unalterably, undeniably her mother's daughter.

Adrienne had figured out a long time ago that Janet Bennett was a woman who couldn't love or be loved. As a child, Adrienne had been hurt by her mother's insensitivity. As an adult, she'd buried the old hurts and responded with sympathy for a woman so lonely, so lost.

But since the pregnancy, she'd been the one to feel lonely and lost. She had her mother's genes and couldn't seem to forget it. Self-reliance and competence were tricks to survival, but there'd never been confidence under the surface. Fear of losing Riley had always affected her being honest with him about who she really was, who she wanted to be. And what if she turned out to be a mother like her own was? How could she risk doing that to Riley's baby?

That's no excuse for running away, ducky.

But I was so scared.

You should be. You're about to lose a man who means the world to you and a baby more precious than life. Is that what you want?

I'm afraid . . .

Is that what you want?

What if I'm a terrible mother? You don't understand how I feel about Riley's baby. How could I possibly risk hurting his child?

Is that what you want? To lose him?

The first hundred miles rushed past, then another hundred. She stopped every hour to find a gas station rest room, and little cardboard containers of milk started to accumulate on the seat beside her.

On every lonely stretch of blacktop, her mind played through long buried insecurities and ancient fears. For centuries women had taken childbirth for granted. It wasn't that way anymore. These were contemporary times. A woman was no longer stuck. She had the choice to do what was right, for her baby, for herself. That's all Adrienne had ever wanted. To do what was right. For Riley, for herself, for the baby.

Her baby.

Mine.

The rush and power of that sweet word took her heart, captured it, wouldn't let go. If love meant anything at all, they were both hers. Riley and the baby.

By the time she crossed into Missouri, she would have given a year of her life to be able to turn around and go home, but it wasn't that easy. She'd come too far to backtrack the entire distance at a stretch, and Riley wouldn't be awake yet. By the time he was, she planned to be stopped and near a telephone.

For the moment she was in the middle of nowhere. It was past dawn but still gloomy. The sun had risen behind a sky mottled with charcoal clouds. Sleet had dulled into a steady driving rain, and winter-barren grain fields stretched for long rolling miles. One farmer's pickup passed her, but that was the only traffic on the road except for the dark car far behind her.

For the third time, she glanced in the rearview mirror. Riley had a dark four-door. More by accident than intention, her feet let up on the gas pedal. When she slowed down to five miles an hour, the car behind her also slowed down. Deliberately she floored the accelerator. The other driver must have responded by flooring his, because the distance between them was kept exactly the same.

She lost sight of her shadow on a curve, but as soon as she reached a straightaway he was there again. The car never came so close that she could see the driver or identify the car's make. Still, it wasn't really a shadow and it wasn't really Riley. Her imagination was running away from her because he was on her mind—

desperately, invasively and lovingly on her mind. *I'm not losing you, Riley. I can't. I won't.*

She was running low on gas when the first cramp cut off her breath. Her first reaction was terror, but that faded quickly. It couldn't be the baby because it couldn't be labor. Not only was the baby not due for three weeks, but labor didn't start like this. She'd read all Riley's hidden books and taken the Lamaze class. Labor started with slow, far apart little twinges that gradually built up into serious cramps. Even if it were the baby, heaven knew she had time. According to the books, especially with a first birth, it could be hours before anything really started happening.

Five minutes later, an invisible vise clamped on her abdomen so hard that her brow broke sweat.

So much for the books.

When Riley saw her car swerve, a ribbon of ice coiled around his heart. He severed the distance between them with his foot flat on the gas. When she pulled off onto the wide shoulder, he was right behind her. She hadn't fully stopped before he jerked his door open.

Wind beat at him as he ran toward her car. Rain ran through his hair, cold and slick and unnoticed. He lost ten years of his life when he looked through the windshield. Adrienne's chestnut head was leaned over the steering wheel; she was limp and still.

Riley didn't start breathing again until he'd wrenched open her door. She turned her head then, saw him and blindly held out her arms. Her eyes were so clotted with thick, soft tears that she turned his entire heart inside out. "Riley, I'm sorry. I've been so stupid, and I know I've put you through hell."

As if he cared. She was alive and okay. He pulled her out of the car—to hell with the pouring rain—and kissed her. And kissed her. And kissed her. He wanted to tell her that he'd shoot her if she ever ran away from him again, but somehow he couldn't work up the anger. She tasted like lost treasure, now found. She smelled like lavender. And her lips were warm under his, wooing warm, heart warm, Adrienne warm.

He felt life flood back through his body—life that had been cold and dead when he'd heard her leave the apartment. Her response had nothing to do with passion and everything to do with love, a love so deep she never felt the rain, so deep that her fingers clutched his hair as if she'd never let him go. And he would probably have kissed her from here to forever if she hadn't suddenly leaned back and doubled over.

"What the—"

"The baby."

He froze on the bleat of a heartbeat. *"Now?"*

"Now, love. I think we'd better find a doctor, Riley."

She smiled at him, all calm and loving. She'd been the frantic one all these months, now it was him. He hustled her into the passenger seat of her car, started the engine and immediately saw she had no gas. In no crisis in her life did Adrienne ever have gas. He grabbed her car key, purse and her, and jogged them back to his car. His hands were slick on the wheel as

he floored the accelerator. The last sign he saw had
been for the town of Hannibal. That had been miles
back. There were no towns on this stretch of highway.
And Adrienne would not be in labor if he hadn't
started the argument earlier that night.

"Riley..."

She started to talk, then closed her eyes and clamped
her teeth together. She was the one in pain, but his
whole forehead was sheened with sweat and his heart
galloped in his chest. He held on to the steering wheel
hard enough to break it. Junction 10 Miles said the
sign, which also pictured gas and thank heavens a
medical facility.

"Riley, I want your baby. I always did."

"Sweetheart, I know that."

"I was just so afraid of being a mother like mine
was. I spent a childhood believing I was just like her."

"Honey, you never had more in common with your
mother than a turkey. Please don't do that. How the
hell often are those pains coming?"

"I don't know. Four, five minutes."

He pushed down the gas pedal.

"Riley...I worked so hard for my career, for that
partnership—and it hasn't meant a bite of fudge in
months. It doesn't matter like I thought it did. I have
to tell you—I *need* to tell you—that I'm not the career woman you fell in love with. I—"

"Honey, breathe. In. Out."

"I want...to be home. I want to diaper and feed my
own baby and I don't want any stranger seeing its first
steps. I want to be a chocolate-chip cookie maker of a

mother. I know that sounds corny, and I was always afraid you'd never be attracted to an old-fashioned housewife. But if I had my choice, if I ever just had one chance to be the woman I want to be . . . I want to make a family like the one I never had, to do it right, to give it everything I have—"

"Adrienne?"

"Hmm?"

"I don't care if you work for the rest of your life, love. I never did. You can work. You can be at home. Either way I always figured you'd love the baby from here to forever, so I don't see a problem. Whatever you want's fine. Except that I'd really appreciate it, love. I would really appreciate it if you'd stop the damned labor pains until I've found a hospital."

She made a sound. It wasn't a scream. It was just a sound coming out of her throat that had something of horrified surprise. She wasn't just hurting. She was dying of pain.

He reached Junction and pulled off to find a sleepy farming town with a farm store, an implement dealer, a grocery store, and unbelievably far down the road, a two-story redbrick building with a sign, Junction General Hospital. The sign was nearly bigger than the place, and the place looked pretty archaic to Riley, but he wasn't floating around with choices.

"Riley?"

"Ssh."

"That last one hurt." But she smiled.

He didn't. Lifting her out of the car, he was in the mood to kill someone. Adrienne was not only exhausted but weak, her eyes dazed with pain. She cramped up again just as he was barreling through the double doors.

A young woman with braided blond hair smiled a greeting at him from the reception desk. She wasn't smiling long.

"I want your entire surgical team," he told her. "Anesthesiologists. Your best OBY-GYN man. A pediatrician. Internist, surgeon—the whole team."

"That's very nice, sir, but could I have your Blue Cross card? I can see she's in labor, but I can't admit her without a—"

"Where the Sam Hill is the delivery room?"

"Upstairs, sir, but I can't admit her without—"

He balanced Adrienne's rear end on the counter, threw the stupid woman his entire wallet and strode toward the elevator.

"Riley, I can walk," Adrienne whispered.

"Ssh." He kissed her, on the brow, on the cheek, fleetingly, tenderly. Then, in his arms, she folded toward him with yet another contraction. It had to take five years for the wheezing elevator to arrive on the second floor.

When the doors finally opened, he strode out with the speed of a cavalry charge, only to find a tomb-quiet corridor painted a pale, dead green. The only sign of life was a gray-haired nurse with the build of a drill sergeant, bending over some forms at a desk. She glanced up. "She's having a baby," he snapped.

"Yes, I can see that."

"The first thing you have to do is put her out of pain. She's hurting. Dammit, do something!"

"My, my, we seem a little distraught—"

"I'm not distraught. I'm mad as hell. Give her something!"

"Riley, you have to calm down, and for heaven's sake put me down before you break your back," Adrienne said firmly.

"Ssh." He kissed her again, lips molded on her brow, but his eyes met the gray-haired battle-ax with fire. "The baby's three weeks early. I want the best doctors flown in from wherever in the country, and more immediately I want drugs. Any of them. All of them. I want her out of pain, you got that? Now!"

The elevator doors cranked open and the young receptionist sprinted out. "Mary, she's not admitted. This man just—"

"It's all right. We'll get it all taken care of," Mary said calmly.

"He didn't sign—"

"I heard you, Anne. Just leave the admitting form on my desk and go back downstairs. I'll handle it." Mary motioned Riley down the hall to the last room on the left, but her shrewd eyes were on her patient. "What's you name, dear?"

As Adrienne exchanged names, she felt the nurse's blunt, strong hand enclose hers. The woman's touch was a woman's bond. Fear, unacknowledged, ebbed out of her. Maybe she was exhausted and the contractions bewilderingly strong and fast, but there was a secret bubble inside her as strong as excitement, as huge as happiness.

"How often, dear?"

"Erratic. But I think around every four minutes."

"Water break?"

"No."

"Anything I need to know about? RH factor, high blood pressure? Anything unusual in the pregnancy, or a reason to expect a difficult delivery?"

"No, everything's been fine until now—except that Liz, my doctor, was a little concerned that the baby was of a size..." A cramp seized Adrienne, hard and sharp. Mary timed it.

"Rough one?" she asked sympathetically.

"A little."

"A little! That's what they've been like for an hour!" Riley snapped to the nurse. He didn't like the room. There was nothing in it but a pristine single bed, table and chair. It smelled sterile and it looked cold. "We need a doctor."

"She'll have a doctor, as soon as we have something to report to him." Mary took a pulse and blood pressure, checking the baby's heartbeat, and then smoothly and efficiently helped Adrienne out of her clothes and folded her into bed. "I'm going to examine you. It'll be a little uncomfortable, but it only takes a moment and then we'll know how dilated you are." She spoke to Adrienne, but her flat, blunt hand was on Riley's chest. He seemed to be moving backward toward the door.

"Forget it. I'm not leaving her."

"There now, I won't argue with you," Mary said pleasantly. "Right past the nurses' station is a waiting room. I just made a fresh pot of coffee. You just pour yourself a nice big mug, and once I've had a chance to examine your wife and page the doctor, you can come right back in here."

"I don't want coffee. I just want . . ." Riley looked past her shoulder at Adrienne.

"I'll be fine," Adrienne promised him.

Mary firmly closed the door, and talked calmly and gently through the short examination. "As I'm sure you noticed, we're not a metropolitan-size facility, but that's not to say you're not in fine hands. Doc Henley was called downstairs—dreadful accident on the highway this morning—but I'll have him up here soon enough. You'll love him, everyone does, but just so you know, I've have five babies of my own, and delivered more babies out of my room 232 here than I can count. Everything's going to be just fine."

She leaned back up, peeled off her glove and reached for the fetal monitor. Within seconds, she had the steady flow of a readout. "That baby's in fine position—absolutely no sign of stress—and you're dilated a full five centimeters. That means you have another five to go, dear, and the best thing you can do for both you and the baby is to rest between contractions."

"Riley—"

"Yes. Riley," Mary murmured dryly. "All in all, I have the feeling you're going to make it through this a great deal easier than your husband."

Adrienne's voice had a catch. "He's not...my husband."

"Well, now..." Mary, unconcerned, covered Adrienne with a cool, smooth sheet. "Some people have always taken a little longer than others to take care of that detail."

"He's so upset—"

Mary nodded. "Try not to worry. I've been nursing for almost twenty-five years and never lost a father yet." She checked the monitor one last time, pulled the shades and moved toward the door. "I'll send in an aide with some ice chips, but after that you just rest until the doctor comes. And I won't be any farther away than that page button if you want me."

"Mary?"

"Yes, dear."

"Are you going to send Riley back in?"

"Once he's calmed down, yes, if you want him."

"I want him." Her heart was in her voice. "You have no idea how much I want him," she whispered fiercely.

The waiting room was painted the same sick green as the halls. Decorations included three Naugahyde chairs, a clanking radiator, a needlepoint picture of a redbrick town hall, and some farming magazines on a well-nicked table. All in all it was an innocuous room. Riley saw it as a torture chamber. He was dragging a hand through his hair for the hundredth time when the stout nurse reappeared in the doorway.

"What took you so long? Is she all right? Is the baby all right? Can I go back in there?"

Mary motioned him to follow her out to the hall to her desk. "The doctor's already been in and gone. She's fine, the baby's fine, and the contractions have let up for a bit. She's catching a ten-minute catnap and she needs it." She took the seat behind her desk and motioned Riley to the chair beside it. "You and I have a few things we need to take care of, and now's a very good time."

The admitting form only needed his signature where she'd marked an X. She'd taken addresses and insurance information from his wallet, which she now tried to hand back to him. He stared at her blankly. With a sigh, she bent low over her bottom drawer and straightened with a half-full bottle of whiskey and a shot glass. She'd seen expectant fathers in worse shape, but not many. His shirt was buttoned wrong; his eyes were bloodshot with panic and anxiety; and he barely glanced at her when she folded his fingers around the shot glass.

"This is all my fault," he said bleakly.

"You think so? In my part of the country, it takes two."

"You don't understand. I started an argument. She was perfectly fine before that. It's my fault she's in labor." The nurse pantomimed his downing the shot glass. "I love her."

"I can see that." When he'd gulped it, she recapped the bottle and packed it neatly back in her bottom drawer.

Riley patted his pocket and drew out a worn sheet of paper. "It's a marriage license. You know how long I've been carrying this around?"

"Tell me," Mary encouraged calmly.

"Liz—that's her doctor—fixed up the blood work, and that's what I was trying to talk to Adrienne about last night. Not the blood work. Getting married. Only she doesn't want to marry me, and I . . ." The whiskey hit him like a slam, first blurring his vision and then clearing it. He focused on Mary as if she were a total stranger, which she was. "I don't know what I'm talking to you for. I'm going back in there with her."

"I think you should," Mary agreed.

When he pelted down the hall, she glanced at the worn sheet he'd laid on her desk, forgotten. She studied it for a moment and then reached for the phone.

Riley looked so worn when he walked through the door; so worn, so frightened, so dear. Adrienne lifted her hand and he took it. His palm was like ice, but his eyes had never been more warm or blue. "Riley, please stop worrying. It's going to be okay."

She looked so small and fragile that he had to lean over and kiss her. "We'll make it okay." Because she was so calm and sure, he even started to believe it. At least he smiled, suddenly, for the first time in hours. "Hey. When'd you get so beautiful?" he murmured.

She chuckled. An hour passed, and then another before her contractions picked up momentum again. The first ones were fleabites by comparison. "Breathe,

Riley," she scolded. "In and out, little puffs. You can do it."

That made him laugh, and the sterile, cold room 232 slowly warmed, became an enclave of two. He fed her ice chips, rubbed her back. She told him bad jokes and they both tolerated the regular arrival of Mary, who seemed to think Adrienne needed regular examinations and a report. "Six centimeters." "Seven. Won't be long now, you two!"

For Adrienne's sake, Riley wanted it over. For his own, there was a growing, incomparable magic seeping into this room. Nothing in his life compared. He'd never felt closer to Adrienne, never imagined that intimacy could have this dimension. Their baby was on its way. Their baby. Not a damn thing in the whole world mattered but this, but her.

Adrienne had been hearing war stories about labor for months. The truth was worse than the stories and exhaustion had become her worst enemy, yet she found herself praying not yet. When it was over, she could never have this moment back with Riley. He was afraid, she knew, and it was the first time since she'd known him that she could be there for him. He needed her. Not the other way around. He needed her—she could feel it, see it, taste it.

"What's wrong with Archibald?" he teased.

"The same thing that's wrong with Hortense. Could you please get serious here?"

"All right, all right. Harold. George. Rudolph. Frederick."

"No, times four. What do you think about your own name?"

"A Riley junior? You'd do that to my son? And I thought I loved you."

The next contraction hit with shattering power. Adrienne forgot about breathing and grabbed on to his hand. Sweat coated her whole body with a fine glaze, and Riley kept counting, counting, counting, promising it would be over...and then it was. She opened her eyes, saw the fierce love in his and whispered, "I'm in trouble."

He instantly jerked up from the chair. "I knew it had to be near time. I'll get Mary, the doctor, the whole damn staff—"

"Ssh. Not that kind of trouble. Or yes...just that kind of trouble, but not quiet yet. Listen to me, Riley."

"Honey, if you—"

"Please listen." It had been an enormous relief to confess her fears and feelings to him—her fears about being a good mother, her feelings about the kind of woman she wanted to be. But she had more to confess than that, a far greater mountain to risk, and she knew she was running out of time. "Through it all, Riley," she said softly, "through biting your head off whenever you mentioned rings, through being grumpy and moody and nasty—"

"Sweetheart, you weren't—"

"Yes, I was. I made too much of a childhood I should have outgrown. I said I didn't trust you, when it was myself I was afraid to trust. What I want you to know, though, is that through it all I loved you. I've always loved you. I was unsure about a hundred things, but never that."

"How much?"

"Pardon?" The declaration had come from her heart, past every fear of rejection, past every milestone of caution she had ever emotionally erected. Somehow she expected him to react a little differently than to jerk off the bed with a rocket's energy and the devil's gleam in his eyes.

"How much do you love me? Enough to take a chance? Enough to marry me?"

Her soothing "Yes" was intended to calm him. Riley responded as though a fire was licking at his heels. "Don't you dare change your mind," he ordered her, smacked a kiss on her forehead and barreled out the door. Down the hall she heard him shouting for Mary.

Mary took care of gowning both men in the scrub room. She was fussy, insisting on the cap and booties and supervising their hands washing as if they were children. Riley was ready first; she sent him through the door where Dr. Henley was already with Adrienne.

Reverend Miller moved slower. Nearing seventy, he wasn't used to being rushed from his lunch. "You've called me at all hours, Mary, but I have to say never for this."

"When you've been a nurse as long as I have, you learn to be prepared for anything," Mary said mildly.

"You told him the license was no good? That the Indiana license isn't valid in Missouri?"

"Of course I didn't tell him that. A marriage in front of God is what counts and besides, they can take care of that legal business any old time. Only if you don't hurry up, Hiram, it's going to be too late. I told you she was already fully dilated—"

Hiram took a long, pompous breath. "It's possible I might have a slight queasy stomach. I've never seen a baby born."

"Well, at your age, it's about time," Mary scolded. "And you're not going to faint. You're not going to have time. You've got both a wedding and a christening to perform—the most efficient piece of work you've done in a long time. Now get in there!"

The minister walked through, took one look at the scene in the operating room, ducked his head fast to the open Bible in his hands and stuttered out a rapid, "Dearly Beloved . . ."

Mary had her hands full. The baby's head was crowning before the first "I do." Hiram tried to go weak-kneed on her; her patient was exhausted; the doctor was in Riley's way—both of them wanted to catch the baby. John David was born to the musical crescendo of clanging radiators and a last "I do," and then there was the christening.

Mary didn't like confusion in her operating room, never tolerated it, and annoying her further were the tears in her eyes. She'd seen far too much life to become emotional at her seasoned age. The miracle of love and life, though…she never tired of it. These two were just starting the cycle, beginning the ultimate romance of a life together.

They say times had changed. Mary knew better.

"What are you doing, Riley?"

"Kissing the bride."

"I think you should unwrap him again and recount his toes. Are you sure?"

"I'm sure. He's perfect."

"He looks red and squished to me."

"He's perfect."

"Yes," she breathed. Every time she blinked away the tears, there was a new batch. If her heart felt fulller, it would probably burst. Their son was tucked at her side; he was warm and perfect and alive and beautiful. So was her new husband of less than thirty minutes, who was leaning over her with an extremely silly smile on his face. Riley's eyes were possessive, proud, loving—a little fierce—and nothing was budging that grin of his. "We could have waited," she murmured.

"For the marriage? You have to be kidding, love. I don't often catch you in a weak moment. I couldn't risk your changing your mind."

"You're out of luck, Mr. Stuart. Nothing this side of the earth was going to change my mind about marrying you. You're stuck with me."

"Are we talking stuck like glue, Mrs. Stuart?"

"We're talking forever, Riley."

"It took you long enough to believe in it," he murmured, and kissed her again. The kiss was a seal and a vow.

She returned the same seal with her lips, the same vow with her eyes, the same love with her heart.

*   *   *   *   *

Jennifer Greene

I grew up in Grosse Pointe, Michigan, a suburb of Detroit. From the time I could read, my nose was always in a book. From the time I could type, I was making up stories. My mother used to shove me out the door, determined to expose me to sunshine and fresh air, but it never took. Sooner or later her back was turned and I'd sneak back in.

In 1970, I graduated from Michigan State with degrees in English and Psychology. MSU gave me a Lantern Night Award—an award they annually hand out to fifty women graduates. Mine was given for a pamphlet I'd written. At that time, it never occurred to me that I was already "hook-line-and-sinkered" on writing.

I married Larry fresh out of college. We were broke—all I had to my name was a suitcase of clothes, seven boxes of books and a typewriter. The transition from a city slicker's life to my new husband's farm was slightly touchy. We moved into a wonderful old farmhouse with all kinds of character, but no one had lived in the place for seventeen years. There was a beehive in the kitchen and bats in the chimney, and the first time I walked out on the front porch, I found a garter snake shedding its skin. It only took me a week of married life to discover that love does not conquer all, and I wanted my mother.

Mom didn't come. Larry and I have now been married nineteen years—a process of discovering that love conquers lots more than I gave it credit for. In the early years I worked as a counselor, teacher and personnel manager...but in my spare time, I was still secretly piling stories in my closet. My husband is a difficult man to keep secrets from. When our two children were small, he bullied me into taking all those stacks of pages out of the closet and giving my writing a serious try.

I found an agent who, thank heaven, believed in me. That was thirty-some books ago.

I write love stories because I believe in them. I always felt sorry for Scarlett O'Hara; she was so sure land was the only thing that lasts. Love not only lasts, it's the glue that holds the days together...and it's that kind of love story I try to share with my readers.

Taylor's Ladies

KAREN KEAST

For M—for always and forever

Chapter One

It seemed like such a good idea at the time, Samantha Capen thought as she fidgeted in the passenger seat of the car moving through the autumn-gold countryside en route to Junction, Missouri. Adopting a baby had seemed like a good idea. But that had been before motherhood was hours away, or perhaps—panic chased down her spine—only minutes away.

She wasn't ready! She just wasn't ready! The baby wasn't due for another two weeks, not until the middle of October, and she needed those two weeks to begin to "feel" like a mother.

"Oh, God," Samantha implored, turning to the man beside her as she recklessly raked her fingers through her short, pixyish brown hair, "you do think the baby's all right, don't you? Coming early and all?" Before her companion could even begin to reply to a question he'd already answered a half-dozen times since leaving St. Louis two hours before, she added, "I should have done more statistical research on early arrivals. I read that book on premature births, but you can't call this premature in the real sense, though it is early. Surely there're statistics indicating the frequency of early arrivals and all the implications— Darn it, Taylor, can't this car go faster? No, no, don't drive faster. I'm not ready to become a mother! A single mother. A—"

Samantha clutched at her chest hidden beneath the layers of a white blouse, a red-and-black plaid flannel shirt and a black pullover sweater, all of which coordinated with tight-legged black pants, red leather boots and dozens of jangly silver bracelets.

Gasping, she wailed, "Oh, God, I'm hyperventilating! Or dying! Or both!"

Taylor Pierce, setting a safe speed despite the delirium loose in the car, glanced calmly at the woman whose wide brown eyes were alight with emotion. "The baby is all right. And furthermore, Sam, *you're* all right. You're not going to hyperventilate, you're not going to die, and you're going to make a wonderful, albeit single, mother."

Sam eyed the sable-haired, gray-eyed oracle as though she wanted to slap his handsome face. "Have I ever told you how much I despise it when you're calm and rational?"

"Yep. In the thirty-five or so years we've known each other, you've told me numerous times. Two thousand, four hundred and twenty-six, to be exact," he added, gently mocking her habit of continually spouting facts and figures. Part of her intimacy with statistics came from her job as a marketing and research analyst, but Taylor suspected the endless charts, columns, and ever-popular percentiles served a more personal purpose, as well. Somehow they categorized life for her, giving her some sense of control she didn't otherwise feel.

"Well, make it two thousand, four hundred and twenty-seven," she said, longing to ruffle his perpetually smooth feathers—if only once in her lifetime.

"Duly noted," Taylor said around a lazy grin that dragged a reluctant smile from her. He reached for her hand. "C'mon, Sam, relax."

Samantha laced her fingers with his and let his warm, comforting touch seep through her. How many times over the years had this man held her hand? It had begun in first grade and continued through high school. It had lasted through college and a disastrous marriage for each, and it was still going on. In short, Taylor Pierce was her best friend—always had been, always would be. It was he who'd encouraged her to adopt when she'd expressed her first speck of interest; it was he who'd told her of a lawyer friend who handled private adoptions; it was he who, she'd just naturally assumed, would go with her to pick up her child.

But she wasn't ready to be a mother!

Mother.

Samantha's thoughts turned sadly to her own mother, whom she'd buried six months before beneath a ground ironically just beginning to awaken with the colorful joys of spring. Even though Margaret Capen had been elderly—she'd been in her mid-seventies—her death had been unexpected. Two strokes, one closely following the other, had ended the life of the vital woman who'd been so much more than a mother to Sam. Because Sam's father had died when she was five, mother and daughter had clung tightly

together. Sam knew that her own career direction had
come directly from her mother's experience. Left to
fend for two with no real work skills, Margaret Capen had had to settle for a low-paying nurse's aide job.
She was determined that her daughter would have an
education, a career; she was determined that Sam
would never have to "settle". And career-wise, Sam
knew she never had. A degree in business administra-
tion and statistical analysis, and ultimately her own
successful marketing research company, had made her
financially independent. She had, however, settled in
an unexpected area.

Her education and career foremost in her mind,
Sam had postponed marriage. Even when she finally
did marry, she postponed having children because the
time hadn't seemed right. All of her energies at that
stage of her life had been channeled into making a go
of her newly founded business. And then, before she
could believe it was really happening, her two-year
marriage was ending as it had begun—with a whim-
per. She and Rick North hadn't even cared enough to
fight. In retrospect, Sam didn't understand why she'd
married him. It had just seemed the thing to do after
Taylor got married. With his marriage, she'd felt
strangely as if she'd lost something precious, as if
she'd lost a piece of herself. Throughout her marriage, throughout her divorce, she hadn't regretted
being childless.

Something had happened, though, when she'd
buried her mother. Maybe staring down at the stark,
cold earth, she'd faced her own mortality for the first

time; maybe the solemn act had simply opened a door to a room that had always been there. Whatever, she'd realized that no one, no son, no daughter, would mourn her death the way she was mourning her mother's, and that seemed an incredibly sad thing. Furthermore, she was past forty. Forty-one, though still in shouting distance of the big four-o, was past forty. Life, a parade whose end was relentlessly marching toward her, was passing her by. Her career, while satisfying and secure, left her incomplete. Suddenly she wanted a child. Typically she'd tried to analyze what was going on inside her head and heart, but found that the feelings couldn't be neatly analyzed, categorized, pigeonholed. Somehow she knew that her mother would approve of her decision to become a last-gasp, mid-life mother.

There was one other something she blamed on her mother's death, a something that made no sense at all. In fact it was so bizarre that she didn't even pretend to understand it. In the months following her mother's demise, as though the death had forever changed her in multiple and intangible ways, she had begun to see Taylor differently. Oh, not all the time. Just occasionally. And always unexpectedly. She equated it with one of those sparkling strobe lights rotating slowly above a dance floor. Every so often, a colored beam would strike Taylor, and she'd see him in a way she'd never seen him before.

The thought challenged her to take a look at him now. The afternoon sun, presiding over the gentle roll of hills, the empty fields that months before had

proudly grown corn and grain, the occasional farm
where woolly sheep grazed, blazed brazenly through
the car window. In its golden glow, Taylor looked...
He looked perfectly normal, Sam decided, feeling inordinately relieved. His hair, thick and vibrant, was
the same sable-brown she was accustomed to seeing.
The same threads of silver streaked the temples, hint-
ing ever so nobly at the fact that he was forty-two and
flirting with middle age. His eyes still were pewter-gray
and inclined toward laughter, while his face still was
angular and sun-kissed from the untold hours his
construction job demanded he be outdoors. His
shoulders filled out a blue-and-red, geometrically-
patterned sweater; his legs, as lean and muscular as an
athlete's, defined a pair of navy cords—all with a degree of familiarity. Yes, he was the Taylor she'd seen
a hundred times, one hundred times a hundred even,
the man she could unhesitatingly call *her* Taylor.

And yet...

And yet she could not forget the times of late when
his hair seemed to cry out for her touch, when his eyes
seemed to draw hers as they never had before, when
she wondered what his lips, lips that had kissed her
cheek a thousand casual times, would feel like against
her mouth in passion. And what would his hand, the
one so accustomed to holding hers, the one even now
holding hers, feel like roaming her body...like a lover?
As always, the questions, bordering on incestuous-
ness, startled her, stunned her, troubled her. Because
they did, she withdrew her hand from his.

Obviously thinking nothing of her action, Taylor placed his hand back on the steering wheel. He glanced over at her. "Okay now?"

"Yeah," she answered, hoping that she truly was. Unconsciously she rubbed one hand with the other, guiltily trying to removed the feel of him. "How much farther?"

"Only a few more miles." They had already passed through Jefferson, headed north. Presently they were stuck behind a rusty pickup that crawled as though suffering with arthritis.

Their imminent arrival jerked Samantha's attention back to the pressing reality of the situation. She groaned. "I'm not ready for this. I needed two more weeks. I haven't even bought diapers or—You do think the baby's all right, don't you, Taylor?" She shoved her fingers back through her hair. "Good grief, can't you pass that decrepit thing? No, no, don't pass it! Just take your time. Lord," she wailed, "I'm not ready for this!"

Throughout her tirade, Taylor smiled faintly and set a calm course.

The hospital, an old two-story, red brick building, sat at the edge of town surrounded by October-bare cornfields. It looked as though it had "grown" there in 1940. As if its seed had been carelessly sown and left to sprout, while the town, with Missouri practicality, had just extended the highway to it and hung a sign in front proclaiming it to be Junction General Hospital. A first-time visitor to the hospital might conclude that green paint had been cheap in the year 1940, or at least in some year thereafter, though by no means a recent year. The interior was painted throughout in that deadly dull, in-need-of-freshening color. Despite its bleakness, however, the hospital's old-fashioned radiators hissed a welcome as Samantha barged through the front door in a state somewhere between exhilaration and out-and-out panic.

"I'm having a baby," she announced to the first person she saw dressed in white—an orderly with a mop. His gaze lowered to Sam's flat tummy, trimly tucked into snug-fitting pants, then raised once more to meet her eyes. He gave her a yeah-sure-you-are-lady look. "No, you don't understand. *I'm* not having the baby. Someone's having it for me." The orderly's expression turned to I've-heard-of-money-buying-everything-but-this-is-ridiculous. "No, no, you don't understand. I'm—"

"Where's the maternity ward?" Taylor asked from behind her in a tone as placid as a still lake.

"Second floor," the orderly replied.

"Thank you," Taylor said, taking Sam's arm and urging her in the direction of the elevator.

"Why didn't I think of that?" she asked, frowning as she stepped quickly aboard.

"You would have. Eventually. Right after you stopped burbling like an idiot."

His teasing smile took the sting out of the words. It also elicited the beginnings of a grin from Sam, that in her harried state of mind was forgotten before it could form.

"Oh, Taylor, what if there're complications?" she asked as the elevator began to wheeze upward. "Sixteen is so young to be having a baby. I know she's been healthy this far, but what if something happens right here at the end? What if it's already happened? What if the baby's already been born?" A dark, panicked expression crossed Samantha's usually smiling face. "What if she changes her mind and doesn't want to give her baby up for adoption?"

She. Her. It was the only way Sam knew to refer to the birthmother. It was the only way the birthmother knew to refer to Sam. Great lengths had been taken to assure everyone's anonymity. All Sam knew was that the daughter of a prominent Missouri family had gotten pregnant and that marriage had been ruled out as an option. The birthmother had equally ruled out abortion. All the birthmother knew about Sam was that she was financially secure, that she'd be a single parent, and that she desperately wanted this baby.

"She's not going to change her mind, babe."

"I know, I know. I'm just having the usual adoption jitters," Samantha said, wondering in some far corner of her mind if Taylor had ever called her *babe* before. It sounded so natural, so comforting. The far corner of her mind decided she liked the sound of what under most conditions was considered an endearment. The same section of her brain noted with just the teensiest bit of resentment that Taylor was his usual calm self. How else could you describe a man whose shoulder was cocked against the elevator wall and whose hands, hands that should have been filled with nervous energy, were buried deep, and casually, in his pants pockets? "Okay! Okay! I also know I'm a basket case. I'll calm down," she said, taking a deep breath as though he'd spoken verbally through his posture. "I promise I will. I prom—Can't this thing go any faster? For the love of Pete, the kid'll be in college before we even get to the second floor!"

"Take it ea-sy," Taylor began, but trailed off as Sam bolted from the slowly opening elevator, leaving only her back to converse with.

Her red boots thudding on the faded linoleum floor, her red shoulder bag whacking her hip, Samantha rushed toward the nurses' station, which was presently attended by a single figure in a crisply starched white uniform.

"I'm going to have a baby. I mean, there's a young girl here having my baby. Do you know how she is? My daughter, I mean. And the mother...the birth-mother...how's she? Has my baby been born? She's early...two weeks...nothing's wrong with the baby, is there? I mean, two weeks isn't a big deal, is it?" Samantha stopped only because she'd run out of breath. She was also aware of a sudden odd buzzing in her head.

The nurse—Mary Condrey, her name tag read— stood behind the station as though she were a commander at the helm of her battleship. Stalwart, thick-shouldered and ample-bosomed, Mary appeared to be in her fifties. She also looked as though she'd been in nursing awhile and, during that while, had seen everything there was to see. Twice over. She looked, too, as if the phrase no-nonsense had been coined for her. Her grayish hair was smoothed slickly beneath a nurse's cap with not even the hint of a frivolous curl, while the cap itself sat rigidly straight, not daring to list a fraction of an inch to the left or the right. She wore not a streak of makeup, although ruby-red garnet studs, at once incongruous and pretty, dotted her ears.

"You must be Ms. Capen," the stalwart ship commander surmised.

"Yes, I must. I mean, I am," Sam returned, the buzzing in her head now sounding like a chorus of honey bees. Each bee seemed to be trying to out-sing the other. "What about my baby—"

"The mother's still in labor."

"How long?"

Mary Condrey glanced at the plain metal watch at her wrist. "Just over three hours."

"How long to go?"

"Have to check with Almighty on that one."

"Oh . . . yeah . . . right. Is everything going okay? I mean, is everything normal?"

"Right as rain," Mary said, her attitude conveying that she subscribed to the theory that nature intended babies to be born with a minimum of fuss.

"She's two weeks early—"

"Babies are often unimpressed with the doctor's scheduling."

"Then it doesn't mean—"

"It means doodly-squat."

"Good . . . great. . . ." The racket in Sam's head was joined by sudden flashing black lights. "That's good . . . great . . ." she repeated, reaching out for the edge of the counter to steady herself. "I, uh...I'm the mother...the adoptive mother...I...I...oh my," she said, the lights growing blacker, "I think I'm going to faint."

Chapter Two

Not while I'm on duty, young lady," Mary said, whisking Sam into a nearby chair and shoving her head between her legs.

Sam heard the voice, gruff though unmistakably caring, as if it were echoing through a long tunnel. She also heard Taylor speaking and, for the first time since picking her up, sounding something other than irritatingly composed. She perceived, from the awkward perspective of her knees, that Taylor had hunched down beside her. She thought he'd also taken her hand in his. Yes, yes, he had. There was no way she could mistake the identity of the hand imbuing hers with strength.

"Sam, are you all right?"

She squeezed his hand in assurance and started to raise her head. Mary shoved it back between her knees. "I'm okay," Sam told the inside of her thigh.

"She's fine," Mary confirmed, stepping away to rifle through the contents of the bottom drawer of her desk. "Been in nursing for twenty-five years, and I've seen a lot of babies born. Even delivered a few single-handedly when the babies weren't too keen on waiting for the doctor. Seen my share of addle-headed fathers-to-be, too. I've never lost a one, and I don't intend to blemish my record by losing a mother-to-be. Here, take this," Mary urged, pressing a shot glass into Sam's free hand. Taylor still held tightly to her other.

Sam raised her head and glanced at the amber liquid.

"Whiskey," Mary said to Sam's silent question. "Best medicine ever distilled. Just ask my Mr. Condrey. He's taken a nip every evening of the thirty years we've been married, and he's healthier than a herd of horses. I've also given a toddy or two to every one of my kids."

Never having read anything on the medicinal value of liquor, Sam didn't feel qualified to discuss the subject. Besides, the situation didn't appear open to discussion. She'd been told, in no uncertain terms, to drink the whiskey. Which she did. She sucked in her breath as the liquor burned down her throat. "You've got kids?" she sputtered.

"Four or five," Mary replied, as if uncertain of the exact number, as though a child one way or the other didn't much matter.

At the rose color returning to Sam's cheeks, Taylor felt relieved enough to revert to his usual calm state. There was even a hint of a tease to his, "Sam's just a tad apprehensive about becoming a mother."

Taking no chances despite her patient's renewed color, Mary took the glass and pushed Sam's head back down.

Feeling much better now that the buzzing had receded and the hospital lights had taken precedence over those in her head, Sam launched into a series of facts. "Motherhood begins over forty for three thousand nine hundred women a year, and statistics reveal that most of the women are apprehensive. Actually studies indicate that late-timers make good mothers, with most being more laid-back, more sure of themselves about mothering than early-timers.'' She stopped, then added on a puzzled note, "Then why aren't I sure of myself? Why aren't I laid-back?" She moaned as though once more realizing the gravity of what was transpiring. "God, I'm not ready to be a mother! I need those two extra weeks!"

"So why don't we leave and come back in two weeks?" Taylor suggested.

Samantha's eyes found his. His were trying hard not to twinkle...but were failing miserably.

"Taylor Pierce, why don't you take your idea, to say nothing of your disgusting self-possession, and stuff it in your ear?"

Taylor grinned, an act that filled his whole face just the way it never failed to fill Sam's heart. Of late, it seemed to be filling it fuller than usual, but now wasn't the time to dwell upon that fact.

Encouraged by the liveliness once more in Sam's voice, Mary made her own suggestion. "Why don't the two of you take a seat in the waiting room? I'll keep you posted."

Paul Simon had once written there were fifty ways to leave your lover. Over the next six hours, Samantha wished there were only half that many ways to leave behind the long, endless minutes. But alas, there seemed none. Not even one tiny one to make the wait just a bit more tolerable. She sat, she paced, she cursed, she prayed—but one second crept into another with maddening slowness.

"Dammit!" Sam cried, jumping to her feet once more and covering the distance of the small waiting room like a tiger roaming its cage.

The room was painted the same deadly dull green as the rest of the hospital, while a couch and three chairs, in a dark green Naugahyde, were haphazardly positioned here and there. Three windows looked out over tilled-under, furrowed cornfields. Pictures of railroads—Junction was the spot where several railroads met—hung on the walls, accompanied by a needlework of the town hall. Farming magazines, all of which Sam had had in her hand at some point, lay scattered about. Compulsive reader that she was, she now knew more about Missouri's apple orchards, soybean crops, cattle and sheep farming than she ever wanted to know. She knew, too, that bass, bluegill, crappies and jack salmon flourished in Missouri streams—and that not one of the scaled little beasties was making the clock tick faster!

"Are you all right?" Taylor asked at her outburst.

"I guess," she said as she folded her arms about her and stepped to the doorway to stare across the hall at the operating room.

Mary had announced an hour before that the birthmother had been rolled into the operating room for delivery. Prior to that, the young woman had been in Room 232, which was the far room at the end of the hall. Though everyone's privacy was being protected—both her lawyer and the birthmother's lawyer had insisted on that—Samantha did know that the woman's parents were with her... or at least had been until this last crucial step. Alone now, except for the hospital attendants, what was the birthmother feeling? Samantha could imagine the physical pain far more vividly than she could the woman's emotional anguish. One would soon be over, the other would never be, for in all of the research she'd done on the subject, she knew it was a myth that the birthmother forgot about the child she carried for nine months before dramatically bringing it into the world. Out of sight was not out of mind.

Samantha sighed, feeling guilty that this woman's sorrow would be her joy. But such were the unbalanced scales of adoption. Sam had no doubt that the woman, the girl, was giving up her baby out of love, wanting the child to have the parenting that she could not provide. Though it had not been openly said, Sam was aware that finances were not the reason the woman had chosen adoption. The family was too prominent for money to be a problem. Sam suspected that that prominence itself was the motivator. A young woman from a respected family had made a mistake; even in a world of liberated morality, that family was not eager to share her mistake with the world, nor make their daughter pay for it for the rest of her life. That was why, Sam was sure, discreet out-of-the-way Junction had been chosen.

In the beginning, Sam had been afraid the birthmother had agreed to adoption under duress. But she quickly had been assured that the young mother did not want the responsibility of raising the child, that she viewed the pregnancy as a blatant mistake. When Sam found out that the birthmother had opted not to see the child, or hold it, after its birth, Sam had begged for the opportunity to do so. She had spouted endless statistics about the importance of bonding. The birthmother had agreed. And thus it was that in a state where an adopted child was often weeks to months old before being placed in the adoptive mother's arms, two lawyers had bent, though never broken, rules to accommodate a needy, and unique, situation.

Though at the moment, Samantha despaired of ever holding her child—her daughter. A sonogram, part of the adoption agreement Sam had signed, to ascertain baby and mother were healthy, had revealed the baby's sex.

"My God, how much longer can it take?" she wailed. "You don't think anything's wrong, do you? You don't think—"

"Nothing's wrong, Sam," Taylor assured her. "And I don't know how long it takes to deliver a baby."

A sudden thought knitted Samantha's brow. "Why didn't you and Laura ever have kids? You would have made a great father."

Taylor studied the woman before him and considered his options. He could tell her the truth, he could lie, or he could just evade the question. Since he didn't think Sam was ready, and probably never would be, for the truth, and since he himself was uncomfortable with a lie, he took the only road left. "It, uh . . . it just never happened." He let his heart strike two unsteady beats before adding, "What about you and North? Why didn't y'all have kids?"

Sam shrugged, then gave a mirthless little laugh. "We weren't married long enough."

"Two years is long enough," Taylor said, not letting her off the hook so easily.

Why hadn't she had a child? Or at least thought about having a child? Or at least tried to have a child? Sam seriously pondered the subject for the first time. She'd always assumed that she'd just been too busy with her job—and that was partly the truth—but what she was feeling now was an even deeper truth. She simply hadn't wanted to make a baby with Richard North. Oh, he'd been a nice man, a very nice man, but she just hadn't seen him in the role of her child's father. For that matter, she couldn't see him in the role of father, period. When she thought of a father, she thought of patience, of smiles, of Tay— She frowned. She thought of Taylor. The realization was disturbing, so Sam didn't pursue it. Instead, she did what Taylor had done so successfully seconds before: she evaded the issue with his very own words. "It, uh...it just never happened."

Taylor's gray gaze delved deeply into hers for what seemed like an eternity. He finally broke eye contact at a sound at the door. They both turned to see only an orderly emptying a wastebasket. Sam sighed heavily with disappointment.

Taylor stood, walked to the coffee maker Mary had set to perking earlier and poured a cup. He added cream and sugar.

"Here," he said, handing the cup to Sam.

"I don't want—"

"Take it. It'll give you something to do besides chew your nails."

Sam smiled. "I do not chew my nails."

"I was speaking metaphorically," Taylor said, grinning back. His smile faded as he felt her trembling hand curve around the cup. He had the sudden overwhelming urge to ease her suffering. Covering her hand with his, he said softly, "The waiting'll be over soon. Hang in just a little longer."

His hand was warm—oh, so warm!—against hers, and Sam greedily soaked in every ounce of the comfort he was offering. He'd always been so giving of himself. So unselfishly giving. That generosity, and the fact that he always seemed to know what she needed, even at those times when she herself hadn't the foggiest clue, was just one of the thousands of things she liked about him.

Her hand felt warm beneath his, Taylor thought. Warm and good. Too good. Abruptly he pulled his hand away and tucked it in a pocket, as though it had been guilty of a treasonous act and had to be locked away. He recrossed the room and poured himself some coffee. When he looked back, Samantha was staring out the window, her back to him.

He simply watched her.

He couldn't remember a time when Sam hadn't been in his life. At first she'd been this sassy little kid with braids in his first grade class, the only kid besides himself willing to stand up to the class bully. Both he and Sam had taken a punch in the nose for it—but not before Taylor had gotten a lick in. No one "pugged" Sam's nose and got away with it! Several years later, she'd been the gangly kid in braces who'd been too self-conscious even to smile. He'd been the only person who could tease her into a grin, the only person she would let see the dental hardware. And then came adolescence with its training bras, followed by the real things, concomitantly followed by a series of suitors. For them both. Through each devastating crush, they'd held each other's hand.

And then came a serious affair or two for each, followed by heartbreak, followed by more hand-holding. After Vietnam, Sam had done more than hold his hand. She'd held him together, body, soul and spirit, when he'd returned emotionally less than he'd gone. Then there'd been a failed marriage—one each, a sort of his-and-hers folly. His for four years, hers for a briefer two, both now almost a year and a half behind them. He wondered if Sam ever thought it peculiar that his marriage had ended on the heels of hers. He wondered, too, what she'd say if she knew that the hand holding his following the breakup and subsequent divorce—namely, her hand—belonged to the person responsible for the marriage's failure. He wondered —He glanced up. Sam had said something,

something he couldn't have repeated had his life depended on it.

"What?"

Her back was still to him. "I said, I want this baby. I didn't realize how much I wanted a child until Mother died. After she was gone, there was this terrible emptiness inside me. Maybe it had been there all along, I don't know. I tried to ignore it, but it just seemed to grow bigger and bigger. I have everything that it's ethical to want—my health, a successful business, a lovely home, a car, Caribbean vacations, chic clothes and too many calories—but sometimes I feel so hollow that I hurt." She turned, her eyes meeting his. "Do you know what I mean?"

Long seconds passed before Taylor said softly, simply, "Yeah, I know what you mean."

He was standing, one broad shoulder braced negligently against the wall. The sun, stealing through a nearby window, cast a fading ray across him. Light. Like the glittery strobe display splashing down on a dance floor. For just a moment that odd, tingly feeling began to step forward. Rather than risking it, Sam removed Taylor from her vision by turning back to the window. She didn't need this new, indefinable Taylor; she needed the old Taylor. She needed her friend.

"I'm afraid," she said quietly, so quietly she wondered if she'd actually given voice to the malign feeling that was smothering her.

"Of what?"

"I'm afraid I won't know what to do with a baby. I haven't been around that many."

"Every new mother's afraid. Instinct'll take over the minute you hold her."

Sam pivoted. "That's just it. I'm not like every other mother. What if all this instinct business is part of pregnancy and the birthing process? What if it's all unleashed in the act of giving birth?"

Taylor pushed slowly from the wall, set down his cup and started toward her. "Maybe. But how does that account for all the adoptive mothers who seem to have caught on quite nicely to mothering? Somewhere along the line instinct kicked in for them."

Sam looked up at the man now towering head and shoulders above her and grinned. "I hate it when you're logical about as much as I hate it when you're calm."

"And I hate it when you sell yourself short, which, I admit, you rarely do."

She angled her head consideringly. "Sometimes I think you see a me in me that no one else sees."

"Maybe. All I know is that you'll make a great mother."

"I want to be a perfect mother."

"There's no such thing as a perfect anything."

"I know, I know! My head tells me that, but my heart says that I need to be her counselor, her confessor, her friend, her teacher—"

"You'll be her mother. That's all you have to be."

"But what exactly is that, Taylor? I haven't seen a job description."

Taylor grinned. "What? In all that research you did on parenting, you didn't find a job description of motherhood?"

Sam tried to hide her smile. "Go ahead. Make fun of my research."

"I'm not making fun. I know you need your statistics like Linus needs his security blanket."

"I don't need—"

"All you need to be a good mother in the beginning, Sam, is to keep the diaper on the right end, feed regularly, love a lot and let nature take its course."

"That's easy for you to say. You're not about to become a moth—"

"Ms. Capen?" came a voice from the doorway.

Sam whirled, her gaze colliding with Mary's. Though Mary's features were as strong and stern as ever, her eyes shone with unconcealed pleasure. "Your daughter just made her appearance. Seven pounds, eight ounces. And she's fit as a fiddle."

A thousand emotions warring for expression, Sam uttered not a single word, made not a single movement.

"Sam?" Taylor called softly when one still second bled into another.

She angled her head toward him and said, as though he hadn't heard at all, "I have a daughter." Her voice was filled with awe.

A slow smile slid across Taylor's lips. "Congratulations, Mom," he whispered.

As he spoke, he lowered his head. Instinctively Sam knew he was going to kiss her. Just the way he'd kissed her a hundred times over the years, his lips casually making contact with her cheek. This time, however, he took her totally by surprise. Instead of her cheek, his mouth brushed across hers. So fleeting was his touch that it held no more substance than a fairy tale. A sugar-spun fairy tale.

Then he raised his head, leaving Sam's heart to race a wild, discordant rhythm that had little to do with the fact that she'd just become a mother.

Chapter Three

Sam told herself that Taylor had meant nothing erotic by the kiss. Sam told herself he had meant it solely as warm congratulations for a special event. But her thudding heart, though in agreement with everything she was thinking, was still acting as though not a word of it were true. Her heart was acting, reacting, as though the kiss had been an eroticism shared between lovers.

Mary cleared her throat.

Startled at the intrusion, Sam pulled her scattered senses together and glanced from Taylor—was he studying her reaction to the kiss, or was it solely her imagination?—to the nurse.

''She'd like to meet her mother,'' Mary said, her tone indicating that beneath her gruffness lay the realization of the tender circumstances.

The simple statement washed all coherent thought from Sam's mind, reducing her to nothing more than feeling—all centered around a newborn baby.

"Go on," Taylor urged, his hand at the small of her back. "Go hold your daughter."

"Come with me," she said, reaching for his hand and clasping it in hers.

Surprise scored Taylor's features, and he held back when she would have pulled him forward. "No, I couldn't . . . I shouldn't . . . I—"

"Please," Samantha whispered.

The word, Sam's pleading voice, her request in general, did things to Taylor. Warm things. Warmer things even than the brush of her lips against his, which was really saying something because the kiss had been the definition of warm. In fact, he could still feel its molten glow.

"Babe, I don't think they'll let me—"

Sam looked at Mary. "Can he?"

"'Course he can. Now, come on, you two," Mary said, "while the baby's still little enough to hold."

Neither dared argue with the imperial command. Especially since neither wanted to argue.

"Seven pounds, eight ounces," Sam reflected as she and Taylor followed along behind Mary. "Statistically that's well within the norm. What about her length?"

"Nearly nineteen inches."

"Good. Good."

"Ten fingers, ten toes," Mary volunteered.

"Great!" Samantha cried, as though her daughter had been the first newborn to ever pull off that phenomenal feat. "What about hair?"

"Yes."

"No, I mean the color."

"Black."

"Black?" Sam said with a pleased smile.

"Black," Mary confirmed.

Suddenly Sam's expression grew anxious, as though she'd just remembered something vital. "What about her Apgars?"

"Apgars?" This came from Taylor, who was at her side.

"Nine," Mary said.

"Thank God!" Sam said, flattening her hand to her chest in unqualified relief. "A ten rating is seldom given," she went on to explain to a perplexed Taylor, whose only comment was, "What in heck are Apgars?"

"They're numbers that represent a newborn's chances for survival based on the baby's color, heart rate, respiration, reflex and muscle tone," Sam answered. "They're taken at one and five minutes after birth."

"You read too much," Taylor muttered, but it was lost in Mary's "If you ask me, a good common sense look-see'll do the same thing as all that highfalutin' Apgar business. Knew every one of mine was healthy the minute I set eyes on them. Here, put these on," she ordered, grabbing two sterile gowns and opening the door to Room 232.

At the threshold, Sam paused. "How's the mother?"

"Just as she should be after giving birth," Mary said. "Her parents are with her."

This last Sam was almost certain was added to reassure her that she would have all the privacy she needed with her daughter. Mary then disappeared, leaving Sam to wait once more.

Room 232 was splashed with the same vapid green paint as the rest of the hospital. It also had a bathroom, a bed, a bedside table and one chair. A window, with a view of the highway and cornfields, faced west. Beyond the window, the night crept closer. Soon the gray gloaming would be gone, and the evening would wrap the little rural town in its nocturnal velvet peace.

At the moment Samantha felt none of that peace. Instead she felt the sharp, knifelike edges of anticipation. Looking around her, she also felt like an intruder in a stranger's world, as though she'd happened upon a diary whose private words she was being forced to read whether she wanted to or not. Tubes hung from the ceiling, and at the bedside rested an oxygen tank and a monitor to measure maternal and fetal heartbeats. These, representing an experience she'd not participated in, and one she could only imagine vaguely, were private enough. The bed, however, represented the true violation of privacy. It was rumpled. As though from impatience. As though from pain. Sam drew her hand across the crumpled sheet, wondering as she did so what the young woman's thoughts had been. Had she been afraid? Remorseful? Glad to be getting it over at last? And had she wondered what kind of woman she was giving her baby up to, just as Sam wondered what kind of woman was giving life to the child that she would call her own?

And how would Sam ever thank this unknown woman for the sacrifice she was making?

Samantha felt Taylor's hand on her shoulder and turned. In his eyes she saw that he knew everything she was thinking, feeling—the way he always seemed to know. He tightened his hand. It was all the communication they needed.

As the door opened, Samantha jerked her head upward. Her heart began to pound at the sight of the pink bundle in Mary's arms.

"Here we are, little miss," Mary cooed to the baby in a voice so foreign to her usual brusqueness that, had Samantha not heard it, she wouldn't have believed it. "Didn't I tell you I had a surprise for you?"

As Mary and the pink bundle approached, an exquisite panic seized Sam. "I—I haven't held many babies," she confessed.

"It's as easy as falling off a log," Mary assured.

Falling. As in dropping. Sam groaned inwardly. She wished the nurse had chosen another comparison.

"In all my years of puttin' babies in mother's arms," Mary said, "I've never seen one broken yet. Baby, that is. Not mother."

"Let's hope you can still say that in a few minutes," Sam muttered. Her panic increased as the pink bundle suddenly left Mary's arms for hers. In fact, the panic exceeded its bounds to become out-and-out fear. Sam ran both sweaty palms down her pants legs and awkwardly positioned her arms, as though ready to receive a tossed football. "What do I do?"

"Just do what comes naturally," Mary said.

Naturally. Didn't anyone understand that she hadn't the least idea what came naturally? That she feared nothing would come naturally? That naturally was a word reserved for those women who'd actually given birth? That—

The thoughts scampered from her head as quickly as mice from a cat when Mary placed the tiny weight in Samantha's arms. Instinctively, naturally, her arms formed a cradle, her hands curling around the small form. She felt a tiny little behind, swaddled in thick diapers, felt short little legs, felt a small head so wobbly it might have been a toy on a spring.

"The only thing you have to watch is her head," Mary cautioned.

Yes, Sam thought, watch her head. But then, somehow she'd known that. Instinctively known it. Naturally known it.

Even as Sam watched, Mary drew back the blanket from the baby's face. It was round and red and still just a bit swollen from delivery. Her eyelids, with an already full sweep of black lashes, were closed. Her cheeks were ruddy and chubby. With her tiny stocking cap—black wisps of renegade hair escaping—she looked as though she'd been out in a chill winter wind. She also looked gorgeous. Beautiful. Unquestionably the prettiest baby ever born.

Sam sighed, trying to vent the pressure that had suddenly built around her heart. It was like no feeling she'd ever had before. It was like Christmas morning, her sixteenth birthday, a school kid's first day of summer all rolled into one. It was like flying to the sun and the moon, with stops at every star.

"Oh, Taylor," Sam whispered in a tone suggesting she'd just approached an altar.

Taylor said nothing, as though he, too, were engaged in worship.

Both simply stared at the baby, barely noticing that Mary slipped quietly from the room.

Finally Sam glanced up. Her eyes were glassy with unshed tears. "She's...she's..."

"...beautiful," Taylor finished.

"Yes," Sam said, adding, "and she's mine."

Taylor smile softly. "And she yours." Reaching out, he swiped away a single tear that glimmered from the crest of Sam's cheek. She sniffed.

At the sound, the baby half cocked an eye, sleepily peered at the two adults—as if checking them out—then gave a little grunt.

Sam beamed with pride. "Did you hear that?"

"I heard it."

"What do you think she was saying?"

"Probably that we're acting like idiots."

Sam smiled. "Yeah, I guess we are...I am." The smiled died abruptly. "Pull back the blanket."

"Why?"

"Just pull it back and count her toes."

"The nurse already said—"

"You trust the numerical count of a woman who can't remember exactly how many children she has?"

Taylor grinned, wide grooves indenting cheeks that were beginning to shadow with end-of-the-day stubble. "Aren't you being just a tad neurotic, Sam?"

Samantha couldn't hide a smile, even though it was at her own expense. "More than a tad. Now, count."

As ordered, Taylor pulled aside the fleecy pink blanket. The baby wore a white gown, from beneath which barely peeked two tiny feet. Taylor pulled up the gown and counted. "Ten little piggies," he confirmed. The baby squirmed, drawing both feet back under the warmth of the gown.

"She's ticklish," Sam said.

"She's protesting," Taylor corrected. "And I don't blame her. I hate it when my feet are warm and some idiot comes along and insists on counting my toes."

"Taylor?"

He looked up after rebundling the baby.

"Shut up. And count her fingers."

"Sorry, kid," Taylor said, checking one perfect little hand, then the other. The baby grunted, flailing one arm. "I know," Taylor sympathized. "She's loony tunes, but really quite harmless. I warn you now, though, she's gonna drive you crazy with her statistics."

The baby's hand flailed again; this time its wrinkled fingers curled around Taylor's index finger. The sight was so stunning, the smallest of small contrasted against the largest of large, newborn pink against weathered bronze, that both Samantha and Taylor sobered instantly.

"She's so little," Sam whispered.

"Yeah. So little."

As though on cue, the baby opened her eyes. Her blue eyes. Eyes so blue they sparkled with innocence.

"Hi, there," Samantha said softly.

The baby blinked.

"Andrea Margaret," Sam continued, "I'd like you to meet Taylor. Taylor, this is Andrea Margaret."

"Hello, Andrea Margaret," Taylor said, wriggling the finger the baby was still clasping.

Andrea Margaret blinked again.

Taylor, who'd had no idea what names Sam was considering, because she carefully guarded them as if doing so would guard the child, thought how very pleased and proud Sam's mother would have been to have a granddaughter named after her.

At the same moment, Sam was thinking how lucky her daughter was to have a man like Taylor in her life. She'd always be able to depend on him, to turn to him, to thrust her problems, big or small, on his wide shoulders. Sam never questioned that Taylor would be Andrea Margaret's best friend—just the way he'd always been hers. The truth was, with their similar sable-colored hair, Andrea Margaret looked as though she could easily have been Taylor's daughter. If she and Taylor had had a child—Sam left the thought unfinished because, even in its partial form, it caused a fluttery feeling in the pit of her stomach.

Samantha was actually relieved when her daughter began to squirm, requiring her full attention elsewhere. The baby's mouth twisted into a fretful little frown at the same time her hands, turning loose of Taylor, swatted at the air. She made a whispering little bleat that sounded suspiciously like a cry. Instinctively she angled her head and began rooting against Sam's breast.

The picture of mother and child was so pristinely perfect that Taylor actually knew a moment of piercing pain. He also knew himself to be a fool. And a coward. A thousand times he'd wanted to lovingly, provocatively caress the same breast that this child was so boldly nudging, but he didn't have the courage. Every time that courage seemed within his grasp, he'd see an image of a shocked Sam. Or of a repulsed Sam. A Sam who'd want nothing more to do with him. Or a Sam who'd now be distanced from him. Always, even though courage fleetingly beckoned, the risk was too great a one for him to take, for he could do nothing to drive her from him. He had to have her in his life. Any form of her was better—infinitely better—than none of her.

The piercing pain grew, and he recognized it for what it was: love. Quite simply, he was madly in love with Samantha. He could remember exactly the first time he'd realized that he loved her. Actually the realization had been preceded by an accusation that had stung the very air through which it had been hurled. That accusation had come from his wife…as she was demanding a divorce that he was more than willing to grant. Only weeks before, Sam had filed for divorce. Though Sam had felt freer than she had for a long while, or so she professed, Taylor inexplicably felt chained, bound, confined within walls he could not define. His wife had defined them for him. Once he'd been accused of loving Sam, he couldn't deny it. And God alone knew how long he'd loved her. Maybe since first grade. Fate had cast them in the role of friends. It was a role Sam had never questioned, and he couldn't rock the boat now.

Could he?

Looking like a madonna, Sam raised her gaze to Taylor. Tears of awe, tears of delight, once more glistened in her eyes as the child nuzzled at her breast. "She . . . she thinks I'm her mother."

"You are," Taylor answered quietly. *You're also my friend and the woman I love. Just as I'm a fool and a coward. A coward for not rocking the boat, a fool for even considering the reckless possibility.*

Chapter Four

Sam was high. As high as the happy moon that smiled down from the black satin sky. So emotionally elevated, so giddy, was she that she could only pick at her food an hour later as she and Taylor sat in a local diner. A short while before, she had replaced her hungry daughter in the capable arms of Mary Condrey. Mary had boldly suggested that Samantha herself might benefit from a meal . . . and some rest.

"Eat," Taylor commanded.

"I am."

"You're playing. There's no nutritional value in shoving food around on a plate."

"Americans consume far too many calories, most of which are for recreational purposes rather than nutritional. We're a society fixated on oral gratification. Researchers say—"

"Eat, Sam." When it was obvious she intended to continue with what researchers say, Taylor nodded sternly toward Sam's virtually untouched plate. "Eat."

"Oh, good grief!" Sam said, scooping some mashed potatoes onto her fork. The fork was almost to her mouth when she halted it suddenly and said, "I need to stop at a mall. I've got to get some diapers and something to dress the baby in to take her home. Oh, Taylor," she said, lowering the fork once more to the plate, her eyes going all gooey, "isn't she the sweetest thing you've ever seen?"

Taylor conceded defeat. On two levels. One, there was no way he could get Sam to eat. Two, there was no way, once the phrase oral gratification had been mentioned, that he could keep at bay the thought of Sam's lips and how heavenly they'd felt brushing against his. He hadn't meant to kiss her mouth. He had just found himself doing it, which led to another concession: there'd been no way, short of death, that he could have stopped himself.

No more than he could stop himself an hour later from being blatantly enchanted with Sam as she shopped. They had easily found a mall, which at the hour of 9:30 p.m. was practically deserted. The department store showed equal signs of emptiness, allowing Samantha and Taylor free rein of the aisles.

"What do you think?" Sam asked. "The white or the pink?"

Taylor made a show of considering the lace on the white dress, the smocking on the pink, when, in actuality, he was far more interested in the rosy glow in Sam's cheeks, the sparkle in her brown eyes. "Uh . . . the pink, I think."

"Yeah, I think so, too," she said, adding, "I'm not going to be one of those parents who gives her child everything."

She announced this as she laid the pink dress atop the mountain of other items—booties, blankets, gowns, seemingly several of everything the baby section of the store offered for sale. Sam had refused to buy anything before the baby's birth, just as she'd refused to announce names. She had called it superstition; Taylor had seen it as a not-so-subtle sign of how much this child meant to her.

"I think that's a wise decision, Sam," Taylor now said, wondering how they were going to cart all this, and presumably the baby, back to St. Louis.

At Sam's lead, with Taylor pushing the buggy, they passed from the clothes department to the toy department. "Researchers say—Oh, Taylor, look!" Samantha cried as she assessed the aisle of dolls. Picking up one, then another, many bigger than Andrea Margaret herself, Sam looked at dolls guaranteed to cry, burp, wet and call, in a singsong voice, for mom-ma.

"Researchers say what?" Taylor prompted.

"Huh? Oh, researchers say it's not healthy for a child, or for an adult, either, for that matter, to get everything he wants. One psychologist calls it beneficial greed. It's the driving force behind wanting to get up every morning." Sam had abandoned the dolls for a china tea service. She looked up into Taylor's gray eyes. "I guess she's a little young for dolls and tea services."

"Just a little, I suspect," he said, fighting a grin. "Give her a week or two."

"That's what I was afraid of," Sam said, turning the corner of the aisle. The row before her was chockfull of stuffed toys. Sam's eyes brightened, as if to say, "Ah, but these are not inappropriate."

In minutes, Sam had lined up a trio of critters—a teddy bear, a fluffy cat and a floppy-eared dog.

"Which?" she asked.

"The teddy bear. Every kid needs a teddy bear."

"Good choice," Sam said, tossing in the bear, adding, "let's check out while there's still a chance I can pay for this." As the clerk rang up the purchases, Sam announced suddenly that she'd forgotten something and raced off toward the toy department. She returned with the floppy-eared dog and a sheepish grin. "Don't say it. I don't want to hear your logical assessment of how I'm spoiling her. And I don't want to hear a lecture on beneficial greed. Frankly, I think I showed great restraint in leaving the cat behind."

Sam's tousled hair tumbled onto her forehead. Her makeup needed freshening. Her rumpled clothes could have used a pressing. But with her eyes glittering with happiness and motherhood settling about her with an appealing graciousness, Taylor thought she'd never looked more beautiful. He smiled—gently, softly, from the depths of his heart.

"I think your excessiveness might be forgiven under the circumstances."

Inwardly his smile died. He wondered if she would as easily forgive him for what he was thinking, which was that he'd never wanted to hold anyone more than he wanted to hold her at that moment—with a need, a greed, that was far from beneficial to his well-being. That he wasn't holding her was testimony to the fact that she wasn't the only one who knew about restraint. He, too, knew its blunt, soul-bludgeoning feel.

* * *

They found a motel at the edge of town. When Taylor asked for adjoining rooms, connected by an inside doorway, Samantha wasn't the least surprised. His protectiveness of her, his sometimes even over-protectiveness, was just another of the things she liked about him. She could never remember not feeling safe with Taylor. From the start, he'd been her personal dragon slayer.

Minutes later, standing at the connecting door between the two rooms, Taylor studied the dying gleam, the sudden fatigue, in Sam's eyes. Clearly she'd had enough excitement for one day.

"Get some sleep," he said, unable to keep his palm from cradling the side of her cheek. As always, she felt like warm gold; as always, he felt her heat deep inside him...just the way he longed, oh so desperately, to feel the heat of himself inside her. Since his divorce he'd thought so often of her as his lover that he was no longer shocked by his desire, and that, in and of itself, shocked him, as did the strength of his need. His outward calm was no reflection of the struggle raging within him. He worried that Sam might somehow read his mind—and his body. Before he could betray himself, he pulled his hand away and repeated, this time thickly, "Get some sleep."

"Taylor?"

He had already turned from her, but now he turned back.

"Thank you."

"For what?"

"For coming with me. For not lecturing me about a floppy-eared dog. For the thousands of things you've done that I've never thanked you for."

Taylor's eyes darkened from misty-gray to slate-gray. "That's what friends are for," he said. His voice rang with an odd timbre that Samantha might have been tempted to interpret as regret had the notion made any sense. But it didn't. No more than did the fact that neither of them appeared to want to be the first to break eye contact. Finally Taylor said, "G'night."

"G'night," Sam repeated and watched as Taylor disappeared into his room. He pushed the door closed behind him, leaving it ajar at an angle that provided privacy while promising that he was nearby.

For long moments, Samantha stared at the door. She felt strangely bereft at Taylor's absence, as though a part of her had been amputated. Cleanly. Aseptically. But without anesthetic. The simple truth was she wanted to be with him. Even though the day was ending. Even though propriety demanded they part. Today had been the most exciting day of her life, and she wasn't ready to stop sharing it with him.

Offering no explanation for her feelings—intuitively she knew the search for answers might set her on a voyage she truly didn't want to take—she turned away and busied herself with bedtime activities. She was tired. Happy, but tired. Excited, but tired. But was she too happy and excited to sleep, even though she was dead on her feet? After showering and donning a pair of red satin pajamas, she slipped beneath the cool sheets of the bed. Within minutes, she had the answer. Yes, she was too happy, too excited to sleep. Tossing and turning, she fought the bed as though it was her mortal enemy.

Thoughts, like a wayward wind, tumbled through her mind—thoughts of her blue-eyed, pink-cheeked daughter, of a pretty smocked dress to carry that daughter home in...of the man next door. Was he asleep? Was he dreaming? What was he wearing? An image rushed forward of bronzed skin—*bare* bronzed skin. The thought heated Samantha until she felt as hot as the earth broiling under a summer sun. Throwing back the cover on an exaggerated sigh, she slung her feet over the side of the bed.

Slight though the commotion was, Taylor heard it. But then he'd heard everything from the small to the barely discernible in the restless hour and a half since he'd gone to bed. He'd heard Sam shower, heard her pad about the room, heard her sink into the bed's thick softness. He would swear he'd even heard her breathing.

Whipping back the blanket, he rose and grabbed his pants, which he yanked over his hair-dusted legs and bare buttocks. He zipped and buttoned the cords as he walked, barefoot, toward the adjoining door. Opening it without hesitation, he passed through.

Both he and his heart stopped abruptly.

Sam stood at the window. The drape was drawn, allowing silver moonlight to spill into the room. A splash, like a streak of platinum paint, drenched her, raining onto her shoulder and running off into a pud-

dle on the floor. In the light, the satin pajamas molded
every feminine curve of her body—the swell of her
breasts, the slope of her hips. Such pure and unadul-
terated womanly perfection had stopped Taylor cold.
That, and the appealing contradiction provided by the
teddy bear she clutched. Woman. Child. No man
could have resisted the sirenlike first nor been un-
moved by the vulnerable second.

"Sam?" Taylor said, the word as light as moon-
beams.

Startled, Samantha turned . . . and watched as the
shadow-dark figure started toward her. The taper of
Taylor's lean, swaggering hips made him look su-
premely virile. As did his bare torso, on which the
moonlight danced to a silent serenade. Hair, the rich
color of charcoal, shaded his chest, spreading out
across well-developed pectorals before dipping in a
linear, provocative pattern into the pants' waist. Sam
heard her breath catch. She'd seen him without a
shirt—numerous times when he wore swim trunks—
but the sight had never affected her so profoundly. She
told herself it was just the moonlight that made him
look different. In any less intimate setting, he wouldn't
look so sexy, so much like a lover. The thought led to
an interesting question. What kind of lover would he
be? Gentle? Demanding? A seductive combination of
both? Appalled by the turn of her thoughts—she had
to stop these shameful imaginings!—she forced them
from her mind.

"I couldn't sleep," she said, willfully ignoring the sensual majesty of the mountainlike shoulders now towering above her.

"Why not?"

Sam shrugged. "Too keyed up, I guess." She grinned. "Actually there's a humongous war going on inside me. Excitement and fear are slugging it out."

The corners of Taylor's mouth lifted. "Any idea who's gonna win?"

"Not a clue. Fear has a sharp right, but excitement has some fancy footwork. I figure the match could go on for hours."

Taylor reached out and brushed back a wisp of hair from Sam's cheek. "Excitement's permissible. Fear's not." He then added, as though he read her mind clearly, "You're gonna make a great mother. A fantastic mother. The best mother that any little girl could ask for. But," he said as he laced her hand with his after taking the teddy bear from her and setting it in a chair, "you're gonna make a cranky mother if you don't get some sleep."

His hand felt warm, big, solid, while his stride was certain and sure as he led her toward the rumpled bed.

Pulling back the cover, he said, "Now, get in."

Because his command brooked no opposition, Samantha slid between the sheets. To her astonishment, Taylor crawled in beside her. Before she could do more than count a skipped heartbeat, he wedged himself against the headboard in a sitting position and drew her to him.

"Go to sleep," he said.

Taylor's chest, strong and vibrant beneath her, cushioned her back, while his arms cradled her tightly...naturally. Though they'd never shared a bed, doing so somehow seemed right, and Samantha could feel her body, as though it were far wiser than her analytical mind, begin to relax into the warm wall of his being. She ignored the appealingly crisp feel of his chest hair, the suggestive caress of his skin, for to acknowledge either would be inappropriate. It also would mean that she had to move—tactfully, of course, but move nonetheless—and that she couldn't do. Because his body felt too good. Besides, she was, surprisingly, growing sleepy.

"Taylor?" she asked drowsily.

"Hmm?"

"You feel good." She was too tired to speak anything but the truth.

Taylor's heart missed a beat. "So do you."

"Taylor?"

"Hmm?"

"You will be Andrea Margaret's godfather—" she yawned hugely "—won't you?"

So exhausted, so sleepy was Sam that she barely heard his hesitation before he answered, "Yeah. Sure."

A long time later, Taylor, unlike the woman in his arms, still lay awake. The truth was he was fighting sleep because he wanted to savor every precious moment of her nearness. Besides, he was pondering the great universal questions of life. Questions like, how could just the quiet stirring of her breath fill him with such pleasure? How could she look more beautiful in sleep than wide awake? How could the feel of satin so exquisitely torture the senses?

The sun peeked cheerily into the motel room, gilding the sleeping forms in its radiant brightness. Sometime during the night—Sam had no idea exactly when or how—she and Taylor had altered their positions. No longer propped against the headboard, they had scooted down into the bed and beneath the covers' cozy warmth. One thing, however, remained the same. Both were still lost, like lovers, in each other's arms.

Sam was groggily aware of the encroaching morning...and of the man beside her. The morning she fought; the man she didn't. In fact, she couldn't have fought him even if she'd wanted to, because he drew her in an irresistible way, forcing her to nuzzle her cheek against his chest. His warm chest. His fuzzy chest. Samantha purred softly, contentedly, and brought her hand to join her cheek.

Splaying her fingers, she buried them deep in the crinkly forest. The curls greedily wrapped themselves about her, ensnaring her in a silken trap she had no wish to escape from. Discontent with knowing only a limited area of his chest, Sam trailed her hand over trim muscle, rippling rib and a hard solid wall, beneath which beat a solid heartbeat. *Boom-boom. Boom-boom.* The consummate rhythm of assurance. Of reliability. Of comfort. She sighed once more and inched her hand a fraction of an inch lower. Her fingertips brushed against a flat nipple.

In reaction, a sleepy Taylor moaned, throatily, and tightened his hold on Samantha. His hand, resting in the middle of her back, tugged her nearer. Sam felt her breasts nestle against him. Nowhere in her dream-fogged brain did she feel a moral urgency to pull away, to end the intimacy. It felt altogether too natural for her breasts to plump against this man. Even if this man was her best friend.

Furthermore, it felt natural for her hand to begin to roam Taylor's body. In fact, it seemed quite eager to make the journey. Lower...lower...past his navel...past his waist...over the waistband of his slacks...to the hard masculine bulge that was straining against the confining fabric. The hard masculine bulge? The unexpectedly, dynamically aroused state of Taylor's body awakened Sam instantly. Just as instantly she realized that her body tingled from head to toe—as though it knew precisely what to do with the treasure she'd just discovered. She snatched her hand away. Her gaze flew upward. Where it collided with Taylor's. A blush began and spread like wildfire to every cell of her being. Every embarrassed, mortified cell.

"I—I'm sorry," she stammered, hearing her tongue trip over itself even as she heard her silent prayer winging heavenward. Please, God, she prayed, let this just be a dream.

Chapter Five

It wasn't a dream.

The gray eyes into which she stared told her that much, though they told her very little else. Except perhaps that this man had only moments before been asleep and that he'd awakened with a start. Beyond that, she perceived nothing. Certainly not a hint of what he was thinking.

What *was* he thinking?

For that matter, what was she thinking? She was thinking, she realized easily enough, that a man often awakened in such a sexually heightened state. Especially if he'd been helped into that state by a bold hand. Taylor's reaction had been mechanical, impersonal. Impersonal. The word sat heavily on Sam's senses, and she understood, without reflection, the why of that. She wanted his reaction to be personal. She wanted the man in him to respond to the woman in her. And that fact was not so easy to understand.

She also wanted him to say something. Anything! But he didn't. He just continued to stare at her, as though he'd never seen her before in his life.

A chilling thought crossed Samantha's mind. What if she'd so shocked him that she'd jeopardized their friendship? The possibility prompted her to speak.

"I'm sorry," she repeated. "I didn't mean to...I didn't know I was...I wouldn't have if...I mean, I...I'm sorry."

Nothing.

Except the loud thudding of her heartbeat and a sudden shrill noise.

"Dammit, say something!" she cried, not even aware she'd spoken aloud.

"The phone's ringing," Taylor said calmly.

It wasn't what she'd expected her bed partner's first words to be. "What?"

Taylor nodded toward the squalling telephone. Sam followed the direction of his gaze. She still seemed incapable of assembling sight and sound into sensible thought.

At the phone's fifth impatient shout, Taylor pushed to an elbow, reached across Sam and grabbed the receiver. Sam was acutely aware of the masculine form sprawled atop her—the bare, hair-dusted chest, the taut flat belly, the full erection he wasn't even trying to hide and which was presently imprinting itself into her thigh. Hotly imprinting itself.

"Hello? Oh, hi, Larry."

At the mention of her lawyer's name, Samantha looked up quickly into Taylor's face. On one level she thought how positively savage Taylor looked with such a wild stubble of beard, how provocatively satyric his smoky-gray eyes suddenly seemed. Why had she never noticed either before? On another level, her thoughts scurried toward the legal issue of the impending adoption.

"Sorry about that," she heard Taylor say to his friend. "Well, look on the bright side. Junction doesn't have that many motels. No, it isn't too early," he said, then glanced at the clock to see what time it was. The clock read 8:10. "No, it isn't too early," he repeated, adding, "I was up." At that, he lowered his gaze to Samantha. She was certain the pun hadn't been accidental. Crimson crawled through her cheeks.

"Yeah, right here," Taylor said, handing the phone to the woman still pinned beneath him. If possible, her blush deepened until her face was the color of her scarlet pajamas, the satin of which had increasingly grown to feel like an irritant to skin that was fire-hot at Taylor's nearness. "For Pete's sake," she chastised, her palm covering the receiver, "you don't have to make it sound as if we slept together!"

"We did, Sam," Taylor pointed out with his usual maddening logic.

"I know we did, but... I mean, technically, but... but..."

"Biblically?" Taylor offered.

"Right... yeah... Biblically..." She was stammering like a first-class idiot. Though she was aware of it, she was unable to stop it.

"Don't sweat it, Sam," Taylor said. "Larry knows we're just friends."

Just friends. Something in the way he said it, something in the way his eyes held hers, challenged Samantha to deny it. Silent moment fled into silent moment, fluttery heartbeat into fluttery heartbeat.

Finally Taylor rolled from her, saying, "Take the call, Sam."

Samantha eased the receiver to her ear, but said nothing as she watched Taylor slip from the bed, cross the room and disappear through the adjoining door. The condition of his body still looked considerably more than friendly. Her own body still felt considerably disturbed.

"Hello?" she forced herself to say.

Samantha had liked Larry Neesom, of the legal firm of Neesom, Sage, Bronner and Shaw, the first time she'd met him. He was bright, savvy and direct.

"Well, is she beautiful?" he now asked.

Everything else, including the sound of Taylor's shower running, took an immediate second place. "Yes," she answered around a grin. Despite her singlemindedness, she found one tiny question forming. Was Taylor's shower a cold one?

"I was sorry I couldn't be there yesterday," the lawyer said, "but I'd been scheduled to be in court on a case that had already been postponed five times."

"No problem," Sam said. "You couldn't have done anything. It was the baby's show."

Larry chuckled. "After three kids, how well I know that. Everything went as arranged, huh?"

Sam knew he was speaking in terms of the legal choreography.

"Everything. We—" She stopped and amended the pronoun, thinking as she did so how strange a slip of the tongue it was, how stranger still to realize that only she was engaged in the adoption of Andrea Margaret.

Somehow, as always, Taylor seemed a part of everything she did. "I was provided the privacy agreed upon."

"You got to hold the baby as stipulated?"

"Precisely."

"Good. I just talked with the birthmother's counsel, and she's signing a surrender form this morning."

Samantha's heart began to pound with happiness. The adoption process was beginning. It was a process that Sam had memorized. First, the birthmother would sign papers of release; second, a court date would be set at which time both the birthmother and birthfather would privately testify that they had entered into the adoption of their own free will; third, Sam would be notified that the adoption had been finalized and that she was now, and forevermore, the legal parent of the child.

"The birthmother's also being released from the hospital," the lawyer added.

Sam frowned in surprise. "So soon?"

"There were no complications during delivery, so the doctor has agreed. I think her parents are eager to get her back home."

"I can understand that."

"Yeah, me, too. Because they're discharging the birthmother this morning, I offered to cancel your morning visitation with the child—sorta give them a chance to clear out in peace. Do you have a problem with that?"

"No, not at all," Samantha said, though she couldn't help being disappointed. She was already looking forward to seeing, to holding, her baby again. "What about this afternoon?"

"As planned. Oh, and by the way, the child will be released in the morning."

"In the morning?" Notes of both anxiety and joy sounded in the question. And a note of disbelief. Sam hadn't expected to be taking her daughter home so soon. Tomorrow night. Andrea Margaret would be home tomorrow night! A vision of an unprepared nursery sailed through Samantha's mind, making her now wish that she'd made some preparations—papered the walls, bought a crib, hung a frilly curtain or something!—but it had seemed too great an emotional risk to take. She hadn't wanted to jinx anything with too cavalier an attitude.

"In the morning," Larry confirmed, a smile of understanding at his lips. He covered a few more legal points before ending with, "I'll talk to you soon. Tell Taylor I'll be in touch with him, too. In fact, I think he and I are playing racketball this weekend. It'll be another opportunity for him to beat the pants off me."

Samantha laughed as was expected of her, but moments later, the receiver returned to its cradle, she simply sat on the edge of the bed, swamped once more by thoughts of Taylor and what had happened earlier. Should she say something? But what could she say? How could she explain what even she didn't understand? And what, dear heaven, must Taylor be thinking?

* * *

Taylor ran the terry towel over a body that was only now beginning to quiet down. His teeth still chattered from the spray of icy water, but he paid the chattering little heed. His mind was too occupied with warm thoughts. Unconsciously, lost to sleep, Sam had acted as a lover, not as a friend. That thought kept playing itself over and over in his head, in his heart, until he thought he would burst wide open from sheer joy. At those moments when his happiness soared the highest, however, caution always urged him back down to earth. Maybe what had happened meant nothing. Maybe Sam had simply been dreaming. Maybe she'd have reacted the same to any man she found beside her.

The unacceptableness, the downright unpleasantness, of this last thought caused Taylor to fling the wet towel into the nearest corner. Naked, he snatched up his electric razor, set it to humming and attacked the dark stubble roughening his cheeks and chin. He willed himself not to think about Sam. He might just as well have willed himself to stop breathing. One memory followed another—memories of her warm, sweet breath wafting against his neck, of her breasts crushed against him, of her hand caressing his— He clamped off the thought before another shower became necessary, but he couldn't stop the hope that rushed through him.

Rubbing a clear spot in the steam-misted mirror, he stepped closer and ran the razor over the patch of skin above his lip. Suddenly, his eye caught the eye of the man in the mirror. Was that man staring back the fool of all time for even entertaining the notion that Sam, at least on some level, thought of him as he thought of her? Taylor was still asking the question forty-five minutes later when he tapped once on the adjoining door.

"Come in," Samantha called in a voice that sounded natural enough until Taylor considered the fact that she didn't look up when he entered her bedroom. "I'll be ready in a minute," she said, dragging a brush through her chocolate-brown hair. Her hairstyle was straight and cropped just above her ears. On someone else, the cut might have appeared too severe. In Sam's case, it emphasized her sky-high cheekbones and showcased her wide brown eyes.

She finally turned those wide brown eyes on him— after she'd brushed her hair, splashed on a sweet-smelling perfume and done a number of other things that Taylor wondered at the necessity of. He wondered, too, when and if she had ever looked as good as she did today in a long khaki skirt, gold sweater and brown boots.

Sam looked over at her friend and acknowledged that if tight jeans were criminal, Taylor Pierce would be serving long and hard time.

For the first time in their lives, neither seemed to know what to say. So for long moments nothing was said. Instead, Sam accepted the fact that something as subtle as starlight, as intangible as sunbeams, had changed between them. She prayed that whatever it

was wasn't heralding the end of a beautiful friendship.

"Larry said the birthmother was being discharged
this morning, so I'm going to wait to visit Andrea
Margaret until this afternoon," Samantha said a little while later as they had breakfast in the motel res-
taurant. Unlike a short while before, Sam now
couldn't stop talking; it was as if she were hiding behind the incessant flow of words. She took a sip of
orange juice before rambling on. "I told you they were
going to discharge the baby in the morning, didn't I?"
Before Taylor could answer that, indeed, she had told
him—twice, as a matter of fact—she rushed on with,
"Now I wish I had fixed up the nursery."

"You'll manage," Taylor managed to squeeze into
the conversation.

"Uhh," Sam muttered around a bite of bacon and
eggs. "I know, but it would just be so much simpler if
I had. Oh, Larry said to tell you he'd be in touch
later."

"You told me."

Sam ignored the remark. "Something about a
racketball game this weekend. Do you beat him
often?"

"Is that what he said?"

"Something about you beating his pants off."

Taylor grinned. "He beats mine off often enough."

The image that jumped to Sam's mind was sinful-
ness in its purest form. Her cheeks pinkened with heat.
She cleared her suddenly dry throat. "I wish I'd at

least painted and papered the nursery. They're gonna release Andrea Margaret tomorrow. The birth-mother—"

"Sam, you've told me all this."

"Oh," she said quietly, sheepishly.

Awkward seconds once more passed.

Finally Samantha could withstand the torment no longer. "Taylor, about this morning—"

"Eat your breakfast," he interrupted. In all probability she didn't know what to say about what happened earlier. With the obvious confusion she was feeling, she'd probably feel obligated to deny, to lessen, to make light of—and, frankly, he was unwilling to hear anything that would dash his fragile hopes. Nodding toward her plate, he repeated, "Eat. I've got some shopping to do."

The shopping he had to do turned out to be the fluffy cat that had gotten left behind at the mall the night before. Taylor plead a godfather's prerogative when Sam, conveniently overlooking the fact that her arms were laden with baby things, accused him of trying to spoil her daughter. By the time they left the mall, they were carrying on with their usual ridiculousness. Their old camaraderie seemed restored.

The refound easiness lasted throughout their visit to the hospital, where they stayed all afternoon. They spent three thirty-minute sessions with the newborn. Sam fed her, burped her, cooed over her and praised her as being the most beautiful baby ever born. Andrea Margaret patiently tolerated all the fuss. In fact, she slept through most of it, contentedly snuggled in the arms of her mother. At the last visit, Samantha insisted that Taylor hold the baby. He was in the middle of explaining that he knew nothing about babies when Sam deposited the small pink bundle in his arms with the admonition that all he had to do was watch her head. A strange emotion squeezed Sam's heart at the sight of Taylor, so large and strong, usually so self-assured, awkwardly holding her daughter as though she were the most precious thing on the face of the earth. Samantha actually had to glance away to catch her breath.

Later that evening, they dined. Before they did, however, Taylor called his construction company, as he had several times before, and spoke with his secretary, Charlotte Sever. Pangs of some dark emotion skipped through Samantha. With a woman's intuition, she knew that the pretty blonde was interested in Taylor. Just how interested he was in her, she had no idea. She did know, however, that they occasionally went out. Sam had always told herself that their relationship was none of her business—and she reminded herself of that fact now. Inexplicably, though, the dark emotion still played havoc with her senses.

At eight forty-five, by mutual agreement, they called it an early night.

"Get a good night's sleep," Taylor said, standing at the adjoining door.

"Yeah," Sam answered, suddenly thinking it would be a lot more likely if he were by her side. Just as suddenly she wondered where the wayward thought had come from.

"I, uh . . . I'll see you in the morning," Taylor said.

"Right."

"Eight o'clock."

"Right."

"Well, g'night," Taylor repeated.

"G'night."

Without further comment, Taylor stepped back and closed the door. This time he didn't leave it ajar. He shut it fully. The act was like a slap in Sam's face. She read his subtle message all too clearly. She had overstepped the boundaries of their friendship that morning, and the closed door, added to the fact that he hadn't even been willing to discuss the matter at breakfast, was his gentle way of reproving her, of redefining his expectations of their relationship.

Unexpectedly Samantha felt like crying. How in heck had she screwed up everything so royally?

Safely on his side of the door, Taylor took a deep breath. Closing the door had been the hardest thing he'd ever done. But it had been necessary. Because if he left it open, he was uncertain just what he might do. And the last thing he wanted was to rush her. Rushing her would lead to only one thing: screwing up the one hope he had.

Chapter Six

Is she still asleep?''

Taylor quietly asked the question the following afternoon as he drew the car to a gentle stop in the driveway of Samantha's two-story condo in a fashionable St. Louis suburb.

Samantha glanced into the back seat. To the right, baby clothes and toys were piled in a heap. To the left, a little black-haired head lolled to the side of the infant car seat. The baby had fretted on the trip home, forcing several stops along the way. Numerous times Sam, who hadn't yet got the hang of the ''Pamper Principle,'' had clumsily changed her daughter's diaper. On one such occasion, as both Andrea Margaret and Taylor looked on—Taylor with a grin, Andrea Margaret with a frown—Samantha had blown a strand of hair back out of her eyes and demanded to see either one of them do any better. Neither had volunteered to try. The baby did voluntarily, greedily, take the bottle offered on another stop. It was during the last hour of the journey that Samantha learned a mother's first prayer of thanksgiving: thank you, Lord, for letting the baby nap.

''I think so,'' Samantha now whispered, as though the two of them were involved in some sinister conspiracy.

Taylor looked over at the woman beside him. She looked frazzled, but glowingly happy... and uncommonly beautiful. "What do you think the chances are of getting her into the house still asleep?" he whispered.

"Little to none."

"That's pretty much how I assess it," Taylor said, "but let's give it the old college try."

Taylor opened his door ever so easily. So did Sam. Stealthily they approached the back door of the car and silently pulled it open. As gently as she could, Sam stooped and unfastened the seat belt that held the baby safe and secure.

"Here goes nothing," she said, easing the baby into her arms. Andrea Margaret whimpered at the disturbance. "Shh," Samantha cooed.

The tiny mouth pouted into a cry; at the same time two heavy little eyelids fluttered, then closed entirely, fanning silky lashes against sugar-pink cheeks. The baby's hand, balled into a Lilliputian fist of protest, relaxed against the slobbered-upon smocking of the dress.

"That's a good girl," Sam crooned.

Both Samantha and Taylor gradually expelled their held breath. At the baby's snorey little sound, they grinned at each other as though they'd just pulled off the coup of the century.

A sudden cold breeze sent Sam's hair swirling. As she draped the ivory crocheted blanket about the baby's head, Taylor reached out to rake the hair from Sam's eyes. A frisson of awareness darted down Samantha's senses, and her gaze flew to Taylor's. After he'd literally closed the door in her face, she'd spent a restless night. It hadn't been a fruitless night, however. She'd made one very important resolution. From that moment on, she'd do nothing that could even remotely be interpreted as other than friendly. Contrarily, though she knew it was nothing more than coincidence—for that matter, maybe nothing more than her imagination—Taylor seemed to have gone out of his way to touch her. In little ways. His hand at the small of her back. His hand at her elbow. His hand brushing back her hair. And did his eyes linger longer in hers? As though trying to read something written deep within?

"C'mon," he said at last, breaking eye contact, "let's get you two inside."

The condo, decorated in blue, rose and cream, was laid out simply with a living area, dining room, kitchen and master bedroom, the latter used as Sam's office, located downstairs; upstairs were three bedrooms. Rosie, the live-in housekeeper recently promoted to housekeeper-nanny, occupied one bedroom. Since Sam worked out of her home, she'd long ago learned that live-in help was not a luxury, but rather a necessity. With the baby, that necessity had increased doubly.

"Rosie won't be here until later this afternoon," Sam explained softly as she climbed the stairs. She could feel Taylor, a diaper bag slung over his shoulder, right behind her. As always, his nearness was comforting. "I gave her the day off. I never dreamed we'd be home so soon. The minute she gets back, I've got to go shopping for a crib." She topped the stairs and started toward her bedroom. "I'll put the baby on my bed and stack pillows around her. That ought to do—"

Taylor grabbed Sam's elbow and gently but forcefully changed her direction until they were headed toward the room set aside for the nursery. Startled, Sam looked up. "Why don't you just see if there's anything in here to lay her on," Taylor said. "Your bed's really not all that safe, even with pillows."

"I use the spare room for storage," Sam said. "Trust me, there's nothing in there to lay—" When Taylor pushed open the door, Sam's voice died in her throat.

The walls had been painted the palest of pink with a border of paper in an animal print in pastel pink, blue and yellow. A white crib with sheets in the same animal print hugged one wall, while a white chest and a bathing and dressing table sat flush with another. A white rocker edged in delicate pink flowers resided in a corner, urging mother and child to try it out. A brightly colored mobile dangled above the bed, and a lamp shaped like a lamb lighted the room the second Taylor's hand found the switch.

Astonished, Sam whirled, her eyes finding Taylor's. Her look begged for an explanation.

Taylor, uncharacteristically uncertain, tucked a hand in his jeans—his tight jeans, though Samantha determinedly ignored the thigh-hugging denim. She also tried to ignore the masculinity she knew lay beyond. "I, uh...I wanted to do something for you and the baby. I know it probably isn't the way you would have done the nursery, but I've been promised it's the latest thing. Fashion-wise, I mean. But if you don't like it—"

"When?" Samantha interrupted, then interrupted herself. "How? You only had two days."

Taylor grinned. "I called in every marker owed me by any of my construction friends. Actually, Charlotte coordinated it through an interior decorator. I threatened that nobody would get a penny if it wasn't finished within forty-eight hours."

Even knowing the nature of the calls, Sam felt proprietary concerning Taylor just at the mention of the woman's name. Sam pushed down the confusing feeling, concentrating instead on the beautifully furnished room.

It was perfect. Absolutely perfect. But not nearly as perfect as the sentiment behind the gift.

"Do you like it?" Taylor asked uncertainly as he watched Samantha survey the room, her eyes roaming from one small detail to another.

Sam turned toward her friend, whom she saw through a haze of tears. "It . . . it's beautiful."

"Ah, Sam," Taylor said softly, stepping toward her and laying his palm alongside her cheek, "I didn't mean to make you cry."

His hand felt warm, incredibly warm, and Samantha's natural inclination was to place her hand atop his. She had done so a hundred times before. This time she didn't, however. Simply because, after he'd closed the door last night, she no longer knew the ground rules of their relationship. She was glad she was holding the baby. It gave her restless hands something to do. Even so, unable to stop herself, she nuzzled her cheek against the strength of his palm.

Her simple, subtle action practically buckled Taylor's knees. He would forever remain grateful to Andrea Margaret for choosing that moment to stir.

"You, uh…you'd better get her into bed," he said. His voice held a husky timbre that got lost in the infant's wail.

"Shh, shh," Samantha sang as she tucked her daughter into the crib. "Doesn't that feel good? You have a beautiful new bed, Andrea Margaret." A few soothing pats to her small patch of back and the baby dozed back to sleep.

This time when Sam glanced up at Taylor, who'd been the one to draw the blanket up around the baby, he whispered, "I'd better go. I need to get to the office."

Sam nodded.

"You two'll be all right?"

Samantha smiled. "Heck if I know."

Taylor grinned. "You two'll be all right."

Sam nodded again. This time she was acutely aware of an emptiness, a loneliness. The depth of it startled her. The source of it confounded her.

"Bye," he said.

"Bye," she answered, silently walking him to the stairway. She watched as his long, lean legs crisply took each step. When his hand reach for the door-knob she called out, "Taylor?"

He turned, his gaze finding her at the head of the stairs. A ray of sun shone through the stained glass of the front door, striping Taylor in a rosy shade of light. The light bounced off his gray eyes, making them look endlessly deep and sexily inviting. The sight was like a swift kick to Samantha's stomach.

"Thank you," she managed to say, gesturing back toward the nursery.

He said nothing for so long that Sam began to wonder if he would. He just kept staring at her with those eyes. Finally, he said, "I'll check on you two later."

And then he was gone.

In his wake, Samantha experienced the empty feeling again. Though the depth of it still startled her, the source no longer confounded her. It had to do with missing Taylor. And the truth was, she'd started missing him even before he had gone.

Blissfully chaotic.

Samantha described the four weeks that followed the baby's arrival that way. Formula always needed to be prepared...and diapers to be changed and changed and changed...and sleepless nights—Andrea Margaret seemed to have her clock turned topsy-turvy—to be endured. Throughout it all, Sam was deliriously happy and perpetually afraid. Now fairly certain that she wasn't going to break the baby, she nonetheless found a million other things to worry about: the rash that developed because of the formula, juggling her job to have quality time with her daughter, pondering whether it was too early to sign her up for pre-preschool, determining what college she would attend! The list was endless.

Sam even found herself sizing up male babies to see if they had any potential as mates for her outstanding, beautiful, bright daughter. None did. Regrettably. Oh, a few came close, but unlike in horseshoes, close didn't count in the mating game. A diligent mother simply could not allow her daughter to throw herself away on someone who drooled excessively, spit up strained carrots on a regular basis or tossed toys in the throes of a temper tantrum.

Throughout the month's madness, Taylor was often at Sam's side, patiently listening to her endless did-you-know? research on the subject of rearing children. When he wasn't at her side, he telephoned... often the last thing at night. Unspoken was the fact that each knew the other was already in bed. Sam fought against seductive visions of a naked Taylor, a bronzed, hair-dusted Taylor, tucked within the folds of masculine bed linen.

Taylor spent his time engaged in his own struggle. He longed to ask Sam if she was wearing the red satin pajamas... and if her breasts still sculpted the fabric with their full, alluring maturity.

On a couple of nights—three, actually, but who was counting?—Taylor neither called nor came by. On those occasions, Sam refused to think of him out with someone. Out as in a date. Out as in a date with Charlotte Sever. Sam refused such mental activities for a very good reason. They were simply too darned painful to engage in.

At the end of the fourth week, Samantha received, via her lawyer to maintain her anonymity, a letter from Andrea Margaret's birthmother. Certain that the woman had changed her mind about the adoption, Sam ripped open the envelope with her heart lodged in her throat. The letter turned out to be a touching message. In a youthful hand, with a painfully inno- cent sentiment, the young woman thanked Sam for adopting her daughter, thanked her for loving her daughter, and begged Sam to one day make the child understand that she, too, the birthmother, had loved her, and that she had simply wanted what was best for her. Moved, Sam wrote back, also via the lawyers, promising to honor the young woman's wishes. As for the finalization of the adoption, Sam waited, hoping daily to hear.

She also hoped daily to make some sense out of her feelings for Taylor. Something she couldn't explain was happening. She felt a dissatisfaction with their friendship. It had come to feel like a skin that no longer fit her. And yet she didn't know what she wanted instead. Or maybe she did. Each time this lat- ter thought crossed her mind, she felt guilty, as though she had somehow defiled their relationship. All she knew was that she couldn't say or do anything that might drive him from her. She couldn't stand for him to close the door on her forever.

"She's grown," Taylor said on the Friday evening of the fifth week.

He had arrived unannounced after dinner, had let himself in with his key as he'd called out a hello, and had coiled his long legs to join Samantha and Andrea Margaret on the floor before the fireplace. Leaning forward, he brushed a kiss to Sam's cheek. Sam pretended her heart didn't change rhythm. She also told herself that she hadn't felt the momentary rasp of Taylor's tongue against her skin. It was just her too-fertile imagination, which seemed to have gone hog-wild. More than once during the past weeks she would have sworn, if she hadn't known better, that Taylor was being deliberately provocative.

Corralling her truant thoughts, Samantha looked down at the baby hungrily guzzling the formula from the bottle. As always, the sight of the chubby-cheeked infant swelled Sam's heart with love. "Yeah. Like a weed."

"She sleeping any better at night?"

"Knock on wood, for the last two nights she's only been up once."

"Mercy, Punkin'," he said, his index finger brushing the baby's tiny hand, "you actually letting Mommy sleep?"

At his voice, at his touch, Andrea Margaret eased up on the bottle's nipple and glanced at Taylor. As if in recognition, she smiled and sent Sam a swift kick in the stomach with her little foot.

"Thanks a lot," Sam groaned, adding, "it's plain to see you've charmed her."

"It's plain to see the kid's got excellent taste. Besides, she's my girl. Aren't you, Punkin'?"

The softly crooned question, coupled with the teasing scent of masculine cologne, caused another kick in Sam's stomach, but this one had nothing to do with her daughter. Samantha sought to ignore it by searching for something to say. She couldn't believe what popped out of her mouth.

"What's wrong, Pierce, you couldn't get a date tonight so you thought you'd drop by here?"

Taylor's eyes grazed hers before he casually leaned back on an elbow and cocked one leg at an angle that had a definitely sexy attitude. Sam told herself that the heat she was feeling was coming from the blazing fire.

"Not every woman has Andrea Margaret's excellent taste," he drawled.

"Poor baby," Sam teased in commiseration, hefting the infant to her shoulder and patting her back. She tried to keep her eyes from the seductive stretch of denim . . . and her mind from what she knew, all too well, was confined within it.

"Yeah," Taylor said with a forty-carat grin, "poor baby."

Andrea Margaret burped her agreement.

Taylor's grin singed the edges of Samantha's senses, and for a moment she thought she was going to drown in the heated waves. She fought again for something to say, this time for something that had nothing to do with grins, denim or cocked legs.

"Ocular bonding," she said, snatching the first thing to stroll along in her head. She was no doubt led to that choice by the replacement of the baby in her arms and the reestablishing of the bottle in said baby's mouth.

Taylor groaned. "You've been researching again."

Sam didn't bother to deny the obvious.

"Okay," Taylor said, "I'll bite. What's ocular bonding?"

"Eye contact between parent and child. If you don't have it, it leads to adult maladjustment. Interestingly, primates are the only species that use gaze as an affiliation signal. That's because only primate infants and mothers are able to look at each other during breast-feeding." Sam frowned as though another thought had superseded the first. "That troubles me a little. Though, of course, it isn't as if I had a choice. I mean, I could hardly breast-feed, could I? But statistics do indicate that breast-fed babies tend, on the whole, to be healthier. They tend—"

Samantha stopped sharply when she glanced at Taylor. His eyes had blatantly lowered to her breasts. Unhurriedly, deliberately, he raised his gaze to hers.

"They tend to be what?" he asked, his voice somewhere between bourbon and whiskey.

"What?" she asked, her voice somewhere between breathing and sighing.

"You were saying that breast-fed babies tend to be something."

She cleared her throat. Then, her gaze melting into his, she repeated, "Healthier. They tend to be healthier."

"Ahh." He sighed. Slowly, he pushed to a sitting position, bringing him right alongside Sam. He reached out a finger and grazed the infant's cheek that was moving in and out with a sucking motion. Suddenly Sam thought that motion looked incredibly suggestive next to Taylor's hand. Or maybe it was the fact that Taylor's hand brushed every so lightly against Sam's breast.

"Breast-fed or bottle-fed," he said with a husky roughness, "really doesn't make a difference in ocular bonding, does it? I mean, either way, mother and child are making eye contact. Don't you think?"

Think?

What Sam thought was that she was losing her mind. Surely the brushing of her breast had been only accidental. Surely the nipple of her breast hadn't knotted in response. Surely the breath caught in her throat would be released.

And then Taylor was taking the baby from her with a casualness that suggested she had imagined everything. "Here, let me burp her this time."

He patted. Andrea Margaret burped. The world spun on its axis just as it should. Yes, everything was as it should be. Except for Samantha. She was clearly losing her mind.

Chapter Seven

Here," Sam said fifteen minutes later as she handed a still-seated Taylor a mug of steaming hot chocolate. She had driven the earlier incident from her mind, or at least had shoved it as far to the back of her mind as she could. Of course his brushing her breast had been accidental. Only a fool would think otherwise.

"Thanks," Taylor said, taking the mug and leaning back against the brick hearth. He had slipped off his shoes and now sat with one socked foot crossed over the other at the ankle.

The baby, its little bottom hiked in the air, lay asleep on its tummy in a basket-weave cradle that rested nearby. Since it was the housekeeper's night off, Samantha had chosen to keep the baby downstairs with her and Taylor. Taylor had insisted on tucking in his godchild, while Samantha prepared the cocoa.

"Is she asleep?" Sam asked.

"Out like a light."

"Good," she said, dropping to the floor beside him. She, too, leaned back against the hearth. Behind them, the fire crackled a sizzling song.

"So, have you heard anything about the finalization of the adoption?" Taylor inquired, bringing the mug to his lips.

Samantha shook her head. "No. Not a word. Except that everything's progressing routinely. Larry said it just takes time, that court dates are often hard to get." She took a sip of the cocoa. "I had a letter from the birthmother." At Taylor's arched eyebrow, she explained.

"That was a nice thing for her to do," Taylor commented.

"Yeah. My heart goes out to her," Sam said. "I can't think of anything sadder than having a baby and not being able to be its mother."

"Sometimes it's sadder to try to be something you're not ready to be."

It's even sadder trying to be something you're not.

Now, where had that thought come from? Samantha wondered. Even as she questioned the statement's origin, she realized that it had been born in the lyrics of the song playing on the radio. A duo of voices, one male, one female, were crooning about being friends and lovers. They were asking the question: why did they have to be one or the other? Sam amended the statement. What could be sadder than trying to be one, namely lovers, when you were and always had been the other? Was that the role she was trying to force on Taylor? Uncomfortable with this whole line of thinking, she dropped it as though it were a too-hot poker.

"I, uh . . . I went by the cemetery today," she said, drastically changing the subject.

Taylor raised his eyes to hers, and for one crazy heartbeat she entertained the notion that he'd been listening to the words of the song, too.

"Eight months, right?" he said.

So piercing were his gray eyes, it took Sam a second to make sense out of his words. When she finally did, she answered, "Yes. It's hard to believe Mother's been gone that long."

"I know. I miss her."

"Yeah, me, too. More than I ever thought it possible to miss anyone. Sometimes it feels as though the memories are going to crush—" She trailed off.

Taylor slid had hand over hers and meshed their fingers. The gesture was a familiar one. One she was grateful for. More than once he'd led the way when she couldn't see clearly; more than once he was the only thing standing between her and loneliness. She tightened her hold, thinking that his hand felt particularly warm, particularly comforting. Unlike in the past, it also made her feel a little breathless.

"Memories are good, though," she heard Taylor saying. She glanced up. "Even though they hurt, they also heal."

"I know," she agreed, pulling her hand from his when it became obvious that she couldn't ignore what his touch was doing to her.

She wrapped her hand around the mug of hot chocolate. Interestingly, his hand had felt warmer than the mug. Far warmer. This, too, she tried to pretend wasn't true. With the same degree of success that she'd ignored her earlier breathlessness. Samantha willed her thoughts to her mother. One of their last conversations came swiftly to mind. It was a conversation she'd shared with no one.

"Whatcha thinking?" Taylor asked softly.

"About Mother. About a conversation we had."

"Want to tell me about it?"

Yes. Yes, she did, she thought.

"After Mother's first stroke, both she and I sensed that the end was near. I don't know how I knew. I just knew." Sam took another swallow of the cocoa, wanting it now for any fortifying property it had. "Anyway, it was one night late. I'd stayed at the hospital even though Momma begged me to go home. She couldn't talk well, but she'd written for me to go home and get some rest. I told her I would in a little bit. When it became obvious that she wasn't going to sleep, I eased to the side of the bed and took her hand. It felt so cold. So damned cold."

Unlike yours, Samantha thought, wanting desperately to reach once more for Taylor's hand. She didn't, however.

Taylor said nothing, neither discouraging her nor encouraging her to go on. He simply sat quietly studying her profile. With an intensity that could have reduced parchment to ashes.

"There had been something that I'd wanted to say to her ever since the stroke," Samantha continued, "and I knew that if I didn't say it soon, I'd never have the chance." She glanced up at Taylor. He was watching her so . . . so closely. So closely that she felt herself going all breathless again. She glanced away, back to a Taylor-less spot where air flowed more freely into her lungs. "I had read an article in a magazine about the near-death experience. I told her that the article said that oftentimes people dying are met by loved ones who've gone before them. I, uh..." The words caught in Sam's throat, and she had to wait until they could squeeze by the constriction.

Still Taylor said nothing.

"I, uh... I asked her if... if she died before I did, if she'd come back for me when it was my time to die. So that I wouldn't be afraid."

Samantha felt her throat tighten even tighter, felt her eyes sting, yet she bit back the tears. Instead, she smiled.

"She acted as though I'd just made the most logical of requests... and in a voice that sounded strong, like her old self, she said simply, 'I'll be there.' Not 'I will if I can,' not 'I'll try,' but an unequivocal, 'I'll be there.'" Sam's eyes misted despite her best intentions. "And damned if I didn't believe her."

Silently Taylor set his mug on the hearth. Just as silently, he took Sam's mug. Then he pulled her into his arms. Sam went. For truly it was the only place she wanted to be. Surely it was all right for one friend to comfort another. Wasn't it? Surely she could pretend again that she didn't feel strange, more-than-friend feelings in his arms. Couldn't she?

She gave up all thought, content to relish the strength of him, content to wallow in the warmth of him. Splaying her hands across his broad back, she rested her cheek on his shoulder... and fought to overlook the fact that her breasts nestled cozily against his chest.

"I've been thinking," she said, sniffing. "About what Mother said. Maybe that's the job description of mothering. Not striving to be the perfect parent. Not always having the right answer. Not always knowing what to do. But just promising to always be there.''

The words fell like a gentle rain and, like a rain, they nourished. This time, they fed Taylor's soul, producing a tender harvest of words. Pushing back until her eyes were forced to meet his, he said, ''Maybe that's what loving is all about, Sam.''

Loving.

Though he'd spoken impersonally, abstractly, the word on his lips sent Sam's heart trebling its beat. That and the fuzzy warm look in his eyes. Eyes that seemed determined not to let hers go. But then, she didn't want them to let her go. Any more than she wanted his arms to release her. And furthermore, there were other things she wanted from him, things that maybe she shouldn't want, but things she wanted just the same. She wanted to feel him caressing her body. She wanted to feel his breath, hot with need, beating against hers. She wanted to feel his lips—

Even as this last thought formed, Taylor's hand slid to her chin, his fingers bracketing her jaw. He tilted her head upward. As his head angled and lowered, Sam's heart went crazy-wild. In anticipation of what she could feel was coming, her eyes closed dreamily. Time passed as quickly as lightning flashing, as slowly as thunder rumbling. And then Sam felt—what? Certainly not the lips she'd been impatiently waiting for. Her eyelids flew open. Taylor, his face so close that she could feel the moist breath, was dabbing the corner of her mouth with the pad of his thumb.

"Chocolate," he said thickly.

The word was obviously foreign, for Sam could make not a single bit of sense out of it. "W-what?" she asked.

"You had chocolate on your mouth."

"Oh," Sam said, so preoccupied with her own run-away heartbeat that she failed to notice that Taylor's, lodged beneath her palm, pounded just as erratically.

All Sam knew was that she'd been wrong. Dead wrong. He hadn't been going to kiss her. And ten to one she'd just made a colossal fool of herself, maybe even jeopardized a friendship of a lifetime. For surely he'd sensed her expectation. And furthermore, she didn't care. At that moment she would have gladly risked either, or both, for the feel of his mouth on hers.

She couldn't sleep.

It had been hours since Taylor, acting as though nothing out of the ordinary had happened, had left . . . with a peck to her cheek, a pat to Andrea Margaret's back and a promise to be in touch. Samantha had thought he'd seemed inordinately pleased with himself. But then, she'd thought he was going to kiss her, too, which just went to show how accurate her perception was.

Kiss.

The thought of his lips melted her until she wondered why she didn't liquefy and flow right out of the rocker and onto the nursery floor. When it had become obvious that rest was going to be scarcer than hen's teeth, Sam had crawled from bed and had started roaming the house. She had ended up in the nursery. Simply because she'd had an overwhelming need to be with someone. A night had never seemed longer. Or lonelier. Or she more confused.

What was happening to her?

The methodic motion of the rocker offered no answer. But then, was one truly necessary? Didn't she know what was wrong, but was afraid to admit it? The bottom line was that she would have sold her soul for Taylor's kiss, then and now. The further bottom line was that she was attracted to him. Totally. Completely. As she'd never been to another man—not even her husband. There, she'd admitted it! Even if she burned in Hades for her carnality, she could no longer hide the truth.

She groaned. Then glanced quickly in the direction of the crib to see if she'd awakened the baby. When she realized she hadn't, she sighed in relief and loosened her thoughts. Did she hear what she was thinking? She lusted after Taylor. She wanted to go to bed with him. She wanted to make love to him...and have him make love to her. She— The friendship might well be over if he ever found out how she felt.

Life without Taylor? The thought filled her with emptiness. He'd always been there for her. She'd always been there for him. She couldn't imagine life any other way. She didn't want to imagine—

Without warning, snippets of their earlier conversation floated back to her.

"Maybe that's the job description of mothering . . . just promising to always be there. . . ."

"Maybe that's what loving is all about . . . loving . . . loving . . . loving . . ."

Suddenly Sam stopped the chair in midrock. A rich warm feeling, like a burst of golden sunshine, flooded her heart. Was it possible? No. Maybe. Oh, my God . . .

"You're sure this is a good idea?" Sam asked as she dialed the telephone several hours later.

Andrea Margaret, fed and burped and reclining in an infant seat that sat on the kitchen cabinet, made a gurgling sound.

"I'll interpret that as a yes," Sam said, tucking the phone between her head and shoulder. She reached for a cloth and dabbed the slobbery mouth of her daughter. Her own mouth was dry from nervous tension. *Oh, God, please let me be doing the right thing!*

On the third ring, a sleepy voice moaned, "Yeah?"

"Oh, God, you were asleep," Sam groaned, glancing at the clock. It read three minutes after seven. "I'm sorry. I just think the whole world gets up early. I mean, Andrea Margaret's been up for hours."

Not to mention how long I was up before that.

"What time is it?" Taylor asked, then moaned again. He'd obviously looked at a clock.

"Sorry," Sam repeated. "Look, I'll call back."

"Don't be silly. Unless, of course, you're expecting me to be coherent or something equally stupid at seven on a Saturday morning."

"No, you don't have to be coherent or something equally stupid. In fact, all you have to do is mutter one word."

"I can probably handle that. If it's nothing fancy."

Samantha heard Taylor shift and knew that he'd scooted up in bed. Had the covers crawled down to reveal a bare chest? And how much more of him was bare? The images that sprang into Sam's mind parched her throat even more. She cleared it.

"I, uh . . . I was wondering if you could come to dinner tonight. Rosie has the weekend off, but I've never given anyone food poisoning before. I thought maybe grilled hamburgers—"

"I'm sorry, Sam," Taylor interrupted, adding, "I have a date."

The one word—date—effectively halted the supply of air to Samantha's lungs. She also experienced a pain in the region of her heart.

"You there?" Taylor asked when a silence settled in the line.

"Yeah. Sure."

"I'm sorry," he repeated. "Charlotte and I are going out to dinner."

Charlotte. Sam wondered what the legal penalty in the state of Missouri was for strangling blond secretaries. "Ah...ah...y'all have a good time. I'll talk to you later."

"Sam, wait. Was it anything special?"

"Special? Ah, no . . . no, nothing special." *I just wanted to tell you that I love you.*

"Can I have a rain check, then?"

"Sure. A rain check."

Sam hung up seconds later. She'd have been unable, even under penalty of death, to repeat anything more she said. Which was pretty much the state she remained in for the rest of the morning and afternoon. The only perk to a downer of a day was a late-afternoon phone call from her lawyer, informing her that the adoption had been finalized. She was legally Andrea Margaret's mother. The elation that Sam felt barely allowed her feet to remain on the floor. She longed desperately to share the news with Taylor.

At ten-thirty that evening, Sam, still hurting from thoughts of Taylor and Charlotte Sever together, dialed Taylor's phone number. She told herself that she wanted to tell him about the adoption. Surely he'd want her to call? But in her heart she knew the adoption was a subterfuge. She wanted to make certain he was home. And out of the clutches of one Charlotte Sever.

But he wasn't home. Not at ten-thirty, nor at eleven or eleven-fifteen. At eleven-thirty, the phone rang and rang and rang.

And a little part of Sam died a slow painful death.

Chapter Eight

She wasn't going to call again. Enough was enough. She didn't care if he stayed out all night with this secretary person. An image of long, flowing blond hair, a beautiful face and an ample chest slinked through Sam's mind. She groaned. She wasn't going to call again. She wasn't going to think about Taylor again. She wasn't— Her fingernail broke as she forcefully redialed the number. She muttered something salty, brought her finger to her mouth for some quick first aid and continued to dial with her other hand. This was it. This was the last time she was going to call. She meant it this time. Just see if she didn't!

As the phone rang, Sam found the bedroom clock. Two minutes till twelve. Midnight. The bewitching hour. The hour of lovers. This last thought produced a vision that sat in her stomach like a pound of lead. She forced herself to concentrate on the phone's endless ringing.

Dammit! Where was he?

At Charlotte Sever's apartment?

Oh, shut up!

You asked.

Well, you didn't have to be so blunt!

Hey, lady, you're the one creating the decadent thoughts. I'm nothing without you. Oh, and by the way, I seriously doubt what you're imagining is pos-

sible. No man can make love that many times in one night. Nor can any man last that long each time.

Seven minutes.

Pardon?

I read that, on the average, copulation takes seven minutes. Sam frowned. Say Taylor had picked her up at seven o'clock...that was five hours...five times sixty minutes equals...three hundred minutes... divided by seven...that was...uh...uh...forty-two point...point eight something. That did suggest a whale of a lot of prowess. Samantha felt better instantly. Until she realized the phone was still ringing. She had just started to hang up the receiver when a voice came on the line. A breathless voice.

"Hello?"

Breathless as in doggedly trying for forty-three?

"Hello?" Taylor said again, reminding Sam of the need to say something.

"Taylor?" She groaned inwardly. What an exquisitely eloquent beginning!

Concern now riddled the voice. "Sam? Is anything wrong?"

"Wrong? No. Nothing's wrong. Why should anything be wrong?"

"It *is* the middle of the night."

Yeah, buster, and just where the heck have you been? "No, nothing's wrong. I mean, I just wanted to talk to you...to tell you the good news. Look, if now's a bad time..."

"Now's fine," Taylor said.

"If it isn't, I could call—"

"Now's fine."

"I mean, if you're not alone..."

She wasn't certain, but she thought he grinned. "I'm alone, Sam."

Relief flooded her. Until she thought of the three hundred minutes that stretched from seven o'clock to midnight. All it took was seven minutes—seven minutes to break her heart in two.

"I just got in," Taylor volunteered.

"I know."

"You do?"

"I mean, I called once or twice before." Once or twice or twenty.

It sounded as if Taylor's grin was back, but why would he be grinning? "What's the good news?"

"What?"

"You said you had some good news?"

"Oh...oh, yeah. Larry called. The adoption has been finalized."

Taylor's mood sobered instantly. "Sam, that's great. How does it feel?"

As though I should be in your arms, sharing the moment with you. "It, uh...it feels good. I'm glad everything's over. I mean, the waiting. I always imagine the worst when I have to wait." *Did you kiss her? Did you take her in your arms? Did you take her to bed?*

"This calls for a celebration," Taylor said, superimposing the suggestion over her too-vivid imagination. "Why don't you come over here tomorrow night? I'll cook spaghetti." A sudden thought occurred to him. "The housekeeper is there on Sunday nights, isn't she? I mean, you do have someone to leave Andrea Margaret with?"

"Yeah, Rosie's here on Sundays, but I've never left Andrea Margaret before. I mean, for several hours."

"Then it's time you did."

"I don't know."

"C'mon, Sam. Every mother deserves an evening off. Besides, I've got some good news to tell you, too."

Curiosity instantly peaked Sam's interest. "What?"

"Uh-uh. Tomorrow night. My place. Seven o'clock." Before she could utter another objection, he added, "Don't argue."

The truth was she had no intention of arguing. She was too eager to hear his good news. Besides, if he spent the evening with her, he could hardly spend the evening with Charlotte Sever, too.

She was going to tell him.

She was going to tell him that she was in love with him.

Regardless of his involvement with his secretary, she owed him the truth. She also owed it to herself to tell him what she was feeling. Even if it meant losing his friendship. All of this she had decided after another sleepless night. The only thing she hadn't decided was *how* she was going to tell him. Every time she came to that part, her feet turned as cold as ice. Her feet were still chilly as she rang the doorbell of Taylor's condo the following night. She blamed it on the snowflakes falling from the midnight-black sky.

Even though she was expecting it, she jumped when
the door opened. Maybe what she wasn't expecting
was for Taylor to look so sexy in a pair of tight jeans
and a plaid flannel shirt. Even the way he was holding the wooden spoon looked sexy...which told her
how far gone she really was.

"C'mon in," he said, starting back for the kitchen.
"I've gotta stir the sauce. Is it still snowing hard?"

Samantha knew her way around Taylor's split-level
condo, and she negotiated it accordingly. "Yeah," she
said, dropping her coat, gloves and purse on the in-
digo-blue sofa. She headed straight for the telephone
on the kitchen wall. "Actually it's getting worse." She
punched in a number and leaned back against the wall.
Her eyes went to Taylor who stood in front of the
stove taste-testing the spaghetti sauce. Specifically her
eyes went to Taylor's tush. Taylor's oh-so-fine, put-
hot-thoughts-in-a-woman's-mind tush. She forced her
eyes upward. To his shoulders. His broad shoulders.
Shoulders a woman could cling to by day and be
sweetly crushed beneath by night. Sam groaned.

"Did you say something?"

Samantha cleared her throat. "No," she growled,
turning away and focusing on the bright fire blazing
away in the nearby hearth. It popped and hissed and
otherwise made wintry noises.

"Rosie," she said when the phone was answered
seconds later, "I'm here. Is she all right? Good. Did
she take all of the bottle? What about the pajamas
with the feet? Did you find them? Good. And did you
remember to powder the rash? Well, if you need me,

you have Mr. Pierce's number. Right. You call now if you need me. Okay? Yeah, okay.'' Hanging up the phone, she turned around.

Taylor, both hands hiked at his hips, stood grinning a mile-wide grin. ''Well, is she surviving?''

Samantha could more easily have died on the spot than hold back a matching smile. ''Yes, apparently she's surviving. And don't you start on me, Taylor Pierce. I don't want to hear your disgusting logic about how Rosie's perfectly capable of taking care of Andrea Margaret. Nor do I want to hear anything about my obsessive compulsiveness or my neuroses concerning motherhood.''

Silently, a smile still at his lips, Taylor crossed his heart in promise. He made an arresting image somewhere between a good little boy and a big naughty man.

God, he looks good! she thought, a syrupy feeling curling in her chest.

''You look great,'' she heard him say, watching as he took in her navy and gold print blouse and her navy corduroy skirt that buttoned down the front. She had fashionably left several buttons unfastened. Through the slit peeked a tantalizing glimpse of legs encased in high-topped leather boots. In the wake of his compliment, she heard herself laugh. ''Did I say something funny?'' he asked.

''You read my mind.''

''You were thinking that you look great?''

She suddenly wished she'd kept her mouth shut. It crossed her mind to wonder how she was going to tell him she loved him if she couldn't even tell him he looked good. "No, I, uh...I was just thinking that...that you did. Look good, I mean."

Taylor's gaze, gray and unwavering, stepped into hers. Or at least that was what it felt like. It felt as if he journeyed right to her soul.

"Were you?" he asked.

The question was casual enough, but Samantha felt a strange, emotionally tugging undercurrent to it. She also felt a strange fluttering in her heart. And the need to sit down. Crossing the floor, she heaved herself onto a tall stool arranged alongside the bar.

"Yeah, sure," she answered, trying to make light of what was fast becoming a bizarre conversation. "You're not too bad to look at."

"Is that 'not to bad to look at' as in sexy?" he asked. Doggedly.

Samantha's heart skipped several beats. Involuntarily, her eyes dropped to his lips. His sexy lips. "What's wrong, Pierce?" she asked in a voice altogether too breathless. "You having trouble scoring lately?"

Taylor grinned. "C'mon, Sam. Am I sexy or not?"

"What does your secretary say?"

His grin broadened, as though the question pleased him beyond measure. "What do *you* think?"

"I think this conversation—"

"Am I sexy, Sam?"

"—is the craziest conversation—"

"Well?"

"I ever—"

"A simple yes or no."

"—had."

"Sam?"

"Yes!" she admitted out of sheer exasperation, then tempered the blunt word by repeating softly, "Yes."

If put under oath, Samantha would have had to swear that, at that exact moment, the kitchen shrank in size. Possibly the entire world. Or to be more precise, the world shrank to the size of the kitchen. Or more accurately, the world shrank to the look in Taylor's eyes. It was a look Sam couldn't interpret. All she knew was that the look was steady, intent, and that she, as though caught in a strong trap, couldn't break away from it. And, furthermore, she wasn't certain she wanted to. In fact, she wasn't certain of anything—her breath, her heartbeat, even the time of night it was.

"I, uh...I think I'll call about Andrea Margaret," she mumbled as she started to slip from the stool. Maybe she could think better on the other side of the room.

Leaning across the bar, Taylor wrapped his fingers around her wrist, halting her. "You just did."

His hand felt warm; her wrist felt like sculptor's clay—eager to be molded and shaped. Still his unreadable eyes bore into hers. One second. Two seconds. Three.

Abruptly he released her and asked, "Are you hungry?"

The unexpected question startled her. As did the sudden loss of his touch. The latter so much that she actually rubbed the spot he'd abandoned. "What?"

"Are you hungry?"

The indiscernible look had fallen from his face. That, coupled with his ordinary question, made her wonder, as she had on more than one occasion of late, if she'd only imagined the earlier look in his eyes. Perhaps she'd even imagined the conversation about whether she thought him sexy. My God, was she going absolutely stark-raving mad?

"Uh . . . yes . . . yes, I'm hungry."

"Good. Dinner'll be ready in about an hour. Until then," he said, reaching up to the overhead rack suspended above the chopping block and taking down two glasses, "let's start celebrating your good news and mine."

Samantha watched as he uncorked a bottle of champagne—expensive champagne—then poured two glasses of the bubbly, straw-yellow liquid. Even from inches away, she could smell the dry, mellow scent. To say nothing of the more intoxicating smell of Taylor's after-shave.

"Let's drink to your news first," he said, holding the wineglass aloft. "To motherhood."

Sam smiled as she thought of the precious little girl in her housekeeper's care, a little girl who'd so quickly changed her life. "To motherhood," Sam said and clinked her glass against Taylor's. Both drank. As Samantha was lowering her glass, Taylor produced a long, narrow jeweler's case seemingly from out of thin air. Sam frowned. "What's this?"

"Open it and see."

Samantha set the wineglass down and picked up the green velvet case. Her gaze raised once to Taylor's before returning to the gift. Inching the lid upward, she stared down at a gold bracelet.

"Oh, Taylor," she whispered, picking up the golden band. Inside was engraved LOVE TO TAYLOR'S LADIES. Her eyes once more found his. "I . . . I don't know what to say," she said, as profoundly moved as when he'd decorated the nursery for her. She was moved not only by the bracelet, but also by the inscription. Maybe, just maybe, he wasn't committed to Charlotte Sever. Maybe, just maybe, now was the time to tell him how she felt about him. Maybe, just maybe, now was the time to tell him she loved him.

"Taylor, I—"

"It's no big deal," Taylor interrupted as he took the bracelet from her numb fingers and fastened it about her wrist. Samantha thought it gleamed in a shade of hope. "It's just a little something to commemorate the occasion." Before she could once more try to express her feelings, he added, "Now, for my good news."

With this, he festively poured more champagne into the glasses. Again, he raised his in salute. Despite the untimeliness of his announcement, Samantha found herself intrigued.

"To marriage," he said simply and with a grin.

What he said might well have been the very last thing Samantha had expected to hear. "Marriage?" she repeated like a first-class, bona fide idiot.

"Yeah," he confirmed, "I'm getting married."

Chapter Nine

Samantha's world shuddered to a stop.

"Aren't you going to congratulate me, Sam?"

She had no idea how much time passed before Taylor posed the question. Probably more than a little time if the tone of his voice indicated anything.

"C-congratulations," Sam stammered, a vision of Charlotte Sever in a white wedding gown stalking her sanity. A pain had begun in Sam's chest and was spreading out like tight, fiery fingers. Cruel fingers that clutched at her heart.

A lopsided grin traipsed across Taylor's mouth. "Ah, c'mon, what kind of congratulations is that for a best friend?"

Sam wasn't sure exactly what he was getting at, but she added, "I, uh...hope you'll be very happy. You know that."

"Thank you. And I do know that," he said, "but what I had in mind was a congratulatory kiss between friends."

His suggestion didn't seem strange—they'd kissed a hundred times over the years for one reason or another, often in congratulations—but she wished to God he hadn't made the request just now. She didn't honestly know if she could bring her lips to his warm skin in celebration of his marrying another woman. She knew, though, that she had no choice. He was standing there waiting for her to kiss him, to act as though everything were perfectly normal between them. She slipped from the stool, praying that her legs held. They did. Somehow. Circling the counter and rising on her toes, she aimed her lips at Taylor's clean-shaven, fragrant-smelling cheek.

"Congrat—"

Taylor's head dipped and angled, his lips brushing lightly across Samantha's. The unexpectedness of the kiss, coupled with the pure pleasure it elicited, clipped her at the back of her knees, and her semishuttered eyes flew wide open.

As though it were the most natural thing in the world, Taylor slid a steadying arm about Sam's waist. "Close your eyes, Sam, and congratulate me."

Too stunned to do anything other than what she'd been told to do, she closed her eyes and whispered, "Congratula—"

This time Taylor's tongue, silken as a balmy night-time breeze, fluttered across her lips, outlining in feathery strokes, teasing the sensitive corners of her mouth in taunting play. Her mind said that she was imagining this, yet her body, her hot and suddenly flushed body, said, "You jolly well better believe he's kissing you! And right into a state of putty!" To confirm that the world was still the world, she opened her eyes again.

Taylor grinned. "You're doing a real good job with this congratulations stuff, Sam. I think one more time and you'll about have it."

Samantha said nothing. She wasn't sure she could.

"Congratulations," Taylor prompted. At her hesitation, he said, "C'mon, Sam, one more time."

"Con-congratulations," she mimicked, her mouth still tingling from the sensual flick of his tongue.

"Atta-girl," he whispered as he lowered his champagne-scented mouth to hers once more.

This time his lips, though gentle, slanted wickedly over hers, making no pretense of giving anything but a pull-out-all-the-stops kiss. His lips moved softly, but boldly, making slow circular motions that devastated Sam's senses. They equally destroyed the strength in her legs. When she sagged, Taylor, his lips never letting up their devil-play, simply tightened his hold by drawing her nearer. Their bodies didn't touch, but the promise was far more potent, far sweeter, than the real thing.

Sam felt that promise and felt, too, the delicious warmth of his mouth. She thought, as coherently as she could think anything, that this was not the kiss of a man about to be married to another woman. And then, even that little bit of coherency fled as the tip of his tongue toyed with the seam of her lips. Toyed. Probed. But never quite penetrated.

Sam moaned, whether in supreme pleasure at what he was doing or abject frustration at what he was not, she wasn't sure. As slowly as a sunrise, Taylor raised his head; as slowly as a moonrise, Samantha opened her eyes. He was still near. Very near. So near she could see the haze in his eyes, the sheen of moisture on his lips. Did her eyes look as hazy? Did her lips look as wet? And could she stand alone if he removed his hand from the small of her back?

Obviously wondering the same thing, Taylor drew a bar stool forward and urged Samantha onto its leather seat. Then, wordlessly, as though nothing extraordinary had happened, he stepped around her and to the stove, where he casually stirred the spaghetti sauce. Sam just stared. With her heart pounding away like a sledgehammer.

"This is gonna be ready sooner than I thought," he said, putting the pasta water on to boil. "You've got to eat it at just the right moment when all the herbs are perfectly blended." He turned, hooking his thumbs in the beltless loops of his jeans. "So what do you think, Sam? Small or large?"

Samantha raised her gaze from his lean waist to his eyes. What she thought was that there was some plot afoot to drive her crazy. The only things she could think about being blended were their lips. Had he really just kissed her? Like a . . . like a lover? At the realization that he was waiting for her to answer some question, she responded in the only honest way she could. "I don't remember the question."

Taylor smiled, her befuddlement obviously amusing him. "Small or large? The wedding. Should it be small or large?"

The mention of the wedding hurt all over again, like fingers picking at a wound still raw. "Really, Taylor, I—"

"If you were getting married, what would you prefer?"

"Uh ... uh ... small, I guess."

He nodded, as though in agreement. "And what about an engagement ring? Should it be ornate, simple, white gold, gold gold, what?"

Sam shrugged. "Simple. And gold. I guess I'd prefer simple and gold."

"Good, that's what I thought, too," Taylor said, adding, as he turned back to the stove to immerse the spaghetti in the water, "Why don't I pick you up first thing in the morning, and you can help me select one?"

The suggestion stung like a slap to Sam's face. There was no way, not even for the sake of friendship, that she would help Taylor pick out an engagement ring for Charlotte Sever. She had just opened her mouth to tactfully decline his suggestion—actually, at this point she didn't really care if it was tactful or not, she was hurting too badly—when Taylor turned back toward her.

"I figure we'll move into your condo, since I've got only the one bedroom, and, besides, the nursery was just decorated. I do most of my work at the office, but I thought I'd put a desk in a corner of your office, to shove papers around on if I have to bring something home. I don't know what we'll do about closet space in your bedroom. But I figure we'll work things out somehow."

Sam's head was swirling with confusion. Evidently it was affecting her hearing.

"Of course, this does screw things up with Andrea Margaret. I can hardly be her godfather now, can I?

But I suppose having a father is more important than having a godfather. Oh, by the way, someone was telling me the other day about a great preschool, but you have to sign up early. I mean, like on the night the kid's conceived, but he knew the owners personally and thought he could get Andrea Margaret in if we wanted. We'll have to decide in the next few weeks.''

"Taylor—"

"Well, maybe we could wait a little longer, but I think we have to move fast. A good preschool's hard to find.''

"Taylor—"

"Maybe I could put the desk in the bedroom if there isn't room in your office.''

"Taylor—"

Throwing his hand in the air in an impatient, halting gesture, as though he knew exactly what Sam was about to say, Taylor said, "I don't want to hear any of your crazy-making analysis, Sam. Not now. In fact, I don't want to hear anything from you right now. I've waited for you to come to your senses." The hand in midair raked through his hair in wild frustration. "God, how I've waited for you to come to your senses! But I'm tired of waiting. Damned tired! Just trust me in this. I'm in love with you. It's that simple, Sam. That damned simple! So don't try to make it complex. And don't try to analyze it in forty-two directions at once. And furthermore, you're in love with me! And don't try to make that complex—"

"I know," Samantha said softly.

"—and don't try to analyze—"

"I know."

"—it inside out. And don't—" He stopped, uncertain he'd heard what he thought he had. Or, more importantly, not daring to hope he'd heard correctly. "You..." His voice was so thick with emotion that he had to start again. "You know what?"

"That I love you," she answered, her own voice so filled with emotion that it was barely audible. Tears glistened in her eyes.

Neither spoke for several heavy heartbeats.

"You mean," Taylor ventured finally, once more raking his hand through his hair, "that I've just been engaged in the biggest bluff of my life and there was really no need for it?"

After the fact, he realized how bold his bluff had been. He hadn't been certain of her reaction, nowhere near it. All he knew was that he'd sensed she cared for him in more than a friendly way—he couldn't forget the way she'd so intimately touched him during sleep the night they'd shared a bed. That incident had been the motivation behind all the sensual little games he'd played since then, games he could have sworn she responded positively to. He'd even played on what he hoped was her jealousy. Though he knew it to be a dirty-dog trick, he'd allowed her to think he'd taken his secretary out on a real date. The truth was that he and Charlotte had been out before, but never romantically, although he wanted to make sure, which he'd done last night, that Charlotte understood they were nothing more than friends. He'd also wanted to thank her for helping

with the nursery. After that, there'd been only one
thing left to do: pile all his eggs in one basket and go
for broke.

"It looks that way," he heard Sam saying in answer to his question.

She was smiling, faintly, with tears in her eyes.
Taylor had no word for what he was feeling. He felt as
royal as a king, as humble as a peasant. He was in
love.

"We, uh . . . we definitely need to check into the
preschool," Sam said, suddenly as uncertain as Taylor was about what came next. As she watched him
walk slowly toward her, she added, her voice quivery,
"And I have room in my office for your desk. And
we'll squeeze your clothes into my closet somehow.
And I don't think Andrea Margaret will mind losing
her godfather. I mean, under the circumstances.
And . . ." She stopped when he stood directly before
her. Simply because the look on his face, the tender
look, the loving look, the oh-God-was-he-sexy! look,
took her breath away.

The pad of Taylor's thumb smeared the tear across
her cheek. Afterward, his hand lingered simply because he couldn't pull it away. In fact, that hand was
joined by the other until both of his palms lay cupping her face.

"Where do we go from here?" Samantha whispered, her heart thudding against her chest as the
warmth of his touch seeped into her like molten sunshine on a May day.

"All the way," Taylor whispered, his head automatically lowering. "We're going all the way, babe."

The broader implication of his words set Sam's soul to burning. Their more singular, sexual implication set her body to tingling, from head to toe and in a most vital spot in between. She was no virgin—she knew about man-woman feelings—but what she was feeling right this moment went beyond anything she'd ever felt before. Its power startled her, stunned her. It even frightened her.

"Taylor!" she whispered, suddenly adrift on an unsure sea.

Sensing her confusion, her fear, he said gently, consolingly, as his head was still descending, "Shh. We'll take it easy."

And then his mouth found hers. As softly as the fluffy snowflakes falling outside. He brushed his lips back and forth across hers—teasingly, playfully, as though having to cautiously lead into the powerful kiss that each could feel coming like a gone-wild wave threatening to crash into wild splendor. His tongue whisked along the curve of her lips before curling into the honeyed corners of her mouth. He kissed her again, fleetingly, promisingly, before drawing the flesh of her bottom lip between his teeth and biting tenderly.

She whimpered and, even though she was still seated, she reached out to steady herself. Her hands found Taylor's flannel shirt, beneath which she could feel the muscles of his chest bunching and balling as he leaned into her. She could also feel the strength of emotion he was keeping on a tight tether. Suddenly she wanted to unleash that restraint. No, she wanted to do more than release it. Considerably more. She wanted to shatter it at the stake. She wanted to make him as hungry for her as she was for him.

The tip of her tongue darted from her lips, seeking any intimate contact with him. What it found was the tip of his tongue, which instantly mated with it. Over and over. A sweet saber's duel. Samantha felt him stiffen with desire, heard him groan with pleasure.

A white-hot current raced through Taylor. "My God, Sam," he rumbled, "are you trying to drive me crazy?"

"Yes."

"Don't you want to take this slow? Don't you want some time to get used to the idea?"

"No, I don't want to take it slow. No, I don't need any time to get used to the idea. And if you don't kiss me, really kiss me, I'll—"

His mouth crushed hers in a fiery kiss filled with passion. Each striving to possess the other, their mouths angled, twisted, until both were breathless. Each remained, however, in agony, for there seemed no way to get as close as they needed to be, to appease the hunger building to painful proportions. Seeking to create a greater intimacy, Taylor thrust his tongue between the seam of her lips. He plundered deeply, sweetly but decisively, sweeping the cove of her mouth with pure and carnal sensuality.

Despite her eagerness of moments before, Taylor sensed that Sam was overwhelmed with the emotions bombarding her. But maybe it was just he who was suddenly overwhelmed. Overwhelmed by feelings he'd never experienced—had never realized existed before. Dragging his mouth from hers, he enfolded her in his arms and buried her face in the hollow of his shoulder. She burrowed deep.

"I know," he whispered. "I know."

She knew exactly what he meant, and she felt wonderfully safe that he understood the stormy, near-painful emotions playing so vividly through her. He stroked her back, molding her body to his in ways that were both soothing and sensual. Her breasts nestled against his chest like plump birds seeking the perfect nest. Somehow, another button of her skirt had come undone, and the fabric fell away at midthigh. Even more inexplicable, those thighs had parted until he stood between them. The suggestion of intimacy was breathtaking. At some point, Sam's hands had slid down Taylor's shirt in search of a surer anchor. Her fingers had fastened in the belt loops of his jeans, which she now clung to tightly. She knew that all she had to do was lower her hand a fraction to touch the powerful male strength of him.

Dare she? Dare she take this one irrevocable step? Loosening her fingers from a belt loop, she whispered the back of her hand across his rigid flesh. Taylor drew in a quiet, dark breath of air.

Both knew that their relationship had forever changed.

* * *

"What about dinner?" Samantha whispered minutes later as she stood in the swath of light gleaming from the bedroom lamp. Her blouse, which Taylor had unbuttoned so slowly she'd thought her heart was going to stop beating, was just being dragged from the waistband of her skirt and off her shoulders.

"To hell with dinner!" Taylor countered.

At least he'd had the forethought to turn off the burners. It had been the last coherent thought he'd had, though. Sam's hair sparkling in the lamplight, her eyes misting with expectation, her shoulders, a shade of cream and honey, coming into glorious view were driving all sane thought out of his mind and below his waist. Painfully below his waist.

At the sight of the pale blue lace cradling her breasts, Taylor, in an attempt to garner just a little composure, closed his eyes and swallowed hard. If simple blue lace was this devastating, how in all that was holy did he expect to withstand what lay beneath it? Perhaps he didn't expect to. Perhaps he was quite prepared to die from pleasure. When he opened his eyes, Sam had removed her boots and was about to unfasten the last button of her corduroy skirt. In the slit of the fabric, he saw the shadowed sensuality of her trim thighs. The sight was almost more than he could withstand.

"Don't," he said softly but firmly, as his hand stilled hers. "Give me a minute." He grinned wolfishly. "We wouldn't want this to be over before it even starts. I've waited too long to let that happen."

The hand smothering hers was trembling. Samantha had often wondered what it would take to ruffle Taylor, to splinter his supreme self-control. Now she knew. It was she herself. That knowledge gave her a power she'd never felt before. Like a siren, she guided his hand through the part of her skirt, placing his palm against her warm leg.

Taylor sucked in his breath. At the same time his eyes darkened to a smoky shade of gray.

"You don't play fair," he whispered, but he didn't move his hand. Except to tauntingly trace the inside of her thigh. With the ball of his thumb, he slid his way down, then up, up, flirting with the lacy edge of her panties. Samantha shivered beneath his carnal caress. She tried to say that he wasn't playing fair, either, but she didn't seem capable of forming the words. She seemed capable only of feeling.

At her oh-so-honest reaction, Taylor groaned and slid his hand to her tight derriere. He roughly pulled her against him at the same time his mouth swooped to hers. His kiss was hot, his body hard, and then Sam felt herself impatiently swung into his strong arms. In seconds, even as his lips continued to sweetly steal from hers, the bed enfolded her within its giant softness. Breaking the kiss, they stared at each other. Like friends. Like lovers.

"Are you certain?" Taylor asked huskily.

"That I love you? Or that I want to go to bed with you?"

"Both."

Samantha brought her hand to his cheek. A muscle jumped beneath her palm. "I love you, Taylor. And I want to go to bed with you. More than I've ever wanted anything."

Taylor's throat worked with emotion as he sought the right words. "I...I...dammit, Sam, I don't even know how to say what I feel!"

The hand at his cheek edged to the nape of his neck. She tugged him down to her. "Then show me," she challenged.

In seconds, his warm skin slid over hers, while their honeyed words flowed—sparkling, light words of love, thick, dark words of passion. Tossing and rolling, one moment on top, the next lost beneath his weight, Sam teased and tangled her legs with Taylor's hair-dusted legs and trailed her fingers through the wealth of hair that covered his chest.

Taylor speared his fingers through the thicket of Sam's short hair, holding her head still for kiss after drugging kiss. He abandoned that pleasing activity only for one more sensual. Ducking his head, his mouth closed over the peak of her breast—kissing, laving, sipping—until Sam arched her back and whimpered helplessly. Easing her passion-riddled body back onto the bed, Taylor kissed her soothingly as his hands traveled her body, undoing every tempering thing his mouth was trying to accomplish.

He'd touched all of her, except for one hidden, hot place. Both his need to touch her and her need to be touched were growing until they quickly became the only needs in the world. In the universe. In the totality of all being. Restlessly, her body tried to capture his touch. Perversely Taylor denied her and himself what they both wanted. When he touched her, he knew there would be no more waiting. Not that his body cared anything for waiting another minute, another second. But he wanted her body to sing forever with the pleasure he knew he was giving it. It was the only time he could remember when the need to give exceeded the need to take.

"Taylor?" she whimpered in frustration, urging her hips upward.

Her timing was impeccable, ensnaring the heat of him until it rested at her body's entryway. She gasped at the hard fullness. He groaned at her moist fire, at the blatantly sensual invitation.

The waiting was over. It had to be. For there was no self-control left.

Parting the soft, sweet folds, he began to slide slowly forward. Samantha moaned as he moved into her. Nothing had ever felt so good, so right, so perfectly natural. In reaction, and surprising herself, Sam felt her body begin an almost instantaneous convulsing. Clutching him to her, she whimpered, gasped, gave herself up to the delicious contractions as, inch by perfect inch, he unhurriedly filled her.

Samantha's unexpected response destroyed Taylor's sanity. With gritted teeth, he forced himself to withhold his own release until he was completely buried within her. At the precise second he was, he felt his body give in to what it so desperately wanted.

At the pinnacle of the moment, he heard Sam's muttered, "I love you." But then, it might have been he who'd uttered the loving words. Or quite possibly, it had been the two of them blending their hearts as they'd just blended their bodies, their spirits, their souls.

Chapter Ten

It was astounding how good overcooked pasta could taste. But then, done, underdone, overdone, the taste wasn't really registering with Sam. She was too preoccupied with Taylor. Just as he was with her—and as she knew they both were with what had transpired over the past two hours.

They had made love over and over—possibly setting the records for prowess that Sam had imagined Taylor setting the night before—both expressing what had too long been bottled inside. Plus, each time they made love they confirmed, at least for one bright second, what neither could truly believe was happening. Some things were just too good to be true.

Sam, warmly ensconced in Taylor's velour robe—and nothing else except the gold bracelet—sat on the floor before the fireplace staring at the man seated across from her. Taylor had once more donned his jeans and flannel shirt, the latter casually hanging open to reveal a hair-matted chest that Sam knew every inch of. Though sated, she still was moved by the sight, particularly the way his dark hair swirled around his navel. His most interesting navel. The navel her tongue had come to know so intimately. Unbelievably, Samantha felt a rush of desire. When her gaze met Taylor's, the message in his eyes mirrored her thoughts.

He grinned like a full-fledged rogue.

She grinned back, saying, "You're a wicked man, Taylor Pierce. How come I never knew that before?"

He shrugged, sending broad shoulders into an impressive performance. "If you want that spaghetti, you'd better eat it and quit making lewd suggestions with your eyes."

"Or else what?" she dared.

Taylor's gaze lowered to the vee neckline of his robe. At the slice of ivory skin that peeped through, at the promise of the softness that lay beyond, his eyes darkened to the color of passion. Touched as surely as if he'd reached out and dragged a finger across the nipples of her breasts, Sam felt the crests pebble to life. This, too, despite the robe's thickness, he seemed to see, for his heated gaze dropped for a meaningful moment.

"Eat," he ordered roughly, adding, "while you have the chance."

Needing to catch her own breath, Sam concentrated on the food on her plate. They had opted to eat before the fireplace. The ivory-colored candles that had once graced the table now sat on the hearth, casting both a wavery light and a faint vanilla fragrance. Alongside them rested wineglasses filled with a full-bodied Bordeaux. The fire, with flames of red, blue and orange, chatted a warm woodsy conversation.

"Finished?" Taylor asked a while later.

"Mmm," Samantha muttered, stacking her plate on top of his. He discarded both to the hearth and picked up the bottle of wine. He refilled her glass, then handed it to her. Their fingers brushed, as did their eyes, before she took a sip.

Taylor, now sitting so close that his leg grazed hers, watched as the ruby-red liquid moistened her lips. Unable to stop himself, he moaned...and leaned into her until his mouth was flush against hers. He nibbled and kissed her lightly, softly, the tip of his tongue dancing across her sweet flesh. She moaned, too, her tongue easing forward to waltz with his.

"You taste good," he whispered.

"So do you," she whispered back.

"I could taste your mouth forever."

"I was hoping for longer than that."

Taylor groaned. Balancing his glass of wine in one hand as he speared the fingers of the other through her silken hair, he claimed her mouth more decisively. His tongue plunged deeply, surely, tasting her in ways as wicked as she'd earlier accused him of being. When their breathing was tattered into shreds, when the wanton kiss demanded cessation or more intimate completion, Taylor dragged his mouth away and braced his forehead against hers.

"Stay the night," he implored, his unraveled breath mingling with hers.

"What about Andrea Margaret?"

"She's getting the best of care with Rosie. Besides, the weather's getting worse." As though to reinforce his point, the wind howled. What had once been only snow was now mixed with sleet, a combination that was fast making the streets dangerous.

"A person *would* have to be crazy to go out in this," Samantha said.

"It would be culpable for one person to let another go out in this."

"I suppose, then," Sam said, her lips quirking into a half-smile, "that it would be foolish for a person to fight another person over the issue."

Taylor's lips slid into a full grin. "It would be damned foolish."

"I, uh...I suppose you could find a place to put me up?" The provocative question dripped with sensuality.

"Oh, I'll find someplace," he said, "though bed space is limited. Would you object to sleeping beneath me?"

"If I must," she whispered, the three words light as homespun lace.

Taylor groaned as he pushed to his feet. "I think we better call Rosie while we can."

Locating the portable phone, Taylor punched in the number of Sam's house and handed her the instrument. Their eyes met and held before he started gathering up their dishes. Leaving the wineglasses behind, he headed for the kitchen.

Despite the cold, he was barefoot. Sam noted this in the same peripheral way she noticed that his jeans cupped his rear end to perfection. Just the way her hands did when they made love. The phone was answered just as this last hot thought burned through her mind. It took Sam a moment to recognize her housekeeper's voice...and to remember just why she was calling.

Taylor returned as the conversation was coming to a close. He had switched off the kitchen light, leaving only the fireplace and the golden glow from the candles. Bending his legs, he once more coiled down in front of Samantha.

"She'll probably sleep on through the night," Sam said, "but check on her, huh? Oh, and I'll be home early in the morning. Right. Okay. You call if you need anything. Okay...okay..."

"Tell her I want to talk to her," Taylor whispered.

"...okay. Listen, Mr. Pierce wants to talk to you. Okay, g'night. Now, call if you need me," she threw in, her maternal instincts unable to rest without one more promise.

Taylor, his fire-shadowed face exhibiting an amused look at her overconcern, took the phone. But only after a fleeting kiss to Sam's lips. "Rosie, Ms. Capen will not be home first thing in the morning. We're going shopping, but we'll be back well before noon. Right. Sure. If you need us, just call. And make sure you keep the house warm enough. It's damned cold out. Just kick the heat up to seventy-four degrees." Sam gave him a look that said he was every bit as bad as she was when it came to overconcern. "Yeah. Okay. Bye," he said, breaking the connection and shoving in the antenna. He tossed the phone into a nearby chair.

"Do, uh...do you think she knows?" Sam ventured.

"That we won't be sleeping alone tonight?"

Samantha nodded, the very thought steaming her senses.

"Do you care?" he asked, the thought playing havoc with him, as well.

"No," Sam breathed.

"My guess would be that she thinks we've been sleeping together all along. If the idea hasn't crossed her mind, however, I'd say she better get used to it. Because I'm not sleeping alone again. Ever. Oh, by the way, we're getting married Friday."

Samantha grinned. "You wouldn't rush a girl, now would you?"

Sam's grin was not returned. In fact, Taylor was deadly serious when he said, "We've got a helluva lot of time to make up for."

His earnestness sobered Samantha, and she reached out a hand to cradle his face. "I know," she said. Feeling a sudden panic, she asked, "This really is happening, isn't it?"

"I don't know, Sam," he answered. "There've been times in the past few hours that I think I must be dreaming. The way I have a thousand times. A hundred thousand times. I'm afraid I'm gonna wake up and find tonight was just a dream." Something in the way he said it suggested he wouldn't survive the disappointment.

The firelight, swollen with heat, flickered across Taylor, reminding Sam once more of the glittery dance light. Unlike before, the Taylor she now saw didn't confuse her or baffle her or cause her to condemn what she was feeling as unnatural, even incestuous.

This Taylor was unquestionably her lover, unmistakably her friend. This Taylor didn't require her to pick one or the other in definition of their relationship.

"It's no dream," she said, cupping her hand to his jaw. "I won't let it be."

Taylor covered her hand with his and drew it to his mouth for a gentle kiss. "I love you," he sighed.

"I love you," she said, a smile suddenly dimpling her cheeks, "maybe from the moment you punched out David Winters for punching me." The smile faded. "I just didn't know I loved you until Mother died." At his perplexed look, she tried to explain what she herself didn't understand. "I don't know what happened, but her death shifted my world. It caused me to look at everything differently. From that moment on, you didn't look the same. I began to have these shameful feelings, these wicked fantasies." She whispered the latter, as if the fantasies had been altogether too sinful to confess to out loud.

"Believe me, I'll put my wicked fantasies up against yours any day."

"Yeah?" she asked, promising herself that one day she'd make him tell her every fantasy, which she'd then personally act out for him, for them.

"Yeah," he answered and started to smile, but a thought changed his mind. "You know, I think your mother knew we were in love."

"What do you mean?"

"About three months before her stroke, she called me over to look at her hot water heater. There was something wrong with the thermostat, which didn't take me but a minute to fix. Anyway, afterward, she poured me a cup of coffee and we talked. At one point she started to say something, but didn't. She said something else, instead. I'm not sure how I knew she switched topics. Maybe her hesitation, maybe the assessing way she looked at me—I don't know. I just knew. I wondered then what she'd been about to say. I wonder now if she didn't see what we were too blind to realize. Although by then I was well aware of my feelings.''

"When did you first know?'' It was a question she was suddenly very curious to have an answer to.

The firelight slid across Taylor's face like a bronzed shadow, illuminating his lean, powerful jaw, his angular chin, his piercing eyes. He tightened his hand over hers, carrying his clasped treasure to his lap.

"Actually, it was pointed out to me. By Laura. Right after you split up with Rick. I simply made the comment that you and Rick had never been suited to each other, that you never should have married. She told me that the only person I really wanted to see married to you was me. I told her she was crazy. She told me I was hiding from the truth.'' Taylor took a deep breath, his eyes never leaving the eyes of the woman before him. "Once the idea was suggested to me, I couldn't run from it. She was right. I had disliked Rick from the beginning for one simple reason. He was your husband.''

"Yes and no,'' Samantha said. "Technically he was my husband—I even told myself I was happy—but he never felt like what I thought a husband should feel like.''

''What should a husband feel like?''

''Like you can't breathe every time you see him. Like your heart stops every time he touches you. Like...like you,'' Sam said breathlessly, her heart skipping beats at the intimate caress of her fingers by his.

Into the sudden, pulsating silence, the fire popped and hissed. Outside, sleet pommeled the roof, pounded on the windows, prayed cold prayers to the frosted gods of winter.

''I thought I'd die every time I thought of him making love to you,'' Taylor said hoarsely.

''I thought I'd die when you married Laura.''

''I tried to pretend it didn't matter that you two were making love, but it did.''

''I think I married Rick only because you married her. I'd never felt so alone.''

''I wanted to be doing to you, with you, everything I imagined him doing!''

This last was said so huskily, so rawly, with such primitive emotion that it was the most powerful aphrodisiac Samantha had ever known. Her bones seemed to melt, her flesh to burn; her senses were seared to ashes.

His body at the same fevered pitch, Taylor tugged her forward as he pushed to his knees. Their bodies collided in a sensual ballet as his mouth roughly, even punishingly for all the worry she'd caused him, fastened to hers. He groaned at her candy-sweet taste, at the corporeal temptation that taste inspired. Molding her to the length of him, he adjusted each feminine curve to fit the counter-curves of his masculine body. Each hill knew its complementary valley.

Emotions dazing her, Samantha slid her hands through the slit of his shirt and to the steadying wall of his bare chest. Beneath her hands hair curled, muscles rippled, skin heated until it threatened to scorch her palms. Fascinated, captivated by the contours of his shoulders, she drew the shirt from him, letting it fall in a heap on the floor. She then eased her hands to his back, splaying her fingers wide to know as much of him as possible. Edging her hands lower, she connected with the denim that sexily clung to his hips. Crowding her fingers into tight hip pockets, she drew him into her. The hardness of his arousal branded her. She moaned as she inched her hips forward and rubbed herself back and forth against him.

Drawing his mouth from hers on a gasp, he unhurriedly trailed his lips down her upturned throat, planting tiny kisses at each stop. "God, I want you!" he whispered savagely, though his movements were slow and maddeningly deliberate. "I can't stop wanting you!"

"Don't stop," she pleaded.

Taylor, desperate to get closer, yanked the belt of the robe. The garment fell invitingly open. His hands moved inside the velour curtain, unerringly finding her breasts, which filled his hands with their weight. He could hardly believe he was holding her so intimately. She was far more priceless than anything he deserved.

Lowering his head, his mouth strung kisses along the lower curve of one breast. Sam closed her eyes and let the sensually stinging feel of his mouth consume her. Nuzzling her breast, Taylor delivered random kisses; he even nipped lightly at the velvet crown with his teeth, sending it to pucker in rigid delight as shudders of pleasure raced down Sam's body. A hoarse groan erupted in his throat when Sam visibly shook in his arms.

Easing the robe from her shoulders, he watched the fire's glow, as though jealous of him, kiss her bare skin. His lips followed in the wake of the gleaming firelight. As the robe fell to the floor, he kissed her shoulders, her arms, the insides of her wrists, the hollow of her neck, the flat of her belly.

"Tell me something," he whispered, his fingers playing gently through the soft curls nesting the heat of her desire.

She whimpered as his fingers teased, but didn't deliver the paradise she sought. "If you keep doing that, I'm not going to be able to tell you anything," she managed to say.

His hand inched up the inside of her thigh, blatantly molding the sensitive mound. She gasped. The sound went through him like a brilliant shot of pain, making him so hard he fought to maintain his breathing. "Have you ever..." His breath cleaved in half, fragmenting the words into incoherent sounds. "Have you ever thought about a brother or sister for Andrea Margaret?"

"In-interesting you should say that," Sam said, her hands seeking to destroy him as he was destroying her. She trailed her fingers down his chest, across his stomach, then to his jeans which she expertly, despite trembling fingers, unfastened. She plunged her hand inside and into sable-brown curls. She found the aching flesh jutting above the zipper-edged vee of denim. Air, and a sweet curse, hissed through Taylor's teeth. "As a matter of fact I have. According to research..."

Taylor growled as her hand swept slowly down him.

"...forty-year-old women..."

She moaned as his finger probed and found the swollen bud.

"...are still capable of producing..."

Taylor groaned.

"...quality embryos in most instances."

"Sam," he whispered suddenly, urgently, pulling her down onto his lap in an unmistakably sensual pose, "if you're going to analyze something, analyze this."

With that, he thrust his hips forward...and thus began a very long, and rewarding, night of research.

Epilogue

Nine months later, in the middle of an August night, as she quoted statistics about how long the average woman spent in labor, Samantha gave birth to a beautiful, healthy, raven-haired daughter. Taylor, by his wife's side, was the first to hold the child. Later when he placed the tiny blanketed bundle in Sam's arms, Sam could have sworn she saw tears in his eyes. She knew there were tears in her own, for suddenly she couldn't have stopped their crystal flow had her life depended on it. Her heart was simply too filled with joy not to have some of it spill over.

In the days that followed, Andrea Margaret called the new arrival ba-by. Samantha simply called her newest daughter a miracle, the kind of blessed event that resulted from friends being lovers, lovers being friends. As for Taylor...well, he simply called the child another of his ladies.

*　*　*　*　*

Karen Keast

Born in Texas, raised in Louisiana, Karen Keast has lived most of her life in Shreveport, Louisiana. She currently resides there with her husband of twenty-four years and her two cats.

Likes: Autumn, rain, the sugar-sand beaches of the Caribbean, lace and silk, and good books that won't turn the reader loose. Also, music, the color pink, and underdogs winning against great odds.

Dislikes: Unfairness, narrow-mindedness, unkindness to animals.

A true introvert, a workaholic, she strives to write books that touch the heart, books that display the spectrum of human emotion. "I want to say something about what it is for me to be a human being and have that something felt by the reader, so that s/he says, 'Yeah, I know what she means. I've felt that way, too.'"

Also known to romance readers as Sandra Canfield and as half of the Sandi Shane writing team, under the name Karen Keast the author has published nearly a dozen contemporary novels and one historical, winning *Romantic Times* awards for Best Series Book of the Year and Best All-Around Series Author.

Labor Dispute

EMILIE
RICHARDS

A Note from Emilie Richards

Eleven years ago, after the joys of giving birth to two healthy sons, my thoughts turned from blue jeans to frilly pink dresses. My husband and I both wanted a girl to round out our family, and this time, concerned about the children of the world in need of parents, we wanted to adopt.

"Easier said than done" was coined for adoptive parents. We quickly discovered all the roadblocks that make adoption so frustrating. In comparison, one night of lovemaking and nine months of vague discomfort seemed simple.

Happily, nine months of pushing the system brought us a tremendous reward. A telephone call began the paperwork that led to our "airport birthing" of Jessamyn, from Calcutta, India, six years old and utterly, unspeakably precious.

On a snowy, frigid night four days after Christmas we made the two-hour journey to Pittsburgh, where Jessie was coming to meet us. Our long labor was finally ending, and our life with this mystery child just beginning.

Who was this daughter who, until that moment, had been no more than a snapshot and paragraphs on transparent Indian stationery? How were we going to communicate with a child who spoke a mixture of Hindi and Bengali but no English? Would we know what to do for her if she was ill? Would we know what to feed her if American food seemed too strange?

The airport wait seemed unbearable. Then, at midnight, as Jessie and her chaperon stepped from the plane, the wait seemed entirely too short. We were overcome with a mixture of emotions not unlike the moments just after a hospital delivery. Our child had arrived, and we had no idea what to do with her. I cried, she stared, my wonderful husband looked as if he'd been struck by a bolt of lightning.

We made it home, with Jessie enduring the two-hour car trip better than her new parents did. The following weeks passed in a blur. She learned English at the speed of light, and learned to say "I love you" first. She showed a marked preference for blue jeans over frilly pink dresses, and quickly became her brothers' favorite toy. She wrote her new name on everything—walls, toys, secret places we didn't find for years—as if proving to herself and to us that she was really Jessie, after all.

It was never easy, as nothing good ever is. She was marvelously stubborn; we were terribly impatient. At times she seemed to have been sent to teach us our faults. At times I'm sure she wondered why she hadn't grabbed a parachute and plunged to another destination on that twenty-four-hour trip from India.

Then one day we woke up and we were a family. Not an adoptive family, or a special family, or a different family. Just a family. We had three children, each wonderful, special and ours. And Jessie had a mom and dad and brothers to love.

Jessie is seventeen now, and one of four children instead of three. She enchants everyone she meets with her beauty, her serenity, her warm smile. She is wise about things most teenagers aren't, kind in a way that's unusual.

All those years ago we knew there was someone missing from our family. We reached across continents and found our daughter. Jessie filled a special place in our family and in our hearts. Not a day goes by that we don't say a silent thank-you.

And yes, at times the needs and challenges of four children overwhelm me. They are completely different, yet I am always the same person. How can I possibly parent them as the individuals they are if I can only be me, altogether too human, too fallible, too quick to judge and, occasionally, too quick to forgive?

Somehow they blossom despite my faults. They grow, they teach, they respond to the love my husband and I give them—not always just as I had hoped, but always in ways that make sense for them. Sometimes I ask myself if I would do it all again. Would I give birth to three headstrong, high-spirited sons? Would I adopt my headstrong, high-spirited daughter? Would I choose once again the chaos of this life?

You bet.

Emilie Richards

Chapter One

Grandmother Schaumbacher always said that no good news ever came over the telephone. The old woman, sight almost gone and heartbeat like the rattle of a diesel engine, still refused to have a phone installed in the tidy-as-a-Sunday-morning Missouri farmhouse where Johanna Groves had spent her childhood. Now Johanna stared at the telephone receiver buzzing angrily in the palm of her hand and thought that, as usual, Grandmother Schaumbacher had been right.

Pregnant. Again. And again and again and...

Her conversation with Mary Condrey, the Junction General nurse who had been Johanna's friend since the birth of her first child, still echoed in her ear, although the words had been uttered minutes before. *"You're pregnant, Johanna. Very pregnant. Pregnant enough to be feeling life any day."*

"But how could this happen, Mary?"

"If you don't know how after three children, you'd better get some books and start reading."

Johanna carefully replaced the receiver. From the living room she heard the shouts of her sons squabbling over what cartoon they were going to watch next. For once she didn't head their way to make peace, popcorn or prophecies of doom. She continued to stare at the telephone.

How was she going to tell David he would be a father again? David, whose laughing gray eyes more often than not these days were bleary with fatigue or narrowed with worry. David, whose broad shoulders already carried more weight than Atlas had ever borne. David, the man she had loved since childhood, married as an adolescent and presented with three sons before she was twenty-three.

David, who had never once by word or deed shown any desire to have another child.

There was the ominous squeak of rubber soles skidding against polished wood floors and the crash of a body against wallpapered walls. Grant Groves, nine in age and ninety in ability to manipulate, stopped just in front of her. "Mom, I want to watch 'Flintstones' and John won't let me."

And what would the baby want to watch? How would the baby *survive* with three active boys whose concept of brotherly love was a hammerlock hug and a pact with one brother to gang up on the other.

"Mom!"

"If you can't settle it yourselves, then turn off the television." Johanna reached for a flannel jacket to throw on over her T-shirt. "I'm going outside to talk to your father."

"Mo-o-om!" Grant added syllables to no avail. The door closed quietly behind his mother as he hummed the last "*m*." He shrugged philosophically and skidded back toward the family room. "Mom said you have to let me!" he shouted.

Outside, Johanna stopped on the back porch and shaded her eyes against the late-afternoon sun. The largest part of the three-hundred-and-twenty-acre farm where she had spent the last thirteen years spread out before her. "The old Grove place," as it was called by all the neighbors, was an undulating patchwork quilt of fields marked by fences and runoffs. Alfalfa was in early bloom, its yard-high stalks highlighted by lavender flowers. The corn was a six-inch carpet of green, and the soybeans were newly leaved. Fertility seemed to rise from the rich black soil like heat waves from desert sand.

Closer to the house, the same rich soil was nothing more than a rutted parking lot for trucks, tractors and a disassembled windrower. Lawn was a concept for city dwellers, and only a fiercely resolute farm wife demanded it. Johanna was one such. She had twelve feet of green rimmed by fragrant lilac bushes and shaded by a tall box elder before the farmyard began. She fared better in front of the house, facing the road. There she had half an acre of grass and flowers—a statistic David had muttered like a profanity on the few occasions when she'd been ill and he'd had to mow it.

Beyond the farmyard parking lot was an assortment of buildings that led downhill, as if in procession, to Jack Salmon Creek. There were a barn, a silo, a nearly abandoned chicken house and a hog house, a corrugated-steel machine shop, two Butler corn dryers and the remains of an old cookhouse that had once served meals for the hands, when men, not machines, farmed the land.

This afternoon, machines—or rather, one machine—was the focus of attention. Johanna spotted

David immediately. He was squatting beside their ancient windrower and he didn't look happy. With him was their closest neighbor to the east, Farley Mason. Farley was cussing. Johanna could just make out his words.

"Dad-blamed thing. Told ya y'oughta get a new one. Told ya not to put your money into more pigs! Pigs is likely throwing money away, when the corn's sellin' high."

David rose in one fluid movement. He was a lithe man, lean and strong, and even now Johanna felt a warm twinge of appreciation for his masculine grace.

"There's no way of knowing if the corn's going to sell high, Farley. You know that," David answered.

Farley spat a stream of tobacco juice. "It will, and you'll be wishin' you hadn't fed it to them pigs."

Johanna made her way down the path lined with the beheaded stalks of tulips. One of the boys, she wasn't sure which, had used them as targets in an impromptu game of baseball-bat golf. Now their denuded green foliage set off the small clumps of marigolds that she had started from seed on her bedroom windowsill.

David turned when he heard her footsteps. His welcoming smile belonged to a man preoccupied.

Farley's smile was tobacco-stained and hearty. He snapped his red suspenders in time to the words of his greeting. "Can't stay for coffee, Johanna. Mighty nice of you to ask."

She managed a smile, too, though just barely. Farley Mason was one of her favorite people. "Did I ask?"

"Nah, but you was gonna." He turned back to David. "Better order a new sickle blade. Could take months to get here."

David nodded.

"Good seein' you, Johanna. Try talkin' some sense into this man of yours for once, how 'bout it?" Farley stomped to his pickup and backed it expertly from between a tractor and the windrower. In moments there was nothing left to show he'd been there except dust settling back on the ground.

David spoke. "I'll have to borrow Farley's windrower to get the first cut of hay this year. The blade on this one's shot."

For a moment Johanna forgot her own unhappiness. David looked tired. The shadow from the bill of his cap couldn't hide the lines of weariness around his eyes. He'd been up since before dawn, and he would work straight through until dark. Spring was the price a farmer paid for a comparatively leisurely winter.

Even though he was weary and unhappy, looking at David still made Johanna feel as shyly expectant as a new bride. He was a large man, six feet two of the muscle and sinew needed to run a successful farm. His skin was deeply tanned except for his forehead, which was a paler hue, because it was perpetually shaded by a hat. His hair was sun-streaked brown, and normally his gray eyes were lit with warmth and laughter. His hands, his callused, long-fingered hands, were equally at home loading hay, delivering calves or stroking his wife's slender body.

Now, as always, she wondered if he ever regretted marrying her and taking on the burdens of a family.

She knew he must regret the way their marriage had come about.

"Jo?"

She realized she had been staring at him. "I'm sorry about the windrower," she said softly. "I know you were hoping to get a few more years out of it."

"Decades." He forced a smile. "Did you want something?"

She was suddenly very, very tired. She wanted things she would never have: David's undying love; David's full attention; David's heartfelt assurance that he wouldn't change a thing about the past thirteen years. More than ever, she wanted those things. And her chance to have them had just grown slimmer. She turned back to the house. "No, it can wait."

"Jo." David laid his hand on her shoulder. "You didn't tell me what the doctor said today after your checkup. Is everything all right?"

She shook her head slowly and spoke without turning. "No. I'm pregnant."

There was a silence, but the hand that spasmodically gripped her shoulder spoke volumes. "Pregnant?" David said at last.

"The night of the VFW dance, as near as I can figure it. We had too many drinks, to celebrate Farley's birthday."

"That was four months ago!"

She heard his condemnation. "I had some spotting the first couple of months after the dance, and I thought my periods were just getting lighter." She paused, because she had to be perfectly honest. "I should have known, anyway. I guess I just haven't wanted to believe it."

"You just found out?"

She turned back to him, because it had become awkward not to. She wished she didn't have to look at his shocked face. "Dr. Landis was sure, but I made him send me over to Junction General for a lab test. Mary just called to give me the news. I thought the doctor was wrong."

David shook his head. "A baby."

She felt a sudden burst of compassion for the tiny life growing inside her. Until that moment she had felt nothing for it at all. "*Our* baby," she said quietly.

David's expression didn't change. She imagined that the fact that they had created this child together had no sentimental significance for him.

"Well, there's nothing to be done about it now." He frowned a little. "Is there?"

"No."

He seemed satisfied with her answer, although she couldn't be sure. He leaned toward her and lightly kissed the tip of her nose. "We'll manage, Jo. We always do."

"Yes." But *she* couldn't manage a smile. She just turned and started back toward the house. She didn't know that David's eyes followed her until she was inside, and only then did he sink to the ground beside the windrower and close them.

Inside Johanna heard an ominous silence. There were no childish voices raised in play or argument, and no television. For a moment she believed that a miracle had occurred and that without being reminded the boys had gone upstairs to change for their evening chores. Then a piercing scream destroyed that bit of optimism.

At a run she followed the sound through the living room and into the kitchen, where she threw open the basement door and switched on the light.

"What is going on down here?" she demanded.

The tear-filled voice that answered was Grant's. "They tied me up! John and Peter tied me up!" He gulped audibly. "Tight!"

Johanna took the stairs two at a time. In the far corner of the spacious basement, where once the first Groves to farm this land had made their home until they could afford to build the house upstairs, Grant stood, his hands tied behind his back and around one of the metal support posts. A bandanna covered his quivering chin.

"I didn't do nothing!" he insisted tearfully.

"Anything," Johanna corrected automatically. She was at his side untying his loosely bound hands in a matter of seconds. With a concentrated effort, Grant could have done it himself in the time it had taken him to scream.

"We were playing space wars. I was the bad guy, and they told me they were gonna pretend to tie me up. Then they really did, and they put this in my mouth." He stripped off the bandanna and threw it to the floor. "They turned off the lights!"

Johanna smoothed back his golden-blond hair. "You're all right, Grant. If you'd tried, you could have gotten your hands loose yourself."

"I was scared!"

Her heart twanged, but even as she murmured sympathetic noises she added and balanced the score-card for each of her sons and came up with a tie. Grant's assaults on his brothers were usually less direct, but no less effective. He was long past the point of needing her protection. Peter, her middle son, was eleven and John, the oldest, was twelve. At nine, Grant was only two inches shorter and five pounds lighter, and since he'd been warring with his brothers since birth, his skills were finely honed.

"We'll go upstairs and see if we can find John and Peter," she promised. "I'll tell them they can't do this again."

Grant's eyes sparkled from more than tears. "Make 'em fill the wood box for me!"

"No." Johanna turned and started across the basement to the stairs. She was almost grateful for this distraction to help her rid herself of the memory of the look on David's face after she'd told him about the baby. "You'll do your chores, same as usual."

With Grant trailing her, Johanna went to find the older boys. She found them in John's room. There was a guilty scuffle as she entered. The angelic expressions on their freckled faces couldn't hide their tension or the glossy paper peeking out from under John's mattress.

"Boy's you seem to have left something in the basement."

John, who except for his mother's freckles was the image of his father, raised one brow as if he couldn't imagine what she meant. "What?"

"Your brother."

Peter giggled nervously. "He was supposed to get loose and come find us. We were waiting for him."

Johanna had been through enough discussions of this type to know what would come next. She would accuse; they would deny. In the end she would warn them not to do it again, and they would obey by finding something different and worse to do next time. She cut the exchange short by skipping right to the warning.

"Don't let me catch either of you doing that again. You frightened your brother."

"We didn't tie him tight enough to scare a flea."

Johanna ignored John's denial. "Now what do you have hidden under your mattress?"

"Mattress?"

If her sense of humor hadn't already disappeared for the day, Johanna might have laughed at the identical looks of horror on John's and Peter's faces. Instead she just held out her hand wearily. "Let's have it, boys."

John opened his mouth to protest, then snapped it shut. He rose slowly from the bed. "It's just a calendar."

"Let me see."

"It's just a calendar," he repeated, reaching slowly between the mattress and box springs to inch it out.

Johanna continued to hold out her hand.

The calendar was the feed-store variety, meant to be tacked to a private spot on a barn wall and enjoyed by farmers who weren't too worn down from years of hard work to appreciate the form and diversity of the female body. The models, who probably believed beef was raised behind the glass mirror of their supermarket's meat department, weren't quite naked and weren't quite clad.

"Do you have any questions about anything here?" Johanna asked nonchalantly after she had flipped clear through to December.

The boys shook their heads in unison.

"Well if you don't have any questions, then you won't need this anymore." Johanna slipped the calendar under her arm.

"But it's Lenny's," Peter said. "And he'll be real mad if I don't give it back to him!"

Lenny lived two farms away. The boys worshiped at his feet because he had already turned the magic age of thirteen. "I'll be sure Lenny gets it back," Johanna promised. "I'll give it to his mother."

The boys groaned.

"Get ready for your chores." She had already turned to leave before she realized she hadn't told any of her sons about the baby. For a moment she hesitated, wondering if she could face another confrontation. Then hope sparked inside her. Someone needed to feel enthusiasm about the coming event. *She* needed to hear enthusiasm in someone's voice. Surely the boys would be excited, if only because they would have another sibling to torment.

"I forgot to tell you," she said, turning back to them. "Something pretty exciting is going to happen to us in September."

Peter and John were still pouting, and Grant was sticking his tongue out at them. Johanna waited for someone to ask what, but no one did. Finally she just told them. "I'm going to have a baby. You'll be getting a new brother or sister in the fall."

Pouts turned to shock, then to dismay. "I'm not giving up my room," John said after a short silence.

"Lenny's baby sister cries all the time," Peter said.

"I don't want to have liver for dinner," Grant said. "I saw it on the counter. Can't we have chicken?"

Johanna searched each childish face. They were so different, these sons of hers, yet mysteriously alike, too. Now they were united in rebellion. She felt another twinge of pity for the child growing inside her. Poor unplanned baby. The pity seemed to mushroom and fill her, until she realized it wasn't just the spark of life inside her for whom she felt sympathy.

She felt sorry for herself. She was exhausted, overworked and vastly unappreciated. Now she carried a new burden, and there was no one she could share it with.

She swallowed tears. "Do your chores," she said simply.

She shut the door on the boys' protests and headed down the hallway.

The tears were flowing by the time she reached her bedroom. She never cried. Tears were for women with time on their hands; tears were for women who weren't married to the man they had loved forever; tears were for women who weren't blessed with three healthy, intelligent sons. When you had been given more than anyone could rightfully expect from life, you didn't cry. You sent prayers of thanksgiving to the heavens, and you worked hard to deserve what you had.

She cried anyway.

The bed beckoned. She couldn't remember the last time she had succumbed to its temptation before nightfall. She usually went to sleep late, often after David had already given in to exhaustion. There was always laundry to do or floors to wax, tomatoes to can or a dress to sew for the women who paid her to finish the projects they had begun and abandoned. She had never, as now, been tempted to cry herself to sleep on the double-wedding-ring quilt that Grandmother Schaumbacher had given her on her wedding day.

She settled against the quilt, tracing the interlocking wedding rings with one finger. The bed felt strangely comfortable, like a neglected old friend who still welcomed her with open arms. She buried her face in the pillow and let its cool surface soothe the hot tears on her cheeks.

A baby.

David thought of himself as a strong man. He had lost a father to heart disease, taken on the full burden of a large farm, married and fathered a child, all before he was twenty-one. Without complaint he rose every morning well before dawn and worked until dark, often with no help from anyone. He provided for his family, even as neighbors lost their farms and drought and fluctuating markets cut severely into his own profits.

He was a strong man, but today he was a strong man who wondered where all his strength had gotten him.

David drove the ailing windrower into the machine shop and parked it where he would be able to get to the blade to remove it, when and if a new blade arrived. There was the screech of gears grinding and echoing off the steel walls. Then silence. He stared at an old tractor that he was dismantling for spare parts.

Johanna was going to have another baby. He remembered the pride he had felt the first time she had told him she was pregnant. He had been young then, and thrilled by this visible proof of his masculinity. He had watched her grow rounder as she grew more beautiful, and he had lain beside her at night, feeling the baby's movements against him.

That first year of their marriage had been a year of miracles. Johanna had been the greatest miracle of all. She had been all his, there when he needed her, there when he wanted her. He had not had to share her with anyone, and the year had passed in a golden glow.

Johanna had no longer been at his beck and call after John was born. He had been as thrilled as she at the baby's birth, pacing outside the delivery-room door like the proverbial nervous father until Mary Condrey, who had been the delivery-room nurse, stepped outside to wink and tell him it was a boy. Afterward, when they took the baby home together, he had been proud and foolishly certain that this child of their creation would be the bond that would hold them together forever.

Instead, the children had become Johanna's whole life. He didn't resent his sons; he loved them more than he had ever believed possible. But he did miss their mother terribly.

And now, just as the boys were growing old enough to need Johanna less and he had a second chance to make her love him, to woo her as he'd never done before their marriage, the cycle was about to begin again.

David climbed down from the windrower, aiming an angry kick at one of its huge tires. Had Johanna gotten pregnant on purpose? Had she wanted this child, afraid that when the boys were gone her own life would be meaningless? Had the promise of more time with her husband held so little appeal?

The questions had been circling in his head in the hour since Johanna had made her announcement. Now, as he started toward the house and supper, he had to admit he knew the answer. Johanna had not gotten pregnant on purpose. He remembered the night of the VFW dance and her laughing protests as he'd made love to her without bothering with birth control. Down deep they had both believed it was safe; nine years of successful prevention had made them cocky.

Johanna had not gotten pregnant on purpose, but she *had* gotten pregnant. And despite the pale hue of her complexion and the absence of a sparkle in her lovely green eyes, he guessed she was glad about it. She was never happier than when she was taking care of others. She had been born to be a mother, born to be a farm wife. She had married him to fulfill that destiny, and he had known it since the day she had accepted his proposal.

He entered the house through the laundry room just off the kitchen, slipping off and hanging up his grease-stained coveralls before he washed his hands in the sink. Surprisingly, the kitchen was empty, cold and dark, with none of the delicious smells of Johanna's cooking. In the family room he found his sons clustered around the television set. "Where's your mother?" he asked, over a conversation between Captain Kirk and Mister Spock.

"I don't know," they chorused without taking their eyes off the set.

"You boys do your chores?"

"Mom didn't tell us what we were supposed to do," John answered.

"You know what you're supposed to do," David told him, walking over to flick off the television. "The same chores you did yesterday. Now get moving."

"We were busy yesterday. Mom did them for us." Peter was the first to stand. "We don't know what we're supposed to do."

"You know what's got to be done. Divide the chores up yourselves." David's voice had the ring of command. The other boys stood, and the three of them started toward the door. David could hear them fighting about who would do what as they left the room.

"Johanna?" David's voice echoed through the house, but no answer was forthcoming. "Johanna?"

He found her upstairs, in their bedroom. It was the last place he had thought to look. She didn't wake up when he entered; she didn't even stir.

It was so rare to find her sleeping that David just stared. Strands of hair, fine and soft, feathered across her cheek. In the glow of the bedside lamp the strands looked more gold than red. Outside in the sunlight the opposite would be true. David could never describe Johanna's hair. She called it brown; he called it glorious. She had cut it pixie-short once when the three boys were no taller than her kneecaps and she'd had no spare time for vanity. In a rare fit of temper David had demanded she grow it back by supper time, and since then she had only trimmed it occasionally, so that now it hung bone-straight to the middle of her back. Usually she clipped it away from her gamine face, but tonight it was a silky fall, caressing her cheek and breast.

Her face was still pale, and even asleep she looked tired, as if someone or something had drained her of all vitality. For a moment David wondered if she had told him the whole truth. Was she ill as well as pregnant? She had never suffered from morning sickness, never slowed down even when she was pregnant with Grant, toilet training Peter and driving John to the church play group three times a week on top of all her other chores. She had always joked that when the time came to give birth she was the modern equivalent of the proverbial pioneer woman who walked to the next row of corn, had her baby, then came back with it strapped on her back to finish her hoeing. Now she looked as if a strong wind might finish her off.

He felt a twinge of alarm. Johanna was always there for her family. And although their time together was limited, when he asked her to be, she tried to be there for him. She was everything any man could ask for, and more than he had a right to have. He loved her so much that the love was a pain deep inside him. If anything were to happen to her...

"Johanna?" he called softly. She didn't move.

"Johanna?"

On the third call her eyes opened slowly. It took her seconds to focus on him, and seconds more to sit up and shake her hair back over her shoulders. She ran her tongue over her lips as if to encourage them to open and move. "What time is it?"

"Half past supper time."

Guilt chased away the bleariness of sleep. "Oh, David, I'm so sorry. I'll get it started right away." She swung her legs over the side of the bed and stood, automatically smoothing and straightening the quilt as she did.

"Why were you sleeping?" David's question came from concern, but it sounded like anger.

"I didn't mean to. I just lay down for a moment." She didn't meet his eyes. She had failed him. Despite a noontime dinner that would fill a city man for a week, she knew that David came in at night famished. She couldn't remember a time when she hadn't had supper on the table waiting for him. It was just one of the ways she tried to show him what he meant to her. She went on before he could question her further. "Did the boys do their chores?"

"They're doing them now. I had to send them out myself."

Her guilt multiplied. "I'm sorry. And after all your problems with the windrower."

Frustration, exhaustion and the growing feeling that the chance for something beautiful was gone colored David's voice. "Let's not forget the baby." He had no sooner said the words than he wished he could cut out his tongue. He ran his hand through his hair. "Look, pretend I didn't say that."

"You don't want this child, do you?"

He wasn't sure about the child, but he was sure he wanted the child's mother. That was the source of his unhappiness, but he couldn't tell her. He tried not to let his feelings show. "I don't know anything except that I'm tired and hungry right now. How about getting some supper together while I take a shower?"

"It'll be ready when you get out." Johanna longed for a reassuring smile, a kiss, a hug. Instead, David turned to begin gathering the clean clothes that she had washed, folded and stacked neatly in his dresser. She went downstairs feeling emptier than she had before her nap. David stood under the warm spray of the shower and wished that he could be twenty again, and that somehow he could make Johanna love him as he loved her.

Chapter Two

Supper was a remarkably subdued affair. Not even the last ears of sweet corn, frozen by Johanna from the previous summer's garden, coaxed anyone at the table to smile. The cherry cobbler might as well have been a second helping of liver and onions.

She stacked the dishwasher and washed pots and pans as David and John went outside to check the hogs and the small flock of chickens. The younger boys went upstairs to the room to get ready for their baths.

The boys were in their pajamas by the time David and John returned. Johanna was slipping on her jacket to go out.

"Checking on your grandmother?" David asked.

She couldn't quite look him in the eye. "I wasn't able to get over there this afternoon. The boys promised they'll go right to bed after you kiss them good night."

"Would you like me to come with you?"

She met his eyes, surprised. The offer was uncharacteristic. Dead tired at the end of a day, David needed sleep, not a social call. He was apologizing. "No." She hesitated; then, because she needed to touch him in some way, she reached up to caress his cheek. "Go to sleep. I'm not going to stay long."

He nodded, then took her hand before it fell to her side. "I'll see you when you get home."

She knew he would be sound asleep, but she smiled anyway. "Maybe I'll be bringing back some of Grandmother Schaumbacher's coffee cake for breakfast."

He squeezed her hand before he dropped it.

The trip to the house where Johanna had been raised was ten minutes by foot or car. By foot it was a straight line through cornfields and over the tiny, rickety footbridge that spanned Jack Salmon Creek. By car the route was a country lane that meandered here and there as if its architect had been uncertain where he wanted to go. Tonight she chose to walk. The sky was a brilliant canopy of stars, and although the air was chilly she knew that with her coat and the child inside her speeding her metabolism she would be warm enough.

Once outside and past the farmyard, she was assaulted by the essence of a Missouri spring night. The air was fragrant with the green of new growth and the rich black of freshly turned soil. Somewhere nearby a nighthawk called its katydid imitation, and overhead bats glided against the moon.

It had been just such a night thirteen years ago when David had asked her to marry him. She had been eighteen and looking forward to graduating from high school. David had been twenty and already weary from trying to single-handedly run his farm on the sparse capital that had been left after his father's sudden death.

But their story had started long before that. Johanna couldn't remember a time when she hadn't known David. Their fathers had been boyhood friends who had remained close until Frank Groves died. She and David had both been motherless, he because his mother had died a year after his birth and she because her mother had left the farm and her family for city life and a new husband when Johanna was three.

Johanna had been raised by her father and grandmother, a warmhearted, stern-faced German immigrant who carried a switch in one pocket and a handful of molasses cookies in the other. David had often made his way to the Schaumbacher farm for the warmth and the cookies—neither he nor Johanna had ever felt the sting of the switch.

From the time she was six, Johanna had known she loved David. A carefree, happy boy, he could make her smile when the world seemed gray, make her forget her freckles and long, skinny legs, make her forget the aching shyness that convinced others she was tongue-tied and boring. They fished together in Jack Salmon Creek, built a tree house in a dying elm that exactly bordered both farms, exchanged vows that they would be rich and famous someday and never again weed a garden or gather eggs.

By the time Johanna was thirteen she realized that although her feelings had only intensified with the years and she was now in the throes of a gigantic crush on the boy-next-farm, David's feelings were different. She was still his pal; he still came to visit; they could still talk about their futures. But sadly, she was nothing more. David's future didn't include her. He loved her as he loved Grandmother Schaumbacher. She was family to him, the sister he had never had.

In the following years she had watched with envy as David dated one lovely, self-assured girl, then another. He was well-liked by everyone, an excellent student, an outstanding athlete. She was a good student, too, but she had none of David's charm or polish. She was a country girl with long legs and a face no one remembered. When she dated, the boys were shy loners like herself. By the time David was a senior, she and the boy she loved had grown worlds apart. David was going to college; David was going to be someone. And although she planned to go to college, too, she knew that by the time she graduated David would be married to a bright and beautiful woman and on the road to success in St. Louis or Kansas City.

Frank Grove's death just after David's high-school graduation changed all that. Now, as Johanna crossed the footbridge over Jack Salmon Creek, she thought of the first night David had come to her for comfort. It had been three weeks after Mr. Grove's death, and the long line of sympathetic callers bringing casseroles, apple pies and advice had finally dwindled.

David had appeared on the front porch as the sun sank behind the windbreak of oaks and maples just beyond Johanna's house. Without words she had taken his hand, and they had walked along the ridge that led up to the windbreak. "I've asked for my tuition back," he said at last. "I'm going to stay here and take over the farm."

She had felt his disappointment like a tangible force. "You've thought about all the alternatives?" she asked. "Selling? Renting?"

"I've thought about them."

Johanna knew David well enough to realize that he would say no more about his decision. Like most of the men she knew, David could talk about anything except his feelings. "It will be hard." She leaned against a maple tree, crossing her arms in front of her.

"Harder than you know. There's not much left to farm with. All the cash that was left went for Dad's hospital bills."

"Can you get a loan?"

"Who would loan money to an eighteen-year-old?"

"If the eighteen-year-old were you, David? Anyone who knows you."

He smiled then, and she imagined it was the first time in three weeks that he had. "You were always my biggest fan, Jo." He lifted the braid that lay across her shoulder and draped it under her nose. "Prettiest, too. A mustache suits you."

She laughed and shook her head until the braid fell back in place. "David, you know I'll help in every way I can."

"I know you will." He leaned forward and kissed her forehead; then he stepped back. "I couldn't let the farm go. It meant too much to my father. I guess it means too much to me."

She was surprised, both by the kiss and the expression of his feelings. "I know," she said softly. "Sometimes I think there's Missouri soil in our veins. Cut either of us and we'd bleed black."

"I thought you'd understand. Not everyone will."

They had walked back to her house after that, but David's evening visits had become a sort of ritual. They continued two or three times a week through

Johanna's junior year and into her senior. Although she and David were still just friends, she began to blossom under his attention. At the same time, the thin, angular body that she had almost given up on began to blossom, too. Maturity gave her new curves and made sense of the button nose and wide mouth she had always disdained. The long legs that had been her greatest trial seemed to perfectly suit her new body, and her freckles seemed to soften and melt together into a healthy glow. Boys who had always looked right through her began to ask her out. Best of all, she was finally able to speak her mind without blushing or stuttering.

Then one evening, just before sunset in the spring of her senior year, her world turned topsy-turvy.

David had come to see her, and hoping that would be the case, she had donned a new green angora turtleneck that made her eyes look like emeralds.

"Let's walk to my place," he'd said, reaching for her hand. "I've got something I want to show you."

Grandmother Schaumbacher had overheard and given her permission, and David and Johanna had set off down the path.

"What do you want to show me?" Johanna asked, as they neared David's farm.

"You'll see."

The surprise was pink and white trillium, masterfully displayed under the grove of dogwoods and redbuds that spread out behind the old cookhouse.

David watched Johanna's delight. "I remember you used to wait for these when we were kids."

"We don't have any at our place. I've always loved trillium." She knelt, ignoring the fact that it had rained that afternoon and the forest floor was wet.

"You love everything about the land, don't you? What are you going to do away at college in the city?"

She left the trillium in place so that they would bloom again the following year and stood, wiping leaves and dirt from the knees of her jeans. "I'm going to miss this, I guess." She looked up at David, who was now a full seven inches taller than she was. She smiled as nonchalantly as she could. "And I'll miss our evening walks."

"From what I can tell, there'll be any number of men who'll want to walk with you."

"But they won't be you, will they?" Johanna realized her hands were trembling slightly. This was as close as she had ever come to telling David what she felt for him.

His gray eyes were serious. He was no longer the laughing young man who had planned to conquer the world. He was a farmer now, and his life was hard work and sacrifice. "Will that matter?" he asked.

"Of course," she said, her voice trembling like her hands.

"Jo, what if you didn't have to leave?"

She shook her head in confusion, afraid to say another word.

David cleared his throat. "What if we got married?"

She could only stare.

"I know this is sudden." David looked away. "We've never talked about marriage.... We've never talked about a future—"

"You've never even kissed me!"

David's eyes swept back to hers. His mouth curved in the beginning of a smile. "I could fix that."

"Oh, don't do me any favors!" She was so filled with emotions that she grabbed the first one she could identify: anger that he could be so casual about something that meant the world to her.

He was grinning now. "Then I think I'll do myself one." His arms wrapped around her, and he pulled her to his chest in one, effortless motion. Her mouth was under his before her heart could beat again.

She had dreamed of this so often that the kiss actually seemed familiar. More important, it seemed right, perfect, endlessly sensual and satisfying. When it ended, she felt that her innocence was a thing of the past.

"It's no—no...wonder," she stuttered, trying to catch her breath, "that the girls beg you to take them out!"

"I don't kiss everybody like that," he promised. "Just the girls I want to marry."

She tried to push him away, but he held hear easily. "Just you, Jo," he said, kissing her hair, her ears, the corner of her mouth, as she turned away from him.

"Why do you want to marry me?" she asked at last, when her knees were weak and her heartbeat as rapid as the trains that sped by their little corner of the earth and gave the town of Junction its name.

"I want to share my life with you."

She wanted to ask him if he loved her, but she couldn't get the words out. He wanted to share her life, but what did that say of love? "Why me?" she asked finally.

"Because you fit here. You're as much a part of this land as I am. You know the life we'll lead. There won't be any surprises."

Disappointment stabbed through her, yet what he said was perfectly true. More, she understood what he hadn't said, too. He was lonely, and tired of trying to run the farm by himself. He needed a woman beside him, someone to feed him and wash his clothes, keep his house clean and share in the chores around the farm. He needed someone who wasn't afraid to work, who wasn't afraid of blood and dirt and sweat, someone who would understand when the corn died of drought and the price of hogs dropped.

If that woman was also a friend, a friend he could kiss the way he had just kissed her, then so much the better.

"And what about love?" she asked, because she had to know, no matter how much it hurt.

"I've always loved you," he said, almost as if he were puzzled she would ask.

"But you'd never even kissed me."

"You had to grow up first, didn't you?" He had kissed her again then, kissed her until she agreed to marry him, kissed her all the way home and for long minutes on her front porch. And when he was finished kissing her, she had known that no matter why David wanted to marry her, she was the luckiest woman in the world.

The months had crept by at a snail's pace after that. The wedding date had been set for June, and high school seemed like nothing more than an obstacle course to get through. David was busy at the farm, and their moments together were rare. When her wedding day dawned bright and sunny, Johanna almost felt as if she were marrying a stranger.

But David was no stranger that night when he came to her, his gray eyes warm with passion, his hands and lips rough yet tender. He rid her of her shyness and her virginity with enthusiastic grace, and when she lay beside him at last and listened to the slow, even rhythm of his breathing, she knew that she had made the right decision for both of them. He was already the husband she needed. She would become the wife he wanted. He would never regret their marriage, never wish that his life had turned out differently. She would do everything in her power to make sure that David was happy.

And that was what she had done for almost thirteen years. Now, as she crossed the final field between the house she lived in with David and the house where she had grown up, she wondered just how well she had succeeded. Through the years it seemed that she and David had grown further apart. Now their own baby seemed to be driving an additional wedge between them. How was it that after almost thirteen years of trying to please the man she adored she couldn't seem to please anyone? Not David, not the boys; and not even herself.

There was only one light on at the Schaumbacher house when she started up the drive. The light was in the kitchen and would burn through the night. Still, Johanna was sure that her grandmother wouldn't yet be asleep. She expected the old woman to be rocking on her front porch, and she wasn't disappointed.

"Grandmother," she called, making a megaphone of her hands. As she drew nearer, she saw that her grandmother was looking toward the sound of her voice. Johanna was climbing the porch steps before she spoke again. "I thought I'd find you here."

"It's a lovely night. I can smell and hear it, even if I can't see it so well." Grandmother Schaumbacher patted the chair next to her in unspoken invitation.

"I'm sorry I didn't come this afternoon. Did Aunt Mattie check on you?"

"She fussed around here like an old hen with a new biddy. What did I ever do to deserve such a daughter?"

"You raised her to be just like you," Johanna said, laughing.

"She's after me to come live with her again."

"She loves you. She worries about you. So does Aunt Wilma."

"Better they should think about something else."

"Well, I've got something for you to think about." Grandmother Schaumbacher stopped rocking. "You finally found out you were pregnant?"

Johanna was stunned. Her grandmother rarely cracked a smile, but now she was grinning with unabashed glee. "How did you know?"

"Do you remember when you were pregnant with John?"

"Like it was yesterday."

"And Peter? And Grant? Every time you'd come over to visit, and I'd give you *flieder* tea. And every time you'd say, 'This tastes funny. What did you put in it?' And then I'd know you were pregnant. You've refused to drink any, *Liebchen*, since about two months ago. What took you so long to know?"

"What took *you* so long to tell me?"

"Better you should find out yourself."

Johanna stared out into the darkness. "Well, I found out."

"And you're not happy."

Johanna thought about all the wisdom her grandmother had garnered over the years. As Johanna had grown up, the stern-faced woman beside her now had been her doctor, her minister, her therapist and her best friend. She had doled out vitamins and herbal teas, sympathy and lectures, along with the eternal molasses cookies that had made her so popular with David. Johanna's mother had rarely visited her, preferring her new family and her life in Chicago, but Johanna had mourned little for the woman who had given her birth. Grandmother Schaumbacher had been the mother she had needed.

So now it was no surprise that her grandmother understood her feelings. "I suppose that seems awful to you, doesn't it?"

"Not awful, *Liebchen*. Sad."

"I hadn't planned on any more children. Sometimes I feel like I've already got fifty. And David isn't happy, either."

"Heaven forbid that our David might not be happy about something."

"What's that supposed to mean?"

"Just that you run in circles, like a dog chasing its tail, to make him happy. I think, maybe, that he sometimes gets dizzy watching you."

Johanna rocked in silence, trying to understand what her grandmother had meant. Finally the old woman spoke again. "I've got *Kaffee Kuchen* for you inside, and a present." She stood. "Take it, then go home to your husband. Perhaps he's waiting up for you."

The inside of the house where Johanna had grown up had hardly changed in the thirteen years since she had moved away. The biggest difference was that her father was no longer there except on weekends. Two years before, after an accident that had pinned him under the wheels of his silage wagon for three hours, he had quit farming to take a job with the Farm Bureau in a town eighty miles away, and the aroma of his pipe and the sound of his cheerful whistle no longer filled the house. To compensate, Johanna and her two aunts paid visits every day to check on Grandmother Schaumbacher, and David and one of Johanna's uncles split the land and farmed it, sharing the profits with her father.

This evening the smell of coffee cake made up for the lack of pipe smoke. Wednesday was Grandmother Schaumbacher's day to bake. The sourdough starter that was the basis for all her creations had been brought with *her* mother from Germany, used, replenished, then used and replenished again, for more years than anyone could trace. It was a piece of history, fueling enough breads and coffee cakes in its time to feed a small nation. And as befitted such an important institution, the starter had been christened *die Mutter*, German for "the mother," because it had birthed so many wonderful baked goods from its yeasty depths. No one knew who was responsible for the name; indeed, no one knew exactly how *die Mutter* had begun. But now Johanna's aunts each had their own share of it, hoarding it to pass down to their children.

"I made a smaller batch than usual," Grandmother Schaumbacher said, making her way to the counter as if her sight were fully intact. "I had to save more of *die Mutter*, because I'm giving you your own to take home with you tonight. I won't always be around to bake for you, Johanna. You must learn to care for *die Mutter* yourself."

Johanna had always known that someday she would be given her own share of the rich yeast-laden batter. It was a ritual, an inheritance bestowed from generation to generation. She would use it in the years to come, and she would remember the smell of her grandmother's kitchen and the love that had been baked into every piece of bread, every crumb of coffee cake.

But she wasn't ready for it yet. *Die Mutter* was one more thing to care for. Right now she had more than she could handle.

"She will give you one hundred times what you give her," Grandmother Schaumbacher said, as if she were reading Johanna's mind. "There is only one thing you must remember. *Die Mutter* must be replenished. You must feed her weekly. If you don't, she will starve and die.''

Johanna knew she couldn't turn down this gift. It was much too important. "I've watched you take care of it for years," she said, hugging her grandmother who still, even bent with age, was taller than she was. "I know what to do."

"You haven't watched closely enough," Grandmother Schaumbacher said mysteriously. "But maybe doing, not watching, is what you need."

Johanna didn't ask what her grandmother meant. The old woman often spoke in riddles, believing that digging for answers made them more precious. Instead she tried to sound grateful. "I know David and the boys will be happy I can bake for them now."

"*Die Mutter* is for you, Johanna, not for David and the boys. It won't be good for them if it's not good for you."

Half an hour later Johanna was entering her own kitchen door, covered crock and foil-wrapped pan of coffee cake tucked securely under her arm. She thought she understood what her grandmother had meant. If she treated the starter as just one more burden, no one in the family could really enjoy what she made from it. She had to show enthusiasm, even if she didn't feel any.

She climbed the stairs after storing both the coffee cake and *die Mutter* in the refrigerator. The boys were all asleep, as angelic now as they had been devilish earlier. Grant still slept with the tattered plush beagle that had been his most prized possession as a baby. Peter, in the bed across the room, had already kicked off his covers, and although Johanna pulled them over him once more, she knew that as soon as she left he would kick them off again.

John, in his own room, slept as if his life depended on it—just the way he did everything else.

Johanna washed and changed into her nightgown in the bathroom. Since she often went to sleep after David, she was used to tiptoeing to bed and gently sliding in between the sheets to keep from waking him. Tonight she walked quietly across the old wooden floor, avoiding the spots where it chronically squeaked, and lifted the blanket.

"Did you have a nice visit with your grandmother?" David murmured as she settled in beside him.

"I did. She was as feisty as usual."

"I know. I stopped by and saw her this morning."

Johanna wasn't surprised that David had seen her grandmother. He stopped to visit her every day if he could. She *was* surprised that he was awake, however. "I thought you'd be dead to the world," she told him, moving closer to absorb his warmth.

"I couldn't get to sleep."

She wondered if he was thinking about the baby, or even if he was wishing that he'd sold the farm all those years ago and found a different life for himself. "Would you like a back rub?" she offered.

"I had something else in mind." David reached for her, sliding his arms around her until she rested fully against him.

David never failed to excite Johanna. She loved him so much that no matter how tired she was, he awoke a response in her. Tonight she needed him more than she ever had. She wondered if he knew. "I'm glad you stayed awake," she whispered against his ear. "You can sleep anytime."

He made quick work of her nightgown and quicker work of any lingering sadness. With his lips on hers and his hands traveling all the familiar pathways, she was quickly ready for lovemaking. David was in no hurry, though. He had always been considerate, never rushing her to completion, but tonight he was more than considerate. He took exquisite care to arouse her.

How was it possible that two people who had grown up and married as friends could drop friendship and become soul-shattering, dimension-altering lovers when they were in bed together? It was one of the mysteries of her marriage that Johanna had never solved.

Now, as David's lips found hollows and planes where they had been a thousand times before, she held him to her, threading her fingers in his sun-lightened hair and moaning softly in response. She loved him with a force that sometimes threatened to tear her apart; she needed him with a desperation born of years of yearning.

When David finally entered her, her body was so in tune with his that they moved together perfectly, wordlessly, in the familiar rhythm, giving, taking, rising closer to the peak until finally, locked tightly together, they found their mutual pleasure. Then, and only then, did they speak again.

"I guess we won't be able to do this much longer." David cuddled Johanna drowsily against him.

She yawned. "No? Why not?"

"The baby."

She smiled a little. "Since when did that stop us?"

David was silent for a while. Then he spoke. "I don't know why we didn't guess, Jo. Your body has changed already."

"I thought I was just gaining weight. I've been eating more."

"You'll be in maternity clothes soon."

"I gave them all away. I'll have to make more."

"You really didn't plan this child, did you?"

The question was so strange that she came rudely awake. "Of course I didn't. Do you think I'd plan something like this without consulting you?"

"You love children."

"I love this farm, too, but I sure don't want another one."

David didn't know what made him continue: guilt; despair that he might lose this special closeness with Johanna when the baby came; the age-old desire to blame problems on someone else; possibly even the hope that somehow they could talk, share their feelings for once, and comfort each other. Whatever it was, he couldn't seem to keep silent. "The boys are growing up. I know you miss having a little one underfoot."

"At times, maybe." Johanna lifted her face to his. "But I hadn't thought about having another baby, and I can't believe you'd think I might have done it on purpose. You were there the night of Farley's birthday, remember? You're a farmer. It takes fertile ground *and* a seed."

He had been there, all right, and his guilt was overwhelming. "I know the facts of life."

"You don't want this baby, do you?"

David was silent. She gulped softly and turned away from him. He wanted to comfort her, but he couldn't answer, because he didn't know. He knew he wanted Johanna, but she wouldn't understand that. She had married a way of life, a plot of ground. She loved him because he had given her those things. But she wouldn't understand his need for her, his deepest desire that she be totally his. And even if she could understand, he had no way to tell her. The words wouldn't come from his farmer's soul. He and Johanna had never talked that way. In fact, if they weren't talking about the crops or their sons, they weren't talking.

"Jo," he said finally, "I couldn't *not* want my own baby. It's just that..." His voice trailed off. *I want you more.*

"The baby will just be one more burden, won't it?"

David could hear the tears in her voice. He gathered her close, even though she resisted. "These are hard times, but we'll manage."

She wanted their life together to be more than managing. She wanted so much more, but there was no way to voice those things to David. She would only embarrass both of them. She sniffed. "If we're going to *manage*, we'll both need some sleep."

David could feel how stiff she was. He felt sorry for her, for himself, and for the baby who was growing innocently inside her. His hands slid down her side and rested on her abdomen. Soon he would feel his child moving against his palm. It would be a miracle, as it had been each time. A child was always a miracle, even if that miracle wasn't appreciated. "Sleep tight, Jo," he whispered, rubbing slow circles on her belly.

It took time, but when Johanna finally fell asleep, his hand was still soothing her.

Chapter Three

The maternity top Johanna slipped over her head was the soft gold of the first two cuts of alfalfa hay, now dried, baled and stored in the hayloft in the barn. Her green elastic-paneled skirt was the color of the shoulder-high corn growing like green waves across the rolling countryside.

In the mirror over her dresser she caught sight of a face prominently freckled from the summer sun. The hands that rose to tie back her sun-bleached hair were callused and chapped from the bushels of weeds she had mercilessly pulled from the half-acre vegetable garden. She was the picture of good health and vitality. Only her eyes, red-rimmed and haunted, signaled a different story.

Summer was almost over. Inside Johanna, the baby was growing and moving, but everything else in her life seemed to have come to a standstill. David was a phantom creature who mysteriously appeared for meals and bedtime but was otherwise absent. Home from school, the boys found new and increasingly innovative ways to avoid working but no new ways to avoid fighting. The garden grew an abundant crop of weeds, but the first crop of beans came and went so fast that the pods were too tough to eat by the time Johanna realized her sons had neglected to harvest most of them.

In the nine years since she had last been pregnant, she had forgotten how the new life growing inside her could sap her strength, distend her body and affect her emotions. Squatting to weed the garden was like lowering a piano from a second-story window. Bending to harvest was like playing double-dare-you with the force of gravity.

Her emotions were even more precarious. She cried over sentimental diaper commercials, yet the tears for her own predicament were frozen inside her. She longed for David's touch, yet she felt too misshapen and unattractive to let him know. She struggled through each day hoping the next would be better and that David would somehow miraculously assure her that no matter how large she grew, how swollen her ankles, how awkward her waddle, he loved her anyway.

That day hadn't yet come. This morning, as she finished her hair, she wondered if it ever would. In the months since she had told him about the baby, David had grown quieter and more distant. He never complained, but—almost worse—he never mentioned the child, as if it didn't matter that in six weeks he would be holding his new son or daughter in his arms.

Johanna wanted to reach out to him, but for once there was nothing inside her to give. She was drained and empty and so tired that even getting out of bed in the mornings was a battle. She had taken to sleeping an extra fifteen minutes while David showered, getting downstairs just before he did to start the coffee and fry eggs. Breakfast was less elaborate than it had been before her pregnancy, but the extra rest helped her get through the day.

This morning she was halfway down the stairs before she realized that David was already in the kitchen. She felt a pang of guilt that he had begun to prepare his own meal. Pans were rattling and silverware clattering when she entered the room.

"You beat me." She sounded exactly the way she felt. She was exhausted, and the day hadn't even started.

"Not hard to do these days."

Johanna frowned at the censure in his voice. She followed him with her eyes as he expertly gathered eggs, bread and milk from the refrigerator. "What are you doing, David?"

"I can't wait around all day for you to decide to get up. I'm fixing my breakfast."

"It's only five in the morning," she said softly. "And I'm up."

He didn't even turn. "The new windrower blade came in yesterday. Farley's going to help me get it on this morning, and I'm not going to keep him waiting. Both of us have farms to run, Jo. You know what it's like this time of year!"

"I didn't know about the blade. You didn't—"

"What's the point?" he exploded. "You don't listen to half the things I say."

"I get ten words a day from you," she said, straightening a little. "You're saying I only hear five?"

"I'm saying your mind's usually somewhere else."

She didn't even bother to remind him that she was pregnant and naturally tired from the extra burden she carried. "It's a busy time for me, too. With the boys out of school it seems like I'm driving them back and forth to baseball or Scout activities every minute. The vegetables are coming in faster than I can put them up—"

David cracked eggs into a cast-iron skillet. "Then don't let me get in your way, Jo. I know how to cook."

Tears sprang to her eyes, but she wouldn't let David see her cry. She blinked them away. "I'll make coffee and toast," she said carefully. "You'll be out of here faster if I help."

They worked in silence until breakfast was ready and on the table. Johanna took one slice of toast; what little appetite she'd awakened with was gone after their fight.

David's appetite was gone, too, but he knew that if he didn't eat, he would suffer for it later. His was a job that demanded all the calories he could consume. As he ate he watched Johanna, who was staring at her coffee cup.

He wished he could call back his angry words. She had slept an extra fifteen minutes, fifteen minutes she certainly needed, and he had treated her like a criminal. But he was no fool. He knew where his feelings came from. Johanna's sleeping late was one more sign that she was backing away from him. They had three noisy sons and a life that sometimes demanded more than it gave. The only time they had together, just the two of them alone, was the few peaceful minutes they spent before they started their day. Now Johanna was sacrificing that time as if it meant nothing.

Baseball and the vegetable garden and Scouts. All those things were more important to Johanna than time spent with her husband. Under stress, her priorities became apparent. Once the baby arrived their time together would vanish like hay under the blade of a windrower.

"David?"

He realized he had been staring at her without really seeing her. He lowered his eyes to his plate.

"I know this is a busy time," she continued. "I'll be sure your breakfast is ready when you come down from now on."

"I know you need the sleep," he said gruffly. "I can manage."

She wondered what they would do without that word in their vocabulary. She blinked back tears again and changed the subject. "Will you be able to use the windrower after you get the new blade installed?"

He nodded as he finished the last bite of his eggs, then stood and carried his plate to the sink. "With some luck. The weather's just right to make the third cut. Low humidity, windy, sunny. If I can get it all cut today, I can get Farley and the Derrick boys to help me bale on Friday."

"Do you remember when I used to help you bale?" she asked wistfully. "Up until Peter was born?"

He leaned against the sink, and for a moment his face lit with a smile as he remembered. "You were the best baler driver I ever had."

"Is that so? That's not what you told me in those days."

"Doesn't pay to flatter the farmhands. You might have asked for a raise."

"It seems to me I had everything I'd ever wanted. What could I have asked for?"

He sobered. "What about all the things you never got to have?"

Johanna was puzzled. "Like what?"

David was serious now. "A college education. Fun. A chance to figure out who you were."

She wondered if those were things *he* had missed. "I had a chance for those things," she reminded him. "And so did you. We both made the choices we wanted to... At least, I always thought we did."

"And now?"

"I don't know. I don't know what I'd change." She tried unsuccessfully to read his expression. "How about you?"

"It doesn't do any good to worry about it, does it?"

She knew he was right. David was an honorable man. Even if he believed he had made a mistake all those years ago, there was nothing he would do about it now. He was a married man who was devoted to his three sons, and he had poured enough sweat and tears into his farm to be bound to it forever.

The stomping of feet at the back door saved her from having to answer. Farley pushed the screen door open and came in through the laundry-room door. "You gonna stand there gabbin' all day with your missus, or you gonna git out here and fix this windrower?" Without taking a breath he turned to Johanna. "Don't have time for coffee, but thanks just the same for askin'."

"I'll bring some out later," Johanna promised. "And coffee cake."

"Not yer grandma's coffee cake?"

"Same recipe."

"That little gal spoils you," Farley told David as they left to go fix the windrower. "Spoils you like a man deserves to be spoiled."

Johanna listened hard, but David didn't answer. She wasn't surprised. These days David only saw what she *didn't* do. He was blind to how hard she worked and how much she wanted to please him.

She was suddenly sadder than she had ever been in her life. She rested her head in her hands and fought back tears, but they slipped down her cheeks anyway. The baby chose that moment to give an extra hard kick, whether to torment or comfort she didn't know, but it was the last straw. She sobbed as if David had kicked her instead.

She had never pretended to herself that David had fallen deeply in love with her over the years. Somehow she had convinced herself that what they shared—common values, affection, childhood memories—was more important to a good marriage than romantic love. Now she wondered how she could have fooled herself for so long. What should have been the central core of their relationship had never existed. And when times got tough, values, affection and memories were not enough to sustain them.

The tears were cleansing. Surprisingly, she felt stronger for having cried them. When she was finished she lifted her head and saw beams of sunlight pouring in through the window that looked over the farmyard. She wasn't superstitious; she didn't believe in signs, but somehow, the sunlight made it easier to face the rest of the morning.

She had washed her face, dusted and straightened the house and finished mixing the coffee cake by the time the boys came down for breakfast. As she had feared, the sourdough starter given to her by her grandmother had become one more thing she had to care for, one more burden. Still, *die Mutter* had more redeeming value than just the wonderful baked goods she made from it. It was true that she had to faithfully take care of *die Mutter* or it would die, but it was also true that when she worked with it she relaxed and enjoyed what she was doing. And when she was finished she had a great feeling of satisfaction, as if she and all the women before her who had used *die Mutter* were part of something larger, a chain of mothers winding from one century into another, feeding their families and upholding family values.

Which was, she knew, a rather broad abstraction to stick on a crock of smelly ancient dough.

"Mom, Peter hit me when I was coming down the stairs," Grant singsonged.

"Mom, John hit me when I was coming down the stairs," Peter singsonged in answer.

"And who hit you, John?" Johanna asked as she pushed the coffee cake into the center of the oven and closed the oven door.

"Nobody hit me, but Grant wanted to," John said, wiping the rim of the sugar bowl with his index finger and popping it into his mouth.

Johanna turned and saw her sons for the first time. Each one of them was dressed in a Scout T-shirt and his best shorts. For a moment she was overwhelmed by how handsome they were, how strong and sturdy. And then she was just overwhelmed.

"Aren't you a little overdressed for your chores?" she asked, dreading their answers.

"No time for chores this morning," John said, as if they had agreed he would be spokesman. "They're starting Scout camp today at Weavers' Farm. We're supposed to be there by eight to help set up tables. Lenny's mom is gonna give us a ride over, and you're supposed to bring us home. Don't you remember?"

"I don't remember because you didn't tell me," Johanna said reasonably.

"Well, it starts today, even if I didn't tell you," John said, just as reasonably.

"And we've gotta eat so we can go," Peter added.

"And we can't be late or *you'll* have to give us a ride," Grant chimed in.

"Why didn't you tell me this last night so I could have gotten you up early enough to finish your work?" Johanna asked.

Three pairs of shoulders rose in identical shrugs.

During the school year the boys' chores were minimal but important. Among the three of them, they checked the calves and mother cows in the pasture near Jack Salmon Creek and distributed hay. They brought milk and pork liver to the cat and kittens who lived in the barn, fed corn to the dozen or so chickens, collected eggs, kept the wood box filled for the cavernous fireplace in the living room that helped heat the house, and assisted their father, if he needed them for special projects.

During the summer, their chores were more extensive and even more important. Unlike many farmers, the Groves grew most of their own food. Farley liked to tease Johanna that she made David farm like a back-to-the-land city boy, but she was convinced that what she and David and the boys could grow was healthier than what they could buy cheaper—if you counted their labor—at the grocery store. So in addition to the garden, the Grove farm had a small orchard with apples, peaches, cherries and a century-old pear tree, a raspberry patch, a blackberry patch, and wild gooseberries for the taking.

The boys were responsible for many of the garden chores. John and Peter could run the small tiller that kept the walkways free of weeds, and all of them were supposed to help with fertilizing, mulching and harvesting. In reality, more often than not Johanna did her share of all the chores and theirs, too.

Today she could see that was exactly what they were expecting again. Some faint flicker of rebellion, lit by her fight with David and nurtured, not extinguished, by her tears, made her shake her head.

"Sorry, boys, but you're not leaving to go anywhere until your chores are done."

"There just isn't time," John said patiently, as if he were speaking to a very small child. "We'll be late if we do, and besides, you don't want to have to give us a ride, do you?"

Johanna wondered when they had become so manipulative. Had it happened all at once? By degrees? Where had she been?

Where had she been? God Almighty, where had she been for thirteen long years?

If it was true that there was a sucker born every minute, then she had lots of company. But truly, was there anyone in the world who had been as big a sucker as Johanna Schaumbacher Groves?

"Mom, we've gotta eat so we can go!"

Johanna didn't even notice which boy had spoken. Suddenly they seemed one entity, a seamless lump of flesh with one purpose in life: to get what they wanted, no matter what the cost to her.

And she wasn't going to take it anymore.

"I am not giving you a ride, boys," she said calmly, although she was not feeling at all calm inside. "And I am not doing your chores. You are not leaving to go anywhere until you've finished them, all of them. Then, if you're still interested in going to camp, you can walk. From this moment on, I'm on strike."

There was a stunned silence. Then they all started to talk at once.

Johanna didn't hear what they were saying. She watched their mouths move as if she were watching television with the sound turned down. Three sons. Three strong sons, each a part of her and David. She had rocked them, nursed them, gotten up in the night with them to soothe and comfort. Then, as they had grown, she had continued to give the same, extraordinarily devoted attention.

And who comforted her? Who soothed her? Who devoted his life to her?

Nobody.

It was that simple, that sad, and that spine-stiffening. If a sucker could be born every minute, one died every minute, too. And the sucker inside her was about to face execution.

She held up her hands for silence, waiting until she had gotten it. "You know what has to be done. Now get busy." Then, with the first real smile to light her face in months, she turned and started out of the room.

"Where are you going?" a dismayed Peter demanded. "Lenny's mom will be here any minute!"

She tossed her head. It felt good, and she did it again. "I'm going to call Lenny's mom and save her a trip. And I'm going to ask her if she's been a sucker, too. Maybe she'd like to go on strike with me."

She could still hear the alarmed buzz of voices as she climbed the stairs to her bedroom. She wasn't without guilt, but it was a faint flutter inside her compared to another feeling.

Overwhelming relief.

The new blade for the windrower was fifteen feet of razor-sharp serrated teeth. David had spent most of the previous afternoon removing the old blade. Now that job seemed simple in comparison to replacing it. He and Farley had been pushing, prying and cursing for most of an hour to get the blade through the guards and in place.

Now they stood back to examine their handiwork.

"Blade's too long," Farley said at last. "By a foot. Sent you the wrong blade."

"Well, let's take it off, wrap it up and send it back," David said.

Farley chortled. He knew David was kidding, although there was no humor in the other man's voice. "Can you take care of it from here?"

"You go on home. It won't be too bad. I'll just take the extra off with my torch. At least the bolt holes fit."

"Yeah, you're as lucky as a man can git."

"Lucky's the word. Now maybe I won't have to cut hay today. I can just relax with my old blowtorch."

"Do it outside in the shade. This shop's already an oven."

"Dad!"

Both men turned as John came running through the open door. "Dad, it's Mom!"

For a moment David felt weak with dread. It was at times like these, when something seemed to threaten Johanna, that he realized the full measure of his love for her. "What is it?" He wiped his greasy hands on his overalls as he started toward John. "Is it the baby?"

"Baby?" John seemed surprised, almost as if the word were foreign. "No, she's acting crazy!"

"Get to the point, son."

"She's upstairs lying in bed reading the paper. And she says she won't drive us to Scout camp. She told us we had to walk! All the way to Weavers' farm! And you know we have to go. My badge depends on my being there!"

"Is she feeling bad? Maybe she's sick." David started through the door.

"She's not sick. I went up and asked her!" John grabbed his father's arm. "She says she feels better than she has in months. She says she's tired of doing things for us."

David felt as if someone had just knocked him to the floor for the count. Johanna was not only backing away from him, she was backing away from their sons. Didn't she want any of them anymore?

"Looks like the spoiling is over," Farley said from behind David. "Sure had something fine while it lasted, though, didn't you?"

"I've got to go up to the house," David said.

"Don't you be hard on that little gal. She's got that baby to think about."

"She's got a family to think about."

John put David's worst fears into words for him. "Mom says she's got herself to think about! What did she mean, Dad?"

"I don't know," David said grimly, "but I guess I'm about to find out."

Chapter Four

David had always loved Johanna. From the day his mother died, Johanna had been the ray of feminine sunshine in his all-male world. As a child she had made pretend tea for him, serving it in her tiny china tea set with the perfect manners of a grand dame with heirloom porcelain. She had taught him to wrap her dolls in receiving blankets, to feed and burp them. She had carpeted their tree house with rag rugs and adorned its windows with gingham curtains. And when he had watched his blue-ribbon 4-H calf being led away by its new owner, she had held his hand tightly, shedding the tears he wasn't allowed to cry.

As a teenager, David had still loved Johanna. She had needed *his* friendship then. She had been terribly shy, and only with him had she come out of her shell. He had loved other girls, too, passionately and temporarily, but it was only with Johanna that he could share his feelings—although the *full* range wasn't shared until she was eighteen and slipping away from him.

David had never expected Johanna to be pretty. Her looks had simply never mattered to him. She had an innate sweetness that soothed his male soul, and it was her sweetness, her shy sense of humor and her warmth and vulnerability, that drew him to her. David had never really thought of a future with Johanna, but he had never thought of one without her, either. Then Mother Nature had pushed the issue.

One day Johanna was the freckled, lovable gawky girl who lived on the farm next door. The next she was a ravishing beauty who was guaranteed to steal the heart of every man who looked at her. It never occurred to David that he was looking at her through the eyes of love, that perhaps not everyone was as smitten as he was. He only knew that he couldn't see enough of her, couldn't talk to her enough, and that when he left her at night to return to his silent house, he couldn't dream about her enough.

He'd known better than to surprise her with his sudden ardor. She was still shy, and she trusted him as she trusted no one else. He was caught in an agony of his own making. They had been friends for so long that he was terrified to risk losing what was now the most important relationship he had. Fear and bone-deep reticence wouldn't allow him to speak. Yet he knew that he couldn't continue holding her hand when what he wanted most was to hold her in his arms.

One night he realized that time had slipped away from him. Johanna was going off to college, and he was staying behind. He was torn between an unselfish love that told him Johanna needed to go, needed to explore the world and face an array of choices about her future, and a purely selfish love that told him to snare Johanna and keep her by his side.

Selfish love had won. He had needed her, desired her, too much to let her go. Surprisingly, she hadn't been hard to convince. They had been friends forever. Johanna was loyal and giving. All he'd had to do was tell her that he needed her and she had given up her future for him. She had accepted his kisses and, later, his lovemaking with an innocence that proclaimed how little she knew of the world of men and women. And she had accepted the humble life he offered with that same innocence.

Now, as David strode toward the farmhouse that had been their home together for thirteen years, he wondered if, at last, Johanna realized what he had done to her.

Had she finally realized the sacrifice he had asked her to make? Did she know what she had given up so she could cook for him, bear his children, clean his house and do endless, thankless farm chores? Sometimes, in his worst nightmares, he dreamed that Johanna finally understood that he had stolen her life. That she left him, taking the warmth, the color, the joy from his.

As he washed his hands, then climbed the stairs to his bedroom, he felt as if he were living that nightmare. He almost expected to find her packing. He didn't expect to find her sleeping.

She was, though. Her cheeks were slightly flushed, and her eyelashes were golden-brown crescents against them. She was breathing slowly, and her hands were clasped on the huge mound of her belly.

He lowered himself gently to the bed so as not to awaken her. He needed to touch her, to reassure himself that she was still there. His hand floated above her hair, then landed, gently stroking the long strands. He often took this intimacy for granted. Now it was as if he were touching her hair for the first time. It was as soft as corn silk, and it clung to his callused finger-tips.

Her eyelids fluttered open. She looked at him as if she didn't know where she was or why.

"Johanna?" he said softly. "Are you ill?"

"I don't think so," she murmured, unconsciously turning her cheek toward his hand. She didn't know what she had done to deserve being petted this way, but she wasn't about to let the opportunity slip away.

"What's going on, then?" David stroked the back of his fingers across her cheek.

Memories of what was going on began to come back to her. She was in bed, in the middle of the morning, not by mistake but on purpose. And she wasn't sick or in labor or giving birth. She was in bed just because that was where she wanted to be.

How was she going to explain it to David?

"I'm resting," she began.

"Are you sure you're not sick?"

Johanna scrutinized the expression on his face. It was close to panic. Had she really always been so strong, so omniscient, that resting now was equated with illness? And why did David seem so worried? She had expected anger, not terror.

"I'm tired," she reassured him. "Tired all the way down to my toes."

"You've never been tired before."

She wondered if she should let him believe that. For a moment pride asserted itself and tried to convince her to tell him that, at least till now, she *had* been the superwoman he seemed to believe in. Honesty asserted itself harder.

"I've been tired a lot," she said. "Some days I wasn't sure I could put one foot in front of the other. Today I really couldn't."

She struggled to sit up, and it wasn't an easy task with a watermelon-sized mound of flesh precisely at the place where she was supposed to bend.

"I know you work hard—"

She waved away both his words and his helping hand. "I work *too* hard." The fight with the boys was now clear in her mind, and she wanted to share it with David right away. "I work harder than I have to, and I'm not going to do it anymore. I told your sons I'm on strike, and I meant it."

David stared at her. She hadn't left him, not physically. But the love she had felt for her family seemed to be fading away. He felt a stab of anger that was almost as painful as his fear.

"Do you know how often I do their chores?" she continued, flushing a little under his gaze. "More than half the time, that's for sure. They run over me, David, because they know they can. What's that teaching them about women? What am I doing to the poor girls they'll marry?"

"You've never exactly been a feminist." David's voice had a decided edge. "Why now?"

"There's no substance that won't resist if it's finally pushed up against a wall. Even water leaves a puddle!"

David looked at her as if she had lost her mind.

Johanna flushed a deeper red. "Did the boys tell you what they did?"

He shook his head curtly.

"They planned to go to Scout camp this morning and didn't tell me. Then they got up just late enough so that they couldn't do their chores before they went. They expected me to do them. Look at me...." She held her blouse away from her bloated belly. "I'm six weeks away from having a baby, and they think I should go out there and bend and shovel and—"

"They weren't asking to go down to the swimming hole. Scout camp is important."

For a moment Johanna couldn't believe she had heard him right. "And I'm not?" she asked softly.

"Of course you are. But they're just kids, and kids are lazy!"

"My kids aren't going to be lazy anymore." Johanna put her hand on David's shoulder. It was as unyielding as the side of their barn. "I always cover for them, David. There's nothing they really have to do, and they know it. As long as it stays that way, I'll do their chores until they leave home, and they'll end up worthless, lazy adults. And *I'll* continue being exhausted."

David didn't hear what she was saying. All he could hear was the sound of her voice as she said goodbye. She had grown tired of all of them. Soon she would be leaving. He moved away from her so that she was no longer touching him. "So you told the boys they could hike to the Weavers' farm? That's going to cure their laziness?"

"I told them if they missed their ride while they were doing their chores, they could walk. What would I be teaching them if I drove them? I'd be rescuing them again. I'm tired of rescuing them."

"Maybe you're just tired of *them*. Maybe you're just tired of all of us."

This time Johanna was the one to stare.

David stood and began to pace the room. "So now you're on strike."

When she'd said the words earlier they had seemed terribly silly. Now, faced with David's anger, they sounded even sillier. Yet she couldn't take them back. She was feeling her way, but there was something vital here that she couldn't renege on.

"I'll do everything I have to do for our survival. I'll cook because we have to eat, but anyone who misses a meal because he's too busy to come to the table can go hungry."

David stopped pacing. "Well, you've thought this out thoroughly, haven't you?"

She hadn't, but once started she was in no mood to quit. "I'll clean the house, but if anyone messes it up, it will stay that way until he straightens it up again."

"What else?" he demanded.

"I'll put up whatever comes out of the garden, but if the boys forget to pick the vegetables, then I'll go to the store and we'll eat whatever the commercial growers harvested this year." She paused and then went on. "And as sorry as I feel for the animals, I'm not feeding another one. The boys will have to deal with the sad eyes of the calves and the yowls of the kittens."

David exploded. Her message was clear, and he didn't want to hear any more. "Why don't I go on strike, too?" He was almost shouting. "I can quit doing all the extra little things I do to make our lives better. How would you like that?"

"I'd like it just fine!" she shouted back. "Maybe we'd see you once in a while, David! Maybe you'd have the time and energy to be a husband and a father!"

The room was suddenly silent. David's face drained of color, but his eyes were two burning coals. "A husband and father provides for his family," he said at last. "If that's not enough for you, Jo, maybe you married the wrong man." He turned on his heel and left the room.

Johanna sat still, stunned, until minutes later when she heard the rumble of their station wagon. She stood and walked to the window just in time to see David and the boys driving away. Even from a distance, she could tell that the boys were still wearing their Scout shirts and that the car was heading in the direction of the Weaver farm.

Johanna's anger carried her all the way up until the noon meal. She forced herself to stay in bed and hem a square-dance skirt for a woman in Junction who was paying her to finish it. She enjoyed sewing, and she had always been good at it. Her reputation as a seamstress brought her more work than she had time to do, and her small but steady income had often bought luxuries for the family that they wouldn't otherwise have had.

Now she found little pleasure in her work. David's words echoed through her head as if he were still in the room shouting at her. As the time passed, her anger changed to guilt, then sadness.

David was a wonderful husband and father. He worked long and hard at an inglorious, unstable profession, and he never complained. If anyone had reason to go on strike, it was David. And what would any of them do if he did?

What would she do if she had to take over David's chores as well as do her own? They had a partnership, each pulling all the weight they could bear. The balance was always precarious; they were always busy. If she went on strike, then David would be forced to do more. She loved him too much to tolerate that.

Yet wasn't she doing what was best for them all by forcing the boys to be responsible? In the long run, wouldn't she be easing David's burden? If she wasn't spoiling the boys, wouldn't there be more time to help David on the farm?

Her arguments were circular. Just when she thought she had an answer, she realized she was right back where she had started.

Finally, the only thing she was sure of was that sitting in bed thinking about the fight wouldn't resolve it. She had to talk to David and make him understand that she was doing what was best for everyone. If he supported her they might see results soon. If he didn't . . .

The coffee cake had been finished hours before. Now she rose and brushed her hair before she went downstairs to slice a large piece to take out to David with some hot coffee. Because she had spent the morning upstairs, the noon meal was going to be a little late. The coffee cake would tide him over until then, and it wasn't a bad peace offering.

On her way out the door she passed the crock where she kept *die Mutter*. The process for keeping it alive was simple. The evening before Johanna was going to bake, she took *die Mutter* from the refrigerator, put it in a large bowl and added flour and warm water. Then she set the bowl in a warm place away from drafts. The next morning she took a cup or two of the resulting batter and put it back in the refrigerator in the starter crock, to use the next time she baked. The rest of the batter went into her coffee cake, along with more flour and other ingredients. As long as she replenished *die Mutter* that way, it continued to live and grow.

Johanna paused, staring at the crock. It should have been in the refrigerator. Something told her to look inside. *Die Mutter* should have been rising there, bubbling gently in yeasty glory. Instead the crock was empty.

She had been so preoccupied this morning that she had added every bit of *die Mutter* to the coffee cake. She hadn't held any back. Now there would be no more sourdough bread or coffee cake unless Grandmother Schaumbacher trusted her with a new starter.

She felt the ridiculous urge to cry. She felt as though she had failed a long line of women, none of whom, she was sure, had ever forgotten to save enough starter to begin a new round of baking. She stood alone. Only she had used up all of *die Mutter* and saved nothing for the future.

Used up. As she went to find David she couldn't get those two words out of her mind. Used up. They seemed to have significance. Until this morning hadn't she allowed *herself* to be used up, again and again, with barely enough left over to start each new day? By not saving *die Mutter*, hadn't she just replayed what happened to *her* every day of the week? She gave and gave, however unnecessarily, saving nothing of herself. She allowed herself to become exhausted, draining away her own health and vitality until she was running on empty.

Even now, with another confrontation with David ahead of her and the loss of *die Mutter* just behind her, she still had more energy than she remembered having for weeks. The enforced rest, rest that still sent tremors of guilt through her, had renewed her.

She wished she could think of a way to convey all this to David. But she was so out of practice at talking about her feelings that she wasn't sure how. Had she and David ever really talked about the way they felt? They had as children. They had shared dreams and plans for the future as only the young can do. Then, as they'd grown older, they had fallen into the roles of the men and women they knew. They no longer talked about what was inside them. They had lived together for thirteen years, but in the important ways, they were strangers.

She found David driving the windrower toward the creek. She took a short cut up the side of a steep hill and waited for him to catch up to her. As he neared, she watched the expert way he maneuvered the old machine. Their windrower had an open cockpit, exposing David to all the elements, and two levers for steering. Newer models were luxurious in comparison, with air-conditioning, a real steering wheel and power-assisted steering. Johanna longed to be able to afford something better for David, but all their equipment was old, draining his time and energy but not the contents of his pockets. David refused to buy on credit unless it was an emergency, and it was that old-fashioned, stubborn common sense that had saved them from foreclosure in the bad years.

He was a good farmer, and a good husband. And as he drew closer, easing off on the throttle and raising the cutter bar and reel before he switched off the ignition, she hoped she could find a way to let him know.

For a moment she wasn't sure David was going to get down. Then he swung his feet over the side and dropped to the ground.

"I see you got the new blade in," she said, holding out the coffee cake.

He shook his head, walking over to wash his hands at a hose beside a narrow irrigation ditch that flowed toward the creek before he accepted her offering.

"The blade's in," he said. "I just cut it to fit."

"Will you have time to get the hay today?"

"Looks like it, if I don't take a break for dinner."

"You'll be starving. Would you like me to bring something out?"

David didn't answer immediately. He examined her, as if he were seeing her for the first time. Then he spoke. "I thought you were on strike."

"You're still angry, aren't you?"

"I don't have time to be angry, Jo. I've got a farm to run and a family to feed. And now, I suppose, I've got your jobs to do, as well."

She could see that they weren't going to communicate. David was in no mood to listen. For a moment she was tempted to give up her pathetic little stand. It was only going to cause more problems, and in the long run that could only be more of a drain on her energy.

Then she remembered *die Mutter*, the starter that *wasn't* anymore, because she hadn't saved any of it. She had used it all up.

She didn't even know that she straightened her shoulders and stood a little taller. "You won't have my jobs to do," she said. "I've never said I won't do *my* jobs. I'm just not going to do anyone else's, and I'm through doing all the little unnecessary things no one appreciates."

David nodded his head. "It should be interesting to see what you think is unnecessary."

"This conversation will be at the top of the list." Johanna turned to go. She would wait until a better time to try to tell David how she felt.

She didn't see the anguish that crossed his face as she turned, and she couldn't read the thoughts that had tumbled through his head all morning. She didn't know the fear he felt, fear that the most wonderful thing in his life was ending.

When he spoke, she didn't know any of the things that fueled his words. "I wonder if this was the way your mother started, Jo. Did she go on strike before she left you and your father?"

She whirled, stunned that he would equate her with her mother. "This isn't the same thing, at all."

"Same thing, different clothing. She left physically. You're leaving emotionally. It all adds up to selfish."

"If selfish means I care about me and this child I'm carrying, then I guess I am!"

Guilt pierced the hard shell of his anger and the fears inside. For a moment he saw how tired she was, how unappreciated. He longed to reach out to her, to hold her and reassure her that he cared about her and the child. He longed to tell her that she was the most important thing in his life. He stepped forward, but she moved away.

"If selfish means I want to get up in the morning and feel like more than the hired help," she continued, "then I guess I am. But it seems to me, David Groves, that you are the one who's being selfish."

"Let's talk about unnecessary." David walked back to the windrower and leaned against the side, pouring himself a cup of coffee to warm the ice inside him.

"You don't want to talk, you want to lecture."

"No, I want to question. Is it unnecessary to clean the house?"

"No. But it's thoughtless of the boys to expect me to clean up their messes. I won't do it anymore."

"What about my messes? Greasy coveralls in the laundry room, muddy shoes on the porch, hair in the sink in the morning."

"Have I ever complained?"

"No, but it seems like maybe you've been saving it up."

"David, it's not you—"

"And what about meals?" David asked, ignoring her protest. "I come in late sometimes. You have to keep food warm or reheat it. You can't clean the kitchen until almost bedtime. Maybe all that's unnecessary."

"There is no point in talking to you. You're refusing to listen to me." Johanna turned to leave, but David's next words stopped her.

"And what about sleeping with me, Jo? How necessary is that? I assume you've got all the kids you want now. Maybe making love isn't necessary anymore. Maybe you'd get more rest if we didn't bother."

She didn't face him, because she didn't want him to see how much he had hurt her. When she spoke her voice was barely steady. "We hardly *bother*, anyway. A pregnant wife doesn't seem to turn you on."

"Jo—"

She ignored him. "Maybe *you* need to think about what's necessary and what isn't. There's more to life than this farm and how much corn you should grow and if the weather turns after the hay is cut. Maybe you need to think about what's necessary for your happiness. I know I'm going to, whether you like it or not."

She was halfway down the hill before she heard David's answer. "If you take me off your necessary list, Jo, don't worry about how it will affect me. I can manage just fine on my own, and you'll just have one less person to worry about. Maybe then you'll be happy."

Chapter Five

During the first week of Johanna's strike the living room was almost impossible to negotiate. She watched the mess pile higher until it reached a point where she couldn't stand it any longer. Then she tied a rope across the door to the living room and tacked up a sign with one word: "Condemned."

The living room was clean by suppertime that night. The meal itself was almost as interesting as the mysterious disappearance of books and papers, toys, games and miscellaneous clothing from the living-room floor. For the first time in Johanna's memory, everyone came to the table early, as if they were afraid the food might be snatched from under their noses if they didn't.

She wasn't sure if the early arrivals were due to the fried chicken with fluffy buttermilk biscuits and cream gravy that she was serving, or just the beginnings of respect. Whichever it was, the meal was the first one she had enjoyed since she and David fought in the field by the windrower. In fact, it was the first *thing* she had enjoyed.

David seemed to be enjoying it, too. She watched him from beneath her lashes like a shy young miss. He hadn't taken many meals with the family since their fight. He ate with them if his schedule permitted, but if he couldn't eat then he didn't touch the food she left out for him. She didn't know what he ate on those nights, but it wasn't the meals she prepared. And she couldn't ask, because the only time they spoke was to put up a front for the boys.

Now he seemed to have no qualms about serving himself seconds—or possibly thirds, she wasn't sure, it had happened so quickly. He ate like a starving man, and the food was disappearing as if inhaled. He caught her looking at him as he reached for another biscuit. For just a moment a smile turned his mouth from grim to wonderful. Then he looked down at his plate as he carefully broke the biscuit and spooned gravy over it.

She wanted to cry. The smile was the best thing that had happened to her in longer than she could remember. She wanted to return it; she wanted to throw her arms around him and beg him to talk to her again. She could do neither, but she did have another trick up her sleeve.

"I've got chocolate meringue pie for dessert," she said, standing to begin gathering plates.

David looked up and watched the way Johanna stood back from the table, leaning forward because their child, their unborn-but-not-for-long child, was in the way. In a moment he was on his feet. "Here, let me help," he said gruffly.

She got a chance to give him the smile she'd wanted to. Their eyes met and held for a moment. "Thank you," she said, "but you're not finished. I'll just clear enough to make room for the pie."

"We haven't had pie since Mom went on strike," Grant announced. "I guess pie's not *necessary*."

David frowned at Grant's words. He sat down to finish eating his biscuit. Johanna couldn't let what had almost been a warm moment end that way.

"It wasn't *necessary*," she agreed as she stacked plates. "I made the pie because I wanted to, and I wanted to because I know all of you like it. That's the best reason to do things, don't you think?"

Grant screwed up his face in thought. Johanna had the urge to kiss each childish wrinkle. "Is that like when we cleaned the living room this afternoon because we knew *you* wanted us to?" he asked.

She nodded. "Yes, sort of. Not because I told you to, not because you had to, but because you knew I'd like it. Because you love me."

Grant still looked serious. "Then does the pie mean that you still love us, Mom?"

She swallowed hard. "I could never *stop* loving you, Grant. Not any of you. But I love me, too, and I love our new baby. I have to take care of all of us the best way I know how."

John stood, stretching, as if that were the only thing on his mind. Then, nonchalantly, he gathered his plate and the serving platter of chicken and headed toward the kitchen.

Johanna watched her oldest son amble through the doorway. She would never doubt the possibility of miracles again.

During the second week of Johanna's strike she came downstairs later than usual one morning to discover a full bushel basket of green beans on the front porch and her three sons snapping them. She hadn't believed they knew how.

"Requirements for a new Scout badge?" she asked, ruffling Peter's hair.

"We don't like those canned beans from the store."

She hadn't known she was raising gourmets. How did they even know what the store's canned beans tasted like, anyway? She pondered this turn of events as she spoke. "I'll freeze these and we'll eat them through most of the fall."

"They won't last longer than that?" John seemed to be calculating beans and days and appetites.

"No, it takes all I plant to last through the winter, and this summer a lot of beans went to waste."

"What else will you have to buy?"

Johanna suspected that John had a career ahead of him in hotel management or accounting. "Well, we have plenty of corn, because your dad planted that back behind the barn and harvested it himself. And it's been a good year for tomatoes, so the ones that weren't harvested didn't hurt us too much."

Grant broke in. "I've picked bushels of tomatoes! Bushels! All by myself!"

Johanna smiled fondly at him. "Peppers didn't do as well as usual. We didn't have enough rain, but I've chopped and frozen enough to take us into the spring. The eggplant was probably the worst disaster."

As one body, the boys cheered.

Johanna was still laughing when David came out on the porch. She felt his presence before she saw he was there. Since she had gone on strike, he hadn't once touched her. She longed for him so much that even being close to him seemed a physical thing.

"What's the joke?" David asked.

"I think your sons sabotaged the eggplant."

"Boys after my own heart."

Johanna turned to see if he were kidding. "You don't like eggplant?"

David's answer was a face that was remarkably like the ones his sons were making.

Johanna made a face, too. "But you never told me!"

"You like it. I didn't want you to quit planting it on account of me."

"I *don't* like it. I've never liked it. I fix it because I thought it was one of your favorites."

"She was showing her love, Dad," Grant said, with a smirk. "And see, it was making you both sick!"

His parents ignored him. "What else don't you like?" Johanna asked. "And what other secrets have you been keeping?"

David hedged. "You were keeping a secret, too, Jo. What don't *you* like?"

She couldn't believe they were having this conversation in the midst of six avidly listening ears, but she wasn't about to stop, now that they had started. It was the first time they had talked in so long.

"I don't like lima beans."

"Me either," Grant put in. The other boys shushed him, fascinated by their parents' exchange.

"Why do you fix them, then?" David sprawled against a porch pillar, obviously enjoying himself.

"Because I thought you liked them. Was I wrong about that, too?"

"No, I like them. I just don't like them a lot. Not enough to grow them, that's for sure."

"They'll go on the compost along with the eggplants today." Johanna couldn't let David think he'd won. "Now it's your turn."

He thought a moment. "Kohlrabi," he said finally. "It tastes like overgrown radishes. I don't care if it prevents cancer or beriberi or athlete's foot. I'd rather take my chances."

"Kohlrabi's one of my favorites."

"Then *you* eat it. Plant some extra broccoli for me."

"I didn't think you liked broccoli. Last time I made it with my special cheese sauce, you didn't even touch it."

"I didn't like the cheese sauce," he explained. "Not the broccoli."

"Why didn't you tell me that?" Johanna put her hands on her hips, but she was smiling. "David, you don't tell me anything!"

"You work so hard to please me, I wouldn't hurt you for the world." The words were out of David's mouth before he had even thought about them. He realized they were true. But what other things hadn't they talked about because they were afraid of hurting each other? What other things were hidden because of the love they shared?

Love. In the past few weeks David had begun to realize the magnitude of his love for Johanna. He had never doubted it; he had just never probed its depths. Now he wondered if, after all, she loved him, too. Not loved as you love your best friend, but loved him as he loved her. She had always worked hard to please him; he had never realized how hard until the past weeks, when she had forced herself to slow down. Now he wondered why she had always tried so hard, if not for love.

"David, talking to me could never hurt me." Not unless you were telling me you didn't want me anymore, Johanna added silently. And that would be a wound from which she would never recover.

"You guys kiss and make up," Grant innocently insisted. "That's what they do on TV."

"You watch too many reruns," David said, but he put his hand tentatively on Johanna's shoulder and leaned over to brush a feather-light kiss across her lips.

"I'll plant an extra row of broccoli next spring." She was dazed and ridiculously happy.

"If I kiss you again, will I get two?"

"One and a half, and that's my final offer." She leaned toward him, and this time the kiss lasted for long, wonderful seconds.

"If *I* kiss you, will you promise not to plant any broccoli at all?" Peter asked.

Everyone was still laughing when David, whistling, went down the steps and out to begin hauling hay in from the fields.

During the third week of Johanna's strike she found the courage to tell her grandmother that she had mistakenly used all of *die Mutter* and needed more. They were sitting together on the Schaumbacher front porch, catching the cooling evening breeze as the sun dipped behind the horizon.

"And you think you're the only one of us who's used it all?" Grandmother Schaumbacher continued to rock steadily, as if the news were no surprise.

"I just wasn't thinking very clearly that morning," she admitted, relieved that her grandmother wasn't hurt.

"It's a wonder a woman can think clearly any morning, *Liebchen*. Children running back and forth, breakfast to fix, chores to do, husbands to flirt with."

"I was doing some of those things."

"You and David, you're not getting along these days?"

Johanna realized she was rocking hard enough to spin the poor baby in her womb. She stopped. "Grandmother, I've gone on strike."

Grandmother Schaumbacher began to laugh.

Amazingly Johanna found that she could laugh, too. She explained between deep, cleansing chuckles. "They were running me ragged. I was doing everything for everybody. I realized one day that I couldn't keep it up. Nobody really understands, but I think they're trying a little. The boys are picking up after themselves better and keeping up with the garden. No one's dared asked me to do their chores in two weeks." She held her stomach as more laughter tore through her. "Two whole weeks! It's a world's record."

The sun was gone before both women had sobered.

"I've wondered when you were going to see what was happening," Grandmother Schaumbacher said at last. "Better it's now than after the baby comes. You'll need all the help you can get."

"It was really *die Mutter* that made me see." Johanna told her grandmother how she had realized that she had become like the empty crock where the starter should have been. "There was just nothing left of me to keep going with," she finished. "Do you know what I mean?"

"I do, *Liebchen*. And now?"

Johanna tried to put her feelings into words. "Now? Well, I feel rested for the first time in longer than I can remember. I wake up in the morning with energy—not a lot, because of the baby—but some. And when I do things for the family, it's because I want to. I don't feel like I have to. And I guess because I'm not so busy I have more time to listen to the boys. Did you know that Peter wants to be a pilot? He wants to go to the Air Force Academy. He's always liked planes, but I had no idea he was so serious."

Grandmother Schaumbacher nodded. "He'll change his mind a dozen times, but this seriousness, it's good. He'll be somebody someday."

"David wanted to be a pilot once. Do you remember? When he was about Peter's age."

"How is David?"

Johanna began to rock again. "I don't know. Angry sometimes. A lot of times, I guess. He doesn't understand what I'm doing and why I'm doing it."

"He doesn't understand when he looks at you and sees the roses in your cheeks now?"

"I don't know."

"Come inside and I'll give you more of *die Mutter*."

Johanna was relieved to be finished talking about David. Despite those few moments of closeness when she'd thought they were about to come to an understanding, she and David were still miles apart. Talking about that distance was painful.

Inside, she stood at the counter as her grandmother measured out two cups of the familiar batter. "I've got plenty today, because I didn't feel like baking as much," she explained, putting *die Mutter* into a clean jar for Johanna to take home.

Johanna held out her hand, but her grandmother didn't give her the jar. "*Die Mutter*, she's a funny lady," Grandmother Schaumbacher mused, speaking, as she always did, as if the starter had human qualities. "You can use her all up, like you did, and she's all gone. Or you can feed her and watch her grow. The funny thing is that no matter how much *die Mutter* can give, she can't grow alone. Someone else has to feed her. She can't feed herself."

Johanna frowned. "Of course it can't. It doesn't have hands. It can't buy flour. It can't turn on the water."

"She's like all of us, isn't she? We can't grow alone. From time to time, someone *must* feed us. If someone doesn't we shrivel and die."

"Grandmother, are you feeling all right?" Johanna was concerned. Maybe her grandmother was trying to tell her that she wasn't being taken care of properly.

Grandmother Schaumbacher laughed. "Johanna, *Liebchen*, I feel wonderful. I'm fed daily by you and my daughters and your father when he's home. I'm fed by your visits and your smiles, because you know I need feeding. Who feeds you, Johanna?"

"I do. I'm taking care of myself now."

"That's not enough. Don't you see? To grow you have to let someone else take care of you sometimes. You can't put yourself in a warm, cozy place to rise and grow."

Johanna understood. "You feed me."

"But I won't always be here. Better you let those closest to you take over now."

"David?" Johanna asked.

"Of course. David. And the boys. You've fed them until they're fat with your feeding, not fat in their bodies, but fat in their hearts and souls. But you've never told them that you needed feeding, too. You've never let them feed you. That's what you must do now."

Johanna put her worst fear into words. "What if David doesn't care enough to feed me? What if he doesn't care at all?"

Johanna's German wasn't good enough to catch all that her grandmother replied, but it was good enough to get the gist of it. Johanna was a silly fool whose own nose was all she could see. She must learn to look beyond the tip of it to find her answers. "David cares," Grandmother Schaumbacher said, after the German flood had ended. "Now go home and see if I'm right. Think of one thing you need from him, anything—the moon, if that's what you really think you want. Then see if David tries to get it for you. Better you find out now if he doesn't love you, before you're an old woman and can't do anything about it!"

* * *

During the fourth week of her strike Johanna decided what she wanted from David. The idea had been constantly with her since her talk with her grandmother, but she was so unaccustomed to asking for anything that it took her most of the week to choose.

Then, one day, her decision was made. There was something she had wanted when she was pregnant with the boys and never requested, something that might be as good for David as it would be for her. If she could ask. If she could *make* herself ask, it might be the thing that helped them make a new start.

But just because she finally knew what she wanted, the asking wasn't easy. She and David were speaking now, even when the children weren't around to hear them, but their fight had never been discussed. They spoke about crops and people they knew. They never spoke about Johanna's strike, or the baby, or the sadness in both their eyes. At night sometimes as she was falling asleep Johanna would feel David move closer, and sometimes she dreamed that he held her, his hand resting on their unborn child. When she awoke in the mornings, though, he was always gone, his breakfast finished, his dishes neatly washed and stacked in the drainer.

There was time for asking now, if not the courage. The boys were back in school, and the majority of the crops were in. Johanna was still refusing to do other people's chores, but, amazingly, their lives were running more smoothly than they ever had before. There had been one morning when the boys had overslept, a morning when she had sadly told them that, no, she would not drive them to school because they had missed the bus while they were finishing their chores, a morning when, surprisingly, David had told them the same thing. A morning when, furious—and possibly just a bit ashamed—the boys had walked the three miles rather than face an unexcused absence.

There was still fighting and mischief, but now that Johanna refused to intervene, there was less of it. The Missouri summer sun and a late summer drought had finished off what was left of the garden, but there were still plenty of full canning jars in the pantry and a freezer filled with produce. The house was always clean but never quite neat. Meals were punctual, and there were always four male bodies around the oak dining-room table when Johanna brought the food in.

So there was time. Johanna had just never realized that she was such a coward in matters of the heart. She was so afraid that David would refuse her request that she couldn't make herself ask. And because the strain was so great, her eyes grew more haunted.

David watched Johanna slipping away from him and knew that he had to speak of the trouble between them. But they had never really spoken about their feelings. He didn't know how to begin; he didn't know what to say. He wondered how he could have known Johanna all his life and still be so frightened to talk to her. What was wrong with their marriage, that they hadn't weathered their first real quarrel, that it had dragged on and dragged them down until he was afraid there might not be a road back to where they had been?

Except that he didn't know if he wanted to return to that place, anyway. Their fight had taught him that he wanted more, needed more. He ached to really talk to Johanna, to tell her how much he cared, to hear those magic words from her, too. He ached to ask her for forgiveness, both for reacting badly when she stood up for her rights and for needing her so much that he had snatched her from the life she might have had without him.

They had reached an impasse. Johanna told herself each morning that this would be the day she asked David for her favor. David told himself each morning this this would be the day he finally told Johanna what he was feeling.

One day melted into the other until it was the fifth week of Johanna's strike.

Chapter Six

Johanna awoke before dawn to the sound of thunder in the distance. The drought that had finished off her garden and stunted the late corn was about to end. She lay in bed for a minute, feeling the baby's restless movements. Soon, in only a little more than two weeks, the baby would be in the bed beside her, nursing contentedly. She tried to remember the feeling of utter peace that had come from early morning feedings, the joy of nourishing and touching and holding her own baby close before the demands of the day intervened.

There had been little time to think of the baby, to cherish the wonder of giving birth. Now she lay in bed as the thunder and the storm it heralded drew closer, and thought about the life inside her.

The bedroom door creaked, pulling her from her dreamy-eyed reverie. She turned her head. "David?"

"I didn't mean to wake you, Jo."

She sat up immediately. His tone was unmistakable. David was worried. "What's wrong?" she asked.

"Nothing. I just don't like the weather."

"We need rain."

"Rain I can handle."

They had been married long enough for her to finish his thought for him. "Are you worried about a tornado?"

"It's too late in the year for there to be much chance of one. But the wind's gusting hard. It took the barn door right off the top hinge."

"You've already been outside?"

"It's later than you think. The sun's up. It's just that nobody can see it."

"Where are the boys?"

"Downstairs. I'm going to drive them in today. I don't want them waiting for the bus in this."

Johanna stood. "Don't be silly. I'll do it. You're needed here."

"No. I'll do it."

Johanna was hurt. She was sure that David was throwing her "strike" back at her by insisting he would drive the boys himself. In the past weeks he had been painfully careful not to ask or accept anything from her. "I can't believe you'd quibble at a time like this," she said, bending down to lift her robe from the corner post of the bed.

"Quibble?" David sounded puzzled.

"You know what I mean."

When she straightened, David was behind her. His hands rested lightly on her shoulders. "No, I don't."

She tried to shrug away his touch, but it grew firmer. "You've never understood what I was trying to do when I went on strike, David. Now you'll drive the boys to school instead of letting me do it, just to prove a point."

He turned her around until she was facing him. "Jo—"

She shook her head. "This isn't any time to fight about it. Do what you want."

One hand left her shoulder and settled softly at her cheek. "What I want to do is keep my wife and the mother of my baby safe at home while I brave the roads. What I *want* to do is take care of her."

She hadn't met his eyes. Now she did. "Take care of me?"

"Yes."

"I thought—"

"I know what you thought." His hand stroked gently past her ear and into her hair. His fingers spread wide, seeking a home. "*I* thought I'd like to keep you here, rosy-cheeked and warm. I thought maybe there would even be a breakfast waiting for me to come home to..." He hesitated, "...unless you're not feeling up to it."

She was ashamed that she'd misjudged him. For a moment she wondered if this was the only time she had. He seemed oddly wistful, as if there were more he wanted to say but didn't know how to. Her expression was probably identical. She risked a small smile. "I'll fix you whatever you'd like."

He exhaled, and it was almost a sigh. "My lovely, warm wife in my arms. That's what I'd like."

She was too amazed to speak. She knew what she looked like: a ten-ton truck after a rear-end collision. Calling her lovely took a poet's soul or more love than any man could possibly possess.

David pulled her closer. "Jo, we're going to have to talk."

"Now?"

"There's no time." David guided her cheek to his chest.

Tentatively Johanna slid her arms around David's waist. When he didn't pull away, she tightened her hold for a moment. "Later, then?" she asked, rubbing her cheek against him.

"Later."

She stepped back reluctantly. "Will we remember how?"

David touched her cheek once more and then turned away. "If we don't, we'll just have to learn again."

That prospect both excited and frightened her. She listened to David's footsteps on the stairs as he left to take the boys to school, and she wondered just what David would say and how it would affect the rest of her life.

The wind picked up gradually, no longer gusting but roaring steadily. Thunder crackled closer still, and the first raindrops fell. Storms were a fact of life in northern Missouri, and Johanna tried not to worry as she prepared David's breakfast. She had set *die Mutter* out the night before; now she added the requisite ingredients to make pancakes a gold-rush prospector would have jumped a claim for.

It was an hour before David came back inside. She had seen the station wagon pull up some time before, and she knew he had gone to check on the animals. When she finally heard his footsteps on the back porch, she poured the first round of batter onto the well-seasoned griddle.

"How's it look out there?" she called.

"It looks like I'd better get right back out." David came into the room, wiping his face on a clean towel from the laundry room. His pants and shirt were damp around the edges, where his slicker hadn't covered them.

"You've got to eat," Johanna insisted, flipping the first batch of pancakes. "These will be finished in less than a minute."

He sat down without a word, and she stopped tending the griddle long enough to pour him a cup of steaming dark coffee. He already looked exhausted, as if the day were ending instead of just beginning. He cradled the coffee cup in his hands, absorbing the warmth. "I stopped off to check on your grandmother. Your Aunt Wilma was there already. Your grandmother's going to go home with her until the storm's over."

Johanna wondered how many men would have been that thoughtful. "You saved me a trip. Thank you."

"I love her, too," he said.

Johanna turned, astonished. David so rarely spoke his feelings that she wondered if she had heard him correctly. "She loves you," she said tentatively. "She always has."

"She was the mother I never had."

Johanna faced the griddle again and blinked back sudden tears. How could she and David have gone so far astray when they shared so much?

"Are the pancakes ready? I've got to get back outside and fix the barn door or we'll lose it for sure."

She nodded, because she couldn't yet speak. Her eyes were dry by the time she brought his plate to the table.

They ate in silence. Johanna picked at her pancakes, her appetite gone. David ate as if the food were fuel for the chores ahead of him. When he was finished he rose to clear his dishes, but she motioned him away. "I'll take care of everything. I just wish I could be more help."

"Come here."

She stood, too. She met David halfway around the table. He framed her face with his hands and bent to kiss her. Perhaps the kiss had been meant to be reassuring, but in an instant it turned into something else. David pulled her as close as he could, wrapping her tightly in his arms. He smelled like rain and coffee and warm man. Johanna absorbed his essence through every pore of her body as she melted into his arms. It had been so long since he'd held her like this. His mouth against hers felt familiar yet strange, as if they had never kissed quite this way before.

She parted her lips and felt the warm probing of his tongue. She ached for his touch in places distended and changed by their child. She ached for all of him.

Johanna threaded her arms around David's neck and held him close. Nothing but this mattered, not their quarrel, not the baby firmly between them, certainly not the barn door. David mattered. She mattered. The way he felt in her arms mattered.

Finally David pulled away. His lips were warm against her cheek. "If you weren't about to have our baby, we'd be in bed right now."

She stiffened. She heard the words as a condemnation. If *you* weren't about to have our baby. The warmth she had felt disappeared, and when she spoke her voice was chilly. "I'm sorry. If you'll remember, I didn't get pregnant on purpose."

David stiffened, too. "Can't I say anything without you taking it the wrong way?"

"What way am I supposed to take it?" Johanna pushed against his shoulders until she was free.

He looked as if he wanted to shake her. "Damn it, Jo, I was just trying to tell you I want you! I'm not a kid! I can wait if I have to, but I thought you just might like to know I still care!" He turned before she could respond. "I'll be outside. Hell, it's a lot more comfortable in the storm than it is in here!"

He was gone before she could find the words to stop him.

He still cared? He wanted her?

Johanna sank to the nearest chair. Her knees were weak from more than David's kiss. They were weak with relief.

David wanted her. And if he *still* cared, then that meant he had cared before. Was caring the same as loving?

She had been married for thirteen years and she didn't know something as simple, as basic, as whether her husband loved her. And why didn't she know? Because she was a coward. She had never asked. The closest she had come was the night David proposed, and then she had been afraid to scrutinize his answer.

He had told her that he'd loved her since then, in the heat of passion, or casually, as if the words were just expected. But she had never asked him to explain, because she had always been afraid to let him know her insecurity. She'd been afraid of what she might find.

Now she was no longer afraid to know. She was afraid of not knowing. She couldn't go on this way any longer.

And suddenly she wasn't afraid to ask him to show his love, either. She had resisted asking him for something she really wanted, even though her grandmother had convinced her that she must. She had resisted, because she had been afraid he would refuse. Now she knew that a refusal couldn't hurt as much as this limbo she was in.

She had to ask. She had to know. Most of all, she had to let David know that *she* cared, because for the first time she realized that he didn't know, not for sure. David didn't know her feelings any more than she knew his.

And they had been married for thirteen years.

The rain was cold, pelting her skin with the icy promise of the fall and winter to come. Johanna hugged one of David's slickers around her—it was the only rain gear that had been able to buckle over her huge belly—and bent her head into the wind.

The rain fell in solid, silver sheets. The churned-up mud of the farmyard was slick, and she picked her way carefully, aware of how disastrous a fall could be. As if in reaction, she felt the baby kicking hard, then she felt a familiar squeezing low in her abdomen. She had been having contractions for weeks now, painless, short-lived contractions that were nothing more than rehearsals for the labor to come. Dr. Landis had told her they were normal, particularly for a woman who had already had several children. She stopped for a moment as the squeezing continued, jabbed uncomfortably and then, finally, drifted into oblivion.

Her labors had all begun this way, slowly building, daylong affairs that had been manageable without painkillers right up until the very end. Fleetingly she wondered if the baby might come early; then she put the idea aside. All the boys had been born two weeks after their official due dates. It was likely that this child would also arrive late. Head bent once more, she continued toward the barn.

The door that she pushed open hung solidly on two hinges. David had already repaired it. He wasn't a man to brood when work had to be done. Johanna stepped inside and closed it behind her. She was overpowered by the sweet odor of new hay and the warm, earthy tang of the livestock.

"David?" She cleared her throat and shouted his name again over the lowing of the calves. "David?"

"What are you doing out here?"

Johanna looked up. David was just above her in the loft. "We have to talk," she said.

He snorted. "Fight, you mean."

She could see she wasn't going to get anywhere shouting over her head at him. The ladder up to the loft looked surprisingly precarious considering that her center of balance was disputable these days. But David had already disappeared back against the wall of the barn, ignoring her presence. If she wanted to talk to him, she could climb up or continue shouting. What she had to say couldn't be shouted.

She was halfway up the ladder when another contraction began. She ignored it, because other than a brief jabbing sensation, it wasn't painful. By the time she reached the loft, however, she felt as if she had run a mile.

She found David forking hay into a chute that led down to the barn floor. "Hi," she said.

"Are you crazy?" He dropped his pitchfork and stalked over to her, clamping his hands on her shoulders. "What are you doing climbing ladders in your condition?"

"We have to talk."

"Can't this wait?"

"No."

He looked completely exasperated with her. "You've gotten to be the stubbornest woman in a state full of stubborn women!"

She lifted her chin a little, and the hood of the slicker fell around her shoulders. "I have to know something right now. It can't wait."

His fingers clamped harder on her shoulders in anger; then, as if he realized he might be hurting her, his hands dropped to his side. "Then ask," he said, biting off the words. "And do it quick. I've got things that have to be done before the whole damn farm blows away."

"Then let it blow, I don't care!"

"Don't care?" He snorted derisively. "This place means everything to you. You've got Missouri soil in your veins, remember? You married me to keep it there."

She wasn't sure why he sounded so sarcastic. "What's the problem with that? Did you want a woman like my mother? Someone who hated the land? Would that have made you happier, David? Maybe I should moan and complain all the time and ask for things I can't have.''

''You're about to ask for something, aren't you?'' he asked coldly.

For a moment she considered not asking. David was in no mood to give her anything. But she knew that if she waited she might never find the courage to ask him again. And if she waited it could be too late.

''Well?'' he asked.

''I want you to stay with me when the baby's born.'' She spat out the words as if they tasted bad. ''And don't say 'no' until you've had a chance to think about it.''

David looked as if someone had just socked him in the stomach.

Johanna felt faint. The rush of adrenaline that had gotten her this far was gone, but she wasn't about to let David know. ''I need you to be with me, David. I don't want to go through this alone.''

David sat down on a bale of hay, like a man whose legs wouldn't hold him any longer. ''Be with you for the birth?''

Johanna sat beside him. Her legs really wouldn't hold her any longer. She shut her eyes and leaned back against another bale. ''Is that so much to ask?''

''You want me there?''

''Of course I want you there. I've always wanted you there when our babies were born.''

''You never told me.''

''You never asked.''

For a long time the only audible sounds were the frightened lowing of the calves and the shrill keening of the wind.

"I don't know if I can be there," David said at last. "I'm sorry."

Johanna squeezed her eyelids together tighter to stop the tears that were brimming behind them. "I'm sorry, too." She felt David's arms around her. She tried to pull away, but he wouldn't let her.

"I don't know if I could stand seeing you in pain, Jo." David forced her head against his chest. "I can't even bear to *think* about anything hurting you."

For a moment she wondered if she had heard him right. David was a farmer, and he had never hesitated to perform any of his jobs, even the most grisly ones. He had witnessed more births than most obstetricians. Certainly a human birth couldn't be worse to watch than the births of the animals he raised. She gave a watery sniff. "I'd be there to help you through it."

"Jo." He stroked her hair. "Jo, do you know how I felt every time they took you into that one-horse delivery room and shut the door? I felt like it was me that was giving you all that pain. If I hadn't been so selfish, if I hadn't wanted the boys and wanted you to have them—"

"I wanted your sons, too!"

"I know you did," he soothed. "But it didn't seem worth it when you were in there having them. And it seemed like it was my fault. If I didn't love to touch you so much, to make love to you, then you wouldn't be in pain."

Johanna could hardly believe the man holding her and confessing his feelings was the man she had married. "I didn't care about the pain," she said, lifting her head to look at him. "I was giving you the best gift I could."

"*I* cared." David brushed her hair back from her face. It was damp, and it slid through his fingers. "I'll care this time, too, only this time, it's really my fault. I wanted to blame this on you, but I know the truth. I was the one who couldn't wait the night of Farley's party. I was the one who had too much to drink."

For months she had thought he still blamed her for the pregnancy. Now for the first time she understood that only his own guilty feelings had made him sound that way. "Do we even have to talk about fault?" she asked gently. "What does fault have to do with the baby growing inside me? This is our child. Ours." She drew David's hand down to her belly. "Maybe he's another Beethoven or Michelangelo. Maybe he'll just be the best darned farmer in Missouri, but whatever he turns out to be, we'll love him and be proud of him and never think about fault again, so why think about it now?"

David's hand traveled over her belly, parting the slicker. It found a resting place between their child and her thigh. "Jo..."

She gasped his name and went suddenly rigid.

"What's wrong?" But before the words were out of David's mouth, he already knew. Moisture seeped against his fingertips.

"David!"

"Your water broke."

She was seized with a pain as sharp as any she had ever felt. She clamped her lips together, but a groan escaped them anyway.

"Are you having a contraction?"

She shook her head. She knew what a contraction felt like. It built from nothing, a cresting wave that finally lapped against the shore and left her drained but at peace. This was a knife in the gut.

David put his hand on her belly. "My God. It feels like a rock!"

"Something's wrong," she said, whimpering.

"We've got to get you down from here. Damn it, Jo, what are you doing in a hayloft, anyway?"

She grabbed his hand as the pain intensified. "I can't move."

"You are not having this baby in the barn," he said.

"Mary did." She bit her lip to keep from crying. She still couldn't move.

David scooped her up as if she hadn't gained an extra twenty-five pounds. "And Joseph would have gotten her to the hospital if there'd been one."

"You can't carry me down the ladder." She punctuated her words with another groan.

"Put your arms around my neck. Tight."

Johanna held on for dear life. On some level she was aware that she was probably strangling David, but she couldn't stop. The sharper the pain the harder she squeezed. Her bottom skimmed the rungs of the ladder as David descended each step. She cried out once, and then it was all over. They were on solid ground.

David set her gently on the pile of hay at the bottom of the chute. "I'm going to get the car. I'll drive it right up to the door, and then I'll come in and get you. Don't move." He turned at the door. "And don't have that baby."

"I'm not having the baby," she gasped pitifully. "Something else is wrong. Hurry, David."

He was already gone.

Chapter Seven

By the time David opened the barn door again, lightning split the sky overhead, followed immediately by shattering claps of thunder. He hardly even noticed, so intent was he on making his way across the floor to Johanna.

"The car wouldn't start," he said grimly, kneeling beside her. "We'll have to take the pickup."

"You go without me." Johanna pushed against his chest as his arms slid under her. "I can't move!"

"Then I'll move you." David lifted her. He wondered if she could feel his arms shaking.

Johanna dug her teeth into her bottom lip, trying not to cry out.

David hurried across the floor. At the door he stopped long enough to pull her slicker around her and the hood over her head. "Once I get you on the seat, can you slide far enough in so that I can close the door?"

She couldn't answer, but he seemed to think the thrashing of her head was a "yes," because he lifted her higher and kicked open the barn door.

Johanna wondered why hell was portrayed as a fiery furnace. Hell was a driving rainstorm. Hell was lightning and thunder and a pain in your middle that felt as if it was tearing you in two. David held her tightly against him, but the wind blew her hood off her head, drenching her face and hair. Once she felt him slip in the mud and almost fall to his knees.

It seemed like forever, although it was really only seconds, before she felt the firm seat of the pickup under her bottom. She gathered what little strength she had left and slid toward the driver's seat so that David could close the door.

He was beside her in moments. "Don't have that baby yet," he said through gritted teeth.

"There's something wrong," Johanna insisted. "This isn't labor." She gasped as the pain deepened once more. "There's something wrong!"

"Johanna, hold on." David's torment sounded in his voice. Despite everything she had said earlier, he was sure he was killing her. This was his fault. She was suffering because of him. He felt every bump in the road as if he were the one in pain.

Johanna was torn between the pain in her belly and the one in her heart. She and David had come so close to telling each other what they felt. Now their chance was gone. And she was dying. She was sure of it. She had waited too long to find out if he loved her. Now she would die not knowing. And David would never know what she felt.

Her moans turned into an undignified yelp.

"Johanna, hold on!"

"David, I...I..." She yelped again.

"Don't try to talk. Just hold on!"

"To what?" she demanded.

"To me. Hold on to my arm. I can drive just fine," he lied. He swerved to miss the limb of a tree that was decorating the middle of the road. He had lived through myriad thunderstorms, even watched a tornado touch down in his front yard once before it swirled off to wreak destruction somewhere miles away, but he had never seen the roads this bad. The rain was a solid wall of water, and the roads were flooding. The dirt lane that ran in front of the farm had been bad enough, slick and potholed, but the blacktop was almost worse. The rain had already filled the shallow drainage ditch that ran beside the road; now water lay inches deep over the surface. They were alone on the road.

David felt Johanna's fingers clamp down on his arm. The resulting pain was reassuring. He deserved it. He welcomed it.

"We should...have...called. My doctor won't...be there." Johanna gripped David's arm tighter.

"If I'd stopped to call, we'd still be at the house. Somebody will be there. Mary will call Dr. Landis as soon as we get there."

"He lives...in the country," she said between groans.

"He'll get there. Somebody will get there. You're going to be all right."

"I'm dying."

"No, you're not. Nobody with a grip like that is dying."

"David," she wailed as the pain grew even sharper. "I'm dying. I know...I am."

"You are not dying," he said firmly, trying to convince himself as well.

"If I do—"

"You are *not* dying!"

"If I do," she gasped, "and the baby doesn't—"

"You are not dying!"

"Will you . . . love it?"

He couldn't believe she would ask such a question. Even under these circumstances. "Of course I'll love our baby. I already love our baby. Now be quiet, Jo. Take deep breaths or something. Save your strength."

"But you didn't . . . want it."

"It wasn't the baby I didn't want, Jo." David shook back a lock of hair dripping in his eye. "I just didn't want to lose you!"

"Lose me?"

"Please, Jo, just shut up. Save your strength."

"Stay with me," she said faintly.

"There's nothing in the world that could tear me away!"

Her next breath was a sob. David wanted to cry, too. He forced himself to concentrate on driving, which was getting more difficult with every moment. He was creeping now, when he wanted to be speeding. He felt no relief when the town proper of Junction came into view. He splashed through the empty streets, leaving them behind in a minute as he pulled onto the highway that would take him to the hospital. Silently he cursed the ancestors who had chosen the middle of nowhere to set down roots. At that moment there was nothing charming or pleasingly country about Junction. It was simply the sticks, and he was a hick farmer who didn't deserve the woman beside him.

"We're almost there," he said, trying to reassure Johanna. Even to his own ears he sounded desperate.

"I love you," she said between sobs. "I've always...loved you."

"I know, Jo," he said, in the same desperate voice. Frantically he bore down on the accelerator, intensely alert to the slightest sway or slide of the truck.

"Really...loved you, I mean," she croaked.

David could hardly understand her, and he was concentrating so hard that the words meant little to him. Just ahead he saw the sign that meant they had finally arrived. "We're here," he said triumphantly. "We're here. We made it."

"Do you love me?" she gasped as David pulled into the parking lot. But he was already out of the pickup, dashing around to get her.

"Come on." He jerked open the door and slid his arms under her. "We're here."

"Do you love me, David?" she asked, against his chest. The words ended on a yelp as the rain hit her full in the face, despite his care with the hood of her slicker.

"Of course I love you," he shouted over the thunder. "I've always loved you."

She couldn't say another word. The pain intensified again until she was light-headed with it. For a moment she was sure the end had come.

The rain stopped suddenly, and she was just conscious enough to realize that they were inside and David was shouting.

There was a scurry of feet and more shouts. Then a familiar face loomed inches from hers. She recognized Mary Condrey, Junction General's head nurse and permanent fixture. "Johanna? Can you hear me?"

Someone answered. Johanna assumed it had been her, although she didn't know what she had said.

"We're going to take you upstairs and examine you. David thinks you might be trying to have that baby." Mary, substantial, gray-haired and well-scrubbed, straightened and gave David a no-nonsense once-over. "You look like hell," she announced. Then she turned and started toward a gurney that was neatly lodged against the wall near the emergency-room entrance. "Put her down here and we'll wheel her up. You stay here and dry off. You can sign all the papers while I examine her."

"I'm not putting her down."

"Hospital rules."

"You know what you can do with them."

Mary snorted. "Don't forget, I've been through this with you when you were a wet-behind-the-ears twenty. You *always* behaved worse than Johanna did." Mary bustled into the elevator, holding the door calmly for David.

Johanna groaned, and David clasped her tighter.

Mary took one look at his anguished face and rolled her eyes. "Thought Johanna was on strike," she said. "Settle the labor dispute, did you?"

"This is no time to be joking!"

"She's having a baby. She's not dying."

David ignored her, lowering his face to Johanna's. "We're almost there," he crooned.

Mary's expression softened just a little. "I'd think you'd be used to this by now."

"There's something wrong," he snapped. "I told you down there. This isn't the way her other labors went."

"And *I* told *you*, every labor is different."

The elevator wheezed to a halt. David was out in the sickly green hallway before the door had opened completely. Mary followed, motioning him left. "She's going in Room 232 for now."

"She's going right to the delivery room! The doctor might have to operate."

"There's someone in there already," Mary said, just a trace of sympathy in her voice. "The tornado knocked a tree onto the roof of Hiram Peters's truck. Worse luck was that he was in it. They're working on him now."

"Tornado?"

"Just a little one. Touched down south of here in the Peters's field. Hiram's going to be fine once he's stitched up."

David's muttered answer had to do with hick-town hospitals with operating rooms that doubled as delivery rooms and were only empty until you needed them.

Mary ignored his complaints, ushering him into the room at the end of the corridor. Through the window David could see cornstalks bent double in the wind.

Johanna whimpered when he laid her on a bed that Mary had efficiently stripped of its spread. Mary was already cranking it to its highest position. "We're shorthanded," she told David. "Some of our staff couldn't make it in on account of the storm. Do you have the stomach to help?" She didn't wait for an answer. "Get her pants off and cover her with that sheet so I can examine her."

David whipped his head around. "You? Where's the doctor?"

"Dr. Henley's stitching up Hiram. Dr. Landis is home. Something ripped out the bridge out by his place."

"Another tornado?"

"Maybe just a little one. No one was hurt, far as we know."

Johanna groaned and clutched David's arm. "David..."

He followed Mary's instructions, wincing each time Johanna groaned. Mary was at the sink in the corner, washing her hands as if *she* were going to have to do surgery.

When Mary came around to Johanna's feet, he vacated his place, holding Johanna's hand while Mary maneuvered her into position to examine her. He bent his head low, next to Johanna's.

"You're going to be fine," he murmured.

She shook her head, wet hair soaking her pillowcase. "David, you didn't understand out there...what I was trying to say—" She stopped, biting her lip until he was sure she was going to bite clean through it.

"You're not going to die," he said, desperate to make her believe it, although he didn't believe it himself.

"Not that." She stopped, panting mournfully as Mary completed the examination.

"There's a perfectly healthy baby planning to arrive before Dr. Landis can ford the old stream." Mary matter-of-factly pulled the sheet back over Johanna's knees and eased her legs from the stirrups. "I'm off to see if Dr. Henley can do the honors."

David straightened. "When?" he demanded. "And what else is wrong with her?"

Mary's eyes twinkled, but her mouth didn't even twitch. "Isn't having a baby enough for one day? You want more?"

"She thinks she's dying!"

"She probably feels like she is. Men ought to have babies now and then, just to see how much fun it is."

Mary was almost out the door before David had recovered. "But this isn't like her other labors!"

"And this baby probably won't be like any of the others, either. It's different every time. Johanna just forgot."

"When is she going to have it?" David shouted as Mary disappeared.

"Hopefully not before I get back...."

David was torn between following Mary to strangle her and weeping.

"David!" Johanna tossed restlessly from side to side. "I was trying to tell you."

"Don't talk," he insisted. "Save your strength, honey. You've got a big job ahead of you."

"I love you!" The strength of Johanna's words grew until she was almost shouting the last one. "Can't you hear me? I've been trying to tell you... really tell you. I don't want to die... without you knowing!"

"You're not going to die." David squeezed her hand. "Jo, you're not going to die. Mary says everything's fine."

Johanna didn't believe Mary for a moment. "I love you!"

David cradled her hand against his cheek. "Jo, I love you, too." He wanted to cry and couldn't. The tears made his voice husky. "You're everything I've ever wanted," he said, the words rushing out like a newly undammed river. "Everything. I couldn't live without you. I was wrong to marry you when I did, to take you away from everything you could have had. But I did it because I loved you so much. I couldn't help myself. Tell me you forgive me."

"Forgive you?" Johanna was weak from fatigue and the incredible strain on her body. Even as she spoke, she felt her body bearing down to begin to push their child from it. She groaned, clamping her lips tightly shut.

"All these years," David said, clasping her hand tighter. "Everything I've done, I've done for you. It hasn't been enough, I know, but it was all I could give you."

"Enough?" The word was squeezed out from compressed lips.

"There's good news and bad news," Mary said, bustling purposefully back into the room. "Bad news is that we've got two more people for Dr. Henley and the rest of the staff to work on. Fairly minor injuries, but they can't really wait. This place is a zoo. Good news is that I've delivered a dozen babies in my time, so I've had plenty of practice. David, are you going to be a help or a hindrance?"

But David had hardly heard her. "Jo, tell me you forgive me."

"There's . . . nothing . . . to . . . forgive! Didn't you hear . . . me?" Johanna panted until the urge to bear down again had passed. "I love you. I always have."

"You have? But you went on strike. You didn't want to do anything for me, and you never seemed to need anything from me. I thought—"

"I wanted you to notice me! I wanted you to love me! That's all I've ever wanted. I've . . . always . . . loved you. I'd do anything for you . . . anything!"

"A hindrance is it, then." Mary pushed David unceremoniously to the side. "Men in delivery rooms!" She shook her head in disgust.

"This isn't a delivery room," David snapped.

"Put on that gown by the door and go wash your hands if you want to stay. Wash them good!"

"David, please stay!" Johanna begged.

He stalked to the sink and turned on the water with an angry twist.

Mary positioned Johanna for another examination. "You're fully dilated. Have you felt like pushing?" she asked.

Johanna gasped and held her breath, bearing down in answer.

"A neat little demonstration," Mary said dryly.

"David!" Johanna shrieked, when the contraction had ended.

Mary looked from husband to wife. She thought she had seen it all in her years at Junction General, but never had she seen such adoration and such distress. Something was very definitely wrong here, but from what she had just heard, it was in the process of being put right.

"Johanna, you're going to be fine!" Mary insisted. "Do you think David would let anything happen to you? He'd fight St. Peter at the Pearly Gates before he'd let him take you. Now get down to business and push that baby out here so we can take a look at him."

David came to Johanna's side, grabbing her hand. "Just do what she say, Jo. She knows what she's doing." He glared at Mary. "Don't you?"

"I've delivered them every which way but inside out," Mary said, eyes twinkling again.

Johanna held her breath and began to push with the next contraction. David gripped her hand and pushed right along with her until his cheeks were red. Mary nodded wisely. "One more push, maybe two. Three at most."

"Can't you say for sure?" David demanded.

"Tell you what, you come down here and watch. Then you tell me."

The color left David's face.

"Come on," Mary insisted. "Come watch your baby being born. Johanna, grab on to the rails and push like you're moving a mountain."

Mary made room for David at Johanna's feet. "This one's going to do it. And here it comes!"

David watched the head crowning and the tiny features coming into view. He was enthralled. He forgot everything, his horrible fear that Jo was really dying, his distress that he had single-handedly brought her to this, the feeling that this baby was one too many.

"Support the head," Mary instructed as David instinctively reached out for the child, beating her by a split second. She watched closely as the rest of the baby came into view. David delivered it like a professional. "Hold it up here." Mary quickly suctioned the mouth and nose, but she could see that the baby was already breathing on its own. "It's a girl," she announced as she waited to cut the cord.

Johanna was in shock. The pain that had become part of her had ceased entirely. Her body felt as if it were in suspension. So she wasn't dying, after all.

"A girl?" David asked wonderingly. "Are you sure?"

"See for yourself. It's unmistakable. Six and a half pounds of one, if my guess is correct." Mary took the baby and laid her on a sterile towel on Johanna's abdomen before she began the simple operation that would separate the child from its mother forever.

Johanna watched, dazed. The baby squirmed against her, and the air was filled with tiny wails. "I'm still alive," she said, astonished.

"A quick labor doesn't kill you—it just doesn't give you time to think," Mary said. "David, give me the blanket over there on the other bed. We'll wrap her up nice and tight."

She did, handing the baby back to David when she was done. Then she finished tending to Johanna, as David swayed from side to side, quieting his new daughter.

When everything was just about completed, a frayed, bleary-eyed man in green surgical garb rushed through the door. "Still need me?" he asked.

Mary humphed. "You can just check her out if you want. Everything went fine. She was made to have babies. Doesn't even need stitches."

In record time Dr. Henley agreed; then, after a quick examination of the baby, he let Mary usher him out of the room. She stopped at the door.

"I'll be back to give the baby a bath in a little while. You three look like you might need some time alone." She started to leave, then turned back. "It's my experience that people usually say exactly what they're feeling when they think there's no time to hedge." Neither Johanna nor David answered her, but she saw that David was no longer rocking the child against him, and Johanna had turned her face toward the window. "You two need to practice talking when you don't think someone's dying." She shut the door behind her.

Johanna didn't know what to do. Through the window she could see the cornstalk ballet. She was afraid to stop looking, afraid to face David after everything that had been said. Did he regret his words? And the baby he held, did he regret her, after all?

Finally she had to turn. The silence wasn't complete. Her new daughter was mewing softly, like a newborn kitten, calling her. And there was another noise she didn't recognize.

David stood, clutching their daughter. His head was bent low. "David?" she whispered.

He looked up, and his eyes were bright with tears that hadn't yet slipped down his cheeks. "She's so beautiful," he said hoarsely. "She looks like you, Jo."

Johanna held out her arms, and he brought the baby to her. She took her daughter, but held out her other arm for David, pulling him tightly against her. "I meant everything I said," she whispered, crying too. "Did you?"

"Everything." He circled them both with his arms.

They held each other tightly, until Mary came back in to take the baby. There would be times in the years to come when they couldn't seem to talk about their feelings, times in the years to come when fear pretended to be anger. But there would never be a time when they doubted again that they were loved.

"We'll name her after your grandmother," David said, when Mary and the baby were gone.

"Grandmother Schaumbacher is a mouthful for such a little thing, don't you think?" Johanna asked sleepily.

"Mina. Mina Johanna Groves."

She lifted his fingers to her lips for a kiss. "That was quick."

"I've been saving the name. I always wanted a daughter."

Johanna could hardly keep her eyes open. "You never told me that."

"I love you, Johanna."

She smiled up at him. "I love you, David."

"Is the strike over?"

"Do I get a night out once a week?"

"If I get to come."

She yawned. "The strike's over, but I'm still not cleaning up after anyone. That's permanent."

He laughed softly. "Then who changes the diapers?"

She wrinkled her nose. "The boys?"

They were still laughing when Mary came back in with Mina for her first feeding. The baby settled against her mother's breast as if she had always been fed there.

Outside, the rain slowly dwindled into a fine mist, and the cornstalks lifted toward the sky that would soon send down sun once more. Inside, David took his sleeping daughter from her sleeping mother's arms and rocked her tenderly.

* * * * *

Emilie Richards

Nowadays it's hard to imagine a life without tale-telling, folk-finding and scenery-snatching, but not so long ago, life held none of those pleasures. I began writing in my thirties, although I was so ready for it, I took off like the proverbial horse who smells water when the idea was suggested to me.

Now I like to think that I had been training to write all those years, even when I wasn't doing it. I graduated from Florida State University one hundred percent unprepared for life. Undaunted and married, my husband Michael and I went into VISTA, the domestic Peace Corps, and spent time in the Ozark Mountains of Arkansas, drinking in the unique culture and hospitable warmth of the people we were supposed to save from poverty. In reality, those same people kept *us* alive by teaching us how to keep a fire going in our wood stove, how to eat on twenty dollars a week, and how to pass a neighborly evening on the front porch listening to stories and folk songs.

We went from the Ozarks to Berkeley, California— a guaranteed route into culture shock—where Michael entered the seminary. Our years in Berkeley were at the height of the Vietnam War, and we watched and listened and argued, coming away forever changed by all we'd seen and done.

We started our family of four in Berkeley and continued it as we moved around the country from Florida to Virginia to Pennsylvania, Louisiana, Australia and finally, recently, to Ohio. Along the way I earned my master's degree in family counseling and pursued a career between children and moves. We made friends and learned how to say goodbye as another church inevitably beckoned. And all the while, I stored up memories and ideas and things I wished I could say.

Now I tell tales and find folks to people them and snatch scenery from my moves and my travels to set them in. For hours I live wholly in my imagination. Sometimes I pinch myself to be sure that I'm not also imagining I have readers. Sharing my stories with you is a frightening experience, because in a way, my stories are me. That you choose to read them is both humbling and gratifying.

Like all of us, I have a million more stories inside me. I sincerely hope they'll continue to speak to you and to remind you of your own lives and the stories you have to tell. And I hope that this book, which was a labor of love for everyone connected with it, will bring you special pleasure.

FOUR UNIQUE SERIES
FOR EVERY WOMAN YOU ARE...

Silhouette Romance

Love, at its most tender, provocative, emotional... in stories that will make you laugh and cry while bringing you the magic of falling in love.

6 titles per month

Silhouette Special Edition

Sophisticated, substantial and packed with emotion, these powerful novels of life and love will capture your imagination and steal your heart.

6 titles per month

SILHOUETTE *Desire*

Open the door to romance and passion. Humorous, emotional, compelling—yet always a believable and sensuous story—Silhouette Desire never fails to deliver on the promise of love.

6 titles per month

Silhouette Intimate Moments

Enter a world of excitement, of romance heightened by suspense, adventure and the passions every woman dreams of. Let us sweep you away.

4 titles per month

SILG-1RR

DIAMOND JUBILEE CELEBRATION!

It's the Silhouette Books tenth anniversary, and what better way to celebrate than to toast *you*, our readers, for making it all possible. Each month in 1990 we'll present you with a DIAMOND JUBILEE Silhouette Romance written by an all-time favorite author! Saying thanks has never been so romantic...

The merry month of May will bring you SECOND TIME LUCKY by Victoria Glenn. And in June, the first volume of Pepper Adams's exciting trilogy Cimarron Stories will be available—CIMARRON KNIGHT. July sizzles with BORROWED BABY by Marie Ferrarella. Suzanne Carey, Lucy Gordon, Annette Broadrick and many more have special gifts of love waiting for you with their DIAMOND JUBILEE Romances.

January: ETHAN by Diana Palmer (#694)
February: THE AMBASSADOR'S DAUGHTER
by Brittany Young (#700)
March: NEVER ON SUNDAE by Rita Rainville (#706)
April: HARVEY'S MISSING by Peggy Webb (#712)

A BIG SISTER
can take her places

She likes that. Her Mom does too.

HARLEQUIN SUPPORTS BIG SISTERS
For more information, contact your local Big Brothers/Big Sisters agency.

BIG BROTHERS
BIG SISTERS
OF AMERICA

BIG BROTHERS/BIG SISTERS AND HARLEQUIN

Harlequin is proud to announce its official sponsorship of Big Brothers/Big Sisters of America. Look for this poster in your local Big Brothers/Big Sisters agency or call them to get one in your favorite bookstore. Love is all about sharing.

BB/BS-1A